A Wrinkle IN TIME

Madeleine L'Engle

WITH RELATED READINGS

THE EMC MASTERPIECE SERIES

Access Editions

EMC/Paradigm Publishing
St. Paul, Minnesota

Staff Credits

Laurie Skiba
Managing Editor

Brenda Owens
High School Editor

Becky Palmer
Associate Editor

Nichola Torbett
Associate Editor

Jennifer J. Anderson
Assistant Editor

Valerie Murphy
Editorial Assistant

Dr. David Darling
Project Consultant

Lori Ann Coleman
Editorial Consultant

Paul Spencer
Art and Photo Researcher

Jennifer Wreisner
Senior Designer

Parkwood Composition
Compositor

Text copyright © 1962 by Madeleine L'Engle Franklin and renewed 1990 by Crosswicks, Ltd. Reprinted by permission of Farrar, Straus & Giroux, Inc. Cover images © Cartesia/Photodisc Imaging (globe); © Randy Allbritton/Getty Images (crystal ball); © StockTrek (starry background).

L'Engle, Madeleine.
A wrinkle in time : with related readings / Madeleine L'Engle.
p. cm. — (The EMC masterpiece series access editions)
Originally published: New York: Farrar, Straus and Giroux, 1962.
Summary: Thirteen-year-old Meg Murry, her little brother Charles Wallace, and their friend Calvin are guided by unearthly strangers as they go on a journey through space and time to search for Meg's and Charles' scientist father who disappeared while experimenting with a new form of space travel. Includes related readings and study questions.
ISBN 0-8219-2532-6
[1. Science fiction. 2. Space and time—Fiction.] I. Title.
PZ7.L5385 Wr 2002
[Fic]—dc21
2002020853

ISBN 0-8219-2532-6

Copyright © 2003 by EMC Corporation

Published by EMC/Paradigm Publishing
875 Montreal Way
St. Paul, Minnesota 55102
800-328-1452
www.emcp.com
E-mail: educate@emcp.com

Printed in the United States of America.
9 10 xxx 16 15 14

Table of Contents

THE LIFE AND WORKS OF

Madeleine L'Engle

Madeleine L'Engle was born Madeleine L'Engle Camp in New York City on November 29, 1918 to Charles Wadsworth Camp, a newspaper writer, and Madeleine Barnett Camp, a pianist. As an only child, raised by a nanny and a governess, Madeleine was often lonely. She filled her time by writing stories, reading books, drawing, and learning to play the piano.

Madeleine L'Engle

Like Meg, the main character in *A Wrinkle in Time,* Madeleine disliked school. She was shy, clumsy, and unpopular, and didn't try hard at her schoolwork. Once, when she was in fifth or sixth grade, a teacher accused her of copying a poem that won a school contest. She couldn't believe that Madeleine had any talent as a writer!

In addition to Madeleine's troubles at school, there was a problem at home: her father, Charles Camp, was not well. While working as a reporter during World War I, his lungs had been badly damaged by mustard gas, a poisonous chemical used in the war. As his illness progressed, the Camps moved to a village high in the French Alps, where the air would be less irritating to Charles Camp's lungs. Twelve-year-old Madeleine was sent to a boarding school nearby in Switzerland. She was the only American girl there, and felt terribly lonely. Even worse, the strict rules meant she had no time to herself to daydream or write stories. Years later, Madeleine used her memories of that school to write a novel entitled *And Both Were Young.*

In 1932, when Madeleine was fourteen, her family moved back to the United States. Madeleine was sent to Ashley Hall Boarding School in Charleston, South Carolina, where she began ninth grade. For the first time, she was happy in school. She participated in school plays and the student council. But during her senior year, her father died. His death left a huge hole in Madeleine's life, and it was a long time before she was able to accept it.

Madeleine went to Smith College and graduated with honors in 1941. She then moved to New York City and worked in the theater, while still pursuing her dream of being an author. She decided to use only her first and middle names—Madeleine L'Engle—as her pen name. During this time she published her first two novels, *A Small Rain* and *Ilsa*. She met her future husband, actor Hugh Franklin, in 1944 when they were both in Anton Chekhov's play *The Cherry Orchard*. They were married in January 1946.

Later that year, the young couple bought an old farmhouse in Connecticut, and named it Crosswicks. For much of their lives, the Franklins lived in New York City where Hugh could find his acting work, but they always returned to Crosswicks in the summer, and grew to regard this place as their true home.

In June 1947 Madeleine and Hugh had a baby girl, Josephine. Madeleine continued to write, working on the novels *And Both Were Young* and *Camilla*. In 1951, when Madeleine was pregnant with their son Bion, they decided to move to Crosswicks full time. Soon after Bion's birth, the couple bought the general store in town, and Hugh began his "longest-running play" in the role of small-town storekeeper. Madeleine loved the small community, but one thing bothered her: some people in the small town didn't like anyone who was different. They tried to pressure everyone to conform, or to act the same. Madeleine struggled against this, believing that it was important for everyone to express his or her individuality. She later expressed that message—that everyone must be free to be different—in her most famous book, *A Wrinkle in Time*.

While living at Crosswicks, Madeleine became active in the local church and began to renew her Christian faith. Christianity became one of Madeleine's greatest sources of inspiration, and her faith is evident in her writing. However, she does not like to be labeled a "Christian writer," because she wants the freedom to write about all kinds of subjects and themes. "I am a writer who is a Christian," she says. "But I would like to be remembered above all else as a writer."

In 1956, Madeleine and Hugh adopted seven-year-old Maria after her parents, close friends of the

Franklins, had died. The three Franklin children filled Crosswicks with, in Madeleine's words, "a joyful noise." After the children went to bed, Madeleine would begin writing. Her family's life inspired her to write a book called *Meet the Austins,* which she said "could easily have been called *Meet the Franklins!*"

In 1959, the Franklins sold their store and planned to move back to New York. But first, they went on a ten-week camping trip across the country. That same year, inspired by the ideas of famous physicists Albert Einstein and Max Planck, Madeleine had an idea for a new story, one that would involve travel through time and space. In the fall of 1959, she finished her book and called it *A Wrinkle in Time.*

"[*A Wrinkle in Time*] was very different from my six earlier published books but I loved it," Madeleine says, "and I hoped that it would mark a turning point."

Unfortunately, many publishers thought *A Wrinkle in Time* was too different, and too difficult. Madeleine received rejection letter after rejection letter. She thought her book would never be published. Finally, after *A Wrinkle in Time* had been rejected 26 times in two years, Madeleine gave up and told her agent to send the book back. Her agent did send it back, but a few months later, she met a publisher who believed in her book. *A Wrinkle in Time* was published in 1962 and became an immediate success. The book won the Newbery Medal in 1963, and went on to win several more awards. Madeleine was thrilled.

Over the next few years, Madeleine published more books. She also began working as a librarian at the Cathedral Church of St. John the Divine in New York. The cathedral library was a quiet place for her to write and think. Hugh continued to act, becoming well known as the suave "Dr. Tyler" on the soap opera *All My Children.* Every summer, the family moved back to Crosswicks. Madeleine published journals about her times there.

In 1973, Madeleine published *A Wind in the Door,* a sequel to *A Wrinkle in Time.* Those two books, along with *A Swiftly Tilting Planet* (1978) and *Many Waters* (1986), continue the adventures of Meg, Charles Wallace, and the rest of the Murry family. They make up what Madeleine calls her "Time Quartet." But Madeleine didn't stop there. Characters from the Murry family and from Calvin O'Keefe's family appear in *The Arm of the Starfish* (1965), *Dragons in the Waters* (1976), and *An Acceptable Time* (1989). Madeleine also wrote many other novels for adults and young people as well as essays and books about faith and prayer. Today, she has written more than sixty books.

In 1986, Madeleine's husband Hugh died of cancer. Hugh and Madeleine had a wonderful marriage, and in losing Hugh she knew she would never be the same again. "We are not supposed to get over our greatest griefs," she wrote. "They are part of what makes us who we are." Not long after he died, Madeleine wrote a book about her marriage to Hugh, called *Two-Part Invention*.

Today, Madeleine lives in her New York City apartment for part of the year, and stays at Crosswicks during the summer. She enjoys spending time with her friends and with her family, which has grown to include grandchildren and great-grandchildren. And, as always, she continues to write.

BOOKS BY MADELEINE L'ENGLE

Fiction for Young Adults

Austin Family Books: *Meet the Austins, The Moon By Night, The Young Unicorns, A Ring of Endless Light, Troubling a Star*

The Time Quartet: *A Wrinkle in Time, A Wind in the Door, A Swiftly Tilting Planet, Many Waters*

Murry/O'Keefe Family Books: *The Arm of the Starfish, Dragons in the Waters, A House Like a Lotus, An Acceptable Time*

Other: *And Both Were Young, Camilla* (originally *Camilla Dickinson*)

Fiction for Adults

The Small Rain (later published as *Prelude*), *Ilsa, A Winter's Love, The Love Letters, The Other Side of the Sun, A Severed Wasp, Certain Women, A Live Coal in the Sea*

Children's Fiction

The Twenty-Four Days Before Christmas, The Anti-Muffins, Miracle on 10th Street, A Full House, The Other Dog

Autobiographical
The Crosswicks Journals: *A Circle of Quiet, The Summer of the Great-Grandmother, The Irrational Season, Two-Part Invention*

Poems
Lines Scribbled on an Envelope, The Risk of Birth, The Weather of the Heart, A Cry Like a Bell

Prayers
Everyday Prayers, Prayers for Sunday, Anytime Prayers, Mothers and Daughters (with Maria Rooney), *Mothers and Sons* (with Maria Rooney), *Prayerbook for Spiritual Friends* (with Luci Shaw)

Reflections on Scripture
And It Was Good, A Stone for a Pillow, Sold Into Egypt, The Rock That Is Higher, Penguins and Golden Calves, Bright Evening Star

Special Books, Plays, and Short Stories
18 Washington Square South, A Journey with Jonah, Dance in the Desert, Spirit and Light, Ladder of Angels, Walking on Water, The Sphinx at Dawn, Trailing Clouds of Glory (with Avery Brooke), *The Glorious Impossible, Glimpses of Grace* (with Carole Chase), *Wintersong* (with Luci Shaw), *Friends for the Journey* (with Luci Shaw), *Madeleine L'Engle Herself* (with Carole Chase)

Time Line of Madeleine L'Engle's Life

➢ = Publications

1918 Madeleine L'Engle Camp is born on November 29 in New York City.

1929 Concerned about her father's health, Madeleine and her family move to a château in the French Alps.

1930 Madeleine is sent to a boarding school in Switzerland.

1932 The Camps return to the United States to care for Madeleine's grandmother, who lives in northern Florida.

1933 Madeleine is sent to Ashley Hall, a boarding school in Charleston, South Carolina.

1935 Charles Camp, Madeleine's father, dies of pneumonia. Madeleine is a senior in high school.

1936 Madeleine enrolls in Smith College, a women's college in Massachusetts. She majors in English.

1941 Madeleine graduates from Smith with honors. She moves to an apartment in New York City.

1943 Madeleine is an understudy in a Broadway play called *Uncle Harry*.
➢ She publishes a one-act play, called *18 Washington Square South*.

1945 Madeleine meets Hugh Franklin while working on the play *The Cherry Orchard*.
➢ *The Small Rain*, Madeleine's first book, is published under the name Madeleine L'Engle, a shortened version of her name that Madeleine felt was "more musical."

1946 Madeleine and Hugh are married. They buy Crosswicks, an old farmhouse in the Connecticut countryside.
➢ *Ilsa* is published.

1947 Daughter Josephine is born.

1949 ➢ *And Both Were Young* is published.

1951 ➢ *Camilla Dickinson* is published.

1952 Son Bion is born. Madeleine and Hugh buy the general store in town; Hugh begins his "longest run" as country storekeeper.

1956 The Franklins adopt Maria.

1957 ➢ *A Winter's Love* is published.

1959 Madeleine and Hugh sell the general store and take their family on a ten-week camping trip across the country before moving to New York. Madeleine writes *A Wrinkle in Time*.

1960 Madeleine begins teaching at St. Hilda's and St. Hugh's Anglican School. She teaches there until 1966.
➢ *Meet the Austins* is published.

➢ After many rejections, *A Wrinkle in Time* is published. **1962**

A Wrinkle in Time wins the John Newbery Medal. **1963**
➢ *The Moon by Night* is published.

➢ *The Twenty-Four Days Before Christmas: An Austin Family Story* is **1964**
published.

Madeleine becomes volunteer librarian and writer-in-residence at the **1965**
Cathedral Church of St. John the Divine in New York City.
➢ *The Arm of the Starfish* is published.

➢ *The Love Letters* is published. **1966**

➢ *The Journey with Jonah* (a play based on a story from the Bible) is **1967**
published.

➢ *The Young Unicorns* is published; the first part of *The Small Rain* is pub- **1968**
lished as *Prelude*.

The Moon by Night wins the Austrian State Literary Prize. **1969**
➢ *Dance in the Desert* and *Lines Scribbled on an Envelope* are published.

Madeleine's mother, Madeleine Camp, dies at age 90. **1971**
➢ *The Other Side of the Sun* is published.

➢ *A Circle of Quiet* is published. **1972**

➢ *A Wind in the Door* is published. **1973**

➢ *Summer of the Great-Grandmother*, the story of Madeleine's mother's **1974**
last year of life, is published. *The Risk of Birth, Prayers for Sunday,* and
Everyday Prayers are also published.

Wheaton College in Illinois creates a special collection of all Madeleine's **1976**
papers and manuscripts.
➢*Dragons in the Waters* and *Spirit and Light: Essays in Historical Theology*
are published.

➢ *The Irrational Season* is published. **1977**

Madeleine wins the University of Southern Mississippi Medal. **1978**
➢ *A Swiftly Tilting Planet* and *The Weather of the Heart* are published.

➢ *Ladder of Angels: Scenes from the Bible Illustrated by Children around the* **1979**
World is published.

A Swiftly Tilting Planet wins the American Book Award; *A Ring of Endless* **1980**
Light is named a Newbery Honor book.
➢ *A Ring of Endless Light, The Anti-Muffins* (an Austin family story), and
Walking on Water: Reflections on Faith and Art are published.

A Swiftly Tilting Planet wins a Newbery Honor Award. **1981**

➢ *The Sphinx at Dawn: Two Stories* and *A Severed Wasp*, a sequel to *A Small* **1982**
Rain, are published.

1983	➤ *And It was Good: Reflections on Beginnings,* is published.
1984	Madeleine wins the Sophia Smith Award, an award given by Smith College for distinction in one's chosen field. ➤ *A House Like a Lotus* is published.
1985	Madeleine wins the Regina Medal. She begins a two-year term as president of the Author's Guild. Hugh retires from "All My Children" and travels with Madeleine on her book tours. They visit Egypt and Austria. ➤ *Trailing Clouds of Glory* is published.
1986	Hugh and Madeleine travel to China together. In September, Hugh dies of cancer. ➤ *Many Waters* is published.
1988	Madeleine celebrates her seventieth birthday with hundreds of friends and relatives at a huge "surprise" party held at the Cathedral Church of St. John the Divine. ➤ *Two-Part Invention: The Story of a Marriage,* a book about Madeleine's marriage to Hugh, is published.
1989	➤ *Sold into Egypt: Joseph's Journey into Human Being* and *An Acceptable Time* are published
1990	➤ *The Glorious Impossible* is published
1992	➤ *Certain Women* is published.
1993	➤ *The Rock That Is Higher* is published.
1994	➤ *Troubling a Star* is published.
1996	➤ *A Live Coal in the Sea* is published. It continues the story of the character Camilla from *Camilla Dickinson; Glimpses of Grace* and *Penguins and Golden Calves* are published.
1997	➤ *Bright Evening Star, Mothers and Daughters,* and *Friends for the Journey* are published.
1998	Madeleine wins the Margaret Edwards Award for achievement in young adult literature.
1999	Madeleine's first great-grandchild, Konstantinos John Voiklis, is born. Her son Bion dies at the age of 47. Madeleine suffers a hip injury. ➤ *A Full House, Mothers and Sons,* and *A Prayerbook for Spiritual Friends* are published.
2000	➤*Madeleine L'Engle Herself: Reflections on a Writing Life,* a collection of Madeleine's essays, put together by Carole Chase, is published.
2001	➤ *The Other Dog,* a children's picture book, is published.

Introducing the Novel
A Wrinkle in Time

In 1958, while Madeleine L'Engle was on a cross-country camping trip with her family, three strange names popped into her mind: *Mrs Whatsit, Mrs Who,* and *Mrs Which.* She immediately decided, "I'll have to write a book about them."

The book she wrote is called *A Wrinkle in Time.* It is about a girl named Meg Murry who, along with her little brother Charles Wallace and a friend named Calvin, takes a journey through time and space to find her missing father—and to fight against an evil force bigger than anything they have ever imagined. On the journey, they are guided by three mysterious beings, whose names you can probably guess.

For two years, Madeleine L'Engle didn't think the book would get published at all. It was rejected time and time again because publishers thought it was too unusual, too difficult, and even too scary for young people. Luckily, one publisher decided to take a chance, and the book became an instant success.

Today, *A Wrinkle in Time* is one of L'Engle's best-known works, and it is considered a classic of young-adult literature. It was awarded the 1963 Newbery Medal and has been translated into over 15 languages. Readers love it just as much today as they did when it was published forty years ago.

Madeleine L'Engle went on to publish three more books about the Murry family's fantastic adventures: *A Wind in the Door* (1973), *A Swiftly Tilting Planet* (1978), and *Many Waters* (1986). Together with *A Wrinkle in Time,* these books are known as the Time Quartet. Characters from *A Wrinkle in Time* also reappear in many of L'Engle's other novels, including *A House Like a Lotus, Dragons in the Waters, The Arm of the Starfish,* and *An Acceptable Time.*

Part Science, Part Fantasy

A Wrinkle in Time is part **science fiction**—imaginative literature based on scientific principles, discoveries, or laws—and part **fantasy**—imaginative literature that can contain magical or supernatural occurrences. This is a combination L'Engle likes to call "science fantasy."

L'Engle says, "What I do in the science fantasies is take a current scientific idea and then, within the limits of possibility, open it up, push it a little further." In *A Wrinkle in Time,* L'Engle used ideas taken from **physics,** a science that deals with matter and energy and how these interact together. The works of famous physicists Albert Einstein and Max Ernst Planck inspired some of the most fantastic occurrences in her novel. Einstein's theory of relativity helped her explain how her characters could "wrinkle" through time and space. Planck's quantum theory helped her explain how the characters could rearrange atoms in order to pass through seemingly solid matter. For more information about the science behind *A Wrinkle in Time,* read the related reading "Wrinkles in Spacetime" on page 215.

Other parts of the book are not explained by scientific ideas. For example, the three Mrs Ws are not based on scientific principles—they are pure fantasy.

Mixing science and fantasy may seem like a strange combination, but Madeleine L'Engle thinks it makes perfect sense. In her speech accepting the Margaret A. Edwards Award, she said, "We live in a fantastic universe, and subatomic particles and quantum mechanics are even more fantastic than the macrocosm [whole universe]. Often the only way to look clearly at this extraordinary universe is through fantasy, fairy tale, myth."

Themes in *A Wrinkle in Time*

One of the **themes,** or main ideas, of *A Wrinkle in Time* is that we all must have the freedom to be different, to think for ourselves and to express our own individual opinions and beliefs. At the beginning of *A Wrinkle in Time,* Meg is upset because she is different, an "oddball." She wishes she were the same as everyone else. But when she goes on her journey, she discovers just how important differences are.

Another important idea in the book is that everyone must do his or her part to fight against evil. In order to illustrate this idea, L'Engle includes quotes from the Bible and from people throughout history who have fought evil with goodness.

Other themes in the book include the idea that things are not always what they seem and the importance of family.

Historical Connections

One of the strongest messages in *A Wrinkle in Time* is that we all must have the freedom to be different, to think for ourselves and to express our own individual opinions and beliefs. This message is important for all times, but it seemed especially urgent in 1962, when the book was first published. At that time, the United States was in the midst of a Cold War—a long period of conflict that never led to full-scale war—with the Soviet Union. Americans criticized the Soviet government because it was very controlling. Unlike American citizens, the Soviets did not enjoy freedom of religion or freedom of the press. People who spoke out against the government could be put in prison.

During the Cold War, many Americans worried that the Soviet form of government would spread, threatening freedom and individuality around the globe. Important books such as George Orwell's *Animal Farm* and *1984* as well as Ray Bradbury's *Fahrenheit 451* depicted what life might be like if all people's freedoms were taken away by controlling leaders. In *A Wrinkle in Time*, Madeleine L'Engle presents her own views about the importance of freedom and individuality.

Space travel is another aspect of the book with a strong link to 1960s history. Madeleine L'Engle started work on her book the year after the Soviets had launched the first orbital satellite, Sputnik, in 1957. This event made everyone around the world go space-crazy, and it set off a Space Race between the U.S. and the Soviet Union that would result in the landing of U.S. astronauts on the moon in 1969.

Characters in
A Wrinkle in Time

Meg Murry. Meg, the main character of *A Wrinkle in Time,* is around thirteen years old. She is very good at math, but not much good at other subjects. She hates school and is always getting in trouble there. Meg thinks she is plain-looking and an oddball.

Charles Wallace Murry. Charles Wallace is Meg's little brother. He is five years old and a genius. Charles Wallace has some extraordinary abilities that Meg is just beginning to understand.

Mr. Murry. Mr. Murry is Meg's father, a physicist who disappeared while working on a top-secret project for the government. Although the family has not heard from him in nearly a year, they still hold out hope that he will return.

Mrs. Murry. Mrs. Murry is Meg's mother. She is a scientist with degrees in biology and bacteriology, and can often be found conducting experiments in her lab off the Murrys' kitchen. Mrs. Murry misses her husband very much, but tries to hide her feelings from her children.

Calvin O'Keefe. Calvin is captain of the basketball team at Meg's high school. Because of his high intelligence, Calvin is already in eleventh grade although he is only fourteen. The tall, orange-haired, blue-eyed boy is popular with all the kids at school. However, Calvin hides certain aspects of himself in order to fit in. Meg and Charles Wallace first meet Calvin in the woods while on their way to see Mrs Whatsit.

Sandy and Dennys. Sandy and Dennys are Meg's ten-year-old twin brothers. They are average students, popular, and athletic. People make fun of Meg and Charles Wallace, but they never make fun of Sandy and Dennys.

Mr. Jenkins. Mr. Jenkins is Meg's high-school principal. He is a cold man who tells Meg that her life would be easier if she just "faced facts" and accepted that her father is not coming back. He also accuses Meg of being "the most belligerent, uncooperative child in school."

Mrs. Buncombe. The wife of the town constable, or police officer, Mrs. Buncombe has twelve bedsheets stolen at the beginning of the book.

Fortinbras. Fortinbras is the Murry family's dog. He arrived on their doorstep as a half-grown puppy. Fortinbras only barks when there is trouble.

Mrs Whatsit, Mrs Who, and Mrs Which. When Meg and Charles Wallace first meet them, these three are living in an abandoned house back in the woods not far from the Murry home. They appear to be old women, but it soon becomes clear that they are only in disguise. Madeleine L'Engle chose to spell the names of these three without a period after "Mrs" (a British style that looks odd to the American reader) in order to make them seem even more mysterious and extraordinary. **Mrs Whatsit** is 2,379,152,497 years old, which makes her younger than her two other companions. When the Murrys first meet her, she is a pleasant-looking old woman dressed in the raggedy clothing of a tramp. **Mrs Who** appears as a plump old lady with enormous glasses. She has a hard time verbalizing her thoughts, so she expresses herself by quoting famous writers and philosophers. **Mrs Which**, the oldest and wisest of the trio, finds it difficult to materialize, so she is most often seen as a shimmering gleam. When she speaks, her voice echoes, or reverberates.

The Dark Thing. The Dark Thing, or Black Thing, is a cold and dark substance like a cloud or a shadow. It represents the forces of evil that threaten to take over the Earth and other parts of the universe.

The Happy Medium. The Happy Medium is a jolly fortune-teller who lives in the constellation of Orion the Hunter. She wears a turban and a long flowing satin gown. The Happy Medium can see everything through her magical crystal ball, and at the command of the three Mrs Ws, she shows the children a view of their home planet being menaced by the Dark Thing.

The Man with Red Eyes. The Man with Red Eyes works for CENTRAL Central Intelligence on the planet Camazotz. Like everyone else on Camazotz, he is controlled by IT. Looking into his glowing red eyes causes people to become hypnotized and drawn into ITs power.

Aunt Beast. Aunt Beast, an inhabitant of the planet Ixchel, is gray and furry with many tentacles. Though repulsive in appearance, she has a wonderful smell and a comforting touch. Like all the other creatures on her planet, Aunt Beast has no eyes. She teaches Meg that it is more important to know what things *are* like than what they *look* like. Aunt Beast saves Meg's life after Meg goes through the Dark Thing.

IT. IT has taken over the minds of everyone on the planet Camazotz and is helping the Dark Thing. IT attempts to brainwash Charles Wallace and Meg as well.

Echoes:

Quotes on Themes
from A Wrinkle in Time

The Universe Is a Mystery

"The most beautiful thing we can experience is a sense of the mysterious. It is the fundamental emotion at the source of all true art and science. The person who knows it not, who can no longer wonder, can no longer feel amazement, is as good as dead, a snuffed-out candle."

—Albert Einstein (1879–1955),
American (German-born) physicist

"[J]ust because we don't understand doesn't mean that the explanation doesn't exist."

—Mrs. Murry to Meg, chapter 3 of *A Wrinkle in Time*

"Nothing important is completely explicable."

—Madeleine L'Engle

The Importance of Freedom and Individuality

"We hold these truths to be self-evident, that all men are created equal, that they are endowed by their creator with certain unalienable rights, that among these are life, liberty, and the pursuit of happiness."

—from The Declaration of Independence, written by Thomas Jefferson (1743–1826), 3rd President of the United States

"As human beings, we are endowed with freedom of choice, and we cannot shuffle off our responsibility upon the shoulders of God or nature. We must shoulder it ourselves. It is up to us."

—A. J. Toynbee (1889–1975), English historian

"It is the ability to choose which makes us human."

—Madeleine L'Engle

"All Fords are exactly alike, but no two people are just alike. Every new life is a new thing under the sun; there has never been anything just like it before, never will be again. [Young people] ought to get that idea . . . [they] should look for the single spark of individuality that makes [them] different from other folks, and develop that. . . . Society and schools may try to iron it out of [them]; their tendency is to put it all in the same mold, but I say don't let that spark be lost; it is your only real claim to importance."

—Henry Ford (1863–1947), American car manufacturer

Courage for the Journey

"The longest journey of any person is the journey inwards."

—Dag Hammarskjöld (1905–1961), Swedish statesman and secretary-general of the United Nations

"We must do the things we think we cannot do."

—Eleanor Roosevelt (1884–1962), American wife of President Franklin D. Roosevelt

"Not I, nor anyone can travel that journey for you. You must travel it for yourself."

—Walt Whitman (1819–1892), American poet

Chapter 1

Mrs Whatsit

It was a dark and stormy night.

In her attic bedroom Margaret Murry, wrapped in an old patchwork quilt, sat on the foot of her bed and watched the trees tossing in the <u>frenzied</u> lashing of the wind. Behind the trees clouds scudded frantically across the sky. Every few moments the moon ripped through them, creating <u>wraithlike</u> shadows that raced along the ground.

The house shook.

Wrapped in her quilt, Meg shook.

She wasn't usually afraid of weather. —It's not just the weather, she thought. —It's the weather on top of everything else. On top of me. On top of Meg Murry doing everything wrong. School. School was all wrong. She'd been dropped down to the lowest section in her grade. That morning one of her teachers had said crossly, "Really, Meg, I don't understand how a child with parents as brilliant as yours are supposed to be can be such a poor student. If you don't manage to do a little better you'll have to stay back next year." During lunch she'd rough-housed a little to try to make herself feel better, and one of the girls said scornfully, "After all, Meg, we aren't grammar-school kids any more. Why do you always act like such a baby?"

And on the way home from school, walking up the road with her arms full of books, one of the boys had said something about her "dumb baby brother." At this she'd thrown the books on the side of the road and tackled him with every ounce of strength she had, and arrived home with her blouse torn and a big bruise under one eye.

Sandy and Dennys, her ten-year-old twin brothers, who got home from school an hour earlier than she

---

words for everyday use

fren • zied (fren'zēd) *adj.,* wild or frantic. *The boat was tossed upon the <u>frenzied</u> sea.*

wraith • like (rāth´līk) *adj.,* ghostly. *The flickering firelight cast <u>wraithlike</u> shadows on the walls, frightening the children.*

did, were disgusted. "Let *us* do the fighting when it's necessary," they told her.

—A <u>delinquent</u>, that's what I am, she thought grimly. —That's what they'll be saying next. Not Mother. But Them. Everybody Else. I wish Father—

But it was still not possible to think about her father without the danger of tears. Only her mother could talk about him in a natural way, saying, "When your father gets back—"

Gets back from where? And when? Surely her mother must know what people were saying, must be aware of the <u>smugly</u> vicious gossip. Surely it must hurt her as it did Meg. But if it did she gave no outward sign. Nothing ruffled the serenity of her expression.

—Why can't I hide it, too? Meg thought. Why do I always have to *show* everything?

The window rattled madly in the wind, and she pulled the quilt close about her. Curled up on one of her pillows a gray fluff of kitten yawned, showing its pink tongue, tucked its head under again, and went back to sleep.

Everybody was asleep. Everybody except Meg. Even Charles Wallace, the "dumb baby brother," who had an uncanny way of knowing when she was awake and unhappy, and who would come, so many nights, tiptoeing up the attic stairs to her—even Charles Wallace was asleep.

How could they sleep? All day on the radio there had been hurricane warnings. How could they leave her up in the attic in the rickety brass bed, knowing that the roof might be blown right off the house, and she tossed out into the wild night sky to land who knows where?

Her shivering grew uncontrollable.

—You asked to have the attic bedroom, she told herself savagely. —Mother let you have it because you're the oldest. It's a privilege, not a punishment.

▶ What quality does Meg dislike in herself?

words for everyday use
de • lin • quent (di liŋ´kwənt) *n.*, person who fails to do what duty or law requires. *Brian had promised to spend more time with his brother, Mitchell, but Brian was a <u>delin-quent</u> with regard to fulfilling his promise.*

smug • ly (smug´lē) *adv.*, in a self-satisfied manner. *"I am a much better actor than you are," Robert said <u>smugly</u>.*

"Not during a hurricane, it isn't a privilege," she said aloud. She tossed the quilt down on the foot of the bed, and stood up. The kitten stretched luxuriously, and looked up at her with huge, innocent eyes.

"Go back to sleep," Meg said. "Just be glad you're a kitten and not a monster like me." She looked at herself in the wardrobe mirror and made a horrible face, baring a mouthful of teeth covered with braces. Automatically she pushed her glasses into position, ran her fingers through her mouse-brown hair, so that it stood wildly on end, and let out a sigh almost as noisy as the wind.

The wide wooden floorboards were cold against her feet. Wind blew in the <u>crevices</u> about the window frame, in spite of the protection the storm sash was supposed to offer. She could hear wind howling in the chimneys. From all the way downstairs she could hear Fortinbras, the big black dog, starting to bark. He must be frightened, too. What was he barking at? Fortinbras never barked without reason.

Suddenly she remembered that when she had gone to the post office to pick up the mail she'd heard about a tramp who was supposed to have stolen twelve sheets from Mrs. Buncombe, the constable's wife. They hadn't caught him, and maybe he was heading for the Murrys' house right now, isolated on a back road as it was; and this time maybe he'd be after more than sheets. Meg hadn't paid much attention to the talk about the tramp at the time, because the postmistress, with a sugary smile, had asked if she'd heard from her father lately.

She left her little room and made her way through the shadows of the main attic, bumping against the ping-pong table. —Now I'll have a bruise on my hip on top of everything else, she thought.

Next she walked into her old dolls' house, Charles Wallace's rocking horse, the twins' electric trains.

words for everyday use crev • ice (krev´is) *n.,* narrow opening. *The rock climber searched for <u>crevices</u> in the face of the rock in which to put her hands and feet.*

"Why must everything happen to me?" she demanded of a large teddy bear.

At the foot of the attic stairs she stood still and listened. Not a sound from Charles Wallace's room on the right. On the left, in her parents' room, not a rustle from her mother sleeping alone in the great double bed. She tiptoed down the hall and into the twins' room, pushing again at her glasses as though they could help her to see better in the dark. Dennys was snoring. Sandy murmured something about baseball and <u>subsided</u>. The twins didn't have any problems. They weren't great students, but they weren't bad ones, either. They were perfectly content with a succession of B's and an occasional A or C. They were strong and fast runners and good at games, and when cracks were made about anybody in the Murry family, they weren't made about Sandy and Dennys.

She left the twins' room and went on downstairs, avoiding the creaking seventh step. Fortinbras had stopped barking. It wasn't the tramp this time, then. Fort would go on barking if anybody was around.

—But suppose the tramp *does* come? Suppose he has a knife? Nobody lives near enough to hear if we screamed and screamed and screamed. Nobody'd care, anyhow.

—I'll make myself some cocoa, she decided. —That'll cheer me up, and if the roof blows off at least I won't go off with it.

In the kitchen a light was already on, and Charles Wallace was sitting at the table drinking milk and eating bread and jam. He looked very small and vulnerable sitting there alone in the big old-fashioned kitchen, a blond little boy in faded blue Dr. Dentons, his feet swinging a good six inches above the floor.

▶ *Why don't the twins have problems at school?*

"Hi," he said cheerfully. "I've been waiting for you."

From under the table where he was lying at Charles Wallace's feet, hoping for a crumb or two, Fortinbras raised his slender dark head in greeting to Meg, and his tail thumped against the floor. Fortinbras had arrived on their doorstep, a half-grown puppy, scrawny and abandoned, one winter night. He was, Meg's father had decided, part Llewellyn setter and part greyhound, and he had a slender, dark beauty that was all his own.

"Why didn't you come up to the attic?" Meg asked her brother, speaking as though he were at least her own age. "I've been scared stiff."

"Too windy up in that attic of yours," the little boy said. "I knew you'd be down. I put some milk on the stove for you. It ought to be hot by now."

How did Charles Wallace always know about her? How could he always tell? He never knew—or seemed to care—what Dennys or Sandy were think-ing. It was his mother's mind, and Meg's, that he probed with frightening accuracy.

Was it because people were a little afraid of him that they whispered about the Murrys' youngest child, who was rumored to be not quite bright? "I've heard that clever people often have subnor-mal children," Meg had once overheard. "The two boys seem to be nice, regular children, but that unattractive girl and the baby boy certainly aren't all there."

It was true that Charles Wallace seldom spoke when anybody was around, so that many people thought he'd never learned to talk. And it was true that he hadn't talked at all until he was almost four. Meg would turn white with fury when people looked at him and clucked, shaking their heads sadly.

"Don't worry about Charles Wallace, Meg," her father had once told her. Meg remembered it very clearly because it was shortly before he went away. "There's nothing the matter with his mind. He just does things in his own way and in his own time."

◄ How would you answer Meg's question, "Was it because people were a little afraid of him . . .?"

"I don't want him to grow up to be dumb like me," Meg had said.

"Oh, my darling, you're not dumb," her father answered. "You're like Charles Wallace. Your development has to go at its own pace. It just doesn't happen to be the usual pace."

"How do you *know?*" Meg had demanded. "How do you *know* I'm not dumb? Isn't it just because you love me?"

"I love you, but that's not what tells me. Mother and I've given you a number of tests, you know."

Yes, that was true. Meg had realized that some of the "games" her parents played with her were tests of some kind, and that there had been more for her and Charles Wallace than for the twins. "IQ tests,[1] you mean?"

"Yes, some of them."

"Is my IQ okay?"

"More than okay."

"What is it?"

"That I'm not going to tell you. But it assures me that both you and Charles Wallace will be able to do pretty much whatever you like when you grow up to yourselves. You just wait till Charles Wallace starts to talk. You'll see."

How right he had been about that, though he himself had left before Charles Wallace began to speak, suddenly, with none of the usual baby <u>preliminaries</u>, using entire sentences. How proud he would have been!

"You'd better check the milk," Charles Wallace said to Meg now, his <u>diction</u> clearer and cleaner than that of most five-year-olds. "You know you don't like it when it gets a skin on top."

"You put in more than twice enough milk." Meg peered into the saucepan.

---

1. **IQ tests.** Intelligence quotient tests: tests designed to measure mental ability

---

words for everyday use

pre • lim • i • na • ries (prē lim´ ə ner´ēz) *n.,* preparatory steps. *Crawling and walking aided by one's family members are the usual <u>preliminaries</u> to a young child's taking his or her first unaided steps.*

dic • tion (dik´shən) *n.,* manner of expression in words. *Because she had a lovely voice and her <u>diction</u> was so clear, we thought that she would be an excellent radio announcer.*

Charles Wallace nodded serenely. "I thought Mother might like some."

"I might like what?" a voice said, and there was their mother standing in the doorway.

"Cocoa," Charles Wallace said. "Would you like a liverwurst-and-cream-cheese sandwich? I'll be happy to make you one."

"That would be lovely," Mrs. Murry said, "but I can make it myself if you're busy."

"No trouble at all." Charles Wallace slid down from his chair and trotted over to the refrigerator, his pajamaed feet padding softly as a kitten's. "How about you, Meg?" he asked. "Sandwich?"

"Yes, please," she said. "But not liverwurst. Do we have any tomatoes?"

Charles Wallace peered into the crisper. "One. All right if I use it on Meg, Mother?"

"To what better use could it be put?" Mrs. Murry smiled. "But not so loud, please, Charles. That is, unless you want the twins downstairs, too."

"Let's be <u>exclusive</u>," Charles Wallace said. "That's my new word for the day. Impressive, isn't it?"

"<u>Prodigious</u>," Mrs. Murry said. "Meg, come let me look at that bruise."

Meg knelt at her mother's feet. The warmth and light of the kitchen had relaxed her so that her attic fears were gone. The cocoa steamed fragrantly in the saucepan; geraniums bloomed on the window sills and there was a bouquet of tiny yellow chrysanthemums in the center of the table. The curtains, red, with a blue and green geometrical pattern, were drawn, and seemed to reflect their cheerfulness throughout the room. The furnace purred like a great, sleepy animal; the lights glowed with steady radiance; outside, alone in the dark, the wind still battered against the house, but the angry power that had frightened Meg while she was alone in the attic was <u>subdued</u> by the familiar comfort of the kitchen.

◄ How does being in the warm kitchen with other people change Meg's feelings about the storm?

words for everyday use

ex • clu • sive (ik sklü´siv) adj., keeping out certain people or groups. *Rather than inviting everyone to their party, they were* <u>exclusive</u> *and kept their guest list brief.*

pro • di • gious (prō dij´əs) adj., wonderful; amazing; of great size. *While the rest of us caught tiny fish, Jason caught one of* <u>prodigious</u> *size.*

sub • due (sub´dü) v., conquer; overcome. *Much to everyone's surprise, Queen Elizabeth's navy* <u>subdued</u> *the mighty Spanish Armada.*

Underneath Mrs. Murry's chair Fortinbras let out a contented sigh.

Mrs. Murry gently touched Meg's bruised cheek. Meg looked up at her mother, half in loving admiration, half in <u>sullen</u> resentment. It was not an advantage to have a mother who was a scientist and a beauty as well. Mrs. Murry's flaming red hair, creamy skin, and violet eyes with long dark lashes seemed even more spectacular in comparison with Meg's outrageous plainness. Meg's hair had been passable as long as she wore it tidily in braids. When she went into high school it was cut, and now she and her mother struggled with putting it up, but one side would come out curly and the other straight, so that she looked even plainer than before.

"You don't know the meaning of <u>moderation</u>, do you, my darling?" Mrs. Murry asked. "A happy medium is something I wonder if you'll ever learn. That's a nasty bruise the Henderson boy gave you. By the way, shortly after you'd gone to bed his mother called up to complain about how badly you'd hurt him. I told her that since he's a year older and at least twenty-five pounds heavier than you are, I thought I was the one who ought to be doing the complaining. But she seemed to think it was all your fault."

"I suppose that depends on how you look at it," Meg said. "Usually no matter what happens people think it's my fault, even if I have nothing to do with it at all. But I'm sorry I tried to fight him. It's just been an awful week. And I'm full of bad feeling."

Mrs. Murry stroked Meg's shaggy head. "Do you know why?"

"I *hate* being an oddball," Meg said. "It's hard on Sandy and Dennys, too. I don't know if they're really like everybody else, or if they're just able to

▶ Why is Meg "full of bad feeling"?

---

words for everyday use

sul • len (sul´ən) *adj.,* showing ill humor by moody and unsociable withdrawal. *Ellen showed her ill humor by sitting alone in the corner with a <u>sullen</u> face.*

mod • er • a • tion (mäd´ər ā´shən) *n.,* avoidance of extremes. *A healthy diet involves eating in <u>moderation</u>—neither gorging nor starving yourself.*

pretend they are. I try to pretend, but it isn't any help."

"You're much too straightforward to be able to pretend to be what you aren't," Mrs. Murry said. "I'm sorry, Meglet. Maybe if Father were here he could help you, but I don't think I can do anything till you've managed to plow through some more time. Then things will be easier for you. But that isn't much help right now, is it?"

"Maybe if I weren't so <u>repulsive</u> looking—maybe if I were pretty like you—"

"Mother's not a bit pretty; she's beautiful," Charles Wallace announced, slicing liverwurst. "Therefore I bet she was awful at your age."

"How right you are," Mrs. Murry said. "Just give yourself time, Meg."

"Lettuce on your sandwich, Mother?" Charles Wallace asked.

"No, thanks."

He cut the sandwich into sections, put it on a plate, and set it in front of his mother. "Yours'll be along in just a minute, Meg. I think I'll talk to Mrs Whatsit about you."

"Who's Mrs Whatsit?" Meg asked.

"I think I want to be exclusive about her for a while," Charles Wallace said. "Onion salt?"

"Yes, please."

"What's Mrs Whatsit stand for?" Mrs. Murry asked.

"That's her name," Charles Wallace answered. "You know the old shingled house back in the woods that the kids won't go near because they say it's haunted? That's where they live."

"They?"

"Mrs Whatsit and her two friends. I was out with Fortinbras a couple of days ago—you and the twins were at school, Meg. We like to walk in the woods,

---

words for everyday use re • pul • sive (ri pul´siv) *adj.*, disgusting. *Renée found the chewing gum left in the drinking fountain <u>repulsive</u>.*

and suddenly he took off after a squirrel and I took off after him and we ended up by the haunted house, so I met them by accident, as you might say."

"But nobody lives there," Meg said.

"Mrs Whatsit and her friends do. They're very enjoyable."

"Why didn't you tell me about it before?" Mrs. Murry asked. "And you know you're not supposed to go off our property without permission, Charles."

"I know," Charles said. "That's one reason I didn't tell you. I just rushed off after Fortinbras without thinking. And then I decided, well, I'd better save them for an emergency, anyhow."

A fresh gust of wind took the house and shook it, and suddenly the rain began to lash against the windows.

"I don't think I like this wind," Meg said nervously.

"We'll lose some shingles off the roof, that's certain," Mrs. Murry said. "But this house has stood for almost two hundred years and I think it will last a little longer, Meg. There's been many a high wind up on this hill."

"But this is a hurricane!" Meg wailed. "The radio kept saying it was a hurricane!"

"It's October," Mrs. Murry told her. "There've been storms in October before."

As Charles Wallace gave Meg her sandwich Fortinbras came out from under the table. He gave a long, low growl, and they could see the dark fur slowly rising on his back. Meg felt her own skin prickle.

"What's wrong?" she asked anxiously.

Fortinbras stared at the door that opened into Mrs. Murry's laboratory which was in the old stone dairy right off the kitchen. Beyond the lab a pantry led outdoors, though Mrs. Murry had done her best to train the family to come into the house through the garage door or the front door and not through her lab. But it was the lab door and not the garage door toward which Fortinbras was growling.

"You didn't leave any nasty-smelling chemicals cooking over a Bunsen burner, did you, Mother?" Charles Wallace asked.

Mrs. Murry stood up. "No. But I think I'd better go see what's upsetting Fort, anyhow."

"It's the tramp, I'm sure it's the tramp," Meg said nervously.

"What tramp?" Charles Wallace asked.

"They were saying at the post office this afternoon that a tramp stole all Mrs. Buncombe's sheets."

"We'd better sit on the pillow cases, then," Mrs. Murry said lightly. "I don't think even a tramp would be out on a night like this, Meg."

"But that's probably why he *is* out," Meg wailed, "trying to find a place *not* to be out."

"In which case I'll offer him the barn till morning." Mrs. Murry went briskly to the door.

"I'll go with you." Meg's voice was <u>shrill</u>.

"No, Meg, you stay with Charles and eat your sandwich."

"Eat!" Meg exclaimed as Mrs. Murry went out through the lab. "How does she expect me to eat?"

"Mother can take care of herself," Charles said. "Physically, that is." But he sat in his father's chair at the table and his legs kicked at the rungs; and Charles Wallace, unlike most small children, had the ability to sit still.

After a few moments that seemed like forever to Meg, Mrs. Murry came back in, holding the door open for—was it the tramp? It seemed small for Meg's idea of a tramp. The age or sex was impossible to tell, for it was completely bundled up in clothes. Several scarves of assorted colors were tied about the head, and a man's felt hat perched atop. A shocking pink stole was knotted about a rough overcoat, and black rubber boots covered the feet.

◀ Who is the most anxious: Mrs. Murry, Meg, or Charles Wallace? What does Charles Wallace mean when he says their mother can take care of herself "physically"?

---

words for everyday use   shrill (shril) *adj.*, having a high-pitched, piercing sound. *To call his dog, Roy let out a <u>shrill</u> whistle.*

"Mrs Whatsit," Charles said suspiciously, "what are you doing here? And at this time of night, too?"

"Now don't you be worried, my honey." A voice emerged from among turned-up coat collar, stole, scarves, and hat, a voice like an unoiled gate, but somehow not unpleasant.

"Mrs—uh—Whatsit—says she lost her way," Mrs. Murry said. "Would you care for some hot chocolate, Mrs Whatsit?"

"Charmed, I'm sure," Mrs Whatsit answered, taking off the hat and the stole. "It isn't so much that I lost my way as that I got blown off course. And when I realized that I was at little Charles Wallace's house I thought I'd just come in and rest a bit before proceeding on my way."

"How did you know this was Charles Wallace's house?" Meg asked.

"By the smell." Mrs Whatsit untied a blue and green paisley scarf, a red and yellow flowered print, a gold Liberty print, a red and black bandanna. Under all this a <u>sparse</u> quantity of grayish hair was tied in a small but tidy knot on top of her head. Her eyes were bright, her nose a round, soft blob, her mouth puckered like an autumn apple. "My, but it's lovely and warm in here," she said.

"Do sit down." Mrs. Murry indicated a chair. "Would you like a sandwich, Mrs Whatsit? I've had liverwurst and cream cheese; Charles has had bread and jam; and Meg, lettuce and tomato."

▶ How could Mrs Whatsit have "peeked"?

"Now, let me see," Mrs Whatsit pondered. "I'm passionately fond of Russian caviar."

"You peeked!" Charles cried indignantly. "We're saving that for Mother's birthday and you can't have any!"

Mrs Whatsit gave a deep and pathetic sigh.

"No," Charles said. "Now, you mustn't give in to her, Mother, or I shall be very angry. How about tuna-fish salad?"

words
for
everyday
use

sparse (spärs) adj., thinly spread. *Because we had just recently seeded our lawn, the new sprouts of grass were still <u>sparse</u>.*

"All right," Mrs Whatsit said meekly.

"I'll fix it," Meg offered, going to the pantry for a can of tuna fish.

—For crying out loud, she thought, —this old woman comes barging in on us in the middle of the night and Mother takes it as though there weren't anything peculiar about it at all. I'll bet she *is* the tramp. I'll bet she *did* steal those sheets. And she's certainly no one Charles Wallace ought to be friends with, especially when he won't even talk to ordinary people.

◀ What does Meg think of Mrs Whatsit?

"I've only been in the neighborhood a short time," Mrs Whatsit was saying as Meg switched off the pantry light and came back into the kitchen with the tuna fish, "and I didn't think I was going to like the neighbors at all until dear little Charles came over with his dog."

"Mrs Whatsit," Charles Wallace demanded severely, "why did you take Mrs. Buncombe's sheets?"

"Well, I *needed* them, Charles dear."

"You must return them at once."

"But Charles, dear, I *can't*. I've *used* them."

"It was very wrong of you," Charles Wallace scolded. "If you needed sheets that badly you should have asked me."

Mrs Whatsit shook her head and clucked. "You can't spare any sheets. Mrs. Buncombe can."

Meg cut up some celery and mixed it in with the tuna. After a moment's hesitation she opened the refrigerator door and brought out a jar of little sweet pickles. —Though why I'm doing it for her I don't know, she thought, as she cut them up. —I don't trust her one bit.

"Tell your sister I'm all right," Mrs Whatsit said to Charles. "Tell her my intentions are good."

"The road to hell is paved with good intentions," Charles <u>intoned</u>.

Charles Wallace repeats a proverb, or common saying. What do you think ◀ the proverb means?

---

words for everyday use

in • tone (in tōn') *v.*, recite in a songlike way. *As their teacher listened, the kindergarteners dutifully <u>intoned</u> the alphabet and the days of the week.*

"My, but isn't he cunning." Mrs Whatsit beamed at him fondly. "It's lucky he has someone to understand him."

"But I'm afraid he doesn't," Mrs. Murry said. "None of us is quite up to Charles."

"But at least you aren't trying to squash him down." Mrs Whatsit nodded her head vigorously. "You're letting him be himself."

◀ What does Mrs Whatsit say is good about the way the Murrys are raising Charles?

"Here's your sandwich," Meg said, bringing it to Mrs Whatsit.

"Do you mind if I take off my boots before I eat?" Mrs Whatsit asked, picking up the sandwich nevertheless. "Listen." She moved her feet up and down in her boots, and they could hear water squelching. "My toes are ever so damp. The trouble is that these boots are a mite too tight for me, and I never can take them off by myself."

◀ Where might Mrs Whatsit have found her clothes?

"I'll help you," Charles offered.

"Not you. You're not strong enough."

"I'll help." Mrs. Murry squatted at Mrs Whatsit's feet, yanking on one slick boot. When the boot came off it came suddenly. Mrs. Murry sat down with a thump. Mrs Whatsit went tumbling backward with the chair onto the floor, sandwich held high in one old claw. Water poured out of the boot and ran over the floor and the big braided rug.

"Oh, dearie me," Mrs Whatsit said, lying on her back in the overturned chair, her feet in the air, one in a red and white striped sock, the other still booted.

Mrs. Murry got to her feet. "Are you all right, Mrs Whatsit?"

◀ How is Mrs Whatsit injured?

"If you have some liniment[2] I'll put it on my <u>dignity</u>," Mrs Whatsit said, still <u>supine</u>. "I think it's sprained. A little oil of cloves mixed well with garlic is rather good." And she took a large bite of sandwich.

---

2. **liniment.** Liquid preparation used to soothe pain or irritation

words for everyday use

dig • ni • ty (dig' nə tē) *n., pride. The important person carried herself with great dignity, her shoulders straight and chin up, her eyes bright with confidence.*

su • pine (sü´pīn) *adj., lying on the back, face upward. The cat lay supine in front of the fire, purring.*

"Do please get up," Charles said. "I don't like to see you lying there that way. You're carrying things too far."

"Have you ever tried to get to your feet with a sprained dignity?" But Mrs Whatsit scrambled up, righted the chair, and then sat back down on the floor, the booted foot stuck out in front of her, and took another bite. She moved with great <u>agility</u> for such an old woman. At least Meg was reasonably sure that she was an old woman, and a very old woman at that.

Mrs Whatsit, her mouth full, ordered Mrs. Murry, "Now pull while I'm already down."

Quite calmly, as though this old woman and her boots were nothing out of the ordinary, Mrs. Murry pulled until the second boot <u>relinquished</u> the foot. This foot was covered with a blue and gray Argyle sock, and Mrs Whatsit sat there, wriggling her toes, contentedly finishing her sandwich before scrambling to her feet. "Ah," she said, "that's ever so much better," and took both boots and shook them out over the sink. "My stomach is full and I'm warm inside and out and it's time I went home."

"Don't you think you'd better stay till morning?" Mrs. Murry asked.

"Oh, thank you, dearie, but there's *so* much to do I just can't waste time sitting around frivoling."[3]

▶ *How do you think Mrs Whatsit has been traveling?*

"It's much too wild a night to travel in."

"Wild nights are my glory," Mrs Whatsit said. "I just got caught in a down draft[4] and blown off course."

"Well, at least till your socks are dry—"

"Wet socks don't bother me. I just didn't like the water squishing around in my boots. Now don't worry about me, lamb." (Lamb was not a word one

---

3. **frivoling.** Wasting time on frivolous, or unimportant, activities
4. **down draft.** Downward air current

a • gil • i • ty (ə jil´ə tē) *n.*, quick and easy movement. *Ballet dancers must possess strength as well as <u>agility</u>.*

re • lin • quish (ri liŋ´kwish) *v.*, give up. *Everyone was shocked when the monarch <u>relinquished</u> his throne.*

would ordinarily think of calling Mrs. Murry.) "I shall just sit down for a moment and pop on my boots and then I'll be on my way. Speaking of ways, pet, by the way, there *is* such a thing as a tesseract."

Mrs. Murry went very white and with one hand reached backward and clutched at a chair for support. Her voice trembled. "What did you say?"

Mrs Whatsit tugged at her second boot. "I said," she grunted, shoving her foot down in, "that there is"—shove—"such a thing"—shove—"as a tesseract." Her foot went down into the boot, and grabbing shawls, scarves, and hat, she hustled out the door. Mrs. Murry stayed very still, making no move to help the old woman. As the door opened, Fortinbras streaked in, panting, wet and shiny as a seal. He looked at Mrs. Murry and whined.

The door slammed.

"Mother, what's the matter!" Meg cried. "What did she say? What is it?"

"The tesseract—" Mrs. Murry whispered. "What did she mean? How could she have known?"

◄ Why is Mrs. Murry surprised?

Chapter 2

Mrs Who

When Meg woke to the jangling of her alarm clock the wind was still blowing but the sun was shining; the worst of the storm was over. She sat up in bed, shaking her head to clear it.

It must have been a dream. She'd been frightened by the storm and worried about the tramp so she'd just dreamed about going down to the kitchen and seeing Mrs Whatsit and having her mother get all frightened and upset by that word—what was it? Tess—tess something.

She dressed hurriedly, picked up the kitten still curled up on the bed, and dumped it unceremoniously on the floor. The kitten yawned, stretched, gave a piteous miaow, trotted out of the attic and down the stairs. Meg made her bed and hurried after it. In the kitchen her mother was making French toast and the twins were already at the table. The kitten was lapping milk out of a saucer.

"Where's Charles?" Meg asked.

"Still asleep. We had rather an interrupted night, if you remember."

"I hoped it was a dream," Meg said.

Her mother carefully turned over four slices of French toast, then said in a steady voice, "No, Meg. Don't hope it was a dream. I don't understand it any more than you do, but one thing I've learned is that you don't have to understand things for them to *be*. I'm sorry I showed you I was upset. Your father and I used to have a joke about tesseract."

"What is a tesseract?" Meg asked.

"It's a concept." Mrs. Murry handed the twins the syrup. "I'll try to explain it to you later. There isn't time before school."

---

words for everyday use   con • cept (kän´sept) *n.*, idea. *The extremely small size of an electron is a difficult concept for many people.*

"I don't see why you didn't wake us up," Dennys said. "It's a gyp[1] we missed out on all the fun."

"You'll be a lot more awake in school today than I will." Meg took her French toast to the table.

"Who cares," Sandy said. "If you're going to let old tramps come into the house in the middle of the night, Mother, you ought to have Den and me around to protect you."

◀ Why do Sandy and Dennys believe Mrs. Murry and the others need them?

"After all, Father would expect us to," Dennys added. "We know you have a great mind and all, Mother," Sandy said, "but you don't have much *sense*. And certainly Meg and Charles don't."

"I know. We're morons." Meg was bitter.

"I wish you wouldn't be such a *dope*, Meg. Syrup, please." Sandy reached across the table. "You don't have to take everything so *person*ally. Use a happy *medium*, for heaven's sake. You just goof around in school and look out the window and don't pay any attention."

◀ Who else told Meg she needed to use a "happy medium"?

"You just make things harder for yourself," Dennys said. "And Charles Wallace is going to have an awful time next year when he starts school. *We* know he's bright, but he's so funny when he's around other people, and they're so used to thinking he's dumb, I don't know what's going to happen to him. Sandy and I'll sock anybody who picks on him, but that's about all we can do."

"Let's not worry about next year till we get through this one," Mrs. Murry said. "More French toast, boys?"

At school Meg was tired and her eyelids sagged and her mind wandered. In social studies she was asked to name the principal imports and exports of Nicaragua, and though she had looked them up dutifully the evening before, now she could remember none of them. The teacher was sarcastic, the rest of the class laughed, and she flung herself down in her seat in a fury. "Who *cares* about the imports and exports of Nicaragua, anyhow?" she muttered.

---

1. **gyp.** A cheat or swindle

"If you're going to be rude, Margaret, you may leave the room," the teacher said.

"Okay, I will." Meg flounced out.

During study hall the principal sent for her. "What seems to be the problem now, Meg?" he asked, pleasantly enough.

Meg looked sulkily down at the floor. "Nothing, Mr. Jenkins."

"Miss Porter tells me you were inexcusably rude."

Meg shrugged.

"Don't you realize that you just make everything harder for yourself by your attitude?" the principal asked. "Now, Meg, *I'm* convinced that you can do the work and keep up with your grade if you will apply yourself, but some of your teachers are not. You're going to have to do something about yourself. Nobody can do it for you." Meg was silent. "Well? What about it, Meg?"

"I don't know what to do," Meg said.

"You could do your homework, for one thing. Wouldn't your mother help you?"

"If I asked her to."

"Meg, is something troubling you? Are you unhappy at home?" Mr. Jenkins asked.

At last Meg looked at him, pushing at her glasses in a <u>characteristic</u> gesture. "Everything's *fine* at home."

"I'm glad to hear it. But I know it must be hard on you to have your father away."

Meg eyed the principal warily, and ran her tongue over the barbed line of her braces.

"Have you had any news from him lately?"

Meg was sure it was not only imagination that made her feel that behind Mr. Jenkins' surface concern was a gleam of <u>avid</u> curiosity. Wouldn't he like to know! she thought. And if I knew anything he's the last person I'd tell. Well, one of the last.

The postmistress must know that it was almost a year now since the last letter, and heaven knows how

▶ *Why does Meg resent the principal's questions? How long has Meg's father been gone?*

words for everyday use

char • ac • ter • is • tic (kar´ək tər is´tik) *adj.,* typical. *Greg wore baseball caps so often that they became <u>characteristic</u> of him.*

a • vid (av´id) *adj.,* eager and enthusiastic. *Lynn was an <u>avid</u> chess player who had participated in several competitions by her sixth birthday.*

many people *she'd* told, or what unkind guesses she'd made about the reason for the long silence.

Mr. Jenkins waited for an answer, but Meg only shrugged.

"Just what was your father's line of business?" Mr. Jenkins asked. "Some kind of scientist, wasn't he?"

"He *is* a <u>physicist</u>." Meg bared her teeth to reveal the two ferocious lines of braces.

◄ What "facts" does Mr. Jenkins want Meg to face?

"Meg, don't you think you'd make a better adjustment to life if you faced facts?"

"I do face facts," Meg said. "They're lots easier to face than people, I can tell you."

"Then why don't you face facts about your father?"

"You leave my father out of it!" Meg shouted.

"Stop bellowing," Mr. Jenkins said sharply. "Do you want the entire school to hear you?"

"So what?" Meg demanded. "I'm not ashamed of anything I'm saying. Are you?"

Mr. Jenkins sighed. "Do you enjoy being the most <u>belligerent</u>, uncooperative child in school?"

Meg ignored this. She leaned over the desk toward the principal. "Mr. Jenkins, you've met my mother, haven't you? You can't accuse her of not facing facts, can you? She's a scientist. She has doctor's degrees in both biology and bacteriology. Her *business* is facts. When she tells me that my father isn't coming home, I'll believe it. As long as she says Father *is* coming home, then I'll believe that."

Mr. Jenkins sighed again. "No doubt your mother wants to believe that your father is coming home, Meg. Very well, I can't do anything else with you. Go on back to study hall. Try to be a little less antagonistic. Maybe your work would improve if your general attitude were more <u>tractable</u>."

---

words for everyday use

phy • si • cist (fiz´i sist) *n.*, expert in the study of matter and energy. *Albert Einstein was a famous <u>physicist</u>.*

bel • lig • er • ent (bə lij´ər ənt) *adj.*, war-like; seeking a fight. *The principal believed that Meg always fought with other students because of her <u>belligerent</u> nature.*

trac • ta • ble (trak´tə b'l) *adj.*, easily managed. *The puppy was so <u>tractable</u> that we never had to send it to obedience school.*

When Meg got home from school her mother was in the lab, the twins were at Little League, and Charles Wallace, the kitten, and Fortinbras were waiting for her. Fortinbras jumped up, put his front paws on her shoulders, and gave her a kiss, and the kitten rushed to his empty saucer and mewed loudly.

"Come on," Charles Wallace said. "Let's go."

"Where?" Meg asked. "I'm hungry, Charles. I don't want to go anywhere till I've had something to eat." She was still sore from the interview with Mr. Jenkins, and her voice sounded cross. Charles Wallace looked at her thoughtfully as she went to the refrigerator and gave the kitten some milk, then drank a mugful herself.

He handed her a paper bag. "Here's a sandwich and some cookies and an apple. I thought we'd better go see Mrs Whatsit."

"Oh, golly," Meg said. "*Why*, Charles?"

"You're still uneasy about her, aren't you?" Charles asked.

"Well, yes."

"Don't be. She's all right. I promise you. She's on our side."

"How do you know?"

"*Meg*," he said impatiently. "I *know*."

"But why should we go see her now?"

"I want to find out more about that tesseract thing. Didn't you see how it upset Mother? You know when Mother can't control the way she feels, when she lets us see she's upset, then it's something big."

Meg thought for a moment. "Okay, let's go. But let's take Fortinbras with us."

"Well, of course. He needs the exercise."

They set off, Fortinbras rushing ahead, then doubling back to the two children, then leaping off again. The Murrys lived about four miles out of the village. Behind the house was a pine woods and it was through this that Charles Wallace took Meg.

"Charles, you know she's going to get in awful trouble—Mrs Whatsit, I mean—if they find out she's

▶ Why does Meg change her mind about going to see Mrs Whatsit?

broken into the haunted house. And taking Mrs. Buncombe's sheets and everything. They could send her to jail."

"One of the reasons I want to go over this afternoon is to warn them."

"Them?"

"I told you she was there with her two friends. I'm not even sure it was Mrs Whatsit herself who took the sheets, though I wouldn't put it past her."

"But what would she want all those sheets for?"

"I intend to ask her," Charles Wallace said, "and to tell them they'd better be more careful. I don't really think they'll let anybody find them, but I just thought we ought to mention the possibility. Sometimes during vacations some of the boys go out there looking for thrills, but I don't think anybody's <u>apt</u> to right now, what with basketball and everything."

They walked in silence for a moment through the fragrant woods, the rusty pine needles gentle under their feet. Up above them the wind made music in the branches. Charles Wallace slipped his hand confidingly in Meg's, and the sweet, little-boy gesture warmed her so that she felt the tense knot inside her begin to loosen. *Charles* loves me at any rate, she thought.

◀ *What is the nature of Meg's relationship with Charles Wallace?*

"School awful again today?" he asked after awhile.

"Yes. I got sent to Mr. Jenkins. He made <u>snide</u> remarks about Father."

◀ *What did Charles know had happened to Meg? How did he know about this?*

Charles Wallace nodded sagely. "I know."

"How do you know?"

Charles Wallace shook his head. "I can't quite explain. You tell me, that's all."

"But I never say anything. You just seem to know."

---

words for everyday use

apt (apt) *adj.*, likely. *If you leave food out, the cat is <u>apt</u> to come back.*

snide (snīd) *adj.*, slyly malicious. *We tried to tell Will that his <u>snide</u> remarks were not winning him any friends, but he continued to make mean comments about other people.*

"Everything about you tells me," Charles said.

"How about the twins?" Meg asked. "Do you know about them, too?"

"I suppose I could if I wanted to. If they needed me. But it's sort of tiring, so I just concentrate on you and Mother."

"You mean you read our minds?"

Charles Wallace looked troubled. "I don't think it's that. It's being able to understand a sort of language, like sometimes if I concentrate very hard I can understand the wind talking with the trees. You tell me, you see, sort of inad—<u>inadvertently</u>. That's a good word, isn't it? I got Mother to look it up in the dictionary for me this morning. I really must learn to read, except I'm afraid it will make it awfully hard for me in school next year if I already know things. I think it will be better if people go on thinking I'm not very bright. They won't hate me quite so much."

Ahead of them Fortinbras started barking loudly, the warning bay that usually told them that a car was coming up the road or that someone was at the door.

"Somebody's here," Charles Wallace said sharply. "Somebody's hanging around the house. Come *on*." He started to run, his short legs straining. At the edge of the woods Fortinbras stood in front of a boy, barking furiously.

As they came panting up the boy said, "For crying out loud, call off your dog."

"Who is he?" Charles Wallace asked Meg.

"Calvin O'Keefe. He's in Regional, but he's older than I am. He's a big bug."

"It's all right, fella. I'm not going to hurt you," the boy said to Fortinbras.

"Sit, Fort," Charles Wallace commanded, and Fortinbras dropped to his haunches in front of the boy, a low growl still pulsing in his dark throat.

▶ *Why doesn't Charles Wallace want to learn how to read?*

words for everyday use in • ad • ver • tent • ly (in´ad vərt´'nt lē) *adv.*, unintentionally; without meaning to. *Rhianna <u>inadvertently</u> overheard her parents' conversation about her upcoming surprise party.*

"Okay." Charles Wallace put his hands on his hips. "Now tell us what you're doing here."

"I might ask the same of you," the boy said with some <u>indignation</u>. "Aren't you two of the Murry kids? This isn't your property, is it?" He started to move, but Fortinbras' growl grew louder and he stopped.

"Tell me about him, Meg," Charles Wallace demanded.

"What would I know about him?" Meg asked. "He's a couple of grades above me, and he's on the basketball team."

"Just because I'm tall." Calvin sounded a little embarrassed. Tall he certainly was, and skinny. His bony wrists stuck out of the sleeves of his blue sweater; his worn corduroy trousers were three inches too short. He had orange hair that needed cutting and the appropriate freckles to go with it. His eyes were an oddly bright blue.

"Tell us what you're doing here," Charles Wallace said.

"What *is* this? The third degree? Aren't you the one who's supposed to be the moron?"

Meg flushed with rage, but Charles Wallace answered placidly, "That's right. If you want me to call my dog off you'd better give."

"Most peculiar moron I've ever met," Calvin said. "I just came to get away from my family."

Charles Wallace nodded. "What kind of family?"

"They all have runny noses. I'm third from the top of eleven kids. I'm a sport."

At that Charles Wallace grinned widely. "So 'm I."

"I don't mean like in baseball," Calvin said.

"Neither do I."

"I mean like in biology," Calvin said suspiciously.

"*A change in gene*," Charles Wallace quoted, "*resulting in the appearance in the offspring of a character which*

◀ *In your own words, what is a "sport"? In what ways are Charles Wallace and Calvin both sports?*

words for everyday use

in • dig • na • tion (in′ dig nā′ shən) *n.*, anger about injustice. *George felt great <u>indignation</u> when he was accused of plagiarizing because he knew he had carefully documented his sources.*

is not present in the parents but which is <u>potentially</u> transmissible to its offspring."

"What gives around here?" Calvin asked. "I was told you couldn't talk."

"Thinking I'm a moron gives people something to feel smug about," Charles Wallace said. "Why should I <u>disillusion</u> them? How old are you, Cal?"

"Fourteen."

"What grade?"

"Junior. Eleventh. I'm bright. Listen, did anybody ask you to come here this afternoon?"

Charles Wallace, holding Fort by the collar, looked at Calvin suspiciously. "What do you mean, *asked?*"

Calvin shrugged. "You still don't trust me, do you?"

"I don't *dis*trust you," Charles Wallace said.

"Do you want to tell me why you're here, then?"

"Fort and Meg and I decided to go for a walk. We often do in the afternoon."

Calvin dug his hands down in his pockets. "You're holding out on me."

"So're you," Charles Wallace said.

"Okay, old sport," Calvin said. "I'll tell you this much. Sometimes I get a feeling about things. You might call it a compulsion. Do you know what compulsion means?"

"<u>Constraint</u>. Obligation. Because one is <u>compelled</u>. Not a very good definition, but it's the Concise Oxford."

"Okay, okay," Calvin sighed. "I must remember I'm preconditioned in my concept of your mentality."

Meg sat down on the coarse grass at the edge of the woods. Fort gently twisted his collar out of Charles Wallace's hands and came over to Meg, lying down beside her and putting his head in her lap.

---

words for everyday use

po • ten • tial • ly (pō ten´shəl lē) adv., possibly. *The meteorologist said that the approaching snowstorm was <u>potentially</u> the worst blizzard in the state's history.*

dis • il • lu • sion (dis´i lü´zhən) v., take away one's illusions or false ideas. *My little sister thinks I am the best football player in the country, but she will probably be <u>disillusioned</u> once she gets a little older.*

con • straint (kən strānt´) n., something that forces or compels. *Because of various <u>constraints</u> Lisa was unable to attend.*

com • pel (kəm pel´) v., force. *You can lead a horse to water, but you can't <u>compel</u> it to drink.*

Calvin tried now politely to direct his words toward Meg as well as Charles Wallace, "When I get this feeling, this compulsion, I always do what it tells me. I can't explain where it comes from or how I get it, and it doesn't happen very often. But I obey it. And this afternoon I had a feeling that I must come over to the haunted house. That's all I know, kid. I'm not holding anything back. Maybe it's because I'm supposed to meet you. You tell *me*."

◀ Why did Calvin come to the woods that day? What ability do you think he has?

Charles Wallace looked at Calvin <u>probingly</u> for a moment; then an almost glazed look came into his eyes, and he seemed to be thinking at him. Calvin stood very still, and waited.

◀ What is Charles Wallace doing?

At last Charles Wallace said, "Okay. I believe you. But I can't tell you. I think I'd like to trust you. Maybe you'd better come home with us and have dinner."

"Well, sure, but—what would your mother say to that?" Calvin asked.

"She'd be delighted. Mother's all right. She's not one of us. But she's all right."

"What about Meg?"

"Meg has it tough," Charles Wallace said. "She's not really one thing or the other."

◀ Into what two categories do you think Charles Wallace divides people? What are the characteristics of each category?

"What do you mean, *one of us?*" Meg demanded. "What do you mean I'm not one thing or the other?"

"Not now, Meg," Charles Wallace said. "Slowly. I'll tell you about it later." He looked at Calvin, then seemed to make a quick decision. "Okay, let's take him to meet Mrs Whatsit. If he's not okay she'll know." He started off on his short legs toward the <u>dilapidated</u> old house.

The haunted house was half in the shadows of the clump of elms in which it stood. The elms were almost bare, now, and the ground around the house was yellow with damp leaves. The late afternoon light had a greenish cast which the blank windows

---

words for everyday use

pro • bing • ly (prōb´iŋ lē) *adv.*, searching with great thoroughness. *Saundra looked* <u>probingly</u> *into the stream to see if there were any trout.*

di • la • pi • da • ted (də lap´ə dāt´id) *adj.*, falling to pieces. *The junkyard was filled with* <u>dilapidated</u> *old cars.*

reflected in a <u>sinister</u> way. An unhinged shutter thumped. Something else creaked. Meg did not wonder that the house had a reputation for being haunted.

A board was nailed across the front door, but Charles Wallace led the way around to the back. The door there appeared to be nailed shut, too, but Charles Wallace knocked, and the door swung slowly outward, creaking on rusty hinges. Up in one of the elms an old black crow gave its raucous cry, and a woodpecker went into a wild ratatattat. A large gray rat scuttled around the corner of the house and Meg let out a stifled shriek.

"They get a lot of fun out of using all the typical props,"[2] Charles Wallace said in a reassuring voice. "Come on. Follow me."

Calvin put a strong hand to Meg's elbow, and Fort pressed against her leg. Happiness at their concern was so strong in her that her panic fled, and she followed Charles Wallace into the dark <u>recesses</u> of the house without fear.

They entered into a sort of kitchen. There was a huge fireplace with a big black pot hanging over a merry fire. Why had there been no smoke visible from the chimney? Something in the pot was bubbling, and it smelled more like one of Mrs. Murry's chemical messes than something to eat. In a dilapidated Boston rocker sat a plump little woman. She wasn't Mrs Whatsit, so she must, Meg decided, be one of Mrs Whatsit's two friends. She wore enormous spectacles, twice as thick and twice as large as Meg's, and she was sewing busily, with rapid jabbing stitches, on a sheet. Several other sheets lay on the dusty floor.

▶ Who is in the kitchen? What does this person look like?

---

2. **props.** Properties; movable items used on a stage or movie set

words for everyday use

sin • is • ter (sin´is tər) *adj.,* threatening harm, evil, or misfortune. *The cartoon villain always wore a <u>sinister</u> sneer on his face.*

re • cess (rē´ses) *n.,* hollow place. *A squirrel built its nest in the <u>recess</u> of the old oak tree.*

Charles Wallace went up to her. "I really don't think you ought to have taken Mrs. Buncombe's sheets without consulting me," he said, as cross and bossy as only a very small boy can be. "What on earth do you want them for?"

The plump little woman beamed at him. "Why, Charlsie, my pet! *Le coeur a ses raisons que la raison ne connait point.* French. Pascal.[3] *The heart has its reasons, whereof reason knows nothing.*"

"But that's not appropriate at all," Charles said crossly.

"Your mother would find it so." A smile seemed to gleam through the roundness of spectacles.

"I'm not talking about my mother's feelings about my father," Charles Wallace scolded. "I'm talking about Mrs. Buncombe's sheets."

The little woman sighed. The enormous glasses caught the light again and shone like an owl's eyes. "In case we need ghosts, of course," she said. "I should think you'd have guessed. If we have to frighten anybody away Whatsit thought we ought to do it appropriately. That's why it's so much fun to stay in a haunted house. But we really didn't mean you to know about the sheets. *Auf frischer Tat ertappt.* German. *In flagrante delicto.* Latin. *Caught in the act.* English. As I was saying—"

◀ *Why did Mrs Whatsit and her friends need sheets?*

But Charles Wallace held up his hand in a peremptory gesture. "Mrs Who, do you know this boy?"

Calvin bowed. "Good afternoon, Ma'am. I didn't quite catch your name."

"Mrs Who will do," the woman said. "He wasn't my idea, Charlsie, but I think he's a good one."

"Where's Mrs Whatsit?" Charles asked.

"She's busy. It's getting near time, Charlsie, getting near time. *Ab honesto virum bonum nihil deterret.*

---

3. **Pascal.** Blaise Pascal (1623–1662), French mathematician and philosopher

words for everyday use   con • sult (kən sult´) v., ask for information. *Dr. Marcus's patients are always welcome to consult another physician for a second opinion.*

per • emp • to • ry (pər emp´tə rē) adj., final; decisive. *Although baseball players may bicker and argue about different plays, the umpire makes the peremptory decision.*

Seneca.[4] *Nothing deters a good man from doing what is honorable.* And he's a very good man, Charlsie, darling, but right now he needs our help."

"Who?" Meg demanded.

"And little Megsie! Lovely to meet you, sweetheart. Your father, of course. Now go home, loves. The time is not yet ripe. Don't worry, we won't go without you. Get plenty of food and rest. Feed Calvin up. Now, off with you! *Justitiae soror fides.* Latin again, of course. *Faith is the sister of justice.* Trust in us! Now, shoo!" And she fluttered up from her chair and pushed them out the door with surprising power.

"Charles," Meg said. "I don't understand."

Charles took her by the hand and dragged her away from the house. Fortinbras ran on ahead, and Calvin was close behind them. "No," he said, "I don't either, yet. Not quite. I'll tell you what I know as soon as I can. But you saw Fort, didn't you? Not a growl. Not a quiver. Just as though there weren't anything strange about it. So you know it's okay. Look, do me a favor, both of you. Let's not talk about it till we've had something to eat. I need fuel so I can sort things out and <u>assimilate</u> them properly."

"Lead on, moron," Calvin cried gaily. "I've never even seen your house, and I have the funniest feeling that for the first time in my life I'm going home!"

> ▶ In what should the children have faith?

---

4. **Seneca.** Lucius Annaeus Seneca (4 BC ?–AD 65), Roman statesman, dramatist, and philosopher

words for everyday use   as • si • mi • late (ə sim´ə lāt´) *v.,* absorb. *The museum has so many pieces that it is difficult for a person to <u>assimilate</u> them all properly on the first visit.*

Respond to the Selection

Charles Wallace would rather let the townspeople go on believing he is a moron than reveal to them that he is a genius. Why is this? Do ordinary people dislike geniuses? Why?

Investigate, Inquire, and Imagine

Recall: GATHERING FACTS

1a. What went wrong with Meg's school day?

2a. What has happened to Meg's father? What does Mrs Who say about Meg's father?

3a. What special ability does Charles Wallace have? How do you know that he has this special ability?

4a. Whom do Meg and Charles Wallace meet in the woods? Why does this person say he has come there? What seems strange about Mrs Whatsit? about Mrs Who?

Interpret: FINDING MEANING

➤ 1b. How does Meg's school day make her feel? Why does Meg feel this way?

➤ 2b. How does Meg feel when people ask about her father? Do these people seem to have good intentions, or do you think they are being malicious? Explain.

➤ 3b. How does Meg feel about Charles Wallace's ability? Why does Charles Wallace not bother concentrating on his twin brothers?

➤ 4b. What does Charles Wallace have in common with the person they meet in the woods? What explanation can you give for the odd behavior of Mrs Whatsit and Mrs Who?

Analyze: TAKING THINGS APART

5a. Compare Sandy and Dennys to Meg and Charles Wallace. Why do the kids pick on Meg and Charles Wallace, but not on the twins?

Synthesize: BRINGING THINGS TOGETHER

➤ 5b. In your opinion, which of the Murry children is the most interesting? Which would you most like to have as a friend?

Evaluate: MAKING JUDGMENTS

6a. Mrs Who asks Meg to "trust in us." If you were Meg, would you trust in Mrs Who and Mrs Whatsit? Why, or why not?

Extend: CONNECTING IDEAS

→ 6b. Meg says that she does not understand the strange events that have occurred and does not know what Mrs Who meant by saying that they would help her father. Does it seem as though Meg, Charles Wallace, and Calvin are being led in a particular direction? Predict what will happen next.

Understanding Literature

CHARACTERIZATION. **Characterization** is the act of creating or describing a character. Writers create characters using three major techniques: by showing what characters say, do, or think; by showing what other characters say or think about them; and by describing what physical features, dress, and personality the characters display. Madeleine L'Engle uses all three techniques in chapters 1–2 to create the character of Meg. Create a character chart like the one below to show examples of all three techniques. One example has been given for you. After you have listed at least three examples in each category, answer the following questions: Do you like Meg? Why do you think she is having problems in school? Do you agree with Mr. Jenkins that she needs to change her attitude?

What Meg says, does, and thinks	What other characters say or think about Meg	Meg's physical features, dress, and personality
	A girl at school says Meg acts like a baby.	

INCITING INCIDENT. The **inciting incident** is the event that introduces the central conflict, or struggle, in a poem, story, or play. Mrs Whatsit's nighttime visit to the Murry home during the middle of a storm may be seen as the inciting incident of *A Wrinkle in Time*. Her arrival begins the series of fantastic events that the children will experience in the novel. Mrs Whatsit's offhand remark about the tesseract indicates that she may know something about the missing Mr. Murry. What techniques does the author use to make Mrs Whatsit's arrival seem important and mysterious?

Chapter 3

Mrs Which

In the forest evening was already beginning to fall, and they walked in silence. Charles and Fortinbras <u>gamboled</u> on ahead. Calvin walked with Meg, his fingers barely touching her arm in a protective gesture.

This has been the most impossible, the most confusing afternoon of my life, she thought, yet I don't feel confused or upset anymore; I only feel happy. Why?

"Maybe we weren't meant to meet before this," Calvin said. "I mean, I knew who you were in school and everything, but I didn't know you. But I'm glad we've met now, Meg. We're going to be friends, you know."

"I'm glad, too," Meg whispered, and they were silent again.

When they got back to the house Mrs. Murry was still in the lab. She was watching a pale blue fluid move slowly through a tube from a beaker to a retort.[1] Over a Bunsen burner[2] bubbled a big, earthenware dish of stew. "Don't tell Sandy and Dennys I'm cooking out here," she said. "They're always suspicious that a few chemicals may get in with the meat, but I had an experiment I wanted to stay with."

"This is Calvin O'Keefe, Mother," Meg said. "Is there enough for him, too? It smells super."

"Hello, Calvin." Mrs. Murry shook hands with him. "Nice to meet you. We aren't having anything but stew tonight, but it's a good thick one."

---

1. **beaker . . . retort.** *Beaker*—jarlike container of glass or metal with a lip for pouring; *retort*—container with a long tube
2. **Bunsen burner.** Small gas burner with a hot, blue flame, used by chemists

---

words for everyday use

gam • bol (gamʹbəl) *v.,* jump or skip about in play. *The children <u>gamboled</u> around the schoolyard during recess.*

"Sounds wonderful to me," Calvin said. "May I use your phone so my mother'll know where I am?"

"Of course. Show him where it is, will you, please, Meg? I won't ask you to use the one out here, if you don't mind. I'd like to finish up this experiment."

Meg led the way into the house. Charles Wallace and Fortinbras had gone off. Outdoors she could hear Sandy and Dennys hammering at the fort they were building up in one of the maples. "This way." Meg went through the kitchen and into the living room.

"I don't know why I call her when I don't come home," Calvin said, his voice bitter. "She wouldn't notice." He sighed and dialed. "Ma?" he said. "Oh, Hinky. Tell Ma I won't be home till late. Now don't forget. I don't want to be locked out again." He hung up, looked at Meg. "Do you know how lucky you are?"

She smiled rather <u>wryly</u>. "Not most of the time."

"A mother like that! A house like this! Gee, your mother's gorgeous! You should see my mother. She had all her upper teeth out and Pop got her a plate but she won't wear it, and most days she doesn't even comb her hair. Not that it makes much difference when she does." He clenched his fists. "But I love her. That's the funny part of it. I love them all, and they don't give a hoot about me. Maybe that's why I call when I'm not going to be home. Because I care. Nobody else does. You don't know how lucky you are to be loved."

▶ Why does Calvin think that Meg is lucky? Why is Meg surprised?

Meg said in a startled way, "I guess I never thought of that. I guess I just took it for granted."

Calvin looked <u>somber</u>; then his enormous smile lit up his face again. "Things are going to happen, Meg! Good things! I feel it!" He began wandering, still slowly, around the pleasant, if shabby, living room. He stopped before a picture on the piano of a small group of men standing together on a beach. "Who's this?"

---

words for everyday use

wry • ly (rī´lē) adv., in a drily funny way. *After he fell while performing his act on stage, Luke got up, smiled <u>wryly</u>, and took a bow.*

som • ber (säm´bər) adj., dark and gloomy; very serious. *We thought that the doctor had bad news because his face was <u>somber</u>.*

"Oh, a bunch of scientists."

"Where?"

Meg went over to the picture. "Cape Canaveral.[3] This one's Father."

"Which?"

"Here."

"The one with glasses?"

"Yup. The one who needs a haircut." Meg giggled, forgetting her worries in her pleasure at showing Calvin the picture. "His hair's sort of the same color as mine, and he keeps forgetting to have it cut. Mother usually ends up doing it for him—she bought clippers and stuff—because he won't take the time to go to the barber."

Calvin studied the picture. "I like him," he announced judiciously. "Looks kind of like Charles Wallace, doesn't he?"

Meg laughed again. "When Charles was a baby he looked *exactly* like Father. It was really funny."

Calvin continued to look at the picture. "He's not handsome or anything. But I like him."

Meg was indignant. "He is too handsome."

Calvin shook his head. "Nah. He's tall and skinny like me."

"Well, I think you're handsome," Meg said. "Father's eyes are kind of like yours, too. You know. Really blue. Only you don't notice his as much because of the glasses."

"Where is he now?"

Meg stiffened. But she didn't have to answer because the door from lab to kitchen slammed, and Mrs. Murry came in, carrying a dish of stew. "Now," she called, "I'll finish this up properly on the stove. Have you done your homework, Meg?"

---

3. **Cape Canaveral** (kə nav´ə rəl). Air Force station located on the east coast of Florida and used for launching spacecraft

---

words for everyday use   ju • di • cious • ly (jü dish´əs lē) *adv.,* showing sound judgment; wisely and carefully. *Sylvia judiciously considered all her options before making a decision.*

"Not quite," Meg said, going back into the kitchen.

"Then I'm sure Calvin won't mind if you finish before dinner."

"Sure, go ahead." Calvin fished in his pocket and pulled out a wad of folded paper. "As a matter of fact I have some junk of mine to finish up. Math. That's one thing I have a hard time keeping up in. I'm okay on anything to do with words, but I don't do as well with numbers."

Mrs. Murry smiled. "Why don't you get Meg to help you?"

"But, see, I'm several grades above Meg."

"Try asking her to help you with your math, anyhow," Mrs. Murry suggested.

"Well, sure," Calvin said. "Here. But it's pretty complicated."

Meg smoothed out the paper and studied it. "Do they care *how* you do it?" she asked. "I mean, can you work it out your own way?"

"Well, sure, as long as I understand and get the answers right."

"Well, *we* have to do it *their* way. Now look, Calvin, don't you see how much easier it would be if you did it *this* way?" Her pencil flew over the paper.

"Hey!" Calvin said. "Hey! I think I get it. Show me once more on another one."

Again Meg's pencil was busy. "All you have to remember is that every ordinary fraction can be converted into an infinite periodic decimal fraction. See? So 3/7 is 0.428571."

▶ Why is Meg "supposed to be dumb" in school? Is she really dumb? What problem does Meg have with math at school?

"This is the craziest family." Calvin grinned at her. "I suppose I should stop being surprised by now, but you're supposed to be dumb in school, always being called up on the carpet."

"Oh, I am."

"The trouble with Meg and math," Mrs. Murry said briskly, "is that Meg and her father used to play with numbers and Meg learned far too many short cuts. So when they want her to do problems the long way around at school she gets sullen and stubborn and sets up a fine mental block for herself."

"Are there any more morons like Meg and Charles around?" Calvin asked. "If so, I should meet more of them."

"It might also help if Meg's handwriting were legible," Mrs. Murry said. "With a good deal of difficulty I can usually <u>decipher</u> it, but I doubt very much if her teachers can, or are willing to take the time. I'm planning on giving her a typewriter for Christmas. That may be a help."

"If I get anything right nobody'll believe it's me," Meg said.

"What's a megaparsec?" Calvin asked.

"One of Father's nicknames for me," Meg said. "It's also 3.26 million light years."

"What's $E = mc^2$?"

"Einstein's equation."

"What's E stand for?"

"Energy."

"m?"

"Mass."

"c^2?"

"The square of the <u>velocity</u> of light in centimeters per second."

"By what countries is Peru[4] bounded?"

"I haven't the faintest idea. I think it's in South America somewhere."

"What's the capital of New York?"[5]

"Well, New York City, of course!"

"Who wrote Boswell's[6] *Life of Johnson?*"

"Oh, Calvin, I'm not any good at English."

Calvin groaned and turned to Mrs. Murry. "I see what you mean. Her I wouldn't want to teach."

---

4. **Peru.** Nation on the west coast of South America bounded by Ecuador, Colombia, Brazil, Bolivia, and Chile
5. **capital of New York.** Albany
6. **Boswell's.** James Boswell (1740–1795), biographer of Samuel Johnson (1709–1784), the English writer and critic

---

words for everyday use

de • ci • pher (dē sī´ fər) v., translate; make understandable. *Until the discovery of the Rosetta stone, people were unable to* <u>decipher</u> *Egyptian hieroglyphs.*

ve • loc • i • ty (və läs´ə tē) n., swiftness, speed. *The* <u>velocity</u> *of the plane was so great that it broke the sound barrier.*

"She's a little one-sided, I grant you," Mrs. Murry said, "though I blame her father and myself for that. She still enjoys playing with her dolls' house, though."

"*Mother!*" Meg shrieked in agony.

"Oh, darling, I'm sorry," Mrs. Murry said swiftly. "But I'm sure Calvin understands what I mean."

With a sudden enthusiastic gesture Calvin flung his arms out wide, as though he were embracing Meg and her mother, the whole house. "How did all this happen? Isn't it wonderful? I feel as though I were just being born! I'm not alone any more! Do you realize what that means to me?"

▶ *Why did Calvin feel alone before now?*

"But you're good at basketball and things," Meg protested. "You're good in school. Everybody likes you."

"For all the most unimportant reasons," Calvin said. "There hasn't been anybody, anybody in the world I could talk to. Sure, I can function on the same level as everybody else, I can hold myself down, but it isn't me."

Meg took a batch of forks from the drawer and turned them over and over, looking at them. "I'm all confused again."

"Oh, so 'm I," Calvin said gaily. "But now at least I know we're going somewhere."

Meg was pleased and a little surprised when the twins were excited at having Calvin for supper. They knew more about his athletic record and were far more impressed by it than she. Calvin ate five bowls of stew, three saucers of Jello, and a dozen cookies, and then Charles Wallace insisted that Calvin take him up to bed and read to him. The twins, who had finished their homework, were allowed to watch half an hour of TV. Meg helped her mother with the dishes and then sat at the table and struggled with her homework. But she could not concentrate.

"Mother, are you upset?" she asked suddenly.

Mrs. Murry looked up from a copy of an English scientific magazine through which she was leafing. For a moment she did not speak. Then, "Yes."

"Why?"

Again Mrs. Murry paused. She held her hands out and looked at them. They were long and strong and beautiful. She touched with the fingers of her right hand the broad gold band on the third finger of her left hand. "I'm still quite a young woman, you know," she said finally, "though I realize that that's difficult for you children to <u>conceive</u>. And I'm still very much in love with your father. I miss him quite dreadfully."

"And you think all this has something to do with Father?"

"I think it must have."

"But what?"

"That I don't know. But it seems the only explanation."

"Do you think things always have an explanation?"

"Yes. I believe that they do. But I think that with our human limitations we're not always able to understand the explanations. But you see, Meg, just because we don't understand doesn't mean that the explanation doesn't exist."

"I like to understand things," Meg said.

"We all do. But it isn't always possible."

"Charles Wallace understands more than the rest of us, doesn't he?"

"Yes."

"Why?"

"I suppose because he's—well, because he's different, Meg."

"Different how?"

"I'm not quite sure. You know yourself he's not like anybody else."

"No. And I wouldn't want him to be," Meg said <u>defensively</u>.

"Wanting doesn't have anything to do with it. Charles Wallace is what he is. Different. New."

◀ What does Mrs. Murry want Meg to realize?

---

words for everyday use

con • ceive (kən sēv´) v., think; imagine; understand. *It is difficult to <u>conceive</u> of something as vast as the universe.*

de • fen • sive • ly (dē fen´siv lē) adv., protectively. *The child lowered his head and folded his arms <u>defensively</u> while he was being scolded.*

▶ What might Mrs.
Murry mean by
"new"?

"New?"

"Yes. That's what your father and I feel."

Meg twisted her pencil so hard that it broke. She laughed. "I'm sorry. I'm really not being destructive. I'm just trying to get things straight."

"I know."

"But Charles Wallace doesn't *look* different from anybody else."

"No, Meg, but people are more than just the way they look. Charles Wallace's difference isn't physical. It's in essence."

Meg sighed heavily, took off her glasses and twirled them, put them back on again. "Well, I know Charles Wallace is different, and I know he's something *more*. I guess I'll just have to accept it without understanding it."

Mrs. Murry smiled at her. "Maybe that's really the point I was trying to put across."

"Yah," Meg said <u>dubiously</u>.

Her mother smiled again. "Maybe that's why our visitor last night didn't surprise me. Maybe that's why I'm able to have a—a willing suspension of disbelief.[7] Because of Charles Wallace."

"Are *you* like Charles?" Meg asked.

"I? Heavens no. I'm blessed with more brains and opportunities than many people, but there's nothing about me that breaks out of the ordinary mold."

"Your looks do," Meg said.

Mrs. Murry laughed. "You just haven't had enough basis for comparison, Meg. I'm very ordinary, really."

Calvin O'Keefe, coming in then, said, "Ha ha."

"Charles all settled?" Mrs. Murry asked.

"Yes."

"What did you read to him?"

"Genesis.[8] His choice. By the way, what kind of an

---

7. **suspension of disbelief.** Audience's or reader's acceptance of impossible or unlikely facts because they are essential to the story
8. **Genesis.** First book of the Bible

---

words for everyday use du • bi • ous • ly (dü' bē əs lē) *adj.,* doubtfully. *Looking at the stack of birthday presents, Sharon <u>dubiously</u> asked, "Are these all for me?"*

experiment were you working on this afternoon, Mrs. Murry?"

"Oh, something my husband and I were cooking up together. I don't want to be *too* far behind him when he gets back."

"Mother," Meg pursued. "Charles says I'm not one thing or the other, not flesh nor fowl nor good red herring."

"Oh, for crying out loud," Calvin said, "you're *Meg*, aren't you? Come on and let's go for a walk."

But Meg was still not satisfied. "And what do you make of Calvin?" she demanded of her mother.

Mrs. Murry laughed. "I don't want to make anything of Calvin. I like him very much, and I'm delighted he's found his way here."

"Mother, you were going to tell me about a tesseract."

"Yes." A troubled look came into Mrs. Murry's eyes. "But not now, Meg. Not now. Go on out for that walk with Calvin. I'm going up to kiss Charles and then I have to see that the twins get to bed."

Outdoors the grass was wet with dew. The moon was halfway up and dimmed the stars for a great arc. Calvin reached out and took Meg's hand with a gesture as simple and friendly as Charles Wallace's. "Were you upsetting your mother?" he asked gently.

"I don't think *I* was. But she's upset."

"What about?"

"Father."

Calvin led Meg across the lawn. The shadows of the trees were long and twisted and there was a heavy, sweet, autumnal smell to the air. Meg stumbled as the land sloped suddenly downhill, but Calvin's strong hand steadied her. They walked carefully across the twins' vegetable garden, picking their way through rows of cabbages, beets, broccoli, pumpkins. Looming on their left were the tall stalks of corn. Ahead of them was a small apple orchard bounded by a stone wall, and beyond this the woods through which they had walked that afternoon. Calvin led the way to the wall, and then sat there, his red hair shining silver in the moonlight, his body dappled with patterns from the tangle of branches. He reached up, pulled an apple off a gnarled limb, and handed it to Meg, then picked one for himself. "Tell me about your father."

"He's a physicist."

"Sure, we all know that. And he's supposed to have left your mother and gone off with some dame."

Meg jerked up from the stone on which she was perched, but Calvin grabbed her by the wrist and pulled her back down. "Hold it, kid. I didn't say anything you hadn't heard already, did I?"

"No," Meg said, but continued to pull away. "Let me go."

"Come on, calm down. *You* know it isn't true, *I* know it isn't true. And how *any*body after one look at your mother could believe any man would leave her for another woman just shows how far jealousy will make people go. Right?"

▶ Why is Meg feeling angry and resentful?

"I guess so," Meg said, but her happiness had fled and she was back in a morass of anger and resentment.

"Look, dope." Calvin shook her gently. "I just want to get things straight, sort of sort out the fact from fiction. Your father's a physicist. That's a fact, yes?"

"Yes."

"He's a Ph.D.[9] several times over."

"Yes."

"Most of the time he works alone but some of the time he was at the Institute for Higher Learning in Princeton. Correct?"

"Yes."

"Then he did some work for the government, didn't he?"

"Yes."

"You take it from there. That's all I know."

"That's about all I know, too," Meg said. "Maybe Mother knows more. I don't know. What he did was—well, it was what they call Classified."

"Top Secret, you mean?"

---

9. **Ph.D.** Doctor of philosophy, the highest degree given by a university. Like his wife, Mr. Murry has earned a Ph.D. in several different subjects.

"That's right."

"And you don't even have any idea what it was about?"

Meg shook her head. "No. Not really. Just an idea because of where he was."

"Well, where?"

"Out in New Mexico for a while; we were with him there; and then he was in Florida at Cape Canaveral, and we were with him there, too. And then he was going to be traveling a lot, so we came here."

"You'd always had this house?"

"Yes. But we used to live in it just in the summer."

"And you don't know where your father was sent?"

"No. At first we got lots of letters. Mother and Father always wrote each other every day. I think Mother still writes him every night. Every once in a while the postmistress makes some kind of a crack about all her letters."

"I suppose they think she's pursuing him or something," Calvin said, rather bitterly. "They can't understand plain, ordinary love when they see it. Well, go on. What happened next?"

◄ What can't the townspeople understand, according to Calvin?

"Nothing happened," Meg said. "That's the trouble."

"Well, what about your father's letters?"

"They just stopped coming."

"You haven't heard anything at all?"

"No," Meg said. "Nothing." Her voice was heavy with misery.

Silence fell between them, as <u>tangible</u> as the dark tree shadows that fell across their laps and that now seemed to rest upon them as heavily as though they possessed a measurable weight of their own.

At last Calvin spoke in a dry, unemotional voice, not looking at Meg. "Do you think he could be dead?"

---

words for everyday use tan • gi • ble (tanʹjə bəl) *adj.,* capable of being touched or felt by touch. *The smell of oranges in the grove was so strong that it was almost <u>tangible</u>.*

Again Meg leaped up, and again Calvin pulled her down. "No! They'd have told us if he were dead! There's always a telegram or something. They always tell you!"

"What *do* they tell you?"

Meg choked down a sob, managed to speak over it. "Oh, Calvin, Mother's tried and tried to find out. She's been down to Washington and everything. And all they'll say is that he's on a secret and dangerous mission, and she can be very proud of him, but he won't be able to—to communicate with us for a while. And they'll give us news as soon as they have it."

"Meg, don't get mad, but do you think maybe *they* don't know?"

A slow tear trickled down Meg's cheek. "That's what I'm afraid of."

"Why don't you cry?" Calvin asked gently. "You're just crazy about your father, aren't you? Go ahead and cry. It'll do you good."

▶ Meg is very critical of herself. Do you think she is too critical? Why, or why not?

Meg's voice came out trembling over tears. "I cry much too much. I should be like Mother. I should be able to control myself."

"Your mother's a completely different person and she's a lot older than you are."

"I wish I were a different person," Meg said shakily. "I hate myself."

Calvin reached over and took off her glasses. Then he pulled a handkerchief out of his pocket and wiped her tears. This gesture of tenderness undid her completely, and she put her head down on her knees and sobbed. Calvin sat quietly beside her, every once in a while patting her head. "I'm sorry," she sobbed finally. "I'm terribly sorry. Now you'll hate me."

"Oh, Meg, you *are* a moron," Calvin said. "Don't you know you're the nicest thing that's happened to me in a long time?"

Meg raised her head, and moonlight shone on her tear-stained face; without the glasses her eyes were unexpectedly beautiful. "If Charles Wallace is a sport, I think I'm a biological mistake." Moonlight flashed against her braces as she spoke.

Now she was waiting to be contradicted. But Calvin said, "Do you know that this is the first time I've seen you without your glasses?"

"I'm blind as a bat without them. I'm near-sighted, like Father."

"Well, you know what, you've got dream-boat eyes," Calvin said. "Listen, you go right on wearing your glasses. I don't think I want anybody else to see what gorgeous eyes you have."

Meg smiled with pleasure. She could feel herself blushing and she wondered if the blush would be visible in the moonlight.

"Okay, hold it, you two," came a voice out of the shadows. Charles Wallace stepped into the moonlight. "I wasn't spying on you," he said quickly, "and I hate to break things up, but this is it, kids, this is it!" His voice quivered with excitement.

"This is what?" Calvin asked.

"We're going."

"Going? Where?" Meg reached out and instinctively grabbed for Calvin's hand.

"I don't know exactly," Charles Wallace said. "But I think it's to find Father."

Suddenly two eyes seemed to spring at them out of the darkness; it was the moonlight striking on Mrs Who's glasses. She was standing next to Charles Wallace, and how she had managed to appear where a moment ago there had been nothing but flickering shadows in the moonlight Meg had no idea. She heard a sound behind her and turned around. There was Mrs Whatsit scrambling over the wall.

"My, but I wish there were no wind," Mrs Whatsit said plaintively. "It's so *difficult* with all these clothes." She wore her outfit of the night before, rubber boots and all, with the addition of one of Mrs. Buncombe's sheets which she had draped over her. As she slid off the wall the sheet caught in a low branch and came off. The felt hat slipped over both eyes, and another branch plucked at the pink stole. "Oh, dear," she sighed. "I shall *never* learn to manage."

Mrs Who <u>wafted</u> over to her, tiny feet scarcely seeming to touch the ground, the lenses of her glasses glittering. *"Come t'è picciol fallo amaro morso!* Dante.[10] *What grievous pain a little fault doth give thee!"* With a clawlike hand she pushed the hat up on Mrs Whatsit's forehead, untangled the stole from the tree, and with a <u>deft</u> gesture took the sheet and folded it.

"Oh, *thank* you," Mrs Whatsit said. "You're *so* clever!"

"Un asno viejo sabe más que un potro. A. Perez. *An old ass knows more than a young colt."*

▶ What do you think Mrs Whatsit was going to say? Do you think Mrs Whatsit, Mrs Who, and Mrs Which are human? Why, or why not?

"Just because you're a paltry few billion years—" Mrs Whatsit was starting indignantly, when a sharp, strange voice cut in.

"Alll rrightt, girrllss. Thiss iss nno ttime forr bbickkering."

"It's Mrs Which," Charles Wallace said.

There was a faint gust of wind, the leaves shivered in it, the patterns of moonlight shifted, and in a circle of silver something shimmered, quivered, and the voice said, "I ddo nott thinkk I willl <u>matterrialize</u> commpletely. I ffindd itt verry ttirinngg, andd wee hhave mmuch ttoo ddoo."

---

10. **Dante** (dän´ tā). Dante Alighieri (1265–1321), Italian poet famed for his epic work *The Divine Comedy*

words for everyday use

waft (wäft) *v.*, float, as on wind. *The butterfly <u>wafted</u> gracefully from flower to flower.*

deft (deft) *adj.*, skillful in a quick and easy way. *With a <u>deft</u> flick of her wrist, Tonya caught the ball.*

ma • te • ri • a • lize (mə tir´ ē ə līz) *v.*, develop into something real or tangible. *Under the sculptor's skilled hands, a face <u>materialized</u> out of formless clay.*

Chapter 4

The Black Thing

The trees were lashed into a violent frenzy. Meg screamed and clutched at Calvin, and Mrs Which's <u>authoritative</u> voice called out, "Qquiett, chilldd!"

Did a shadow fall across the moon or did the moon simply go out, extinguished as abruptly and completely as a candle? There was still the sound of leaves, a terrified, terrifying rushing. All light was gone. Darkness was complete. Suddenly the wind was gone, and all sound. Meg felt that Calvin was being torn from her. When she reached for him her fingers touched nothing.

She screamed out, "Charles!" and whether it was to help him or for him to help her, she did not know. The word was flung back down her throat and she choked on it.

She was completely alone.

She had lost the protection of Calvin's hand. Charles was nowhere, either to save or to turn to. She was alone in a fragment of nothingness. No light, no sound, no feeling. Where was her body? She tried to move in her panic, but there was nothing to move. Just as light and sound had vanished, she was gone, too. The <u>corporeal</u> Meg simply was not.

◀ *Describe what Meg is feeling. What do you think is happening to her?*

Then she felt her limbs again. Her legs and arms were tingling faintly, as though they had been asleep. She blinked her eyes rapidly, but though she herself was somehow back, nothing else was. It was not as simple as darkness, or absence of light. Darkness has a tangible quality; it can be moved through and felt; in darkness you can bark[1] your shins; the world of things still exists around you. She was lost in a horrifying <u>void</u>.

---

1. **bark.** Scrape or skin

words for everyday use

au • thor • i • ta • tive (ə thôr´ ə tāt´iv) *adj.,* having or showing power. *Although the ruler was very large and commanding in appearance, he did not have a very <u>authoritative</u> voice.*

cor • po • re • al (kôr pôr´ē əl) *adj.,* phys-ical, bodily. *The computer-enhanced images looked real enough to be <u>corporeal</u>.*

void (void) *n.,* empty space. *Because of the incredible distances between planets, stars, and other galaxies, most of space is a <u>void</u>.*

It was the same way with the silence. This was more than silence. A deaf person can feel vibrations. Here there was nothing to feel.

Suddenly she was aware of her heart beating rapidly within the cage of her ribs. Had it stopped before? What had made it start again? The tingling in her arms and legs grew stronger, and suddenly she felt movement. This movement, she felt, must be the turning of the earth, rotating on its axis, traveling its elliptic course about the sun. And this feeling of moving with the earth was somewhat like the feeling of being in the ocean, out in the ocean beyond this rising and falling of the breakers, lying on the moving water, pulsing gently with the swells, and feeling the gentle, <u>inexorable</u> tug of the moon.

I am asleep; I am dreaming, she thought. I'm having a nightmare. I want to wake up. Let me wake up.

"Well!" Charles Wallace's voice said. "That was quite a trip. I do think you might have warned us."

Light began to pulse and quiver. Meg blinked and shoved shakily at her glasses and there was Charles Wallace standing indignantly in front of her, his hands on his hips. "Meg!" he shouted. "Calvin! Where are you?"

She saw Charles, she heard him, but she could not go to him. She could not shove through the strange, trembling light to meet him.

Calvin's voice came as though it were pushing through a cloud. "Well, just give me time, will you? I'm older than you are."

Meg gasped. It wasn't that Calvin wasn't there and then that he was. It wasn't that part of him came first and then the rest of him followed, like a hand and then an arm, an eye and then a nose. It was a sort of shimmering, a looking at Calvin through water, through smoke, through fire, and then there he was, solid and reassuring.

▶ Charles Wallace refers to his experience as a trip. Through what did he and the others travel?

▶ What is Calvin's materialization like?

"Meg!" Charles Wallace's voice came. "Meg! Calvin, where's Meg?"

"I'm right here," she tried to say, but her voice seemed to be caught at its source.

"Meg!" Calvin cried, and he turned around, looking about wildly.

"Mrs Which, you haven't left Meg *behind,* have you?" Charles Wallace shouted.

"If you've hurt Meg, any of you—" Calvin started, but suddenly Meg felt a violent push and a shattering as though she had been thrust through a wall of glass.

"Oh, *there* you are!" Charles Wallace said, and rushed over to her and hugged her.

"But *where* am I?" Meg asked breathlessly, relieved to hear that her voice was now coming out of her in more or less a normal way.

She looked around rather wildly. They were standing in a sunlit field, and the air about them was moving with the delicious fragrance that comes only on the rarest of spring days when the sun's touch is gentle and the apple blossoms are just beginning to unfold. She pushed her glasses up on her nose to reassure herself that what she was seeing was real.

They had left the silver glint of a biting autumn evening; and now around them everything was golden with light. The grasses of the field were a tender new green, and scattered about were tiny, multicolored flowers. Meg turned slowly to face a mountain reaching so high into the sky that its peak was lost in a crown of puffy white clouds. From the trees at the base of the mountain came a sudden singing of birds. There was an air of such <u>ineffable</u> peace and joy all around her that her heart's wild thumping slowed.

"When shall we three meet again,
In thunder, lightning, or in rain,"[2]

---

2. *"When shall we . . . again, / In thunder . . . rain."* Line spoken by the three witches at the beginning of *Macbeth,* a play by William Shakespeare (1564–1616)

---

words for everyday use in • ef • fa • ble (in ef´ə bəl) *adj.,* too overwhelming to be expressed or described in words. *We could not express the <u>ineffable</u> contentment we felt when we finally escaped from the cold and snow and lay on a warm, sandy beach.*

came Mrs Who's voice. Suddenly the three of them were there, Mrs Whatsit with her pink stole askew; Mrs Who with her spectacles gleaming; and Mrs Which still little more than a shimmer. Delicate, multicolored butterflies were fluttering about them, as though in greeting.

▶ What do Mrs Whatsit, Mrs Who, and Mrs Which find so funny?

Mrs Whatsit and Mrs Who began to giggle, and they giggled until it seemed that, whatever their private joke was, they would fall down with the wild fun of it. The shimmer seemed to be laughing, too. It became vaguely darker and more solid; and then there appeared a figure in a black robe and a black peaked hat, beady eyes, a beaked nose, and long gray hair; one bony claw clutched a broomstick.

"Wwell, jusstt ttoo kkeepp yyou girrlls happpy," the strange voice said, and Mrs Whatsit and Mrs Who fell into each other's arms in gales of laughter.

"If you ladies have had your fun I think you should tell Calvin and Meg a little more about all this," Charles Wallace said coldly. "You scared Meg half out of her wits, whisking her off this way without any warning."

"*Finxerunt animi, raro et perpauca loquentis,*" Mrs Who intoned. "Horace.[3] *To action little, less to words inclined.*"

▶ Why does Mrs Who quote all the time?

"Mrs Who, I wish you'd stop quoting!" Charles Wallace sounded very annoyed.

Mrs Whatsit adjusted her stole. "But she finds it so difficult to <u>verbalize</u>, Charles dear. It helps her if she can quote instead of working out words of her own."

▶ Why is it important not to lose one's sense of humor?

"Anndd wee mussttn'tt looose ourr sensses of hummorr," Mrs Which said. "Thee onnlly wway ttoo ccope withh ssometthingg ddeadly sseriouss iss ttoo ttry ttoo trreatt itt a llittlle lliigghtly."

"But that's going to be hard for Meg," Mrs Whatsit said. "It's going to be hard for her to realize that we *are* serious."

"What about me?" Calvin asked.

---

3. **Horace.** Quintus Horatius Flaccus (65–8 BC), Roman poet and satirist

**words
for
everyday
use**   ver • ba • lize (vər´bə līz) *v.*, express something in words. *ShaVonda knew that her father loved her even though he rarely <u>verbalized</u> his feelings.*

"The life of your father isn't at stake," Mrs Whatsit told him.

"What about Charles Wallace, then?"

Mrs Whatsit's unoiled-door-hinge voice was warm with affection and pride. "Charles Wallace knows. Charles Wallace knows that it's far more than just the life of his father. Charles Wallace knows what's at stake."

"But remember," Mrs Who said, *"Αεηπου ουδεὶ ν̓, πὰυτα δ' εηπί ζεί νχρεωτ."* Euripides.[4] *Nothing is hopeless; we must hope for everything."*

"Where are we now, and how did we get here?" Calvin asked.

◀ Where have Mrs Whatsit, Mrs Who, and Mrs Which brought the children?

"Uriel, the third planet of the star Malak in the spiral nebula[5] Messier 101."

"This I'm supposed to believe?" Calvin asked indignantly.

"Aas yyou llike," Mrs Which said coldly.

For some reason Meg felt that Mrs Which, despite her looks and <u>ephemeral</u> broomstick, was someone in whom one could put complete trust. "It doesn't seem any more peculiar than anything else that's happened."

◀ Why does Meg feel Mrs Which can be trusted?

"Well, then, someone just tell me how we got here!" Calvin's voice was still angry and his freckles seemed to stand out on his face. "Even traveling at the speed of light[6] it would take us years and years to get here."

"Oh, we don't travel at the speed of *anything*," Mrs Whatsit explained earnestly. "We *tesser*. Or you might say, we *wrinkle*."

"Clear as mud," Calvin said.

Tesser, Meg thought. Could that have anything to do with Mother's tesseract?

She was about to ask when Mrs Which started to speak, and one did not interrupt when Mrs Which

◀ Why doesn't Calvin believe that they have actually traveled to a distant planet? How does Mrs Whatsit say they got there?

---

4. **Euripides** (yù ri´ pə dēz). Greek dramatist who lived from *circa* 484–406 BC
5. **nebula.** Cloud of gas or dust in space; or, a galaxy other than Earth's
6. **speed of light.** 186,282 miles per second. No object can move as fast as light.

---

words for everyday use
e • phem • er • al (e fem´ ər əl) *adj.,* lasting for only a brief time; short-lived. *The <u>ephemeral</u> flowers bloomed for only a few fragrant hours before they wilted and died.*

was speaking. "Mrs Whatsit iss yyoungg andd nnaïve."

"She keeps thinking she can explain things in words," Mrs Who said. *"Qui plus sait, plus se tait.* French, you know. *The more a man knows, the less he talks."*

▶ Why doesn't Charles need them to use words?

"But she has to use words for Meg and Calvin," Charles reminded Mrs Who. "If you brought them along, they have a right to know what's going on."

Meg went up to Mrs Which. In the intensity of her question she had forgotten all about the tesseract. "Is my father here?"

Mrs Which shook her head. "Nnott heeere, Megg. Llett Mrs Whatsitt expllainn. Shee isss yyoungg annd thee llanguage of worrds iss eeasierr fforr hherr thann itt iss fforr Mrs Whoo andd mee."

▶ Why has the group stopped on Uriel? What does Meg demand? What does Mrs Who say Meg will have to learn in order to help her father?

"We stopped here," Mrs Whatsit explained, "more or less to catch our breaths. And to give you a chance to know what you're up against."

"But what about Father?" Meg asked. "Is he all right?"

"For the moment, love, yes. He's one of the reasons we're here. But you see, he's only one."

"Well, where is he? Please take me to him!"

"We can't, not yet," Charles said. "You have to be patient, Meg."

"But I'm *not* patient!" Meg cried passionately. "I've never been patient!"

Mrs Who's glasses shone at her gently. "If you want to help your father then you must learn patience. *Vitam impendere vero. To stake one's life for the truth.* That is what we must do."

"That is what your father is doing." Mrs Whatsit nodded, her voice, like Mrs Who's, very serious, very solemn. Then she smiled her radiant smile. "Now! Why don't you three children wander around and Charles can explain things a little. You're perfectly safe on Uriel. That's why we stopped here to rest."

"But aren't you coming with us?" Meg asked fearfully.

There was silence for a moment. Then Mrs Which raised her authoritative hand. "Sshoww themm," she said to Mrs Whatsit, and at something in her voice Meg felt prickles of <u>apprehension</u>.

"Now?" Mrs Whatsit asked, her creaky voice rising to a squeak. Whatever it was Mrs Which wanted them to see, it was something that made Mrs Whatsit uncomfortable, too.

"Nnoww," Mrs Which said. "Tthey mmay aas welll knoww."

"Should—should I *change?"* Mrs Whatsit asked.

"Bbetter."

"I hope it won't upset the children too much," Mrs Whatsit murmured, as though to herself.

"Should I change, too?" Mrs Who asked. "Oh, but I've had *fun* in these clothes. But I'll have to admit Mrs Whatsit is the best at it. *Das Werk lobt den Meister.* German. *The work proves the craftsman.* Shall I transform now, too?"

Mrs Which shook her head. "Nnott yett. Nnott heere. Yyou mmay wwaitt."

"Now, don't be frightened, loves," Mrs Whatsit said. Her plump little body began to shimmer, to quiver, to shift. The wild colors of her clothes became muted, whitened. The pudding-bag shape stretched, lengthened, merged. And suddenly before the children was a creature more beautiful than any Meg had even imagined, and the beauty lay in far more than the outward description. Outwardly Mrs Whatsit was surely no longer a Mrs Whatsit. She was a marble white body with powerful flanks, something like a horse but at the same time completely unlike a horse, for from the magnificently modeled back sprang a nobly formed torso, arms, and a head resembling a man's, but a man with a perfection of dignity and virtue, an exaltation of joy[7] such as Meg had never before seen. No, she thought, it's not like a Greek centaur.[8] Not in the least.

◀ *What special ability does Mrs Whatsit have?*

---

7. **exaltation of joy.** Intense, glorified state of joy
8. **Greek centaur.** Mythical creature with a horse's body and the torso, arms, and head of a human. Greek centaurs were often depicted as savage and uncouth, quite different than Mrs Whatsit's version, which is all dignity and virtue.

---

words for everyday use   ap • pre • hen • sion (ap´rē hen´shən) *n.,* dread; uneasy or fearful anticipation of the future. *Sally felt great <u>apprehension</u> before going on a roller coaster for the first time.*

From the shoulders slowly a pair of wings unfolded, wings made of rainbows, of light upon water, of poetry.

Calvin fell to his knees.

"No," Mrs Whatsit said, though her voice was not Mrs Whatsit's voice. "Not to me, Calvin. Never to me. Stand up."

"Ccarrry themm," Mrs Which commanded.

With a gesture both delicate and strong Mrs Whatsit knelt in front of the children, stretching her wings wide and holding them steady, but quivering. "Onto my back, now," the new voice said.

The children took hesitant steps toward the beautiful creature.

"But what do we call you now?" Calvin asked.

"Oh, my dears," came the new voice, a rich voice with the warmth of a woodwind, the clarity of a trumpet, the mystery of an English horn. "You can't go on changing my name each time I <u>metamorphose</u>. And I've had such pleasure being Mrs Whatsit I think you'd better keep to that." She? he? it? smiled at them, and the radiance of the smile was as tangible as a soft breeze, as directly warming as the rays of the sun.

"Come." Charles Wallace clambered up.

Meg and Calvin followed him, Meg sitting between the two boys. A <u>tremor</u> went through the great wings and then Mrs Whatsit lifted and they were moving through the air.

Meg soon found that there was no need to cling to Charles Wallace or Calvin. The great creature's flight was serenely smooth. The boys were eagerly looking around the landscape.

"Look." Charles Wallace pointed. "The mountains are so tall that you can't see where they end."

Meg looked upwards and indeed the mountains seemed to be reaching into infinity.

They left the fertile fields and flew across a great plateau of granite-like rock shaped into enormous

◀ Why doesn't Mrs Whatsit want the children to think of a new name for her?

---

words for everyday use

met • a • mor • phose (met′ə môr′fōz) v., change in form or nature; transform. *The caterpillar <u>metamorphosed</u> into a beautiful butterfly.*

trem • or (trem′ər) n., trembling, shaking, or shivering. *The <u>tremors</u> that follow an earthquake are known as aftershocks.*

monoliths.[9] These had a definite, rhythmic form, but they were not statues; they were like nothing Meg had ever seen before, and she wondered if they had been made by wind and weather, by the formation of this earth, or if they were a creation of beings like the one on which she rode.

They left the great granite plain and flew over a garden even more beautiful than anything in a dream. In it were gathered many of the creatures like the one Mrs Whatsit had become, some lying among the flowers, some swimming in a broad, crystal river that flowed through the garden, some flying in what Meg was sure must be a kind of dance, moving in and out above the trees. They were making music, music that came not only from their throats but from the movement of their great wings as well.

"What are they singing?" Meg asked excitedly.

Mrs Whatsit shook her beautiful head. "It won't go into your words. I can't possibly transfer it to your words. Are you getting any of it, Charles?"

Charles Wallace sat very still on the broad back, on his face an intently listening look, the look he had when he <u>delved</u> into Meg or his mother. "A little. Just a very little. But I think I could get more in time."

"Yes. You could learn it, Charles. But there isn't time. We can only stay here long enough to rest up and make a few preparations."

Meg hardly listened to her. "I want to know what they're saying! I want to know what it means."

"Try, Charles," Mrs Whatsit urged. "Try to translate. You can let yourself go, now. You don't have to hold back."

"But I can't!" Charles Wallace cried in an <u>anguished</u> voice. "I don't know enough! Not yet!"

"Then try to work with me and I'll see if I can't verbalize it a little for them."

---

9. **monoliths.** A monolith is a single giant stone in the form of a pillar or column.

words for everyday use

delve (delv) v., search deeply. *Because Liz was interested in Ugaritic, or Syrian, mythology, she <u>delved</u> into the stacks of the library to learn more.*

an • guished (aŋ´gwisht) adj., feeling great suffering, as from worry, grief, or pain. *I knew from Jessica's <u>anguished</u> expression that she had not done well on the test.*

Charles Wallace got his look of probing, of listening.

I know that look! Meg thought suddenly. Now I think I know what it means! Because I've had it myself, sometimes, doing math with Father, when a problem is just about to come clear—

Mrs Whatsit seemed to be listening to Charles's thoughts. "Well, yes, that's an idea. I can try. Too bad you don't really know it so you can give it to me direct, Charles. It's so much more work this way."

"Don't be lazy," Charles said.

Mrs Whatsit did not take offense. She explained, "Oh, it's my favorite kind of work, Charles. That's why they chose me to go along, even though I'm so much younger. It's my one real talent. But it takes a tremendous amount of energy, and we're going to need every ounce of energy for what's ahead of us. But I'll try. For Calvin and Meg I'll try." She was silent; the great wings almost stopped moving; only a delicate stirring seemed to keep them aloft. "Listen, then," Mrs Whatsit said. The <u>resonant</u> voice rose and the words seemed to be all around them so that Meg felt that she could almost reach out and touch them: *"Sing unto the Lord a new song, and his praise from the end of the earth, ye that go down to the sea, and all that is therein; the isles, and the inhabitants thereof. Let the wilderness and the cities thereof lift their voice; let the inhabitants of the rock sing, let them shout from the top of the mountains. Let them give glory unto the Lord!"*[10]

◀ *Translate the creatures' song into your own words.*

Throughout her entire body Meg felt a pulse of joy such as she had never known before. Calvin's hand reached out; he did not clasp her hand in his; he moved his fingers so that they were barely touching hers, but joy flowed through them, back and forth between them, around them and about them and inside them.

When Mrs Whatsit sighed it seemed completely incomprehensible that through this bliss could come the faintest whisper of doubt.

---

10. *"Sing . . . unto the Lord!"* Quotation from the Bible, Isaiah 42:10–12

words for everyday use   re • so • nant (rez′ə nənt) *adj.*, resounding or reechoing; strong or deep in tone. *The church bells let out <u>resonant</u> tones that could be heard in every farm in the village.*

"We must go now, children." Mrs Whatsit's voice was deep with sadness, and Meg could not understand. Raising her head, Mrs Whatsit gave a call that seemed to be a command, and one of the creatures flying above the trees nearest them raised its head to listen, and then flew off and picked three flowers from a tree growing near the river and brought them over. "Each of you take one," Mrs Whatsit said. "I'll tell you how to use them later."

As Meg took her flower she realized that it was not a single blossom, but hundreds of tiny flowerets forming a kind of hollow bell.

"Where are we going?" Calvin asked.

"Up."

The wings moved steadily, swiftly. The garden was left behind, the stretch of granite, the mighty shapes, and then Mrs Whatsit was flying upward, climbing steadily up, up. Below them the trees of the mountain dwindled, became sparse, were replaced by bushes and then small, dry grasses, and then vegetation ceased entirely and there were only rocks, points and peaks of rock, sharp and dangerous. "Hold on tight," Mrs Whatsit said. "Don't slip."

Meg felt Calvin's arm circle her waist in a secure hold.

Still they moved upward.

Now they were in clouds. They could see nothing but drifting whiteness, and the moisture clung to them and condensed in icy droplets. As Meg shivered, Calvin's grip tightened. In front of her Charles Wallace sat quietly. Once he turned just long enough to give her a swift glance of tenderness and concern. But Meg felt as each moment passed that he was growing farther and farther away, that he was becoming less and less her adored baby brother and more and more one with whatever kind of being Mrs Whatsit, Mrs Who, and Mrs Which in actuality were.

Abruptly they burst out of the clouds into a shaft of light. Below them there were still rocks; above them the rocks continued to reach up into the sky, but now, though it seemed miles upward, Meg could see where the mountain at last came to an end.

Mrs Whatsit continued to climb, her wings straining a little. Meg felt her heart racing; cold sweat

▶ In what way does Charles Wallace appear to be changing?

began to gather on her face and her lips felt as though they were turning blue. She began to gasp.

"All right, children, use your flowers now," Mrs Whatsit said. "The atmosphere will continue to get thinner from now on. Hold the flowers up to your face and breathe through them and they will give you enough oxygen. It won't be as much as you're used to, but it will be enough."

Meg had almost forgotten the flowers, and was grateful to realize that she was still clasping them, that she hadn't let them fall from her fingers. She pressed her face into the blossoms and breathed deeply.

Calvin still held her with one arm, but he, too, held the flowers to his face.

Charles Wallace moved the hand with the flowers slowly, almost as though he were in a dream.

Mrs Whatsit's wings strained against the thinness of the atmosphere. The summit was only a little way above them, and then they were there. Mrs Whatsit came to rest on a small plateau of smooth silvery rock. There ahead of them was a great white disk.

"One of Uriel's moons," Mrs Whatsit told them, her mighty voice faintly breathless.

"Oh, it's beautiful!" Meg cried. "It's beautiful!"

The silver light from the enormous moon poured over them, blending with the golden quality of the day, flowing over the children, over Mrs Whatsit, over the mountain peak.

"Now we will turn around," Mrs Whatsit said, and at the quality of her voice, Meg was afraid again.

But when they turned she saw nothing. Ahead of them was the thin clear blue of sky; below them the rocks thrusting out of the shifting sea of white clouds.

"Now we will wait," Mrs Whatsit said, "for sunset and moonset."

Almost as she spoke the light began to deepen, to darken.

"I want to watch the moon set," Charles Wallace said.

"No, child. Do not turn around, any of you. Face out towards the dark. What I have to show you will be more visible then. Look ahead, straight ahead, as far as you can possibly look."

▶ What does Mrs Whatsit command them to see?

Meg's eyes ached from the strain of looking and seeing nothing. Then, above the clouds which encircled the mountain, she seemed to see a shadow, a faint thing of darkness so far off that she was scarcely sure she was really seeing it.

Charles Wallace said, "What's that?"

"That sort of shadow out there," Calvin gestured. "What is it? I don't like it."

"Watch," Mrs Whatsit commanded.

It was a shadow, nothing but a shadow. It was not even as tangible as a cloud. Was it cast by something? Or was it a Thing in itself?

The sky darkened. The gold left the light and they were surrounded by blue, blue deepening until where there had been nothing but the evening sky there was now a faint pulse of star, and then another and another and another. There were more stars than Meg had ever seen before.

"The atmosphere is so thin here," Mrs Whatsit said as though in answer to her unasked question, "that it does not obscure your vision as it would at home. Now look. Look straight ahead."

Meg looked. The dark shadow was still there. It had not lessened or dispersed with the coming of night. And where the shadow was the stars were not visible.

What could there be about a shadow that was so terrible that she knew that there had never been before or ever would be again, anything that would chill her with a fear that was beyond shuddering, beyond crying or screaming, beyond the possibility of comfort?

Meg's hand holding the blossoms slowly dropped and it seemed as though a knife gashed through her lungs. She gasped, but there was no air for her to breathe. Darkness glazed her eyes and mind, but as she started to fall into unconsciousness her head dropped down into the flowers which she was still clutching; and as she inhaled the fragrance of their purity her mind and body revived, and she sat up again.

The shadow was still there, dark and dreadful.

▶ Why can't Calvin's hand reassure Meg?

Calvin held her hand strongly in his, but she felt neither strength nor reassurance in his touch. Beside her a tremor went through Charles Wallace, but he sat very still.

He shouldn't be seeing this, Meg thought. This is too much for so little a boy, no matter how different and extraordinary a little boy.

Calvin turned, rejecting the dark Thing that blotted out the light of the stars. "Make it go away, Mrs Whatsit," he whispered. "Make it go away. It's evil."

Slowly the great creature turned around so that the shadow was behind them, so that they saw only the stars <u>unobscured</u>, the soft throb of starlight on the mountain, the descending circle of the great moon swiftly slipping over the horizon. Then, without a word from Mrs Whatsit, they were traveling downward, down, down. When they reached the corona of clouds Mrs Whatsit said, "You can breathe without the flowers now, my children."

Silence again. Not a word. It was as though the shadow had somehow reached out with its dark power and touched them so that they were incapable of speech. When they got back to the flowery field, bathed now in starlight, and moonlight from another, smaller, yellower, rising moon, a little of the tenseness went out of their bodies, and they realized that the body of the beautiful creature on which they rode had been as rigid as theirs.

◀ Why might Mrs Whatsit have been tense also?

With a graceful gesture it dropped to the ground and folded its great wings. Charles Wallace was the first to slide off. "Mrs Who! Mrs Which!" he called, and there was an immediate quivering in the air. Mrs Who's familiar glasses gleamed at them. Mrs Which appeared, too; but, as she had told the children, it was difficult for her to materialize completely, and though there was the robe and peaked hat, Meg could look through them to mountain and stars. She slid off Mrs Whatsit's back and walked, rather unsteadily after the long ride, over to Mrs Which.

"That dark Thing we saw," she said. "Is that what my father is fighting?"

---

words for everyday use

un • ob • scured (un əb skyùrd´) *adj.,* clear or distinct; easily seen. *It was a beautiful summer night, and the constellations were <u>unobscured</u> by clouds.*

Respond to the Selection

When Calvin sees the dark Thing above the planet Uriel, he says, "Make it go away, Mrs Whatsit . . . it's evil." What do you think the dark Thing is? Why is it terrifying? What would you think or feel if you saw the dark Thing?

Investigate, Inquire, and Imagine

Recall: GATHERING FACTS

1a. What does Meg show Calvin how to do? What does Mrs. Murry say is the cause of Meg's trouble with math at school?

2a. What does Meg say happened to her father? What does Calvin say about Meg's father? Where does Charles tell Meg and Calvin they are going?

3a. Where do Meg, Calvin, and Charles suddenly find themselves? How do they get there? Into what does Mrs Whatsit transform?

4a. Where does Mrs Whatsit bring the children once she has transformed? Why do the children need the flowers? What do the children see once they get there?

Interpret: FINDING MEANING

➤ 1b. Why is Calvin surprised that Meg can help him with his homework? Why does Calvin say that he wants to meet "more morons like Meg and Charles"?

➤ 2b. How does talking to Calvin about her father make Meg feel? Why? How do you think Meg feels about finding her father?

➤ 3b. How does Meg feel during her sudden journey? How do the children feel when Mrs Whatsit transforms?

➤ 4b. Why does Meg think that Charles should not be allowed to see the Thing that Mrs Whatsit shows them? Why does Mrs Whatsit show them this Thing?

Analyze: TAKING THINGS APART

5a. Identify Meg's strengths and weaknesses. Do you think Meg is too critical of herself? Explain.

Synthesize: BRINGING THINGS TOGETHER

➤ 5b. Mrs Whatsit undergoes a physical transformation, or change, in chapter 4. Meg undergoes, in chapters 3 and 4, an emotional change. What major change occurs in Meg's emotional state in these chapters? In what ways do you predict Meg will continue to change over the course of the journey?

6a. *A Wrinkle in Time* is about the battle between good and evil. In chapter 4, Mrs Whatsit introduces the children to the planet Uriel and to something called the Black Thing. What details about Uriel make it a fitting example of pure goodness? What details about the Black Thing make it a fitting example of pure evil?

6b. In your opinion, what is goodness? What is evil? With a partner, brainstorm a list of things that you associate with goodness; then, brainstorm another list of things you associate with evil. When everyone has finished brainstorming, you may discuss your answers as a class.

Goodness	Evil

Understanding Literature

ALLUSION. An **allusion** is a reference in a literary work to something famous. Mrs Who alludes to the three witches in William Shakespeare's *Macbeth* when she says, "When shall we three meet again, / In thunder, lightning, or in rain?" The three witches in *Macbeth* have supernatural powers that enable them to tell the future and to cause storms. Why do you think Mrs Who alludes to the witches in *Macbeth* immediately after the group tessers? Who or what are Mrs Whatsit, Mrs Who, and Mrs Which pretending to be? Who or what do you think they actually are?

FANTASY AND SCIENCE FICTION. **Fantasy** is a type of writing that is very imaginative and unrealistic. Fantasy stories may involve imaginary beings such as elves, dragons, or unicorns, as well as magical or supernatural occurrences. **Science fiction** is imaginative literature based on scientific principles, discoveries, or laws. It is similar to fantasy in that it deals with imaginary worlds, but differs from fantasy in having a scientific basis. Often science fiction deals with the future, the distant past, or with worlds other than our own. *A Wrinkle in Time* contains elements of both fantasy and science fiction. Which parts of the story so far seem like fantasy? Which parts seem like science fiction?

THEME. A **theme** is a main idea in a literary work. A work can have more than one theme. One theme of *A Wrinkle in Time* is that things are not always what they seem, and that a person should not make a judgment before learning all the facts. Which of the characters you have met so far in the book are not what they seem to be? Explain. According to the townspeople, what seems to have happened to Mr. Murry? How are the circumstances different from what they might appear to be?

Chapter 5

The Tesseract

"Yes," Mrs Which said. "Hhee iss beehindd thee ddarrkness, sso thatt eevenn wee cannott seee hhimm."

Meg began to cry, to sob aloud. Through her tears she could see Charles Wallace standing there, very small, very white. Calvin put his arms around her, but she shuddered and broke away, sobbing wildly. Then she was enfolded in the great wings of Mrs Whatsit and she felt comfort and strength pouring through her. Mrs Whatsit was not speaking aloud, and yet through the wings Meg understood words.

◀ Why do you suppose that Mrs Whatsit is able to comfort Meg when Calvin is unable to do so?

"My child, do not despair. Do you think we would have brought you here if there were no hope? We are asking you to do a difficult thing, but we are confident that you can do it. Your father needs help, he needs courage, and for his children he may be able to do what he cannot do for himself."

"Nnow," Mrs Which said. "Arre wee rreaddy?"

"Where are we going?" Calvin asked.

Again Meg felt an actual physical tingling of fear as Mrs Which spoke.

"Wwee musstt ggo bbehindd thee sshaddow."

"But we will not do it all at once," Mrs Whatsit comforted them. "We will do it in short stages." She looked at Meg. "Now we will tesser, we will wrinkle again. Do you understand?"

"No," Meg said flatly.

Mrs Whatsit sighed. "Explanations are not easy when they are about things for which your civilization still has no words. Calvin talked about traveling at the speed of light. You understand that, little Meg?"

"Yes," Meg nodded.

"That, of course, is the impractical, long way around. We have learned to take short cuts wherever possible."

"Sort of like in math?" Meg asked.

"Like in math." Mrs Whatsit looked over at Mrs Who. "Take your skirt and show them."

"*La experiencia es la madre de la ciencia.* Spanish, my dears. Cervantes.[1] *Experience is the mother of knowledge.*" Mrs Who took a portion of her white robe in her hands and held it tight.

"You see," Mrs Whatsit said, "if a very small insect were to move from the section of skirt in Mrs Who's right hand to that in her left, it would be quite a long walk for him if he had to walk straight across."

Swiftly Mrs Who brought her hands, still holding the skirt, together.

"Now, you see," Mrs Whatsit said, "he would *be* there, without that long trip. That is how we travel."

Charles Wallace accepted the explanation serenely. Even Calvin did not seem perturbed. "Oh, *dear,*" Meg sighed. "I guess I *am* a moron. I just don't get it."

"That is because you think of space only in three dimensions," Mrs Whatsit told her. "We travel in the fifth dimension. This is something you can understand, Meg. Don't be afraid to try. Was your mother able to explain a tesseract to you?"

"Well, she never did," Meg said. "She got so upset about it. Why, Mrs Whatsit? She said it had something to do with her and Father."

"It was a concept they were playing with," Mrs Whatsit said, "going beyond the fourth dimension to the fifth. Did your mother explain it to you, Charles?"

---

1. **Cervantes.** Miguel de Cervantes Saavedra (1547–1616), Spanish writer famous for his novel *Don Quijote*

"Well, yes." Charles looked a little embarrassed. "Please don't be hurt, Meg. I just kept at her while you were at school till I got it out of her."

Meg sighed. "Just explain it to me."

"Okay," Charles said. "What is the first dimension?"

"Well—a line: ——————— "

"Okay. And the second dimension?"

"Well, you'd square the line. A flat square would be in the second dimension."

"And the third?"

"Well, you'd square the second dimension. Then the square wouldn't be flat any more. It would have a bottom, and sides, and a top."

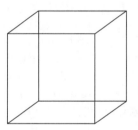

"And the fourth?"

"Well, I guess if you want to put it into mathematical terms you'd square the square. But you can't take a pencil and draw it the way you can the first three. I know it's got something to do with Einstein and time. I guess maybe you could call the fourth dimension Time."

"That's right," Charles said. "Good girl. Okay, then, for the fifth dimension you'd square the fourth, wouldn't you?"

"I guess so."

"Well, the fifth dimension's a tesseract. You add that to the other four dimensions and you can travel through space without having to go the long way

◄ Why does Charles think Meg might be hurt?

around. In other words, to put it into Euclid,[2] or old-fashioned plane geometry, a straight line is *not* the shortest distance between two points."

For a brief, illuminating second Meg's face had the listening, probing expression that was so often seen on Charles's. "I see!" she cried. "I got it! For just a moment I got it! I can't possibly explain it now, but there for a second I saw it!" She turned excitedly to Calvin. "Did you get it?"

He nodded. "Enough. I don't understand it the way Charles Wallace does, but enough to get the idea."

"Sso nnow wee ggo," Mrs Which said. "Tthere iss nott all thee ttime inn tthe worrlld."

"Could we hold hands?" Meg asked.

Calvin took her hand and held it tightly in his.

"You can try," Mrs Whatsit said, "though I'm not sure how it will work. You see, though we travel together, we travel alone. We will go first and take you afterward in the backwash. That may be easier for you." As she spoke the great white body began to waver, the wings to dissolve into mist. Mrs Who seemed to evaporate until there was nothing but the glasses, and then the glasses, too, disappeared. It reminded Meg of the Cheshire Cat.

—I've often seen a face without glasses, she thought; —but glasses without a face![3] I wonder if I go that way, too. First me and then my glasses?

She looked over at Mrs Which. Mrs Which was there and then she wasn't.

There was a gust of wind and a great thrust and a sharp shattering as she was shoved through—what? Then darkness; silence; nothingness. If Calvin was still holding her hand she could not feel it. But this time she was prepared for the sudden and complete dissolution of her body. When she felt the tingling

---

2. **Euclid.** Ancient Greek mathematician who lived around 300 BC; he established some of the basic principles of geometry.

3. **Cheshire Cat . . . glasses without a face.** Paraphrased from a passage in Lewis Carroll's *Alice in Wonderland*

---

words for everyday use

dis • so • lu • tion (dis'ə lü´shən) n., breaking up or into parts; dissolving. *After the dissolution of the club, the members went their separate ways, and the club's remaining funds were given to charity.*

coming back to her fingertips she knew that this journey was almost over and she could feel again the pressure of Calvin's hand about hers.

Without warning, coming as a complete and unexpected shock, she felt a pressure she had never imagined, as though she were being completely flattened out by an enormous steam roller. This was far worse than the nothingness had been; while she was nothing there was no need to breathe, but now her lungs were squeezed together so that although she was dying for want of air there was no way for her lungs to expand and contract, to take in the air that she must have to stay alive. This was completely different from the thinning of atmosphere when they flew up the mountain and she had had to put the flowers to her face to breathe. She tried to gasp, but a paper doll can't gasp. She thought she was trying to think, but her flattened-out mind was as unable to function as her lungs; her thoughts were squashed along with the rest of her. Her heart tried to beat; it gave a knife-like, sidewise movement, but it could not expand.

But then she seemed to hear a voice, or if not a voice, at least words, words flattened out like printed words on paper, "Oh, no! We can't stop here! This is a *two*-dimensional planet and the children can't manage here!"

◀ Why can't the children survive on this planet?

She was whizzed into nothingness again, and nothingness was wonderful. She did not mind that she could not feel Calvin's hand, that she could not see or feel or be. The relief from the <u>intolerable</u> pressure was all she needed.

Then the tingling began to come back to her fingers, her toes; she could feel Calvin holding her tightly. Her heart beat regularly; blood coursed through her veins. Whatever had happened, whatever mistake had been made, it was over now. She thought she heard Charles Wallace saying, his words

words for everyday use   in • tol • er • able (in täl´ər ə bəl) *adj.,* not able to be endured. *Residents complained that the smell coming from the new factory was <u>intolerable</u>.*

round and full as spoken words ought to be, *"Really,* Mrs Which, you might have killed us!"

This time she was pushed out of the frightening fifth dimension with a sudden, immediate jerk. There she was, herself again, standing with Calvin beside her, holding onto her hand for dear life, and Charles Wallace in front of her, looking indignant. Mrs Whatsit, Mrs Who, and Mrs Which were not visible, but she knew that they were there; the fact of their presence was strong about her.

"Cchilldrenn, I appolloggize," came Mrs Which's voice.

"Now, Charles, calm down," Mrs Whatsit said, appearing not as the great and beautiful beast she had been when they last saw her, but in her familiar wild garb of shawls and scarves and the old tramp's coat and hat. "You know how difficult it is for her to materialize. If you are not substantial yourself it's *very* difficult to realize how limiting protoplasm[4] is."

"I *ammm* ssorry," Mrs Which's voice came again; but there was more than a hint of amusement in it.

"It is *not* funny." Charles Wallace gave a childish stamp of his foot.

Mrs Who's glasses shone out, and the rest of her appeared more slowly behind them. *"We are such stuff as dreams are made on."* She smiled broadly. "Prospero in *The Tempest.*[5] I *do* like that play."

"You didn't do it on *purpose?"* Charles demanded.

▶ How does Mrs Whatsit explain Mrs Which's mistake?

"Oh, my darling, of course not," Mrs Whatsit said quickly. "It was just a very understandable mistake. It's very difficult for Mrs Which to think in a corporeal way. She wouldn't hurt you deliberately; you know that. And it's really a very pleasant little planet, and rather amusing to be flat. We always enjoy our visits there."

"Where are we now, then?" Charles Wallace demanded. "And why?"

"In Orion's belt.[6] We have a friend here, and we want you to have a look at your own planet."

---

4. **protoplasm.** The essential living matter of all plant and animal cells

5. **Prospero in *The Tempest.*** Prospero is a character in Shakespeare's play *The Tempest,* first produced in 1611.

6. **Orion's belt.** Central part of the constellation nicknamed "the Hunter"; this constellation contains the stars Rigel and Betelgeuse

"When are we going home?" Meg asked anxiously. "What about Mother? What about the twins? They'll be terribly worried about us. When we didn't come in at bedtime—well, Mother must be frantic by now. She and the twins and Fort will have been looking and looking for us, and of course we aren't there to be found!"

"Now, don't worry, my pet," Mrs Whatsit said cheerfully. "We took care of that before we left. Your mother has had enough to worry her with you and Charles to cope with, and not knowing about your father, without our adding to her anxieties. We took a time wrinkle as well as a space wrinkle. It's very easy to do if you just know how."

◀ Why won't Mrs. Murry worry about the children?

"What do you mean?" Meg asked <u>plaintively</u>. "Please, Mrs Whatsit, it's all so confusing."

"Just relax and don't worry over things that needn't trouble you," Mrs Whatsit said. "We made a nice, tidy little time tesser, and unless something goes terribly wrong we'll have you back about five minutes before you left, so there'll be time to spare and nobody'll ever need to know you were gone at all, though of course you'll be telling your mother, dear lamb that she is. And if something goes terribly wrong it won't matter whether we ever get back at all."

"Ddon'tt ffrrightenn themm," Mrs Which's voice came. "Aare yyou llosingg ffaith?"

"Oh, no. No, I'm not."

But Meg thought her voice sounded a little faint.

"I hope *this* is a nice planet," Calvin said. "We can't *see* much of it. Does it ever clear up?"

Meg looked around her, realizing that she had been so breathless from the journey and the stop on the two-dimensional planet that she had not noticed her surroundings. And perhaps this was not very surprising, for the main thing about the surroundings was exactly that they *were* unnoticeable. They seemed to be standing on some kind of <u>nondescript</u>, flat surface.

---

words for everyday use

plain • tive • ly (plān′tiv lē) *adv.*, in a sorrowful or sad way. *"Please, oh please, can I have a puppy?" my little brother asked* <u>plaintively</u>.

non • de • script (nän′di skript′) *adj.*, hard to describe; colorless; drab. *Gina said that the girl's outfit was so <u>nondescript</u> that she could not possibly tell me what it looked like.*

The air around them was gray. It was not exactly fog, but she could see nothing through it. Visibility was limited to the nicely definite bodies of Charles Wallace and Calvin, the rather unbelievable bodies of Mrs Whatsit and Mrs Who, and a faint occasional glimmer that was Mrs Which.

"Come, children," Mrs Whatsit said. "We don't have far to go, and we might as well walk. It will do you good to stretch your legs a little."

As they moved through the grayness Meg caught an occasional glimpse of slaglike rocks, but there were no traces of trees or bushes, nothing but flat ground under their feet, no sign of any vegetation at all.

▶ Who are the children going to meet?

Finally, ahead of them there loomed what seemed to be a hill of stone. As they approached it Meg could see that there was an entrance that led into a deep, dark cavern. "Are we going in there?" she asked nervously.

"Don't be afraid," Mrs Whatsit said. "It's easier for the Happy Medium to work within. Oh, you'll like her, children. She's very jolly. If ever I saw her looking unhappy I would be very depressed myself. As long as she can laugh I'm sure everything is going to come out right in the end."

"Mmrs Whattsitt," came Mrs Which's voice severely, "jusstt beccause yyou arre verry youngg iss nno exxcuse forr tallkingg tooo muchh."

Mrs Whatsit looked hurt, but she subsided.

"Just how old *are* you?" Calvin asked her.

"Just a moment," Mrs Whatsit murmured, and appeared to calculate rapidly upon her fingers. She nodded triumphantly. "Exactly 2,379,152,497 years, 8 months, and 3 days. That is according to *your* calendar, of course, which even you know isn't very accurate." She leaned closer to Meg and Calvin and whispered, "It was really a *very* great honor for me to be chosen for this mission. It's just because of my verbalizing and <u>materializing</u> so well, you know. But of

words for everyday use ma • te • ri • a • lize (mə tir´ē ə līz) *v.*, develop into something real or tangible. *The approaching car's headlights <u>materialized</u> suddenly out of the darkness.*

course we can't take any credit for our talents. It's how we use them that counts. And I make far too many mistakes. That's why Mrs Who and I enjoyed seeing Mrs Which make a mistake when she tried to land you on a two-dimensional planet. It was *that* we were laughing at, not at you. She was laughing at herself, you see. She's really terribly nice to us younger ones."

Meg was listening with such interest to what Mrs Whatsit was saying that she hardly noticed when they went into the cave; the <u>transition</u> from the grayness of outside to the grayness of inside was almost unnoticeable. She saw a flickering light ahead of them, ahead and down, and it was toward this that they went. As they drew closer she realized that it was a fire.

"It gets very cold in here," Mrs Whatsit said, "so we asked her to have a good bonfire going for you."

As they approached the fire they could see a dark shadow against it, and as they went closer still they could see that the shadow was a woman. She wore a turban of beautiful pale mauve silk, and a long, flowing, purple satin gown. In her hands was a crystal ball into which she was gazing raptly. She did not appear to see the children, Mrs Whatsit, Mrs Who, and Mrs Which, but continued to stare into the crystal ball; and as she stared she began to laugh; and she laughed and laughed at whatever it was that she was seeing.

Mrs Which's voice rang out clear and strong, echoing against the walls of the cavern, and the words fell with a sonorous clang.

"WWEE ARRE HHERRE!"

The woman looked up from the ball, and when she saw them she got up and curtsied deeply. Mrs Whatsit and Mrs Who dropped small curtsies in return, and the shimmer seemed to bow slightly.

"Oh, Medium, dear," Mrs Whatsit said, "these are the children. Charles Wallace Murry." Charles Wallace

---

words for everyday use **tran • si • tion** (tran zish'ən) *n.*, passage, or change, from one condition to another. *We watched the water's <u>transition</u> from a liquid to a gaseous state.*

bowed. "Margaret Murry." Meg felt that if Mrs Whatsit and Mrs Who had curtsied, she ought to, also; so she did, rather awkwardly. "And Calvin O'Keefe." Calvin bobbed his head. "We want them to see their home planet," Mrs Whatsit said.

The Medium lost the delighted smile she had worn till then. "Oh, *why* must you make me look at unpleasant things when there are so many delightful ones to see?"

Again Mrs Which's voice <u>reverberated</u> through the cave. "Therre willl nno llonggerr bee sso manyy ppl-leasanntt thinggss too llookk att iff rressponssible ppeoplle ddo nnott ddoo ssomethingg abboutt thee unnppleassanntt oness."

The Medium sighed and held the ball high.

"Look, children," Mrs Whatsit said. "Look into it well."

"*Que la terre est petite à qui la voit des cieux!* Delille.[7] *How small is the earth to him who looks from heaven,*" Mrs Who intoned musically.

Meg looked into the crystal ball, at first with caution, then with increasing eagerness, as she seemed to see an enormous sweep of dark and empty space, and then galaxies swinging across it. Finally they seemed to move in closer on one of the galaxies.

"Your own Milky Way,"[8] Mrs Whatsit whispered to Meg.

They were headed directly toward the center of the galaxy; then they moved off to one side; stars seemed to be rushing at them. Meg flung her arm up over her face as though to ward off the blow.

"Llookk!" Mrs Which commanded.

Meg dropped her arm. They seemed to be moving in toward a planet. She thought she could make out polar ice caps. Everything seemed sparkling clear.

---

7. **Delille.** Jacques Delille (1738–1813), French poet and classicist
8. **Milky Way.** Galaxy that is home to our solar system

words for everyday use

re • ver • be • ra • te (ri vər´ bə rāt) *v.*, echo. *The children's shouts <u>reverberated</u> off the walls of the canyon.*

"No, no, Medium dear, that's Mars," Mrs Whatsit reproved gently.

"Do I *have* to?" the Medium asked.

"NNOWW!" Mrs Which commanded.

The bright planet moved out of their vision. For a moment there was the darkness of space; then another planet. The outlines of this planet were not clean and clear. It seemed to be covered with a smoky haze. Through the haze Meg thought she could make out the familiar outlines of continents like pictures in her Social Studies books.

"Is it because of our atmosphere that we can't see properly?" she asked anxiously.

"Nno, Mmegg, yyou knnoww thatt itt iss nnott tthee attmosspheeere," Mrs Which said. "Yyou mmusstt bee brrave."

"It's the Thing!" Charles Wallace cried. "It's the Dark Thing we saw from the mountain peak on Uriel when we were riding on Mrs Whatsit's back!"

◄ What is casting a shadow over the earth? How long has it been there?

"Did it just come?" Meg asked in agony, unable to take her eyes from the sickness of the shadow which darkened the beauty of the earth. "Did it just come while we've been gone?"

Mrs Which's voice seemed very tired. "Ttell herr," she said to Mrs Whatsit.

Mrs Whatsit sighed. "No, Meg. It hasn't just come. It has been there for a great many years. That is why your planet is such a troubled one."

"But why—" Calvin started to ask, his voice croaking hoarsely.

Mrs Whatsit raised her hand to silence him. "We showed you the Dark Thing on Uriel first—oh, for many reasons. First, because the atmosphere on the mountain peaks there is so clear and thin you could see it for what it is. And we thought it would be easier for you to understand it if you saw it—well, someplace *else* first, not your own earth."

"I hate it!" Charles Wallace cried passionately. "I hate the Dark Thing!"

Mrs Whatsit nodded. "Yes, Charles dear. We all do. That's another reason we wanted to prepare you on Uriel. We thought it would be too frightening for you to see it first of all about your own, beloved world."

"But what is it?" Calvin demanded. "We know that it's evil, but what is it?"

"Yyouu hhave ssaidd itt!" Mrs Which's voice rang out. "Itt iss Eevill. Itt iss thee Ppowers of Ddarrkknesss!"

"But what's going to happen?" Meg's voice trembled. "Oh, please, Mrs Which, tell us what's going to happen!"

"Wee wwill cconnttinnue tto ffightt!"

▶ Why do the children stand straighter?

Something in Mrs Which's voice made all three of the children stand straighter, throwing back their shoulders with determination, looking at the glimmer that was Mrs Which with pride and confidence.

"And we're not alone, you know, children," came Mrs Whatsit, the comforter. "All through the universe it's being fought, all through the cosmos, and my, but it's a grand and exciting battle. I know it's hard for you to understand about size, how there's very little difference in the size of the tiniest microbe and the greatest galaxy. You think about that, and maybe it won't seem strange to you that some of our very best fighters have come right from your own planet, and it's a *little* planet, dears, out on the edge of a little galaxy. You can be proud that it's done so well."

"Who have our fighters been?" Calvin asked.

"Oh, *you* must know them, dear," Mrs Whatsit said.

Mrs Who's spectacles shone out at them triumphantly, *"And the light shineth in darkness; and the darkness comprehended it not."* [9]

"Jesus!" Charles Wallace said. "Why of course, Jesus!"

"Of course!" Mrs Whatsit said. "Go on, Charles, love. There were others. All your great artists. They've been lights for us to see by."

▶ What sorts of people have fought against the Dark Thing?

"Leonardo da Vinci?" Calvin suggested tentatively. "And Michelangelo?"

"And Shakespeare," Charles Wallace called out, "and Bach! And Pasteur and Madame Curie and Einstein!"

---

9. *"And the light . . . not."* Quotation from the Bible, John 1:5

Now Calvin's voice rang with confidence. "And Schweitzer and Gandhi and Buddha and Beethoven and Rembrandt and St. Francis!"

"Now you, Meg," Mrs Whatsit ordered.

"Oh, Euclid, I suppose." Meg was in such an <u>agony</u> of impatience that her voice grated irritably. "And Copernicus. But what about Father? Please, what about Father?"

"Wee aarre ggoingg tto yourr ffatherr," Mrs Which said.

"But where is he?" Meg went over to Mrs Which and stamped as though she were as young as Charles Wallace.

Mrs Whatsit answered in a voice that was low but quite firm. "On a planet that has given in. So you must prepare to be very strong."

◀ What does Mrs Whatsit mean when she says the planet has "given in"?

All traces of cheer had left the Happy Medium's face. She sat holding the great ball, looking down at the shadowed earth, and a slow tear coursed down her cheek. "I can't stand it any longer," she sobbed. "Watch now, children, watch!"

words for everyday use   ag • o • ny (ag´ə nē) *n.*, intense pain; torture. *The injured football player grasped his knee and cringed in <u>agony</u>.*

Chapter 6

The Happy Medium

Again they focused their eyes on the crystal ball. The earth with its fearful covering of dark shadow swam out of view and they moved rapidly through the Milky Way. And there was the Thing again.

"Watch!" the Medium told them.

The Darkness seemed to seethe and writhe. Was this meant to *comfort* them?

Suddenly there was a great burst of light through the Darkness. The light spread out and where it touched the Darkness the Darkness disappeared. The light spread until the patch of Dark Thing had vanished, and there was only a gentle shining, and through the shining came the stars, clear and pure. Then, slowly, the shining dwindled until it, too, was gone, and there was nothing but stars and starlight. No shadows. No fear. Only the stars and the clear darkness of space, quite different from the fearful darkness of the Thing.

"You see!" the Medium cried, smiling happily. "It can be overcome! It is being overcome all the time!"

Mrs Whatsit sighed, a sigh so sad that Meg wanted to put her arms around her and comfort her.

"Tell us exactly what happened, then, please," Charles Wallace said in a small voice.

"It was a star," Mrs Whatsit said sadly. "A star giving up its life in battle with the Thing. It won, oh, yes, my children, it won. But it lost its life in the winning."

Mrs Which spoke again. Her voice sounded tired, and they knew that speaking was a tremendous effort for her. "Itt wass nnott sso llongg aggo fforr yyou, wwass itt?" she asked gently.

Mrs Whatsit shook her head.

---

words for everyday use

writhe (rīth) *v.*, twist or squirm as if in pain. *Wendell writhed to free himself from his brother's grasp.*

▶ What happened to Mrs Whatsit? Why is Charles grateful?

Charles Wallace went up to Mrs Whatsit. "I see. Now I understand. You were a star, once, weren't you?"

Mrs Whatsit covered her face with her hands as though she were embarrassed, and nodded.

"And you did—you did what that star just did?"

With her face still covered, Mrs Whatsit nodded again.

Charles Wallace looked at her, very solemnly. "I should like to kiss you."

Mrs Whatsit took her hands down from her face and pulled Charles Wallace to her in a quick embrace. He put his arms about her neck, pressed his cheek against hers, and then kissed her.

Meg felt that she would have liked to kiss Mrs Whatsit, too, but that after Charles Wallace, anything that she or Calvin did or said would be <u>anticlimax</u>. She contented herself with looking at Mrs Whatsit. Even though she was used to Mrs Whatsit's odd getup (and the very oddness of it was what made her seem so comforting), she realized with a fresh shock that it was not Mrs Whatsit herself that she was seeing at all. The complete, the true Mrs Whatsit, Meg realized, was beyond human understanding. What she saw was only the game Mrs Whatsit was playing; it was an amusing and charming game, a game full of both laughter and comfort, but it was only the tiniest <u>facet</u> of all the things Mrs Whatsit *could* be.

"I didn't mean to tell you," Mrs Whatsit <u>faltered</u>. "I didn't mean ever to let you know. But, oh, my dears, I did so love being a star!"

"Yyouu arre sstill verry yyoungg," Mrs Which said, her voice faintly <u>chiding</u>.

The Medium sat looking happily at the star-filled sky in her ball, smiling and nodding and chuckling gently. But Meg noticed that her eyes were drooping,

---

words for everyday use

an • ti • cli • max (an tĭ klī´maks) *n.*, sudden drop from the important to the commonplace. *The movie built up so much suspense and anticipation that the ending seemed like an <u>anticlimax</u>.*

fa • cet (fas'it) *n.*, one of a number of sides or aspects. *A cube has six <u>facets</u>.*

fal • ter (fôl'tər) *v.*, stumble. *Ben <u>faltered</u> as he was climbing the steep stairway.*

chide (chīd) *v.*, scold. *"You forgot to call me," Derek <u>chided</u> me.*

and suddenly her head fell forward and she gave a faint snore.

"Poor thing," Mrs Whatsit said, "we've worn her out. It's very hard work for her."

"Please, Mrs Whatsit," Meg asked, "what happens now? Why are we here? What do we do next? Where is Father? When are we going to him?" She clasped her hands pleadingly.

"One thing at a time, love!" Mrs Whatsit said.

Mrs Who cut in. *"As paredes tem ouvidos.* That's Portuguese. *Walls have ears."*

"Yes, let us go outside," Mrs Whatsit said. "Come, we'll let her sleep."

But as they turned to go, the Medium jerked her head up and smiled at them radiantly. "You weren't going to go without saying good-by to me, were you?" she asked.

"We thought we'd just let you sleep, dear." Mrs Whatsit patted the Medium's shoulder. "We worked you terribly hard and we know you must be very tired."

"But I was going to give you some ambrosia or nectar[1] or at least some tea—"

At this Meg realized that she was hungry. How much time had passed since they had had their bowls of stew? she wondered.

But Mrs Whatsit said, "Oh, thank you, dear, but I think we'd better be going."

"They don't need to eat, you know," Charles Wallace whispered to Meg. "At least not food, the way we do. Eating's just a game with them. As soon as we get organized again I'd better remind them that they'll have to feed us sooner or later."

The Medium smiled and nodded. "It does seem as though I should be able to do something *nice* for you, after having had to show those poor children such horrid things. Would they like to see their mother before they go?"

"Could we see Father?" Meg asked eagerly.

"Nno," Mrs Which said. "Wwee aare ggoingg tto yourr ffatherr, Mmegg. Doo nnott bbee immpatientt."

---

1. **ambrosia or nectar.** Mythological foods of the gods and immortals

"But she *could* see her mother, couldn't she?" the Medium wheedled.

"Oh, why not," Mrs Whatsit put in. "It won't take long and it can't do any harm."

"And Calvin, too?" Meg asked. "Could he see his mother, too?"

Calvin touched Meg in a quick gesture, and whether it was of thanks or apprehension she was not sure.

"I tthinkk itt iss a misstake." Mrs Which was disapproving. "Bbutt ssince yyou hhave menttionedd itt I ssupposse yyouu musstt ggo aheadd."

"I hate it when she gets cross," Mrs Whatsit said, glancing over at Mrs Which, "and the trouble is, she always seems to be right. But I really don't see how it could hurt, and it might make you all feel better. Go on, Medium dear."

The Medium, smiling and humming softly, turned the crystal ball a little between her hands. Stars, comets, planets, flashed across the sky, and then the earth came into view again, the darkened earth, closer, closer, till it filled the globe, and they had somehow gone through the darkness until the soft white of clouds and the gentle outline of continents shone clearly.

"Calvin's mother first," Meg whispered to the Medium.

▶ What is Calvin's home life like?

The globe became hazy, cloudy, then shadows began to solidify, to <u>clarify</u>, and they were looking into an untidy kitchen with a sink full of unwashed dishes. In front of the sink stood an <u>unkempt</u> woman with gray hair stringing about her face. Her mouth was open and Meg could see the toothless gums and it seemed that she could almost hear her screaming at two small children who were standing by her. Then she grabbed a long wooden spoon from the sink and began whacking one of the children.

words for everyday use

cla • ri • fy (klar´ə fī´) v., make clear. *Our discussion had become so muddled that we were happy when Andre spoke up to clarify certain issues.*

un • kempt (un kempt´) adj., untidy. *While Ricardo was always tidy in appearance, Vincent was usually unkempt.*

"Oh, dear—" the Medium murmured, and the picture began to dissolve. "I didn't really—"

"It's all right," Calvin said in a low voice. "I think I'd rather you knew."

Now instead of reaching out to Calvin for safety, Meg took his hand in hers, not saying anything in words but trying to tell him by the pressure of her fingers what she felt. If anyone had told her only the day before that she, Meg, the snaggle-toothed, the <u>myopic</u>, the clumsy, would be taking a boy's hand to offer him comfort and strength, particularly a popular and important boy like Calvin, the idea would have been beyond her comprehension. But now it seemed as natural to want to help and protect Calvin as it did Charles Wallace.

The shadows were swirling in the crystal again, and as they cleared Meg began to recognize her mother's lab at home. Mrs. Murry was sitting perched on her high stool, writing away at a sheet of paper on a clipboard on her lap. She's writing Father, Meg thought. The way she always does. Every night.

The tears that she could never learn to control swam to her eyes as she watched. Mrs. Murry looked up from her letter, almost as though she were looking toward the children, and then her head drooped and she put it down on the paper, and sat there, huddled up, letting herself relax into an unhappiness that she never allowed her children to see.

And now the desire for tears left Meg. The hot, protective anger she had felt for Calvin when she looked into his home she now felt turned toward her mother.

"Let's go!" she cried harshly. "Let's *do* something!"

"She's always so right," Mrs Whatsit murmured, looking toward Mrs Which. "Sometimes I wish she'd just say I told you so and have done with it."

"I only meant to help—" the Medium wailed.

◄ Why does Mrs Whatsit say that Mrs Which is always right?

<u>words for everyday use</u> my • o • pic (mī äp´ik) *adj.,* nearsighted. *Because I am <u>myopic</u>, I need my glasses to focus on things that are more than ten feet away.*

"Oh, Medium, dear, *don't* feel badly," Mrs Whatsit said swiftly. "Look at something cheerful, do. I can't bear to have you distressed!"

"It's all right," Meg assured the Medium earnestly. "Truly it is, Mrs. Medium, and we thank you very much."

"Are you sure?" the Medium asked, brightening.

"Of course! It really helped ever so much because it made me mad, and when I'm mad I don't have room to be scared."

"Well, kiss me good-by for good luck, then," the Medium said.

Meg went over to her and gave her a quick kiss, and so did Charles Wallace. The Medium looked smilingly at Calvin, and winked. "I want the young man to kiss me, too. I always did love red hair. And it'll give you good luck, Laddie-me-love."

Calvin bent down, blushing, and awkwardly kissed her cheek.

The Medium tweaked his nose. "You've got a lot to learn, my boy," she told him.

"Now, good-by, Medium dear, and many thanks," Mrs Whatsit said. "I dare say we'll see you in an eon[2] or two."

"Where are you going in case I want to tune in?" the Medium asked.

"Camazotz," Mrs Whatsit told her. (Where and what was Camazotz? Meg did not like the sound of the word or the way in which Mrs Whatsit pronounced it.) "But please don't distress yourself on our behalf. You know you don't like looking in on the dark planets, and it's very upsetting to us when you aren't happy."

"But I must know what happens to the children," the Medium said. "It's my worst trouble, getting fond. If I didn't get fond I could be happy all the time. *Oh,* well, *ho* hum, I manage to keep pretty jolly, and a little snooze will do wonders for me right now. Good-by, everyb—" and her word got lost in the general b-b-bz-z of a snore.

▶ In what way does seeing her mother help Meg?

---

2. **eon.** An extremely long, indefinite period of time; thousands of years

"Ccome," Mrs Which ordered, and they followed her out of the darkness of the cave to the <u>impersonal</u> grayness of the Medium's planet.

"Nnoww, cchilldrenn, yyouu musstt nott bee frrightennedd att whatt iss ggoingg tto hhappenn," Mrs Which warned.

"Stay angry, little Meg," Mrs Whatsit whispered. "You will need all your anger now."

Without warning Meg was swept into nothingness again. This time the nothingness was interrupted by a feeling of clammy coldness such as she had never felt before. The coldness deepened and swirled all about her and through her, and was filled with a new and strange kind of darkness that was a completely tangible thing, a thing that wanted to eat and digest her like some enormous <u>malignant</u> beast of prey.

Then the darkness was gone. Had it been the shadow, the Black Thing? Had they had to travel through it to get to her father?

There was the by-now-familiar tingling in her hands and feet and the push through hardness, and she was on her feet, breathless but unharmed, standing beside Calvin and Charles Wallace.

"Is this Camazotz?" Charles Wallace asked as Mrs Whatsit materialized in front of him.

"Yes," she answered. "Now let us just stand and get our breath and look around."

They were standing on a hill and as Meg looked about her she felt that it could easily be a hill on earth. There were the familiar trees she knew so well at home: birches, pines, maples. And though it was warmer than it had been when they so <u>precipitously</u> left the apple orchard, there was a faintly autumnal touch to the air; near them were several small trees with reddened leaves very like sumac, and a big patch of goldenrod-like flowers. As she looked down

◄ A simile *is a comparison using* like *or as. What simile does the author use to describe the darkness Meg experiences while tessering?*

words for everyday use

im • per • so • nal (im pər´sə nəl) *adj.*, not related to an individual. *The Johnsons send out <u>impersonal</u> photocopies of a letter each holiday season, but the Greens take the time to write individual cards.*

ma • lig • nant (mə lig´nənt) *adj.*, having a harmful influence; threatening. *The croc-* odile's toothy smile seemed <u>malignant</u>.

pre • ci • pi • tous • ly (prē sip´ə təs lē) *adv.*, suddenly or unexpectedly. *Cars screeched and skidded to avoid hitting the motorcycle, which had zoomed <u>precipitously</u> out into the intersection.*

the hill she could see the smokestacks of a town, and it might have been one of any number of familiar towns. There seemed to be nothing strange, or different, or frightening, in the landscape.

But Mrs Whatsit came to her and put an arm around her comfortingly. "I can't stay with you here, you know, love," she said. "You three children will be on your own. We will be near you; we will be watching you. But you will not be able to see us or to ask us for help, and we will not be able to come to you."

"But is Father here?" Meg asked tremblingly.

"Yes."

"But where? When will we see him?" She was poised for running, as though she were going to sprint off, immediately, to wherever her father was.

"That I cannot tell you. You will just have to wait until the <u>propitious</u> moment."

Charles Wallace looked steadily at Mrs Whatsit. "Are you afraid for us?"

"A little."

"But if you weren't afraid to do what you did when you were a star, why should you be afraid for us now?"

"But I was afraid," Mrs Whatsit said gently. She looked steadily at each of the three children in turn. "You will need help," she told them, "but all I am allowed to give you is a little talisman.[3] Calvin, your great gift is your ability to communicate, to communicate with all kinds of people. So, for you, I will strengthen this gift. Meg, I give you your faults."

"My faults!" Meg cried.

"Your faults."

"But I'm always trying to get rid of my faults!"

"Yes," Mrs Whatsit said. "However, I think you'll find they'll come in very handy on Camazotz. Charles Wallace, to you I can give only the <u>resilience</u> of your childhood."

▶ Why might Meg's faults be useful on Camazotz?

---

3. **talisman.** Something that is supposed to bring good luck or keep away evil

From somewhere Mrs Who's glasses glimmered and they heard her voice. "Calvin," she said, "a hint. For you a hint. Listen well:

. . . For that he was a spirit too delicate
To act their earthy and <u>abhorr'd</u> commands,
Refusing their grand hests, they did confine him
By help of their most <u>potent</u> ministers,
And in their most <u>unmitigable</u> rage,
Into a cloven pine; within which rift
Imprisoned, he didst painfully remain. . . .

Shakespeare. *The Tempest.*"[4]

"Where are you, Mrs Who?" Charles Wallace asked. "Where is Mrs Which?"

"We cannot come to you now," Mrs Who's voice blew to them like the wind. *"Allwissend bin ich nicht; doch viel ist mir bewisst.* Goethe.[5] *I do not know everything; still many things I understand.* That is for you, Charles. Remember that you do not know everything." Then the voice was directed to Meg. "To you I leave my glasses, little blind-as-a-bat. But do not use them except as a last resort. Save them for the final moment of peril." As she spoke there was another shimmer of spectacles, and then it was gone, and the voice faded out with it. The spectacles were in Meg's hand. She put them carefully into the breast pocket of her blazer, and the knowledge that they were there somehow made her a little less afraid.

"Tto alll tthreee off yyou I ggive mmy ccommandd," Mrs Which said. "Ggo ddownn innttoo tthee ttownn. Ggo ttogetherr. Ddoo nnott llett tthemm ssepparate yyou. Bbee sstrongg." There was a flicker and then it vanished. Meg shivered.

◀ *Why might Mrs Who remind Charles of this?*

---

4. *". . . For that . . . The Tempest."* Mrs Who's hint is a quotation from act 1, scene 2 of William Shakespeare's *The Tempest*. This passage tells how one of the characters, a spirit called Ariel, was once imprisoned in a tree by an evil witch named Sycorax because he refused to do her bidding.

5. **Goethe** (gər´ tə). Johann Wolfgang von Goethe (1749–1832), German poet and dramatist

words for everyday use

ab • horred (ab hòrd´) *adj.,* hated. *The people booed when shown a picture of their <u>abhorred</u> dictator, General Freedomcrusher.*

po • tent (pōt´'nt) *adj.,* having power. *Although it is a tiny blossom, it has a <u>potent</u> and lovely scent.*

un • mi • ti • ga • ble (un mit´ə gə bəl) *adj.,* absolute; not lessened or eased. *I felt <u>unmitigable</u> sorrow when my best friend moved across the country.*

Mrs Whatsit must have seen the shiver, for she patted Meg on the shoulder. Then she turned to Calvin. "Take care of Meg."

"I can take care of Meg," Charles Wallace said rather sharply. "I always have."

Mrs Whatsit looked at Charles Wallace, and the creaky voice seemed somehow both to soften and to deepen at the same time. "Charles Wallace, the danger here is greatest for you."

"Why?"

▶ How could Charles's special abilities make him more vulnerable?

"Because of what you are. Just exactly because of what you are you will be by far the most <u>vulnerable</u>. You *must* stay with Meg and Calvin. You must *not* go off on your own. Beware of pride and arrogance, Charles, for they may betray you."

At the tone of Mrs Whatsit's voice, both warning and frightening, Meg shivered again. And Charles Wallace butted up against Mrs Whatsit in the way he often did with his mother, whispering, "Now I think I know what you meant about being afraid."

"Only a fool is not afraid," Mrs Whatsit told him. "Now go." And where she had been there was only sky and grasses and a small rock.

"Come *on*," Meg said impatiently. "Come on, let's *go!*" She was completely unaware that her voice was trembling like an aspen leaf. She took Charles Wallace and Calvin each by the hand and started down the hill.

Below them the town was laid out in harsh <u>angular</u> patterns. The houses in the outskirts were all exactly alike, small square boxes painted gray. Each had a small, rectangular plot of lawn in front, with a straight line of dull-looking flowers edging the path to the door. Meg had a feeling that if she could count the flowers there would be exactly the same number for each house. In front of all the houses children

---

words for everyday use

vul • ne • ra • ble (vul´nər ə bəl) *adj.*, open to attack. *Baby rabbits are blind, unable to run, and very <u>vulnerable</u>.*

an • gu • lar (aŋ´gyü lər) *adj.*, having sharp corners. *Jesse liked his paintings to have only <u>angular</u> forms and no soft, rounded ones.*

were playing. Some were skipping rope, some were bouncing balls. Meg felt vaguely that something was wrong with their play. It seemed exactly like children playing around any housing development at home, and yet there was something different about it. She looked at Calvin, and saw that he, too, was puzzled.

"Look!" Charles Wallace said suddenly. "They're skipping and bouncing in rhythm! Everyone's doing it at exactly the same moment."

◀ What is strange about the children's play?

This was so. As the skipping rope hit the pavement, so did the ball. As the rope curved over the head of the jumping child, the child with the ball caught the ball. Down came the ropes. Down came the balls. Over and over again. Up. Down. All in rhythm. All identical. Like the houses. Like the paths. Like the flowers.

Then the doors of all the houses opened simultaneously, and out came women like a row of paper dolls. The print of their dresses was different, but they all gave the appearance of being the same. Each woman stood on the steps of her house. Each clapped. Each child with the ball caught the ball. Each child with the skipping rope folded the rope. Each child turned and walked into the house. The doors clicked shut behind them.

◀ What simile does the author use to describe the women? Why do you think she makes this comparison?

"How can they do it?" Meg asked wonderingly. "We couldn't do it that way if we tried. What does it mean?"

"Let's go back." Calvin's voice was urgent.

"Back?" Charles Wallace asked. "Where?"

"I don't know. Anywhere. Back to the hill. Back to Mrs Whatsit and Mrs Who and Mrs Which. I don't like this."

"But they aren't there. Do you think they'd come to us if we turned back now?"

"I don't like it," Calvin said again.

"Come *on*." Impatience made Meg squeak. "You *know* we can't go back. Mrs Whatsit *said* to go into the town." She started on down the street, and the two boys followed her. The houses, all identical, continued, as far as the eye could reach.

◀ How is Meg responding to the situation?

Then, all at once, they saw the same thing, and stopped to watch. In front of one of the houses stood a little boy with a ball, and he was bouncing it. But he bounced it rather badly and with no particular rhythm, sometimes dropping it and running after it with awkward, <u>furtive</u> leaps, sometimes throwing it up into the air and trying to catch it. The door of his house opened and out ran one of the mother figures. She looked wildly up and down the street, saw the children and put her hand to her mouth as though to stifle a scream, grabbed the little boy and rushed indoors with him. The ball dropped from his fingers and rolled out into the street.

▶ What is strange about the mother's behavior?

Charles Wallace ran after it and picked it up, holding it out for Meg and Calvin to see. It seemed like a perfectly ordinary, brown rubber ball.

"Let's take it in to him and see what happens," Charles Wallace suggested.

Meg pulled at him. "Mrs Whatsit said for us to go on into the town."

"Well, we *are* in the town, aren't we? The outskirts anyhow. I want to know more about this. I have a hunch it may help us later. You go on if you don't want to come with me."

"No," Calvin said firmly. "We're going to stay together. Mrs Whatsit said we weren't to let them separate us. But I'm with you on this. Let's knock and see what happens."

They went up the path to the house, Meg reluctant, eager to get on into the town. "Let's hurry," she begged, *"please!* Don't you want to find Father?"

"Yes," Charles Wallace said, "but not blindly. How can we help him if we don't know what we're up against? And it's obvious we've been brought here to help him, not just to find him." He walked briskly up the steps and knocked at the door. They waited. Nothing happened. Then Charles Wallace saw a bell, and this he rang. They could hear the bell buzzing in the house, and the sound of it echoed down the street. After a moment the mother figure opened the

---

words for everyday use fur • tive (fər´tiv) adj., sneaky. The _furtive_ thief crept around the corner, but the detective cleverly spotted him.

door. All up and down the street other doors opened, but only a crack, and eyes peered toward the three children and the woman looking fearfully out the door at them.

"What do you want?" she asked. "It isn't paper time yet; we've had milk time; we've had this month's Puller Prush Person;[6] and I've given my Decency Donations regularly. All my papers are in order."

"I think your little boy dropped his ball," Charles Wallace said, holding it out.

The woman pushed the ball away. "Oh, no! The children in our section *never* drop balls! They're all perfectly trained. We haven't had an <u>Aberration</u> for three years."

All up and down the block, heads nodded in agreement.

Charles Wallace moved closer to the woman and looked past her into the house. Behind her in the shadows he could see the little boy, who must have been about his own age.

"You can't come in," the woman said. "You haven't shown me any papers. I don't have to let you in if you haven't any papers."

Charles Wallace held the ball out beyond the woman so that the little boy could see it. Quick as a flash the boy leaped forward and grabbed the ball from Charles Wallace's hand, then darted back into the shadows. The woman went very white, opened her mouth as though to say something, then slammed the door in their faces instead. All up and down the street doors slammed.

"What are they afraid of?" Charles Wallace asked. "What's the matter with them?"

◀ *What might be the reason for the woman's reaction?*

---

6. **Puller Prush Person.** "Puller Prush" is a twist on Fuller Brush, a household-goods company that used to sell its products door to door. The "Fuller Brush Man" was a common sight in American neighborhoods in the 1950s and 1960s.

---

words for everyday use

a • ber • ra • tion (ab´ər ā′shən) *n.*, departure from the normal. *For Mark, who was generally very awkward and shy and hated going out to clubs, taking salsa dancing lessons was a serious* <u>aberration</u>.

▶ In what way was Charles trying to "get through"?

"Don't *you* know?" Meg asked him. "Don't you know what all this is about, Charles?"

"Not yet," Charles Wallace said. "Not even an inkling. And I'm trying. But I didn't get through anywhere. Not even a chink. Let's go." He stumped down the steps.

After several blocks the houses gave way to apartment buildings; at least Meg felt sure that that was what they must be. They were fairly tall, rectangular buildings, absolutely plain, each window, each entrance exactly like every other. Then, coming toward them down the street, was a boy about Calvin's age riding a machine that was something like a combination of a bicycle and a motorcycle. It had the slimness and lightness of a bicycle, and yet as the foot pedals turned they seemed to generate an unseen source of power, so that the boy could pedal very slowly and yet move along the street quite swiftly. As he reached each entrance he thrust one hand into a bag he wore slung over his shoulder, pulled out a roll of papers, and tossed it into the entrance. It might have been Dennys or Sandy or any one of hundreds of boys with a newspaper route in any one of hundreds of towns back home, and yet, as with the children playing ball and jumping rope, there was something wrong about it. The rhythm of the gesture never varied. The paper flew in identically the same arc at each doorway, landed in identically the same spot. It was impossible for anybody to throw with such consistent perfection.

Calvin whistled. "I wonder if they play baseball here?"

As the boy saw them he slowed down on his machine and stopped, his hand arrested as it was about to plunge into the paper bag. "What are you kids doing out on the street?" he demanded. "Only route boys are allowed out now, you know that."

"No, we don't know it," Charles Wallace said. "We're strangers here. How about telling us something about this place?"

"You mean you've had your entrance papers processed and everything?" the boy asked. "You must have if you're here," he answered himself.

"And what are you doing here if you don't know about us?"

"You tell me," Charles Wallace said.

"Are you examiners?" the boy asked a little anxiously. "Everybody knows our city has the best Central Intelligence Center on the planet. Our production levels are the highest. Our factories never close; our machines never stop rolling. Added to this we have five poets, one musician, three artists, and six sculptors, all perfectly channeled."

"What are you quoting from?" Charles Wallace asked.

"The Manual, of course," the boy said. "We are the most oriented city on the planet. There has been no trouble of any kind for centuries. All Camazotz knows our record. That is why we are the capital city of Camazotz. That is why CENTRAL Central Intelligence is located here. That is why IT makes ITs home here." There was something about the way he said "IT" that made a shiver run up and down Meg's spine.

But Charles Wallace asked briskly, "Where is this Central Intelligence Center of yours?"

"CENTRAL Central," the boy corrected. "Just keep going and you can't miss it. You *are* strangers, aren't you! What are you doing here?"

"Are you supposed to ask questions?" Charles Wallace demanded severely.

The boy went white, just as the woman had. "I humbly beg your pardon. I must continue my route now or I will have to talk my timing into the explainer." And he shot off down the street on his machine.

Charles Wallace stared after him. "What is it?" he asked Meg and Calvin. "There was something funny about the way he talked, as though—well, as though he weren't really doing the talking. Know what I mean?"

Calvin nodded, thoughtfully. "Funny is right. Funny peculiar. Not only the way he talked, either. The whole thing smells."

"Come *on.*" Meg pulled at them. How many times was it she had urged them on? "Let's go find Father. He'll be able to explain it all to us."

◀ Why does Charles Wallace think that the boy is quoting from something?

◀ Why does the boy become flustered?

They walked on. After several more blocks they began to see other people, grown-up people, not children, walking up and down and across the streets. These people ignored the children entirely, seeming to be completely intent on their own business. Some of them went into the apartment buildings. Most of them were heading in the same direction as the children. As these people came to the main street from the side streets they would swing around the corners with an odd, automatic stride, as though they were so deep in their own problems and the route was so familiar that they didn't have to pay any attention to where they were going.

After a while the apartment buildings gave way to what must have been office buildings, great stern structures with enormous entrances. Men and women with briefcases poured in and out.

Charles Wallace went up to one of the women, saying politely, "Excuse me, but could you please tell me—" But she hardly glanced at him as she continued on her way.

"Look." Meg pointed. Ahead of them, across a square, was the largest building they had ever seen, higher than the Empire State Building, and almost as long as it was high.

"This must be it," Charles Wallace said, "their CENTRAL Central Intelligence or whatever it is. Let's go on."

"But if Father's in some kind of trouble with this planet," Meg objected, "isn't that exactly where we *shouldn't* go?"

"Well, how do you propose finding him?" Charles Wallace demanded.

"I certainly wouldn't ask *there!*"

"I didn't say anything about asking. But we aren't going to have the faintest idea where or how to begin to look for him until we find out something more about this place, and I have a hunch that that's the place to start. If you have a better idea, Meg, why of course just say so."

"Oh, get down off your high horse," Meg said crossly. "Let's go to your old CENTRAL Central Intelligence and get it over with."

▶ Why does Meg tell Charles to "get off [his] high horse"? How is Charles behaving? Who warned him about this behavior?

"I think we ought to have passports or some-thing," Calvin suggested. "This is much more than leaving America to go to Europe. And that boy and the woman both seemed to care so much about hav-ing things in proper order. We certainly haven't got any papers in proper order."

"If we needed passports or papers Mrs Whatsit would have told us so," Charles Wallace said.

Calvin put his hands on his hips and looked down at Charles Wallace. "Now look here, old sport. I love those three old girls just as much as you do, but I'm not sure they know *everything*."

"They know a lot more than we do."

"Granted. But you know Mrs Whatsit talked about having been a star. I wouldn't think that being a star would give her much practice in knowing about peo-ple. When she tried to be a person she came pretty close to goofing it up. There was never anybody on land or sea like Mrs Whatsit the way she got herself up."

"She was just having fun," Charles said. "If she'd wanted to look like you or Meg I'm sure she could have."

Calvin shook his head. "I'm not so sure. And these people seem to be *people*, if you know what I mean. They aren't like us, I grant you that, there's some-thing very off-beat about them. But they're lots more like ordinary people than the ones on Uriel."

"Do you suppose they're robots?" Meg suggested.

Charles Wallace shook his head. "No. That boy who dropped the ball wasn't any robot. And I don't think the rest of them are, either. Let me listen for a minute."

They stood very still, side by side, in the shadow of one of the big office buildings. Six large doors kept swinging open, shut, open, shut, as people went in and out, in and out, looking straight ahead, straight ahead, paying no attention to the children whatso-ever, whatsoever. Charles wore his listening, probing look. "They're not robots," he said suddenly and def-initely. "I'm not sure *what* they are, but they're not robots. I can feel minds there. I can't get at them at all, but I can feel them sort of pulsing. Let me try a minute more."

▶ What image is used to describe the people moving in and out of the buildings?

The three of them stood there very quietly. The doors kept opening and shutting, opening and shutting, and the stiff people hurried in and out, in and out, walking jerkily like figures in an old silent movie. Then, abruptly, the stream of movement thinned. There were only a few people and these moved more rapidly, as if the film had been speeded up. One white-faced man in a dark suit looked directly at the children, said, "Oh, dear, I shall be late," and flickered into the building.

"He's like the white rabbit,"[7] Meg giggled nervously.

"I'm scared," Charles said. "I can't reach them at all. I'm completely shut out."

"We have to find Father—" Meg started again.

▶ What worries Charles Wallace about meeting his father?

"Meg—" Charles Wallace's eyes were wide and frightened. "I'm not sure I'll even know Father. It's been so long, and I was only a baby—"

Meg's reassurance came quickly. "You'll know him! Of course you'll know him! The way you'd know me even without looking because I'm always there for you, you can always reach in—"

"Yes." Charles punched one small fist into an open palm with a gesture of great decision. "Let's go to CENTRAL Central Intelligence."

Calvin reached out and caught both Charles and Meg by the arm. "You remember when we met, you asked me why I was there? And I told you it was because I had a compulsion, a feeling I just had to come to that particular place at that particular moment?"

"Yes, sure."

"I've got another feeling. Not the same kind, a different one, a feeling that if we go into that building we're going into terrible danger."

---

7. **the white rabbit.** Character in Lewis Carroll's *Alice in Wonderland*

Respond to the Selection

How would you feel if, like Meg, Calvin, and Charles, you were suddenly in a place where everything was identical and people seemed to move in rhythm and without free will? Would you try to assert your individuality? If so, how? Discuss with your classmates what it would be like to visit Camazotz.

Investigate, Inquire, and Imagine

Recall: GATHERING FACTS

1a. How do Mrs Who and Mrs Whatsit explain their ability to travel long distances through space? In what dimension do they travel? What does Charles tell Meg a tesseract is?

2a. What friend do Mrs Whatsit, Mrs Who, and Mrs Which take the children to see on the planet in Orion's belt? What does this friend show the children?

3a. What do the children learn about Mrs Whatsit, Mrs Who, and Mrs Which? What did Mrs Whatsit used to be? What did she do?

4a. What do Mrs Whatsit and Mrs Who give Meg on Camazotz? What does Mrs Whatsit give Calvin? What warnings do Mrs Who and Mrs Whatsit give Charles? What does Charles say is peculiar about the minds of the people on Camazotz?

Interpret: FINDING MEANING

➤ 1b. Why does Charles think Meg might be hurt that their mother explained the tesseract to him first? How does Meg feel when she glimpses the nature of the tesseract?

➤ 2b. Why does what Meg sees make her angry? Why does Meg thank Mrs Whatsit, Mrs Who, and Mrs Which's friend for making her angry?

➤ 3b. Why does Charles say he would like to kiss Mrs Whatsit when she tells him what she used to be?

➤ 4b. Why does Mrs Whatsit say she gives this warning to Charles? How do Meg, Charles, and Calvin feel about Camazotz?

Analyze: TAKING THINGS APART

5a. Identify the things that are strange about the people on Camazotz. How is the city on Camazotz similar to communities you are familiar with? How is it eerily different?

Synthesize: BRINGING THINGS TOGETHER

➤ 5b. If the people on Camazotz are not robots, what do you think they are? What might be causing them to behave as they do? Predict how the "gifts" and advice the children received might prove useful on Camazotz.

Evaluate: Making Judgments

6a. Near the end of chapter 6, Charles, Calvin, and Meg name some people they think have been fighters of evil, or "lights for us to see by," on the planet Earth. Look up each of these people in an encyclopedia and record some information about his or her accomplishments. Do you think these people are good examples of "lights" on Earth? Explain why, or why not.

Extend: Connecting Ideas

➤ 6b. With a partner, brainstorm a list of other people—great artists, scientists, thinkers, leaders, or fighters—who have been "lights for us to see by." What did these individuals offer to others? In what ways did these people fight against darkness, ignorance, or evil?

Understanding Literature

PUN. A **pun** is a play on words, one that cleverly makes use of a double meaning. Earlier in the book, both Meg's mother and her twin brothers tell Meg that she needs to find a "happy medium." What did they mean by this? What kind of "happy medium" does Meg find in chapter 5? Explain the pun created by the two meanings of "happy medium."

SUSPENSE. **Suspense** is a feeling of anxiousness or curiosity. Writers create suspense by raising questions in the reader's mind and by using details that create strong emotions. Calvin says that the CENTRAL Central Intelligence building gives him "a feeling that if we go into that building we're going into terrible danger." What earlier premonition, or strong feeling, did Calvin have? What makes this final line of chapter 6 suspenseful? What makes it seem as if this building may be dangerous?

Chapter 7

The Man with Red Eyes

"We knew we were going to be in danger," Charles Wallace said. "Mrs Whatsit told us that."

"Yes, and she told us that it was going to be worse for you than for Meg and me, and that you must be careful. You stay right here with Meg, old sport, and let me go in and case the joint and then report to you."

"No," Charles Wallace said firmly. "She told us to stay together. She told us not to go off by ourselves."

"She told *you* not to go off by yourself. I'm the oldest and I should go in first."

"No." Meg's voice was flat. "Charles is right, Cal. We have to stay together. Suppose you didn't come out and we had to go in after you? Unh-unh. Come on. But let's hold hands if you don't mind."

Holding hands, they crossed the square. The huge CENTRAL Central Intelligence Building had only one door, but it was an enormous one, at least two stories high and wider than a room, made of a dull, bronze-like material.

"Do we just knock?" Meg giggled.

Calvin studied the door. "There isn't any handle or knob or latch or anything. Maybe there's another way to get in."

"Let's try knocking anyhow," Charles said. He raised his hand, but before he touched the door it slid up from the top and to each side, splitting into three sections that had been completely invisible a moment before. The startled children looked into a great entrance hall of dull, greeny marble. Marble benches lined three of the walls. People were sitting there like statues. The green of the marble reflecting on their faces made them look <u>bilious</u>. They turned

---

words for everyday use   bil • ious (bil′yəs) *adj.*, having a greenish color to the skin, as if suffering from liver disease. *Sam's <u>bilious</u> face was the first sign of his seasickness.*

their heads as the door opened, saw the children, looked away again.

"Come on," Charles said, and, still holding hands, they stepped in. As they crossed the threshold the door shut silently behind them. Meg looked at Calvin and Charles and they, like the waiting people, were a sickly green.

The children went up to the blank fourth wall. It seemed <u>unsubstantial</u>, as though one might almost be able to walk through it. Charles put out his hand. "It's solid, and icy cold."

Calvin touched it, too. "Ugh."

Meg's left hand was held by Charles, her right by Calvin, and she had no desire to let go either of them to touch the wall.

"Let's ask somebody something." Charles led them over to one of the benches. "Er, could you tell us what's the procedure around here?" he asked one of the men. The men all wore nondescript business suits, and though their features were as different one from the other as the features of men on earth, there was also a sameness to them.

▶ How are the people on Camazotz similar to people on Earth?

—Like the sameness of people riding in a subway, Meg thought. —Only on a subway every once in a while there's somebody different and here there isn't.

The man looked at the children <u>warily</u>. "The procedure for what?"

"How do we see whoever's in authority?" Charles asked.

"You present your papers to the A machine. You ought to know that," the man said severely.

"Where is the A machine?" Calvin asked.

The man pointed to the blank wall.

"But there isn't a door or anything," Calvin said. "How do we get in?"

"You put your S papers in the B slot," the man said. "Why are you asking me these stupid questions? Do

---

words for everyday use

un • sub • stan • tial (un´səb stan´shəl) adj., not solid or heavy. There appeared to be a city in the distance, but we realized that it was <u>unsubstantial</u>, a mere mirage.

war • i • ly (wer´ə lē) adv., cautiously. Llewellyn approached the barking dog <u>warily</u>.

you think I don't know the answers? You'd better not play any games around here or you'll have to go through the Process machine again and you don't want to do *that*."

"We're strangers here," Calvin said. "That's why we don't know about things. Please tell us, sir, who you are and what you do."

"I run a number-one spelling machine on the second-grade level."

"But what are you doing here now?" Charles Wallace asked.

"I am here to report that one of my letters is jamming, and until it can be properly oiled by an F Grade oiler there is danger of jammed minds."

"Strawberry jam or raspberry?" Charles Wallace murmured. Calvin looked down at Charles and shook his head warningly. Meg gave the little boy's hand a slight, understanding pressure. Charles Wallace, she was quite sure, was not trying to be rude or funny; it was his way of whistling in the dark.

The man looked at Charles sharply. "I think I shall have to report you. I'm fond of children, due to the nature of my work, and I don't like to get them in trouble, but rather than run the risk myself of <u>reprocessing</u> I must report you."

"Maybe that's a good idea," Charles said. "Who do you report us to?"

"To *whom* do I report you."

"Well, to whom, then. I'm not on the second-grade level yet."

—I wish he wouldn't act so sure of himself, Meg thought, looking anxiously at Charles and holding his hand more and more tightly until he wriggled his fingers in protest. That's what Mrs Whatsit said he had to watch, being proud. —Don't, please don't, she thought hard at Charles Wallace. She wondered if Calvin realized that a lot of the arrogance was <u>bravado</u>.

◀ What do you think the school system on Camazotz is like?

---

words for everyday use

re • proc • ess • ing (rē prä́s΄es iŋ) *n.*, the act of processing again. *Now that we have adequate information we are <u>reprocessing</u> your request.*

bra • va • do (brə vä΄dō) *n.*, pretended courage. *Shibani's <u>bravado</u> masked her fear in the face of danger.*

▶ What is the man afraid of? What do you suppose it means to be "reprocessed"?

The man stood up, moving jerkily as though he had been sitting for a long time. "I hope he isn't too hard on you," he murmured as he led the children toward the empty fourth wall. "But I've been reprocessed once and that was more than enough. And I don't want to get sent to IT. I've never been sent to IT and I can't risk having that happen."

There was IT again. What was this IT?

The man took from his pocket a folder filled with papers of every color. He shuffled through them carefully, finally withdrawing one. "I've had several reports to make lately. I shall have to ask for a requisition for more A-21 cards." He took the card and put it against the wall. It slid through the marble, as though it were being sucked in, and disappeared. "You may be detained for a few days," the man said, "but I'm sure they won't be too hard on you because of your youth. Just relax and don't fight and it will all be much easier for you." He went back to his seat, leaving the children standing and staring at the blank wall.

And suddenly the wall was no longer there and they were looking into an enormous room lined with machines. They were not unlike the great computing machines Meg had seen in her science books and that she knew her father sometimes worked with. Some did not seem to be in use; in others lights were flickering on and off. In one machine a long tape was being eaten; in another a series of dotdashes were being punched. Several white-robed attendants were moving about, tending the machines. If they saw the children they gave no sign.

Calvin muttered something.

"What?" Meg asked him.

"There is nothing to fear except fear itself,"[1] Calvin said. "I'm quoting. Like Mrs Who. Meg, I'm scared stiff."

"So 'm I." Meg held his hand more tightly. "Come on."

They stepped into the room with the machines. In spite of the enormous width of the room it was even longer than it was wide. Perspective made the

---

1. **There is nothing to fear . . . itself.** Paraphrased from the first Inaugural Address of President Franklin Delano Roosevelt

long rows of machines seem almost to meet. The children walked down the center of the room, keeping as far from the machines as possible.

"Though I don't suppose they're radioactive[2] or anything," Charles Wallace said, "or that they're going to reach out and grab us and chew us up."

After they had walked for what seemed like miles, they could see that the enormous room did have an end, and that at the end there was something.

Charles Wallace said suddenly, and his voice held panic, "Don't let go my hands! Hold me tight! He's trying to get at me!"

"Who?" Meg squeaked.

"I don't know. But he's trying to get in at me! I can feel him!"

"Let's go back." Calvin started to pull away.

"No," Charles Wallace said. "I have to go on. We have to make decisions, and we can't make them if they're based on fear." His voice sounded old and strange and remote. Meg, clasping his small hand tightly, could feel it sweating in hers.

As they approached the end of the room their steps slowed. Before them was a platform. On the platform was a chair, and on the chair was a man.

What was there about him that seemed to contain all the coldness and darkness they had felt as they <u>plunged</u> through the Black Thing on their way to this planet?

"I have been waiting for you, my dears," the man said. His voice was kind and gentle, not at all the cold and frightening voice Meg had expected. It took her a moment to realize that though the voice came from the man, he had not opened his mouth or moved his lips at all, that no real words had been spoken to fall upon her ears, that he had somehow communicated directly into their brains.

◀ What is strange about the way the man talks?

---

2. **radioactive.** Giving off electromagnetic radiation, waves of energy that can harm body tissues. Exposure to large amounts of radiation can cause genetic mutation and death.

---

words for everyday use

plunge (plunj) *v.,* move rapidly downward or forward. *Sage kicked off her shoes and <u>plunged</u> into the icy water to save the drowning child.*

"But how does it happen that there are three of you?" the man asked.

Charles Wallace spoke with harsh boldness, but Meg could feel him trembling. "Oh, Calvin just came along for the ride."

"Oh, he did, did he?" For a moment there was a sharpness to the voice that spoke inside their minds. Then it relaxed and became soothing again. "I hope that it has been a pleasant one so far."

"Very educational," Charles Wallace said.

"Let Calvin speak for himself," the man ordered.

Calvin growled, his lips tight, his body rigid. "I have nothing to say."

Meg stared at the man in horrified fascination. His eyes were bright and had a reddish glow. Above his head was a light, and it glowed in the same manner as the eyes, pulsing, throbbing, in steady rhythm.

Charles Wallace shut his eyes tightly. "Close your eyes," he said to Meg and Calvin. "Don't look at the light. Don't look at his eyes. He'll hypnotize you."

"Clever, aren't you? Focusing your eyes would, of course, help," the soothing voice went on, "but there are other ways, my little man. Oh, yes, there are other ways."

"If you try it on me I shall kick you!" Charles Wallace said. It was the first time Meg had ever heard Charles Wallace suggesting violence.

"Oh, will you, indeed, my little man?" The thought was tolerant, amused, but four men in dark smocks appeared and <u>flanked</u> the children.

"Now, my dears," the words continued, "I shall of course have no need of <u>recourse</u> to violence, but I thought perhaps it would save you pain if I showed you at once that it would do you no good to try to oppose me. You see, what you will soon realize is that there is no need to fight me. Not only is there no need, but you will not have the slightest desire to do

▶ *What is the man with the red eyes offering to the children?*

so. For why should you wish to fight someone who is here only to save you pain and trouble? For you, as well as for the rest of all the happy, useful people on this planet, *I*, in my own strength, am willing to assume all the pain, all the responsibility, all the burdens of thought and decision."

"We will make our own decisions, thank you," Charles Wallace said.

"But of *course*. And our decisions will be one, yours and mine. Don't you see how much better, how much *easier* for you that is? Let me show you. Let us say the multiplication table together."

"No," Charles Wallace said.

"Once one is one. Once two is two. Once three is three."

"Mary had a little lamb!" Charles Wallace shouted. "Its fleece was white as snow!"

◀ Why does Charles Wallace recite nursery rhymes?

"Once four is four. Once five is five. Once six is six."

"And everywhere that Mary went the lamb was sure to go!"

"Once seven is seven. Once eight is eight. Once nine is nine."

"Peter, Peter, pumpkin eater, had a wife and couldn't keep her—"

"Once ten is ten. Once eleven is eleven. Once twelve is twelve."

The number words pounded insistently against Meg's brain. They seemed to be boring their way into her skull.

"Twice one is two. Twice two is four. Twice three is six."

Calvin's voice came out in an angry shout. "Fourscore and seven years ago our fathers brought forth on this continent a new nation, conceived in liberty, and dedicated to the proposition that all men are created equal."[3]

"Twice four is eight. Twice five is ten. Twice six is twelve."

---

3. **Fourscore and seven years ago . . . created equal.** Quoted from President Abraham Lincoln's "Gettysburg Address"

"Father!" Meg screamed. "Father!" The scream, half involuntary, jerked her mind back out of darkness.

The words of the multiplication table seemed to break up into laughter. "Splendid! Splendid! You have passed your preliminary tests with flying colors."

"You didn't think we were as easy as all that, falling for that old stuff, did you?" Charles Wallace demanded.

"Ah, I hoped not. I most sincerely hoped not. But after all you are very young and very impressionable, and the younger the better, my little man. The younger the better."

Meg looked up at the fiery eyes, at the light pulsing above them, and then away. She tried looking at the mouth, at the thin, almost colorless lips, and this was more possible, even though she had to look obliquely, so that she was not sure exactly what the face really looked like, whether it was young or old, cruel or kind, human or alien.

"If you please," she said, trying to sound calm and brave. "The only reason we are here is because we think our father is here. Can you tell us where to find him?"

"Ah, your father!" There seemed to be a great chortling of delight. "Ah, yes, your father! It is not *can* I, you know, young lady, but *will* I?"

"Will you, then?"

"That depends on a number of things. Why do you want your father?"

"Didn't you ever have a father yourself?" Meg demanded. "You don't want him for a *reason*. You want him because he's your *father*."

"Ah, but he hasn't been *acting* very like a father, lately, has he? Abandoning his wife and his four little

▶ *What doesn't the man with red eyes understand about family?*

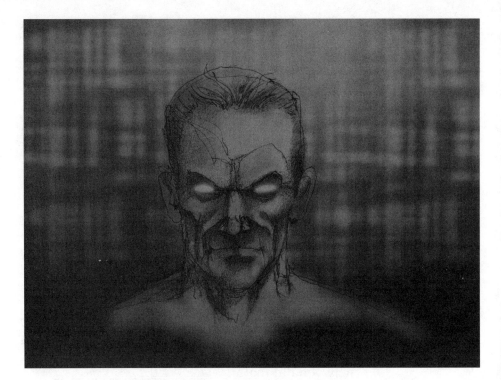

children to go gallivanting off on wild adventures of his own."

"He was working for the government. He'd never have left us otherwise. And we want to see him, please. Right now."

"My, but the little miss is impatient! Patience, patience, young lady."

Meg did not tell the man on the chair that patience was not one of her virtues.

"And by the way, my children," he continued <u>blandly</u>, "you don't need to vocalize verbally with me, you know. I can understand you quite as well as you can understand me."

Charles Wallace put his hands on his hips defiantly. "The spoken word is one of the triumphs of man," he proclaimed, "and I intend to continue using it, particularly with people I don't trust." But

◄ *Why does Charles Wallace insist on communicating aloud?*

words
for
everyday
use

bland • ly (bland´lē) *adv.*, smoothly. *"I really don't care what you do,"* said Lionel <u>blandly</u>.

his voice was shaking. Charles Wallace, who even as an infant had seldom cried, was near tears.

"And you don't trust me?"

"What reason have you given us to trust you?"

"What cause have I given you for *dis*trust?" The thin lips curled slightly.

Suddenly Charles Wallace darted forward and hit the man as hard as he could, which was fairly hard, as he had had a good deal of coaching from the twins.

"Charles!" Meg screamed.

The men in dark smocks moved smoothly but with swiftness to Charles. The man in the chair casually raised one finger, and the men dropped back.

"Hold it—" Calvin whispered, and together he and Meg darted forward and grabbed Charles Wallace, pulling him back from the platform.

The man gave a wince and the thought of his voice was a little breathless, as though Charles Wallace's punch had succeeded in winding him. "May I ask why you did that?"

▶ Why does Charles Wallace hit the man with red eyes?

"Because you aren't you," Charles Wallace said. "I'm not sure what you are, but you"—he pointed to the man on the chair—"aren't what's talking to us. I'm sorry if I hurt you. I didn't think you were real. I thought perhaps you were a robot, because I don't feel anything coming directly from you. I'm not sure where it's coming from, but it's coming *through* you. It isn't you."

"Pretty smart, aren't you?" the thought asked, and Meg had an uncomfortable feeling that she detected a snarl.

"It's not that I'm smart," Charles Wallace said, and again Meg could feel the palm of his hand sweating inside hers.

"Try to find out who I am, then," the thought probed.

"I have been trying," Charles Wallace said, his voice high and troubled.

"Look into my eyes. Look deep within them and I will tell you."

Charles Wallace looked quickly at Meg and Calvin, then said, as though to himself, "I have to," and focused his clear blue eyes on the red ones of the man in the chair. Meg looked not at the man but at her brother. After a moment it seemed that his eyes were no longer focusing. The pupils grew smaller and smaller, as though he were looking into an intensely bright light, until they seemed to close entirely, until his eyes were nothing but an opaque blue. He slipped his hands out of Meg's and Calvin's and started walking slowly toward the man on the chair.

◀ What is happening to Charles Wallace?

"No!" Meg screamed. "No!"

But Charles Wallace continued his slow walk forward, and she knew that he had not heard her.

"No!" she screamed again, and ran after him. With her inefficient flying tackle she landed on him. She was so much larger than he that he fell sprawling, hitting his head a sharp crack against the marble floor. She knelt by him, sobbing. After a moment of lying there as though he had been knocked out by the blow, he opened his eyes, shook his head, and sat up. Slowly the pupils of his eyes dilated until they were back to normal, and the blood came back to his white cheeks.

The man on the chair spoke directly into Meg's mind, and now there was a distinct <u>menace</u> to the words. "I am not pleased," he said to her. "I could very easily lose patience with you, and that, for your information, young lady, would not be good for your father. If you have the slightest desire to see your father again, you had better cooperate."

◀ How might the man with red eyes remind Meg of Mr. Jenkins?

Meg reacted as she sometimes reacted to Mr. Jenkins at school. She scowled down at the ground in sullen fury. "It might help if you gave us something to eat," she complained. "We're all starved. If you're going to be horrible to us you might as well give us full stomachs first."

Again the thoughts coming at her broke into laughter. "Isn't she the funny girl, though! It's lucky for you that you amuse me, my dear, or I shouldn't

---

words for everyday use

men • ace (men′əs) *n.*, threat. *There was a strong <u>menace</u> in the low, throaty growl of the watchdog.*

be so easy on you. The boys I find not nearly so <u>diverting</u>. Ah, well. Now, tell me, young lady, if I feed you will you stop interfering with me?"

"No," Meg said.

"Starvation does work wonders, of course," the man told her. "I hate to use such primitive methods on you, but of course you realize that you force them on me."

"I wouldn't eat your old food, anyhow." Meg was still all churned up and angry as though she were in Mr. Jenkins' office. "I wouldn't trust it."

"Of course our food, being synthetic, is not superior to your messes of beans and bacon and so forth, but I assure you that it's far more nourishing, and though it has no taste of its own, a slight conditioning is all that is necessary to give you the illusion that you are eating a roast turkey dinner."

"If I ate now I'd throw up, anyhow," Meg said.

Still holding Meg's and Calvin's hands, Charles Wallace stepped forward. "Okay, what next?" he asked the man on the chair. "We've had enough of these preliminaries. Let's get on with it."

"That's exactly what we were doing," the man said, "until your sister interfered by practically giving you a brain concussion. Shall we try again?"

"No!" Meg cried. "No, Charles. *Please.* Let me do it. Or Calvin."

"But it is only the little boy whose neurological system is complex enough. If you tried to conduct the necessary neurons your brains would explode."

"And Charles's wouldn't?"

"I think not."

"But there's a possibility?"

"There's always a possibility."

"Then he mustn't do it."

"I think you will have to grant him the right to make his own decisions."

---

words for everyday use

di • vert • ing (də vərt´iŋ) *adj.,* amusing or entertaining. *Dino's <u>diverting</u> antics stopped the baby from crying.*

But Meg, with the dogged <u>tenacity</u> that had so often caused her trouble, continued. "You mean Calvin and I can't know who you really are?"

◄ How are Meg's faults helping her?

"Oh, no, I didn't say that. You can't know it in the same way, nor is it as important to me to have you know. Ah, here we are!" From somewhere in the shadows appeared four more men in dark smocks carrying a table. It was covered with a white cloth, like the tables used by Room Service in hotels, and held a metal hot box containing something that smelled delicious, something that smelled like a turkey dinner.

There's something phoney in the whole setup, Meg thought. There is definitely something rotten in the state of Camazotz.[4]

Again the thoughts seemed to break into laughter. "Of course it doesn't *really* smell, but isn't it as good as though it really did?"

"I don't smell anything," Charles Wallace said.

"I know, young man, and think how much you're missing. This will all taste to you as though you were eating sand. But I suggest that you force it down. I would rather not have your decisions come from the weakness of an empty stomach."

The table was set up in front of them, and the dark smocked men heaped their plates with turkey and dressing and mashed potatoes and gravy and little green peas with big yellow blobs of butter melting in them and cranberries and sweet potatoes topped with gooey browned marshmallows and olives and celery and rosebud radishes and—

Meg felt her stomach rumbling loudly. The saliva came to her mouth.

"Oh, Jeeminy—" Calvin mumbled.

Chairs appeared and the four men who had provided the feast slid back into the shadows.

---

4. **There is . . . in the state of Camazotz.** Paraphrased from "Something is rotten in the state of Denmark," a line from William Shakespeare's tragedy *Hamlet*

words for everyday use te • nac • i • ty (te nas'ə tē) *n.*, quality of holding firmly; stubbornness. *Although her first attempts were unsuccessful, Irma continued to try with <u>tenacity</u>.*

Charles Wallace freed his hands from Meg and Calvin and plunked himself down on one of the chairs.

"Come on," he said. "If it's poisoned it's poisoned, but I don't think it is."

Calvin sat down. Meg continued to stand indecisively.

Calvin took a bite. He chewed. He swallowed. He looked at Meg. "If this isn't real, it's the best imitation you'll ever get."

Charles Wallace took a bite, made a face, and spit out his mouthful. "It's unfair!" he shouted at the man.

Laughter again. "Go on, little fellow. Eat."

Meg sighed and sat. "I don't think we should eat this stuff, but if you're going to, I'd better, too." She took a mouthful. "It tastes all right. Try some of mine, Charles." She held out a forkful of turkey.

Charles Wallace took it, made another face, but managed to swallow. "Still tastes like sand," he said. He looked at the man. "Why?"

▶ Why does the food taste bad to Charles and not to Meg and Calvin?

"You know perfectly well why. You've shut your mind entirely to me. The other two can't. I can get in through the chinks. Not all the way in, but enough to give them a turkey dinner. You see, I'm really just a kind, jolly old gentleman."

"Ha," Charles Wallace said.

The man lifted his lips into a smile, and his smile was the most horrible thing Meg had ever seen. "Why don't you trust me, Charles? Why don't you trust me enough to come in and find out what I am? I am peace and utter rest. I am freedom from all responsibility. To come in to me is the last difficult decision you need ever make."

"If I come in can I get out again?" Charles Wallace asked.

"But of course, if you want to. But I don't think you will want to."

"If I come—not to stay, you understand—just to find out about you, will you tell us where Father is?"

"Yes. That is a promise. And I don't make promises lightly."

"Can I speak to Meg and Calvin alone, without your listening in?"

"No."

Charles shrugged. "Listen," he said to Meg and Calvin. "I have to find out what he really is. You know that. I'm going to try to hold back. I'm going to try to keep part of myself out. You mustn't stop me this time, Meg."

"But you won't be able to, Charles! He's stronger than you are! You know that!"

"I have to try."

"But Mrs Whatsit warned you!"

"I have to try. For Father, Meg. Please. I want—I want to know my father—" For a moment his lips trembled. Then he was back in control. "But it isn't only Father, Meg. You know that, now. It's the Black Thing. We have to do what Mrs Which sent us to do."

"Calvin—" Meg begged.

But Calvin shook his head. "He's right, Meg. And we'll be with him, no matter what happens."

"But what's going to happen?" Meg cried.

Charles Wallace looked up at the man. "Okay," he said. "Let's go."

Now the red eyes and the light above seemed to bore into Charles, and again the pupils of the little boy's eyes contracted. When the final point of black was lost in blue he turned away from the red eyes, looked at Meg, and smiled sweetly, but the smile was not Charles Wallace's smile.

"Come on, Meg, eat this delicious food that has been prepared for us," he said.

Meg snatched Charles Wallace's plate and threw it on the floor, so that the dinner splashed about and the plate broke into fragments. "No!" She cried, her voice rising shrilly. "No! No! No!"

From the shadows came one of the dark-smocked men and put another plate in front of Charles Wallace, and he began to eat eagerly. "What's wrong, Meg?" Charles Wallace asked. "Why are you being so belligerent and uncooperative?" The voice was Charles Wallace's voice, and yet it was different, too, somehow flattened out, almost as a voice might have sounded on the two-dimensional planet.

Meg grabbed wildly at Calvin, shrieking, "That isn't Charles! Charles is gone!"

◀ What is Charles Wallace planning to do?

◀ Why can Charles Wallace now enjoy the food? Why is Meg upset?

◀ Who else accused Meg of being "belligerent and uncooperative" back before they began their journey?

Chapter 8

The Transparent Column

Charles Wallace sat there tucking away turkey and dressing as though it were the most delicious thing he had ever tasted. He was dressed like Charles Wallace; he looked like Charles Wallace; he had the same sandy brown hair, the same face that had not yet lost its baby roundness. Only the eyes were different, for the black was still swallowed up in blue. But it was far more than this that made Meg feel that Charles Wallace was gone, that the little boy in his place was only a copy of Charles Wallace, only a doll.

She fought down a sob. "Where is he?" she demanded of the man with red eyes. "What have you done with him? Where is Charles Wallace?"

"But my dear child, you are hysterical," the man thought at her. "He is right there, before you, well and happy. Completely well and happy for the first time in his life. And he is finishing his dinner, which you also would be wise to do."

"You know it isn't Charles!" Meg shouted. "You've got him somehow."

"Hush, Meg. There's no use trying to talk to him," Calvin said, speaking in a low voice into her ear. "What we have to do is hold Charles Wallace tight. He's there, somewhere, underneath, and we mustn't let them take him away from us. Help me hold him, Meg. Don't lose control of yourself. Not now. You've got to help me hold Charles!" He took the little boy firmly by one arm.

Fighting down her hysteria, Meg took Charles's other arm and held it tightly.

"You're hurting me, Meg!" Charles said sharply. "Let me go!"

"No," Meg said grimly.

"We've been all wrong." Charles Wallace's voice, Meg thought, might have been a recording. There was a canned quality to it. "He isn't an enemy at all. He's our friend."

"Nuts," Calvin said rudely.

"You don't understand, Calvin," Charles Wallace said. "Mrs Whatsit, Mrs Who, and Mrs Which have confused us. They're the ones who are really our enemies. We never should have trusted them for a minute." He spoke in his calmest, most reasonable voice, the voice which infuriated the twins. He seemed to be looking directly at Calvin as he spoke, and yet Meg was sure that the bland blue eyes could not see, and that someone, something else was looking at Calvin through Charles.

◀ What does Charles Wallace say about Mrs Whatsit, Mrs Who, and Mrs Which? Do you agree?

Now the cold, strange eyes turned to her. "Meg, let go. I will explain it all to you, but you must let go."

"No." Meg gritted her teeth. She did not release her grasp, and Charles Wallace began to pull away with a power that was not his own, and her own spindly strength was no match against it. "Calvin!" she gasped as Charles Wallace wrenched his arm from her and stood up.

Calvin the athlete, Calvin the boy who split firewood and brought it in for his mother, whose muscles were strong and controlled, let go Charles Wallace's wrist and tackled him as though he were a football. Meg, in her panic and rage, darted at the man on the chair, intending to hit him as Charles Wallace had done, but the black-smocked men were too quick for her, and one of them held her with her arms <u>pinioned</u> behind her back.

"Calvin, I advise you to let me go," came Charles Wallace's voice from under Calvin.

Calvin, his face screwed up with grim determination, did not relax his hold. The man with red eyes nodded and three of the men moved in on Calvin (at least it took three of them), pried him loose, and held him as Meg was being held.

"Mrs Whatsit!" Meg called despairingly. "Oh, Mrs Whatsit!"

But Mrs Whatsit did not come.

"Meg," Charles Wallace said. "Meg, just listen to me."

words for everyday use   pin • ioned (pin′yənd) adj., bound. *A bird cannot fly with <u>pinioned</u> wings.*

"Okay, I'm listening."

"We've been all wrong, I told you; we haven't understood. We've been fighting our friend, and Father's friend."

"If Father tells me he's our friend maybe I'll believe it. Maybe. Unless he's got Father—under—under a spell, or whatever it is, like you."

▶ What is Meg afraid of now?

"This isn't a fairy tale. Spells indeed," Charles Wallace said. "Meg, you've got to stop fighting and relax. Relax and be happy. Oh, Meg, if you'd just relax you'd realize that all our troubles are over. You don't understand what a wonderful place we've come to. You see, on this planet everything is in perfect order because everybody has learned to relax, to give in, to submit. All you have to do is look quietly and steadily into the eyes of our good friend here, for he is our friend, dear sister, and he will take you in as he has taken me."

"Taken you in is right!" Meg said. "You know you're not you. You know you've never in your life called me *dear sister*."

"Shut up a minute, Meg," Calvin whispered to her. He looked up at the man with red eyes. "Okay, have your henchmen[1] let us go and stop talking to us through Charles. We know it's you talking, or whatever's talking through you. Anyhow, we know you have Charles hypnotized."

"A most <u>primitive</u> way of putting it," the man with red eyes murmured. He gestured slightly with one finger, and Meg and Calvin were released.

"Thanks," Calvin said wryly. "Now, if you are our friend, will you tell us who—or what—you are?"

"It is not necessary for you to know who I am. I am the Prime Coordinator, that is all you need to know."

"But you're being spoken through, aren't you, just like Charles Wallace? Are you hypnotized, too?"

---

1. **henchmen.** Trusted helpers or followers as of a political leader or gang leader

---

words for everyday use

prim • i • tive (pri´mə tiv) *adj.,* belonging to or characteristic of an early age or stage of development; little evolved. *Europeans of past centuries looked down on peoples of Africa, calling them "<u>primitive</u>" because they believed they were not as highly developed.*

"I told you that was too primitive a word, without the correct <u>connotations</u>."

"Is it you who are going to take us to Mr. Murry?"

"No. It is not necessary, nor is it possible, for me to leave here. Charles Wallace will conduct you."

"Charles Wallace?"

"Yes."

"When?"

"Now." The man with red eyes made the frightening grimace that passed for his smile. "Yes, I think it might as well be now."

Charles Wallace gave a slight jerk of his head, saying, "Come," and started to walk in a strange, gliding, mechanical manner. Calvin followed him. Meg hesitated, looking from the man with red eyes to Charles and Calvin. She wanted to reach out and grab Calvin's hand, but it seemed that ever since they had begun their journeyings she had been looking for a hand to hold, so she stuffed her fists into her pockets and walked along behind the two boys. —I've got to be brave, she said to herself. —I *will* be.

They moved down a long, white, and seemingly endless corridor. Charles Wallace continued the jerky rhythm of his walk and did not once look back to see if they were with him.

Suddenly Meg broke into a run and caught up with Calvin. "Cal," she said, "listen. Quick. Remember Mrs Whatsit said your gift was communication and that was what she was giving you. We've been trying to fight Charles physically, and that isn't any good. Can't you try to communicate with him? Can't you try to get in to him?"

"Golly day, you're right." Calvin's face lit up with hope, and his eyes, which had been somber, regained their usual sparkle. "I've been in such a swivet—It may not do any good, but at least I can try." They quickened their pace until they were level with

◀ Why does Meg decide not to hold Calvin's hand?

---

words for everyday use

con • no • ta • tion (kän´ə tā´shən) *n.*, idea suggested by or associated with a word. *Although* inexpensive *and* cheap *both mean "having a low cost," the word* cheap *has* connotations *of inferior quality that* inexpensive *does not have.*

Charles Wallace. Calvin reached out for his arm, but Charles flung it off.

"Leave me alone," he snarled.

"I'm not going to hurt you, old sport," Calvin said. "I'm just trying to be friendly. Let's make it up, hunh?"

"You mean you're coming around?" Charles Wallace asked.

▶ What happens between Calvin and Charles Wallace?

"Sure," Calvin's voice was coaxing. "We're reasonable people, after all. Just look at me for a minute, Charlibus."

Charles Wallace stopped and turned slowly to look at Calvin with his cold, vacant eyes. Calvin looked back, and Meg could feel the intensity of his concentration. An enormous shudder shook Charles Wallace. For a brief flash his eyes seemed to see. Then his whole body twirled wildly, and went rigid. He started his marionette's[2] walk again. "I should have known better," he said. "If you want to see Murry you'd better come with me and not try any more hanky-panky."

"Is that what you call your father—Murry?" Calvin asked. Meg could see that he was angry and upset at his near success.

"Father? What is a father?" Charles Wallace intoned. "Merely another <u>misconception</u>. If you feel the need of a father, then I would suggest that you turn to IT."

IT again.

"Who's this IT?" Meg asked.

"All in good time," Charles Wallace said. "You're not ready for IT yet. First of all I will tell you something about this beautiful, enlightened planet of Camazotz." His voice took on the dry, <u>pedantic</u> tones of Mr. Jenkins. "Perhaps you do not realize that on Camazotz we have conquered all illness, all deformity—"

▶ What happens when a person on Camazotz becomes ill?

---

2. **marionette.** Puppet or jointed doll moved by strings or wires from above

words for everyday use

mis • con • cep • tion (mis´kən səp´shən) n., mistaken thought or idea. *The belief that the world is flat was once a common <u>misconception</u>.*

pe • dan • tic (pe dan´tik) adj., laying unnecessary stress on minor or trivial points of learning. *The students were bored by Mr. Jenkins's <u>pedantic</u> style.*

"We?" Calvin interrupted.

Charles continued as though he had not heard. And of course he hadn't, Meg thought. "We let no one suffer. It is so much kinder simply to <u>annihilate</u> anyone who is ill. Nobody has weeks and weeks of runny noses and sore throats. Rather than endure such discomfort they are simply put to sleep."

"You mean they're put to sleep while they have a cold, or that they're murdered?" Calvin demanded.

"Murder is a most primitive word," Charles Wallace said. "There is no such thing as murder on Camazotz. IT takes care of all such things." He moved jerkily to the wall of the corridor, stood still for a moment, then raised his hand. The wall flickered, quivered, grew transparent. Charles Wallace walked through it, beckoned to Meg and Calvin, and they followed. They were in a small, square room from which radiated a dull, sulphurous[3] light. There was something <u>ominous</u> to Meg in the very compactness of the room, as though the walls, the ceiling, the floor might move together and crush anybody rash enough to enter.

"How did you do that?" Calvin asked Charles.

"Do what?"

"Make the wall—open—like that."

"I merely rearranged the atoms," Charles Wallace said loftily. "You've studied atoms in school, haven't you?"

"Sure, but—"

"Then you know enough to know that matter isn't solid, don't you? That you, Calvin, consist mostly of empty space? That if all the matter in you came together you'd be the size of the head of a pin? That's plain scientific fact, isn't it?"

"Yes, but—"

"So I simply pushed the atoms aside and we walked through the space between them."

---

3. **sulphurous.** Of or like a pale yellow, nonmetallic chemical element, also suggesting the fires of hell

words for everyday use

an • ni • hi • late (ə nīˊə lātˊ) v., destroy completely. "We will <u>annihilate</u> the city and everyone in it!" shouted the leader of the attacking force.

om • i • nous (ämˊə nəs) adj., threatening. The <u>ominous</u>, dark clouds loomed overhead as we hurried to seek shelter from the storm.

Meg's stomach seemed to drop, and she realized that the square box in which they stood must be an elevator and that they had started to move upward with great speed. The yellow light lit up their faces, and the pale blue of Charles's eyes absorbed the yellow and turned green.

Calvin licked his lips. "Where are we going?"

"Up." Charles continued his lecture. "On Camazotz we are all happy because we are all alike. Differences create problems. You know that, don't you, dear sister?"

"No," Meg said.

"Oh, yes, you do. You've seen at home how true it is. You know that's the reason you're not happy at school. Because you're different."

"*I'm* different, and I'm happy," Calvin said.

"But you pretend that you *aren't* different."

"I'm different, and I like being different." Calvin's voice was unnaturally loud.

"Maybe I don't like being different," Meg said, "but I don't want to be like everybody else, either."

Charles Wallace raised his hand and the motion of the square box ceased and one of the walls seemed to disappear. Charles stepped out, Meg and Calvin following him, Calvin just barely making it before the wall came into being again, and they could no longer see where the opening had been.

"You wanted Calvin to get left behind, didn't you?" Meg said.

"I am merely trying to teach you to stay on your toes. I warn you, if I have any more trouble from either of you, I shall have to take you to IT."

As the word IT fell from Charles's lips, again Meg felt as though she had been touched by something slimy and horrible. "So what is this IT?" she asked.

"You might call IT the Boss." Then Charles Wallace giggled, a giggle that was the most sinister sound Meg had ever heard. "IT sometimes calls ITself the Happiest Sadist."[4]

Meg spoke coldly, to cover her fear. "I don't know what you're talking about."

▶ *What does Charles say about differences? Do Meg and Calvin agree with him?*

▶ *Explain the pun, or play on words, Charles Wallace is making.*

---

4. **Sadist** (sā' dist or sa' dist). One who takes delight in cruelty

"That's s-a-d-i-s-t, not s-a-d-d-e-s-t, you know," Charles Wallace said, and giggled again. "Lots of people don't pronounce it correctly."

"Well, I don't care," Meg said defiantly. "I don't ever want to see IT, and that's that."

Charles Wallace's strange, monotonous voice ground against her ears. "Meg, you're supposed to have *some* mind. Why do you think we have wars at home? Why do you think people get confused and unhappy? Because they all live their own, separate, individual lives. I've been trying to explain to you in the simplest possible way that on Camazotz individuals have been done away with. Camazotz is ONE mind. It's IT. And that's why everybody's so happy and efficient. That's what old witches like Mrs Whatsit don't want to have happen at home."

◄ *Who is IT?*

"She's not a witch," Meg interrupted.

"No?"

"No," Calvin said. "You know she's not. You know that's just their game. Their way, maybe, of laughing in the dark."

"In the dark is correct," Charles continued. "They want us to go on being confused instead of properly organized."

Meg shook her head violently. "No!" she shouted. "I know our world isn't perfect, Charles, but it's better than this. This isn't the only alternative! It can't be!"

"Nobody suffers here," Charles intoned. "Nobody is ever unhappy."

"But nobody's ever happy, either," Meg said earnestly. "Maybe if you aren't unhappy sometimes you don't know how to be happy. Calvin, I want to go home."

"We can't leave Charles," Calvin told her, "and we can't go before we've found your father. You know that. But you're right, Meg, and Mrs Which is right. This is Evil."

Charles Wallace shook his head, and scorn and disapproval seemed to <u>emanate</u> from him. "Come.

words for everyday use
em • a • nate (em´ə nāt´) v., come forth. *A musty aroma <u>emanated</u> from the cave.*

▶ What does Charles Wallace criticize?

We're wasting time." He moved rapidly down the corridor, but continued to speak. "How dreadful it is to be low, individual organisms. Tch-tch-tch." His pace quickened from step to step, his short legs flashing, so that Meg and Calvin almost had to run to keep up with him. "Now see this," he said. He raised his hand and suddenly they could see through one of the walls into a small room. In the room a little boy was bouncing a ball. He was bouncing it in rhythm, and the walls of his little cell seemed to pulse with the rhythm of the ball. And each time the ball bounced he screamed as though he were in pain.

"That's the little boy we saw this afternoon." Calvin said sharply, "the little boy who wasn't bouncing the ball like the others."

Charles Wallace giggled again. "Yes. Every once in a while there's a little trouble with cooperation, but it's easily taken care of. After today he'll never desire to <u>deviate</u> again. Ah, here we are."

He moved rapidly down the corridor and again held up his hand to make the wall transparent. They looked into another small room or cell. In the center of it was a large, round, transparent column, and inside this column was a man.

"FATHER!" Meg screamed.

---

words for everyday use de • vi • ate (dē′vē āt′) v., turn aside from a particular course or direction. *Michaela <u>deviated</u> from her original plan and followed a different course of action.*

Respond to the Selection

List some ways in which you are different from other people. Do you enjoy being unique in some ways? Are there times when you wish you were not so different? Write about being different in your journal.

Investigate, Inquire, and Imagine

Recall: Gathering Facts

1a. What does the man with red eyes ask Meg, Calvin, and Charles Wallace to do? What does each of them do instead?

2a. What does Meg do to stop Charles Wallace the first time he tries to see who the man with red eyes really is?

3a. What is the first thing Calvin and Meg do to try to rescue Charles Wallace from the man with red eyes? Is this attempt successful?

4a. What do differences cause, according to Charles Wallace?

Interpret: Finding Meaning

1b. Why do Meg, Calvin, and Charles Wallace resist the suggestion of the man with red eyes?

2b. Do you think Charles Wallace makes a good decision about finding out who the man with red eyes really is? Why, or why not?

3b. What happens when Calvin uses his gift to try to reach Charles Wallace? Is physical strength or communication more powerful?

4b. Give examples of differences being positive.

Analyze: Taking Things Apart

5a. Reread pages 20–21. Then, compare the way Meg reacts to Mr. Jenkins to the way she reacts to the man with red eyes. How does Charles Wallace, at the end of chapter 7, echo Mr. Jenkins's words? What do both Mr. Jenkins and IT (who is speaking through Charles Wallace and the man with red eyes) want from Meg?

Synthesize: Bringing Things Together

5b. When might it be good not to be too cooperative or too eager to fit in with everyone else? How are Meg's faults helping her on Camazotz? How might they help her when she is taken to IT?

Evaluate: MAKING JUDGMENTS

6a. Charles Wallace tells Meg and Calvin that "Camazotz is ONE mind. It's IT. And that's why everybody is so happy and efficient." The man with the red eyes says, "I am peace and utter rest. I am freedom from all responsibility. To come in to me is the last difficult decision you need ever make." Do you think the people of Camazotz are truly happy and at peace? Does Camazotz offer positive solutions to the problems of Earth? Why, or why not?

Extend: CONNECTING IDEAS

➤ 6b. Do you think your life would be easier if you didn't have any difficult choices to make? Would you enjoy a life that was completely free of all pain and unhappiness? If you were offered happiness in exchange for your individuality and free will, would you take it? Why, or why not?

Understanding Literature

DESCRIPTION AND MOOD. A **description** gives a picture in words of a character, object, or scene. **Mood** is the emotion, or general feeling created by a piece of writing. A mood can be any kind of feeling—tense or peaceful, suspenseful or silly, gloomy or joyful, happy or sad, festive or lonely. In your own words, describe the inside of the CENTRAL Central Intelligence Building. What is the lobby like? How would you describe the second room that Meg, Calvin, and Charles Wallace enter? What mood is created by the description of the CENTRAL Central Intelligence Building?

THEME. A **theme** is a main idea in a literary work. A work can have more than one theme. One theme of *A Wrinkle in Time* is that things are not always what they seem. In what way is the man with red eyes not what he seems? How is the dinner he serves them not what it seems to be? It might seem that a world like Camazotz, in which everyone agrees, would be a happy and peaceful place. How is reality different?

Chapter 9

IT

Meg rushed at the man imprisoned in the column, but as she reached what seemed to be the open door she was hurled back as though she had crashed into a brick wall.

Calvin caught her. "It's just transparent like glass this time," he told her. "We can't go through it."

Meg was so sick and dizzy from the impact that she could not answer. For a moment she was afraid that she would throw up or faint. Charles Wallace laughed again, the laugh that was not his own, and it was this that saved her, for once more anger overcame her pain and fear. Charles Wallace, her own real, dear Charles Wallace, never laughed at her when she hurt herself. Instead, his arms would go quickly around her neck and he would press his soft cheek against hers in loving comfort. But the demon Charles Wallace snickered. She turned away from him and looked again at the man in the column.

◀ How does Meg know that this is not the "real" Charles Wallace?

"Oh, Father—" she whispered longingly, but the man in the column did not move to look at her. The horn-rimmed glasses, which always seemed so much a part of him, were gone, and the expression of his eyes was turned inward, as though he were deep in thought. He had grown a beard, and the silky brown was shot with gray. His hair, too, had not been cut. It wasn't just the overlong hair of the man in the snapshot at Cape Canaveral; it was pushed back from his high forehead and fell softly almost to his shoulders, so that he looked like someone in another century, or a shipwrecked sailor. But there was no question, despite the change in him, that he was her father, her own beloved father.

"My, he looks a mess, doesn't he?" Charles Wallace said, and sniggered.

Meg swung on him with sick rage. "Charles, that's Father! Father!"

"So what?"

Meg turned away from him and held out her arms to the man in the column.

"He doesn't see us, Meg," Calvin said gently.

"Why? Why?"

"I think it's sort of like those little peepholes they have in apartments, in the front doors," Calvin explained. "You know. From inside you can look through and see everything. And from outside you can't see anything at all. We can see him, but he can't see us."

"Charles!" Meg pleaded. "Let me in to Father!"

"Why?" Charles asked <u>placidly</u>.

Meg remembered that when they were in the room with the man with red eyes she had knocked Charles Wallace back into himself when she tackled him and his head cracked the floor; so she hurled herself at him. But before she could reach him his fist shot out and punched her hard in the stomach. She gasped for breath. Sickly, she turned away from her brother, back to the transparent wall. There was the cell, there was the column with her father inside. Although she could see him, although she was almost close enough to touch him, he seemed farther away than he had been when she had pointed him out to Calvin in the picture on the piano. He stood there quietly as though frozen in a column of ice, an expression of suffering and endurance on his face that pierced into her heart like an arrow.

"You say you want to help Father?" Charles Wallace's voice came from behind her, with no emotion whatsoever.

"Yes. Don't you?" Meg demanded, swinging around and glaring at him.

"But of course. That is why we are here."

"Then what do we *do?*" Meg tried to keep the franticness out of her voice, trying to sound as drained of feeling as Charles, but nevertheless ending on a squeak.

"You must do as I have done, and go in to IT," Charles said.

words
for
everyday
use

pla • cid • ly (plas´id lē) *adv.*, calmly. *The clouds floated <u>placidly</u> along on a gentle breeze.*

"No."

"I can see you don't really want to save Father."

"How will my being a <u>zombie</u> save Father?"

"You will just have to take my word for it, Margaret," came the cold, flat voice from Charles Wallace. "IT wants you and IT will get you. Don't forget that I, too, am part of IT, now. You know I wouldn't have done IT if IT weren't the right thing to do."

"Calvin," Meg asked in agony, "will it really save Father?"

But Calvin was paying no attention to her. He seemed to be concentrating with all his power on Charles Wallace. He stared into the pale blue that was all that was left of Charles Wallace's eyes. *"And, for thou wast a spirit too delicate/To act her earthy and abhorr'd commands . . ./she did confine thee . . . into a cloven pine—"* he whispered, and Meg recognized Mrs Who's words to him.

For a moment Charles Wallace seemed to listen. Then he shrugged and turned away. Calvin followed him, trying to keep his eyes focused on Charles's. "If you want a witch, Charles," he said, "IT's the witch. Not our ladies. Good thing I had *The Tempest* at school this year, isn't it, Charles? It was the witch who put Ariel in the cloven pine, wasn't it?"

Charles Wallace's voice seemed to come from a great distance. "Stop staring at me."

Breathing quickly with excitement, Calvin continued to pin Charles Wallace with his stare. "You're like Ariel in the cloven pine, Charles. And I can let you out. Look at me, Charles. Come back to us."

◀ *What is Calvin trying to do?*

Again the shudder went through Charles Wallace.

Calvin's intense voice hit at him. "Come back, Charles. Come back to us."

Again Charles shuddered. And then it was as though an invisible hand had smacked against his chest and knocked him to the ground, and the stare

---

words for everyday use

zom • bie (zäm´bē) *n.,* person showing mechanical, listless behavior; literally, a dead person who has come to life. *After two days without sleep, Charlie moved like a zombie.*

with which Calvin had held him was broken. Charles sat there on the floor of the corridor whimpering, not a small boy's sound, but a fearful, animal noise.

"Calvin." Meg turned on him, clasping her hands intensely. "Try to get to Father."

Calvin shook his head. "Charles almost came out. I almost did it. He almost came back to us."

"Try Father," Meg said again.

"How?"

"Your cloven pine thing. Isn't Father imprisoned in a cloven pine even more than Charles? Look at him, in that column there. Get him out, Calvin."

Calvin spoke in an exhausted way. "Meg. I don't know what to do. I don't know how to get in. Meg, they're asking too much of us."

"Mrs Who's spectacles!" Meg said suddenly. Mrs Who had told her to use them only as a last resort, and surely that was now. She reached into her pocket and the spectacles were there, cool and light and comforting. With trembling fingers she pulled them out.

"Give me those spectacles!" Charles Wallace's voice came in a harsh command, and he scrambled up off the floor and ran at her.

She barely had time to snatch off her own glasses and put on Mrs Who's, and, as it was, one earpiece dropped down her cheek and they barely stayed on her nose. As Charles Wallace lunged at her she flung herself against the transparent door and she was through it. She was in the cell with the imprisoning column that held her father. With trembling fingers she straightened Mrs Who's glasses and put her own in her pocket.

"Give them to me," came Charles Wallace's menacing voice, and he was in the cell with her, with Calvin on the outside pounding frantically to get in.

▶ How is Meg able to reach her father?

Meg kicked at Charles Wallace and ran at the column. She felt as though she were going through something dark and cold. But she was through. "Father!" she cried. And she was in his arms.

This was the moment for which she had been waiting, not only since Mrs Which whisked them off on their journeys, but during the long months and years before, when the letters had stopped coming, when people made remarks about Charles Wallace, when Mrs. Murry showed a rare flash of loneliness or grief. This was the moment that meant that now and forever everything would be all right.

As she pressed against her father all was forgotten except joy. There was only the peace and comfort of leaning against him, the wonder of the protecting circle of his arms, the feeling of complete reassurance and safety that his presence always gave her.

Her voice broke on a happy sob. "Oh, Father! Oh, Father!"

"Meg!" he cried in glad surprise. "Meg, what are you doing here? Where's your mother? Where are the boys?"

She looked out of the column, and there was Charles Wallace in the cell, an <u>alien</u> expression <u>distorting</u> his face. She turned back to her father. There was no more time for greeting, for joy, for explanations. "We have to go to Charles Wallace," she said, her words tense. "Quickly."

Her father's hands were moving gropingly over her face, and as she felt the touch of his strong, gentle fingers, she realized with a flooding of horror that she could see him, that she could see Charles in the cell and Calvin in the corridor, but her father could not see them, could not see her. She looked at him in panic, but his eyes were the same steady blue that she remembered. She moved her hand <u>brusquely</u> across his line of vision, but he did not blink.

"Father!" she cried. "Father! Can't you see me?"

His arms went around her again in a comforting, reassuring gesture. "No, Meg."

"But, Father, I can see you—" Her voice trailed off. Suddenly she shoved Mrs Who's glasses down her nose and peered over them, and immediately she was

---

words for everyday use

a • li • en (āʹlē ən) adj., strange; foreign. *The sight and feel of snow was an <u>alien</u> experience to the boy who had lived in the tropics all his life.*

dis • tort (di stôrtʹ) v., change from its usual shape. *The fun house mirrors <u>distorted</u> our appearance, making us look shorter, taller, wider, or thinner than we really were.*

brusque • ly (bruskʹlē) adv., abruptly. *Phil turned away <u>brusquely</u> so that Bea would not see the tears in his eyes.*

in complete and utter darkness. She snatched them off her face and thrust them at her father. "Here."

His fingers closed about the spectacles. "Darling," he said, "I'm afraid your glasses won't help."

"But they're Mrs Who's, they aren't mine," she explained, not realizing that her words would sound like gibberish to him. "Please try them, Father. Please!" She waited while she felt him fumbling in the dark. "Can you see now?" she asked. "Can you see now, Father?"

"Yes," he said. "Yes. The wall is transparent, now. How extraordinary! I could almost see the atoms rearranging!" His voice had its old, familiar sound of excitement and discovery. It was the way he sounded sometimes when he came home from his laboratory after a good day and began to tell his wife about his work. Then he cried out, "Charles! Charles Wallace!" And then, "Meg, what's happened to him? What's wrong? That *is* Charles, isn't it?"

"IT has him, Father," she explained tensely. "He's gone into IT. Father, we have to help him."

For a long moment Mr. Murry was silent. The silence was filled with the words he was thinking and would not speak out loud to his daughter. Then he said, "Meg, I'm in prison here. I have been for—"

"Father, these walls. You can go through them. I came through the column to get in to you. It was Mrs Who's glasses."

◀ What power do Mrs Who's glasses have?

Mr. Murry did not stop to ask who Mrs Who was. He slapped his hand against the <u>translucent</u> column. "It seems solid enough."

"But I got in," Meg repeated. "I'm here. Maybe the glasses help the atoms rearrange. Try it, Father."

She waited, breathlessly, and after a moment she realized that she was alone in the column. She put out her hands in the darkness and felt its smooth surface curving about her on all sides. She seemed utterly alone, the silence and darkness <u>impenetrable</u> forever. She fought down panic until she heard her father's voice coming to her very faintly.

"I'm coming back in for you, Meg."

It was almost a tangible feeling as the atoms of the strange material seemed to part to let him through to her. In their beach house at Cape Canaveral there had been a curtain between dining and living room made of long strands of rice. It looked like a solid curtain, but you could walk right through it. At first Meg had flinched each time she came up to the curtain; but gradually she got used to it and would go running right through, leaving the long strands of rice swinging behind her. Perhaps the atoms of these walls were arranged in somewhat the same fashion.

◀ To what does Meg compare the parting rearrangement of atoms as they move through the wall?

"Put your arms around my neck, Meg," Mr. Murry said. "Hold on to me tightly. Close your eyes and don't be afraid." He picked her up and she wrapped her long legs around his waist and clung to his neck. With Mrs Who's spectacles on she had felt only a faint darkness and coldness as she moved through the column. Without the glasses she felt the same awful

---

words for everyday use

trans • lu • cent (trans lü´sənt) adj., letting light pass through. *The sunlight streamed through the translucent panels of colored glass.*

im • pe • ne • tra • ble (im pen´i trə bəl) adj., not able to be passed through or understood. *No light shines through the impenetrable leaf cover to the forest floor.*

clamminess she had felt when they tessered through the outer darkness of Camazotz. Whatever the Black Thing was to which Camazotz had submitted, it was within as well as without the planet. For a moment it seemed that the chill darkness would tear her from her father's arms. She tried to scream, but within that icy horror no sound was possible. Her father's arms tightened about her, and she clung to his neck in a strangle hold, but she was no longer lost in panic. She knew that if her father could not get her through the wall he would stay with her rather than leave her; she knew that she was safe as long as she was in his arms.

Then they were outside. The column rose up in the middle of the room, crystal clear and empty.

Meg blinked at the blurred figures of Charles and her father, and wondered why they did not clear. Then she grabbed her own glasses out of her pocket and put them on, and her myopic eyes were able to focus.

▶ Why is IT displeased?

Charles Wallace was tapping one foot impatiently against the floor. "IT is not pleased," he said. "IT is not pleased at all."

Mr. Murry released Meg and knelt in front of the little boy. "Charles," his voice was tender. "Charles Wallace."

"What do you want?"

"I'm your father, Charles. Look at me."

The pale blue eyes seemed to focus on Mr. Murry's face. "Hi, Pop," came an <u>insolent</u> voice.

"That isn't Charles!" Meg cried. "Oh, Father, Charles isn't like that. IT has him."

"Yes." Mr. Murry sounded tired. "I see." He held his arms out. "Charles. Come here."

Father will make it all right, Meg thought. Everything will be all right now.

Charles did not move toward the outstretched arms. He stood a few feet away from his father, and he did not look at him.

---

words for everyday use   in • so • lent (in´sə lənt) adj., boldly disrespectful. *Mr. Marengo fired the <u>insolent</u> waiter after he insulted every customer in the restaurant.*

"Look at me," Mr. Murry commanded.

"No."

Mr. Murry's voice became harsh. "When you speak to me you will say 'No, Father,' or 'No, sir.'"

"Come off it, Pop," came the cold voice from Charles Wallace—Charles Wallace who, outside Camazotz, had been strange, had been different, but never rude. "You're not the boss around here."

Meg could see Calvin pounding again on the glass wall. "Calvin!" she called.

"He can't hear you," Charles said. He made a horrible face at Calvin, and then he thumbed his nose.

"Who's Calvin?" Mr. Murry asked.

"He's—" Meg started, but Charles Wallace cut her short.

"You'll have to defer your explanations. Let's go."

"Go where?"

"To IT."

"No," Mr. Murry said. "You can't take Meg there."

"Oh, can't I!"

"No, you cannot. You're my son, Charles, and I'm afraid you will have to do as I say."

"But he *isn't* Charles!" Meg cried in anguish. Why didn't her father understand? "Charles is nothing like that, Father! You know he's nothing like that!"

"He was only a baby when I left," Mr. Murry said heavily.

"Father, it's IT talking through Charles. IT isn't Charles. He's—he's bewitched."

"Fairy tales again," Charles said.

"You know IT, Father?" Meg asked.

"Yes."

"Have you seen IT?"

"Yes, Meg." Again his voice sounded exhausted. "Yes. I have." He turned to Charles. "You know she wouldn't be able to hold out."

"Exactly," Charles said.

"Father, you can't talk to him as though he were Charles! Ask Calvin! Calvin will tell you."

"Come along," Charles Wallace said. "We must go." He held up his hand carelessly and walked out of the cell, and there was nothing for Meg and Mr. Murry to do but to follow.

As they stepped into the corridor Meg caught at her father's sleeve. "Calvin, here's Father!"

Calvin turned anxiously toward them. His freckles and his hair stood out brilliantly against his white face.

"Make your introductions later," Charles Wallace said. "IT does not like to be kept waiting." He walked down the corridor, his <u>gait</u> seeming to get more jerky with each step. The others followed, walking rapidly to keep up.

"Does your father know about the Mrs Ws?" Calvin asked Meg.

▶ After finding her father, what does Meg discover about her problems?

"There hasn't been time for anything. Everything's awful." Despair settled like a stone in the pit of Meg's stomach. She had been so certain that the moment she found her father everything would be all right. Everything would be settled. All the problems would be taken out of her hands. She would no longer be responsible for anything.

And instead of this happy and expected outcome, they seemed to be encountering all kinds of new troubles.

"He doesn't understand about Charles," she whispered to Calvin, looking unhappily at her father's back as he walked behind the little boy.

"Where are we going?" Calvin asked.

"To IT. Calvin, I don't want to go! I can't!" She stopped, but Charles continued his jerky pace.

"We can't leave Charles," Calvin said. "They wouldn't like it."

"Who wouldn't?"

"Mrs Whatsit & Co."

"But they've betrayed us! They brought us here to this terrible place and abandoned us!"

Calvin looked at her in surprise. "You sit down and give up if you like," he said. "I'm sticking with Charles." He ran to keep up with Charles Wallace and Mr. Murry.

---

words for everyday use **gait** (gāt) *n.*, manner of walking. *Ethan's ambling <u>gait</u> is much slower than Darcy's fast-paced stride.*

"I didn't mean—" Meg started, and pounded after them.

Just as she caught up with them Charles Wallace stopped and raised his hand, and there was the elevator again, its yellow light sinister. Meg felt her stomach jerk as the swift descent began. They were silent until the motion stopped, silent as they followed Charles Wallace through long corridors and out into the street. The CENTRAL Central Intelligence Building loomed up, stark and angular, behind them.

—Do something, Meg implored her father silently. —Do something. Help. Save us.

They turned a corner, and at the end of the street was a strange, domelike building. Its walls glowed with a flicker of violet flame. Its silvery roof pulsed with ominous light. The light was neither warm nor cold, but it seemed to reach out and touch them. This, Meg was sure, must be where IT was waiting for them.

They moved down the street, more slowly now, and as they came closer to the domed building the violet flickering seemed to reach out, to envelop them, to suck them in: they were inside.

Meg could feel a rhythmical pulsing. It was a pulsing not only about her, but in her as well, as though the rhythm of her heart and lungs was no longer her own but was being worked by some outside force. The closest she had come to the feeling before was when she had been practicing artificial respiration[1] with Girl Scouts, and the leader, an immensely powerful woman, had been working on Meg, intoning OUT goes the bad air, IN comes the good! while her heavy hands pressed, released, pressed, released.

Meg gasped, trying to breathe at her own normal rate, but the inexorable beat within and without

---

1. **artificial respiration.** Emergency lifesaving procedure that involves breathing air from one's own lungs into the mouth and lungs of someone else

---

words for everyday use

im • plore (im plôr´) v., beseech or beg. *Ted implored the coach to give him another chance.*

en • ve • lop (en vel´əp) v., wrap up or cover completely. *The baby was enveloped in a bundle of blankets.*

▶ What does Meg experience as they approach IT?

continued. For a moment she could neither move nor look around to see what was happening to the others. She simply had to stand there, trying to balance herself into the artificial rhythm of her heart and lungs. Her eyes seemed to swim in a sea of red.

Then things began to clear, and she could breathe without gasping like a beached fish, and she could look about the great, circular, domed building. It was completely empty except for the pulse, which seemed a tangible thing, and a round dais[2] exactly in the center. On the dais lay—what? Meg could not tell, and yet she knew that it was from this that the rhythm came. She stepped forward <u>tentatively</u>. She felt that she was beyond fear now. Charles Wallace was no longer Charles Wallace. Her father had been found but he had not made everything all right. Instead everything was worse than ever, and her adored father was bearded and thin and white and not <u>omnipotent</u> after all. No matter what happened next, things could be no more terrible or frightening than they already were.

Oh, couldn't they?

As she continued to step slowly forward, at last she realized what the Thing on the dais was.

IT was a brain.

▶ Why is Meg even more frightened when she realizes that IT is a brain?

A disembodied brain. An oversized brain, just enough larger than normal to be completely revolting and terrifying. A living brain. A brain that pulsed and quivered, that seized and commanded. No wonder the brain was called IT. IT was the most horrible, the most repellent thing she had ever seen, far more nauseating than anything she had ever imagined with her conscious mind, or that had ever tormented her in her most terrible nightmares.

But as she had felt she was beyond fear, so now she was beyond screaming.

---

2. **dais.** Platform raised above the floor as for a throne

words for everyday use	ten • ta • tive • ly (ten´tə tiv lē) adv., experimentally; uncertainly. Eva stepped tentatively on her sprained ankle and then limped off the court.	om • ni • po • tent (äm nip´ə tənt) adj., all-powerful. The king insisted that he be referred to as King Darius the Omnipotent, ruler of the world.

She looked at Charles Wallace, and he stood there, turned towards IT, his jaw hanging slightly loose; and his vacant blue eyes slowly twirled.

Oh, yes, things could always be worse. These twirling eyes within Charles Wallace's soft round face made Meg icy cold inside and out.

She looked away from Charles Wallace and at her father. Her father stood there with Mrs Who's glasses still perched on his nose—did he remember that he had them on?—and he shouted to Calvin, "Don't give in!"

"I won't! Help Meg!" Calvin yelled back. It was absolutely silent within the dome, and yet Meg realized that the only way to speak was to shout with all the power possible. For everywhere she looked, everywhere she turned, was the rhythm, and as it continued to control the systole and diastole of her heart,[3] the intake and outlet of her breath, the red <u>miasma</u> began to creep before her eyes again, and she was afraid that she was going to lose consciousness, and if she did that she would be completely in the power of IT.

Mrs Whatsit had said, "Meg, I give you your faults."

What were her greatest faults? Anger, impatience, stubbornness. Yes, it was to her faults that she turned to save herself now.

With an immense effort she tried to breathe against the rhythm of IT. But ITs power was too strong. Each time she managed to take a breath out of rhythm an iron hand seemed to squeeze her heart and lungs.

Then she remembered that when they had been standing before the man with red eyes, and the man with red eyes had been intoning the multiplication table at them, Charles Wallace had fought against his

---

3. **systole and diastole of her heart.** Rhythmic contraction (systole) and expansion (diastole) of the chambers of the heart

words for everyday use mi • as • ma (mī az′mə) *n.*, unwholesome vapor. *Pilar tried not to breathe in the <u>miasma</u> of the swamp.*

power by shouting out nursery rhymes, and Calvin by the Gettysburg Address.

"Georgie, porgie, pudding and pie," she yelled. *"Kissed the girls and made them cry."*

That was no good. It was too easy for nursery rhymes to fall into the rhythm of IT.

She didn't know the Gettysburg Address. How did the Declaration of Independence begin? She had memorized it only that winter, not because she was required to at school, but simply because she liked it.

▶ What happens when Meg recites the Declaration of Independence?

"We hold these truths to be self-evident!" she shouted, "that all men are created equal, that they are endowed by their creator with certain unalienable rights, that among these are life, liberty, and the pursuit of happiness."

As she cried out the words she felt a mind moving in on her own, felt IT seizing, squeezing her brain. Then she realized that Charles Wallace was speaking, or being spoken through by IT.

"But that's exactly what we have on Camazotz. Complete equality. Everybody exactly alike."

For a moment her brain reeled with confusion. Then came a moment of blazing truth. "No!" she cried triumphantly. *"Like* and *equal* are not the same thing at all!"

▶ In what ways are like *and* equal different?

"Good girl, Meg!" her father shouted at her.

But Charles Wallace continued as though there had been no interruption. "In Camazotz all are equal. In Camazotz everybody is the same as everybody else," but he gave her no argument, provided no answer, and she held on to her moment of revelation.

Like and equal are two entirely different things.

For the moment she had escaped from the power of IT.

But how?

She knew that her own puny little brain was no match for this great, bodiless, pulsing, writhing mass on the round dais. She shuddered as she looked at IT. In the lab at school there was a human brain preserved in formaldehyde,[4] and the seniors

---

4. **formaldehyde.** Colorless, strong-smelling substance used as a disinfectant and preservative

preparing for college had to take it out and look at it and study it. Meg had felt that when that day came she would never be able to endure it. But now she thought that if only she had a dissecting knife[5] she would slash at IT, cutting ruthlessly through cerebrum, cerebellum.[6]

Words spoke within her, directly this time, not through Charles. "Don't you realize that if you destroy me, you also destroy your little brother?"

◀ What might happen if IT were destroyed?

If that great brain were cut, were crushed, would every mind under ITs control on Camazotz die, too? Charles Wallace and the man with red eyes and the man who ran the number-one spelling machine on the second-grade level and all the children playing ball and skipping rope and all the mothers and all the men and women going in and out of the buildings? Was their life completely dependent on IT? Were they beyond all possibility of salvation?

She felt the brain reaching at her again as she let her stubborn control slip. Red fog glazed her eyes.

Faintly she heard her father's voice, though she knew he was shouting at the top of his lungs. "The periodic table of elements,[7] Meg! Say it!"

A picture flashed into her mind of winter evenings spent sitting before the open fire and studying with her father. "Hydrogen. Helium," she started obediently. Keep them in their proper atomic order. What next. She knew it. Yes. "Lithium, Beryllium, Boron, Carbon, Nitrogen, Oxygen, Fluorine." She shouted the words at her father, turned away from IT. "Neon. Sodium. Magnesium. Aluminum. Silicon. Phosphorus."

"Too rhythmical," her father shouted. "What's the square root of five?"

For a moment she was able to concentrate. Rack your brains yourself, Meg. Don't let IT rack them.

---

5. **dissecting knife.** Sharp knife for cutting plant or animal tissue to be analyzed

6. **cerebrum, cerebellum.** *Cerebrum*—upper main part of the brain in vertebrates, believed to control conscious and voluntary processes; *cerebellum*—section of the brain behind and below the cerebrum, which coordinates muscular movement

7. **periodic table of elements.** Chart showing the arrangement of the chemical elements according to the number of protons in the nucleus of each element

"The square root of five is 2.236," she cried triumphantly, "because 2.236 times 2.236 equals 5!"

"What's the square root of seven?"

"The square root of seven is—" She broke off. She wasn't holding out. IT was getting at her, and she couldn't concentrate, not even on math, and soon she, too, would be absorbed in IT, she would *be* an IT.

"Tesser, sir!" she heard Calvin's voice through the red darkness. "Tesser!"

She felt her father grab her by the wrist, there was a terrible jerk that seemed to break every bone in her body, then the dark nothing of tessering.

If tessering with Mrs Whatsit, Mrs Who, and Mrs Which had been a strange and fearful experience, it was nothing like tessering with her father. After all, Mrs Which was experienced at it, and Mr. Murry— how did he know anything about it at all? Meg felt that she was being torn apart by a <u>whirlwind</u>. She was lost in an agony of pain that finally dissolved into the darkness of complete unconsciousness.

---

words for everyday use
whirl • wind (hwərl´wind´) *n.*, current of air spinning violently upward in a spiral that has a forward motion. *Imogene was caught up in a <u>whirlwind</u> of activity, and she did not have a spare minute of time to herself.*

Chapter 10

Absolute Zero[1]

The first sign of returning consciousness was cold. Then sound. She was aware of voices that seemed to be traveling through her across an arctic waste. Slowly the icy sounds cleared and she realized that the voices belonged to her father and Calvin. She did not hear Charles Wallace. She tried to open her eyes but the lids would not move. She tried to sit up, but she could not stir. She struggled to turn over, to move her hands, her feet, but nothing happened. She knew that she had a body, but it was as lifeless as marble.

She heard Calvin's frozen voice: "Her heart is beating so slowly—"

Her father's voice: "But it's beating. She's alive."

"Barely."

"We couldn't find a heartbeat at all at first. We thought she was dead."

"Yes."

"And then we could feel her heart, very faintly, the beats very far apart. And then it got stronger. So all we have to do is wait." Her father's words sounded brittle in her ears, as though they were being chipped out of ice.

Calvin: "Yes. You're right, sir."

She wanted to call out to them, "I'm alive! I'm very much alive! Only I've been turned to stone."

But she could not call out any more than she could move.

Calvin's voice again. "Anyhow you got her away from IT. You got us both away and we couldn't have gone on holding out. IT's so much more powerful and strong than— How *did* we stay out, sir? How did we manage as long as we did?"

Her father: "Because IT's completely unused to being refused. That's the only reason I could keep from being absorbed, too. No mind has tried to hold out against IT for so many thousands of centuries that certain centers

◀ *Why were Calvin, Meg, and Mr. Murry able to "hold out against IT"?*

---

1. **Absolute Zero.** Absolute zero is –273 degrees Celsius, a temperature so cold that all motion, down to the level of molecules, is stopped.

have become soft and <u>atrophied</u> through lack of use. If you hadn't come to me when you did I'm not sure how much longer I would have lasted. I was on the point of giving in."

Calvin: "Oh, no, sir—"

Her father: "Yes. Nothing seemed important any more but rest, and of course IT offered me complete rest. I had almost come to the conclusion that I was wrong to fight, that IT was right after all, and everything I believed in most passionately was nothing but a madman's dream. But then you and Meg came in to me, broke through my prison, and hope and faith returned."

Calvin: "Sir, why were you on Camazotz at all? Was there a particular reason for going there?"

▶ How did Mr. Murry get to Camazotz?

Her father, with a <u>frigid</u> laugh: "Going to Camazotz was a complete accident. I never intended even to leave our own solar system. I was heading for Mars. Tessering is even more complicated than we had expected."

Calvin: "Sir, how was IT able to get Charles Wallace before it got Meg and me?"

▶ How did Charles Wallace's arrogance lead to his being captured by IT?

Her father: "From what you've told me it's because Charles Wallace thought he could deliberately go into IT and return. He trusted too much to his own strength—listen!—I think the heartbeat is getting stronger!"

His words no longer sounded to her quite as frozen. Was it his words that were ice, or her ears? Why did she hear only her father and Calvin? Why didn't Charles Wallace speak?

Silence. A long silence. Then Calvin's voice again: "Can't we do anything? Can't we look for help? Do we just have to go on waiting?"

Her father: "We can't leave her. And we must stay together. We must *not* be afraid to take time."

Calvin: "You mean we were? We rushed into things on Camazotz too fast, and Charles Wallace rushed in too fast, and that's why he got caught?"

words for everyday use

at • ro • phied (a´trə fēd) *adj.*, wasted away. *Verity worked with a physical therapist to regain the strength in her <u>atrophied</u> muscles.*

fri • gid (frij´id) *adj.*, extremely cold. *The danger of frostbite is great during <u>frigid</u> weather.*

"Maybe. I'm not sure. I don't know enough yet. Time is different on Camazotz, anyhow. Our time, inadequate though it is, at least is straightforward. It may not be even fully one-dimensional, because it can't move back and forth on its line, only ahead; but at least it's <u>consistent</u> in its direction. Time on Camazotz seems to be <u>inverted</u>, turned in on itself. So I have no idea whether I was imprisoned in that column for centuries or only for minutes." Silence for a moment. Then her father's voice again. "I think I feel a pulse in her wrist now."

Meg could not feel his fingers against her wrist. She could not feel her wrist at all. Her body was still stone, but her mind was beginning to be capable of movement. She tried desperately to make some kind of a sound, a signal to them, but nothing happened.

Their voices started again. Calvin: "About your project, sir. Were you on it alone?"

Her father: "Oh, no. There were half a dozen of us working on it and I daresay a number of others we don't know about. Certainly we weren't the only nation to investigate along that line. It's not really a new idea. But we did try very hard not to let it be known abroad that we were trying to make it <u>practicable</u>."

"Did you come to Camazotz alone? Or were there others with you?"

"I came alone. You see, Calvin, there was no way to try it out ahead with rats or monkeys or dogs. And we had no idea whether it would really work or whether it would be complete bodily disintegration. Playing with time and space is a dangerous game."

"But why you, sir?"

"I wasn't the first. We drew straws, and I was second."

"What happened to the first man?"

"We don't—look! Did her eyelids move?" Silence. Then: "No. It was only a shadow."

---

words for everyday use

con • sis • tent (kən sisʹtənt) *adj.*, holding always to the same principle or practice; steady. *Cameron's <u>consistent</u> effort was appreciated by Ms. Alfonso.*

in • ver • ted (in vərʹtəd) *adj.*, turned upside down. *Tally found the missing kitten under an <u>inverted</u> bucket.*

prac • ti • ca • ble (prakʹti kə bəl) *adj.*, usable; that can be put into practice. *Many unsuccessful attempts were made before human flight became <u>practicable</u>.*

But I *did* blink, Meg tried to tell them. I'm sure I did. And I can hear you! *Do* something!

But there was only another long silence, during which perhaps they were looking at her, watching for another shadow, another flicker. Then she heard her father's voice again, quiet, a little warmer, more like his own voice. "We drew straws, and I was second. We know Hank went. We saw him go. We saw him vanish right in front of the rest of us. He was there and then he wasn't. We were to wait for a year for his return or for some message. We waited. Nothing."

Calvin, his voice cracking: "Jeepers, sir. You must have been in sort of a flap."

Her father: "Yes. It's a frightening as well as an exciting thing to discover that matter and energy *are* the same thing, that size is an illusion, and that time is a material substance. We can know this, but it's far more than we can understand with our puny little brains. I think you will be able to comprehend far more than I. And Charles Wallace even more than you."

"Yes, but what happened, please, sir, after the first man?"

Meg could hear her father sigh. "Then it was my turn. I went. And here I am. A wiser and a humbler man. I'm sure I haven't been gone two years. Now that you've come I have some hope that I may be able to return in time. One thing I have to tell the others is that we know nothing."

Calvin: "What do you mean, sir?"

Her father: "Just what I say. We're children playing with dynamite. In our mad rush we've plunged into this before—"

With a desperate effort Meg made a sound. It wasn't a very loud sound, but it was a sound. Mr. Murry stopped. "Hush. Listen."

Meg made a strange, croaking noise. She found that she could pull open her eyelids. They felt heavier than marble but she managed to raise them. Her father and Calvin were hovering over her. She did not see Charles Wallace. Where was he?

She was lying in an open field of what looked like rusty, stubby grass. She blinked, slowly, and with difficulty.

▶ What happened to the other scientist who tessered?

▶ In what ways might Mr. Murry be humbler and wiser?

"Meg," her father said. "Meg. Are you all right?"

Her tongue felt like a stone tongue in her mouth, but she managed to croak, "I can't move."

"Try," Calvin urged. He sounded now as though he were very angry with her. "Wiggle your toes. Wiggle your fingers."

"I can't. Where's Charles Wallace?" Her words were blunted by the stone tongue. Perhaps they could not understand her, for there was no answer.

"We were knocked out for a minute, too," Calvin was saying. "You'll be all right, Meg. Don't get panicky." He was crouched over her, and though his voice continued to sound cross he was peering at her with anxious eyes. She knew that she must still have her glasses on because she could see him clearly, his freckles, his stubby black lashes, the bright blue of his eyes.

Her father was kneeling on her other side. The round lenses of Mrs Who's glasses still blurred his eyes. He took one of her hands and rubbed it between his. "Can you feel my fingers?" He sounded quite calm, as though there were nothing extraordinary in having her completely paralyzed. At the quiet of his voice she felt calmer. Then she saw that there were great drops of sweat standing out on his forehead, and she noticed vaguely that the gentle breeze that touched her cheeks was cool. At first his words had been frozen and now the wind was mild: was it icy cold here or warm? "Can you feel my fingers?" he asked again.

Yes, now she could feel a pressure against her wrist, but she could not nod. "Where's Charles Wallace?" Her words were a little less blurred. Her tongue, her lips were beginning to feel cold and numb, as though she had been given a massive dose of novocaine at the dentist's. She realized with a start that her body and limbs were cold, that not only was she not warm, she was frozen from head to toe, and it was this that had made her father's words seem like ice, that had paralyzed her.

◀ Why is Meg paralyzed?

"I'm frozen—" she said faintly. Camazotz hadn't been this cold, a cold that cut deeper than the wind on the bitterest of winter days at home. She was away from IT, but this unexplained iciness was almost as bad. Her father had not saved her.

Now she was able to look around a little, and everything she could see was rusty and gray. There were trees edging the field in which she lay, and their leaves were the same brown as the grass. There were plants that might have been flowers, except that they were dull and gray. In contrast to the drabness of color, to the cold that numbed her, the air was filled with a delicate, springlike fragrance, almost <u>imperceptible</u> as it blew softly against her face. She looked at her father and Calvin. They were both in their shirt sleeves and they looked perfectly comfortable. It was she, wrapped in their clothes, who was frozen too solid even to shiver.

"Why am I so cold?" she asked. "Where's Charles Wallace?" They did not answer. "Father, where are we?"

▶ What has made Meg so cold?

Mr. Murry looked at her soberly. "I don't know, Meg. I don't tesser very well. I must have overshot, somehow. We're not on Camazotz. I don't know where we are. I think you're so cold because we went through the Black Thing, and I thought for a moment it was going to tear you away from me."

"Is this a dark planet?" Slowly her tongue was beginning to thaw; her words were less blurred.

"I don't think so," Mr. Murry said, "but I know so little about anything that I can't be sure."

"You shouldn't have tried to tesser, then." She had never spoken to her father in this way before. The words seemed hardly to be hers.

Calvin looked at her, shaking his head. "It was the only thing to do. At least it got us off Camazotz."

"Why did we go without Charles Wallace? Did we just leave him there?" The words that were not really hers came out cold and accusing.

"We didn't 'just leave him,'" her father said. "Remember that the human brain is a very delicate <u>organism</u>, and it can be easily damaged."

---

words for everyday use

im • per • cep • ti • ble (im′pər sep′tə bəl) *adj.*, not plain or distinct; difficult to see or understand. *The keen nose of the bloodhound picked up the scent that was* <u>*imperceptible*</u> *to everyone else.*

or • gan • ism (ȯr′gə niz′əm) *n.*, living being. *An amoeba is a one-celled* <u>*organism*</u>.

"See, Meg," Calvin crouched over her, tense and worried, "if your father had tried to yank Charles away when he tessered us, and if IT had kept grabbing hold of Charles, it might have been too much for him, and we'd have lost him forever. And we had to do something right then."

"Why?"

"IT was taking us. You and I were slipping, and if your father had gone on trying to help us he wouldn't have been able to hold out much longer, either."

"*You* told him to tesser," Meg charged Calvin.

"There isn't any question of blame," Mr. Murry cut in severely. "Can you move yet?"

All Meg's faults were uppermost in her now, and they were no longer helping her. "No! And you'd better take me back to Camazotz and Charles Wallace quickly. You're supposed to be able to help!" Disappointment was as dark and <u>corrosive</u> in her as the Black Thing. The ugly words tumbled from her cold lips even as she herself could not believe that it was to her father, her beloved, longed-for father, that she was talking to in this way. If her tears had not still been frozen they would have gushed from her eyes.

She had found her father and he had not made everything all right. Everything kept getting worse and worse. If the long search for her father was ended, and he wasn't able to overcome all their difficulties, there was nothing to guarantee that it would all come out right in the end. There was nothing left to hope for. She was frozen, and Charles Wallace was being devoured by IT, and her omnipotent father was doing nothing. She teetered on the seesaw of love and hate, and the Black Thing pushed her down into hate. "You don't even know where we are!" she cried out at her father. "We'll never see Mother or the twins again! We don't know where earth is! Or even where Camazotz is! We're lost out in space! What are you going to *do!*"

◄ *In what way is Meg in the grip of the Black Thing?*

words for everyday use   cor • ro • sive (kə rōs′iv) *adj.,* eating away. *Corrosive* plaque can cause cavities in teeth.

She did not realize that she was as much in the power of the Black Thing as Charles Wallace.

Mr. Murry bent over her, massaging her cold fingers. She could not see his face. "My daughter, I am not a Mrs Whatsit, a Mrs Who, or a Mrs Which. Yes, Calvin has told me everything he could. I am a human being, and a very <u>fallible</u> one. But I agree with Calvin. We were sent here for something. And we know that all things work together for good to them that love God, to them who are the called according to His purpose."[2]

▶ Whose purpose does Mr. Murry say they are working for?

"The Black Thing!" Meg cried out at him. "Why did you let it almost get me?"

"You've never tessered as well as the rest of us," Calvin reminded her. "It never bothered Charles and me as much as it did you."

"He shouldn't have taken me, then," Meg said, "until he learned to do it better."

Neither her father nor Calvin spoke. Her father continued his gentle massage. Her fingers came back to life with tingling pain. "You're hurting me!"

"Then you're feeling again," her father said quietly. "I'm afraid it *is* going to hurt, Meg."

The piercing pain moved slowly up her arms, began in her toes and legs. She started to cry out against her father when Calvin exclaimed, "Look!"

Coming toward them, moving in silence across the brown grass, were three figures.

What were they?

On Uriel there had been the magnificent creatures. On Camazotz the inhabitants had at least resembled people. What were these three strange things approaching?

They were the same dull gray color as the flowers. If they hadn't walked upright they would have seemed like animals. They moved directly toward the three

---

2. **And we know . . . according to His purpose.** Quotation from the Bible, Romans 8:28

---

words for everyday use

fal • li • ble (fal´ə bəl) *adj.*, likely to be mistaken or fooled. *Kendra is <u>fallible</u>, although she never likes to admit that she is wrong.*

human beings. They had four arms and far more than five fingers to each hand, and the fingers were not fingers, but long waving tentacles. They had heads, and they had faces. But where the faces of the creatures on Uriel had seemed far more than human faces, these seemed far less. Where the features would normally be there were several <u>indentations</u>, and in place of ears and hair were more tentacles. They were tall, Meg realized as they came closer, far taller than any man. They had no eyes. Just soft indentations.

Meg's rigid, frozen body tried to shudder with terror, but instead of the shudder all that came was pain. She moaned.

The Things stood over them. They appeared to be looking down at them, except that they had no eyes with which to see. Mr. Murry continued to kneel by Meg, massaging her.

He's killed us, bringing us here, Meg thought. I'll never see Charles Wallace again, or Mother, or the twins. . . .

Calvin rose to his feet. He bowed to the beasts as though they could see him. He said, "How do you do, sir—ma'am—?"

"Who are you?" the tallest of the beasts said. His voice was neither hostile nor welcoming, and it came not from the mouthlike indentation in the furry face, but from the waving tentacles.

—They'll eat us, Meg thought wildly. —They're making me hurt. My toes—my fingers—I hurt. . . .

Calvin answered the beast's question. "We're—we're from earth. I'm not sure how we got here. We've had an accident. Meg—this girl—is—is paralyzed. She can't move. She's terribly cold. We think that's why she can't move."

One of them came up to Meg and squatted down on its huge haunches beside her, and she felt utter loathing and <u>revulsion</u> as it reached out a tentacle to touch her face.

◀ Does the beast seem like a friend or an enemy? What makes you think so?

But with the tentacle came the same delicate fragrance that moved across her with the breeze, and she felt a soft, tingling warmth go all through her that momentarily <u>assuaged</u> her pain. She felt suddenly sleepy.

I must look as strange to it as it looks to me, she thought drowsily and then realized with a shock that of course the beast couldn't see her at all. Nevertheless a reassuring sense of safety flowed through her with the warmth which continued to seep deep into her as the beast touched her. Then it picked her up, cradling her in two of its four arms.

Mr. Murry stood up quickly. "What are you doing?"

"Taking the child."

---

words for everyday use

as • suage (ə swāj´) v., lessen; relieve. *Beryl's reassurances <u>assuaged</u> Adrian's fear.*

Respond to the Selection

Imagine that you are Calvin. How do you feel about the adventure up to this point? Are you happy to be part of it, or do you wish that you had never run into Meg and Charles Wallace? What do you think of the way Meg behaves when she comes out of her frozen state?

Investigate, Inquire, and Imagine

Recall: GATHERING FACTS

1a. What did Meg think would happen when she found her father?

2a. What does Meg recite when she is brought to IT?

3a. Why had Mr. Murry been on Camazotz?

4a. What has made Meg so cold? Why are Mr. Murry and Calvin not suffering as Meg is?

Interpret: FINDING MEANING

1b. Why might Meg have had unrealistic expectations of her father?

2b. How do their thoughts keep Meg, Mr. Murry, and Calvin from being taken into IT?

3b. Do you think Mr. Murry will continue to work on the study of time and space travel if he returns to Earth? Why, or why not?

4b. Why is Meg beginning to give up hope?

Analyze: TAKING THINGS APART

5a. Meg screams at Charles Wallace, who is being spoken through by IT, "*Like* and *equal* are not the same thing at all!" Explain the difference between *like* and *equal*.

Synthesize: BRINGING THINGS TOGETHER

5b. Meg quotes from the Declaration of Independence in an attempt to fight IT. Why do you think she chose this particular quote? Reread the quote, and explain how the ideas in it compare to the ideas of IT.

Evaluate: MAKING JUDGMENTS

6a. Before she experiences IT, Meg complains that Mrs Whatsit, Mrs Who, and Mrs Which have betrayed them. Does she have good reason for feeling this way? Why do you think Mrs Whatsit, Mrs Who, and Mrs Which do not or cannot help the four earthlings? What might the author be saying about each person's responsibility to combat evil on his or her own?

Extend: CONNECTING IDEAS

→ 6b. Think of a time when you had to do something very difficult by yourself. Did you have any support from others? How did you feel about facing this challenge? How did you feel when you were done? If you cannot think of a good example, write instead of a time when you felt your parent or another adult let you down.

Understanding Literature

DIALOGUE. **Dialogue** is conversation involving two or more people or characters. Examine the dialogue between Calvin and Mr. Murry in chapter 10. What information is revealed by this dialogue? What questions does this dialogue answer for the reader? What do you think Mr. Murry was about to say when he heard Meg make a sound?

SUSPENSE. **Suspense** is a feeling of anxiousness or curiosity. Writers create suspense by raising questions in the reader's mind and by using details that create strong emotions. The end of chapter 10 is suspenseful because the creature is leaving with Meg. What feelings do the humans have toward the creatures they see? What do the humans think might happen when the creature picks up Meg? What do you think will happen to Meg?

Chapter 11

Aunt Beast

"No!" Mr. Murry said sharply. "Please put her down."

A sense of amusement seemed to emanate from the beasts. The tallest, who seemed to be the spokesman, said, "We frighten you?"

"What are you going to do with us?" Mr. Murry asked.

The beast said, "I'm sorry, we communicate better with the other one." He turned toward Calvin. "Who are you?"

"I'm Calvin O'Keefe."

"What's that?"

"I'm a boy. A—a young man."

"You, too, are afraid?"

"I'm—not sure."

"Tell me," the beast said. "What do you suppose you'd do if three of *us* suddenly arrived on your home planet."

"Shoot you, I guess," Calvin admitted.

"Then isn't that what we should do with you?"

Calvin's freckles seemed to deepen, but he answered quietly. "I'd really rather you didn't. I mean, the earth's my home, and I'd rather be there than anywhere in the world—I mean, the universe— and I can't wait to get back, but we make some awful bloopers there."

The smallest beast, the one holding Meg, said, "And perhaps they aren't used to visitors from other planets."

"Used to it!" Calvin exclaimed. "We've never had any, as far as I know."

"Why?"

"I don't know."

The middle beast, a tremor of <u>trepidation</u> in his words, said, "You aren't from a dark planet, are you?"

◀ What does Calvin say he would do to the beasts if they landed on his planet? What does the beast ask Calvin in return?

words for everyday use

trep • i • da • tion (trep´ə dā´shən) n., anxiety; fear. *Farley entered the dark room with <u>trepidation</u>, uncertain of what he would find there.*

"No." Calvin shook his head firmly, though the beast couldn't see him. "We're—we're shadowed. But we're fighting the shadow."

The beast holding Meg questioned, "You three are fighting?"

"Yes," Calvin answered. "Now that we know about it."

The tall one turned back to Mr. Murry, speaking sternly. "You. The oldest. Man. From where have you come? Now."

Mr. Murry answered steadily. "From a planet called Camazotz." There was a mutter from the three beasts. "We do not belong there," Mr. Murry said, slowly and distinctly. "We were strangers there as we are here. I was a prisoner there, and these children rescued me. My youngest son, my baby, is still there, trapped in the dark mind of IT."

Meg tried to twist around in the beast's arms to glare at her father and Calvin. Why were they being so frank? Weren't they aware of the danger? But again her anger dissolved as the gentle warmth from the tentacles flowed through her. She realized that she could move her fingers and toes with comparative freedom, and the pain was no longer so <u>acute</u>.

"We must take this child back with us," the beast holding her said.

Meg shouted at her father. "Don't leave me the way you left Charles!" With this burst of terror a spasm of pain wracked her body and she gasped.

"Stop fighting," the beast told her. "You make it worse. Relax."

"That's what IT said," Meg cried. "Father! Calvin! Help!"

The beast turned toward Calvin and Mr. Murry. "This child is in danger. You must trust us."

"We have no alternative," Mr. Murry said. "Can you save her?"

"I think so."

words for everyday use

a • cute (ə kyüt´) adj., sharp; severe. *Kyra went to the doctor because she was experiencing* <u>*acute*</u> *pain in her abdomen.*

"May I stay with her?"

"No. But you will not be far away. We feel that you are hungry, tired, that you would like to bathe and rest. And this little—what is the word?" the beast cocked its tentacles at Calvin.

"Girl," Calvin said.

"This little girl needs prompt and special care. The coldness of the—what is it you call it?"

◀ What is wrong with Meg?

"The Black Thing?"

"The Black Thing. Yes. The Black Thing burns unless it is <u>counteracted</u> properly." The three beasts stood around Meg, and it seemed that they were feeling into her with their softly waving tentacles. The movement of the tentacles was as rhythmic and flowing as the dance of an undersea plant, and lying there, cradled in the four strange arms, Meg, despite herself, felt a sense of security that was deeper than anything she had known since the days when she lay in her mother's arms in the old rocking chair and was sung to sleep. With her father's help she had been able to resist IT. Now she could hold out no longer. She leaned her head against the beast's chest, and realized that the gray body was covered with the softest, most delicate fur imaginable, and the fur had the same beautiful odor as the air.

◀ How does Meg feel while in the beast's arms?

I hope I don't smell awful to it, she thought. But then she knew with a deep sense of comfort that even if she did smell awful the beasts would forgive her. As the tall figure cradled her she could feel the frigid stiffness of her body relaxing against it. This bliss could not come to her from a thing like IT. IT could only give pain, never relieve it. The beasts must be good. They had to be good. She sighed deeply, like a very small child, and suddenly she was asleep.

When she came to herself again there was in the back of her mind a memory of pain, of agonizing pain. But the pain was over now and her body was lapped in comfort. She was lying on something wonderfully

words for everyday use

coun • ter • act (kount′ər akt′) v., act directly against. *The antidote <u>counteracted</u> the poison.*

soft in an enclosed chamber. It was dark. All she could see were occasional tall moving shadows which she realized were beasts walking about. She had been stripped of her clothes, and something warm and pungent was gently being rubbed into her body. She sighed and stretched and discovered that she *could* stretch. She could move again, she was no longer paralyzed, and her body was bathed in waves of warmth. Her father had not saved her; the beasts had.

"So you are awake, little one?" The words came gently to her ears. "What a funny little tadpole you are! Is the pain gone now?"

"All gone."

"Are you warm and alive again?"

"Yes, I'm fine." She struggled to sit up.

"No, lie still, small one. You must not exert yourself as yet. We will have a fur garment for you in a moment, and then we will feed you. You must not even try to feed yourself. You must be as an infant again. The Black Thing does not relinquish its victims willingly."

"Where are Father and Calvin? Have they gone back for Charles Wallace?"

"They are eating and resting," the beast said, "and we are trying to learn about each other and see what is best to help you. We feel now that you are not dangerous, and that we will be allowed to help you."

"Why is it so dark in here?" Meg asked. She tried to look around, but all she could see was shadows. Nevertheless there was a sense of openness, a feel of a gentle breeze moving lightly about, that kept the darkness from being oppressive.

Perplexity came to her from the beast. "What is this dark? What is this light? We do not understand. Your father and the boy, Calvin, have asked this, too. They say that it is night now on our planet, and that they cannot see. They have told us that our atmosphere is what they call opaque, so that the stars are not visible,

words for everyday use

per • plex • i • ty (pər pleks´ə tē) *n.*, bewilderment; confusion. *The teacher's explanation cleared the perplexity from Luke's mind.*

o • paque (ō pāk´) *adj.*, not transparent: blocking out light. *The opaque curtains kept out the sunlight.*

and then they were surprised that we know stars, that we know their music and the movements of their dance far better than beings like you who spend hours studying them through what you call telescopes. We do not understand what this means, to *see.*"

"Well, it's what things look like," Meg said helplessly.

"We do not know what things *look* like, as you say," the beast said. "We know what things *are* like. It must be a very limiting thing, this seeing."

"Oh, no!" Meg cried. "It's—it's the most wonderful thing in the world!"

"What a very strange world yours must be!" the beast said, "that such a peculiar-seeming thing should be of such importance. Try to tell me, what is this thing called *light* that you are able to do so little without?"

"Well, we can't see without it," Meg said, realizing that she was completely unable to explain vision and light and dark. How can you explain sight on a world where no one has ever seen and where there is no need of eyes? "Well, on this planet," she fumbled, "you have a sun, don't you?"

◀ What does Meg realize she can't explain?

"A most wonderful sun, from which comes our warmth, and the rays which give us our flowers, our food, our music, and all the things which make life and growth."

"Well," Meg said, "when we are turned toward the sun—our earth, our planet, I mean, toward our sun— we receive its light. And when we're turned away from it, it is night. And if we want to see we have to use artificial lights."

"Artificial lights," the beast sighed. "How very complicated life on your planet must be. Later on you must try to explain some more to me."

"All right," Meg promised, and yet she knew that to try to explain anything that could be seen with the eyes would be impossible, because the beasts in some way saw, knew, understood, far more completely than she, or her parents, or Calvin, or even Charles Wallace.

◀ What does Meg realize about the beasts?

"Charles Wallace!" she cried. "What are they doing about Charles Wallace? We don't know what IT's

doing to him or making him do. Please, oh, please, help us!"

"Yes, yes, little one, of course we will help you. A meeting is in session right now to study what is best to do. We have never before been able to talk to anyone who has managed to escape from a dark planet, so although your father is blaming himself for everything that has happened, we feel that he must be quite an extraordinary person to get out of Camazotz with you at all. But the little boy, and I understand that he is a very special, a very important little boy—ah, my child, you must accept that this will not be easy. To go *back* through the Black Thing, *back* to Camazotz—I don't know. I don't know."

"But Father left him!" Meg said. "He's got to bring him back! He can't just abandon Charles Wallace!"

The beast's communication suddenly became crisp. "Nobody said anything about abandoning anybody. That is not our way. But we know that just because we want something does not mean that we will get what we want, and we still do not know *what* to do. And we cannot allow you, in your present state, to do anything that would <u>jeopardize</u> us all. I can see that you wish your father to go rushing back to Camazotz, and you could probably make him do this, and then where would we be? No. No. You must wait until you are more calm. Now, my darling, here is a robe for you to keep you warm and comfortable." Meg felt herself being lifted again, and a soft, light garment was slipped about her. "Don't worry about your little brother." The tentacles' musical words were soft against her. "We would *never* leave him behind the shadow. But for now you must relax, you must be happy, you must get well."

The gentle words, the feeling that this beast would be able to love her no matter what she said or did, lapped Meg in warmth and peace. She felt a delicate

---

words for everyday use jeo • par • dize (jep´ ər dīz´) v., put at risk; endanger. *The fire <u>jeopardized</u> the lives of everyone in the building.*

touch of tentacle to her cheek, as tender as her mother's kiss.

"It is so long since my own small ones were grown and gone," the beast said. "You are so tiny and vulnerable. Now I will feed you. You must eat slowly and quietly. I know that you are half starved, that you have been without food far too long, but you must not rush things or you will not get well."

Something completely and indescribably and incredibly delicious was put to Meg's lips, and she swallowed gratefully. With each swallow she felt strength returning to her body, and she realized that she had had nothing to eat since the horrible fake turkey dinner on Camazotz which she had barely tasted. How long ago was her mother's stew? Time no longer had any meaning.

"How long does night last here?" she murmured sleepily. "It will be day again, won't it?"

"Hush," the beast said. "Eat, small one. During the coolness, which is now, we sleep. And, when you waken, there will be warmth again and many things to do. You must eat now, and sleep, and I will stay with you."

"What should I call you, please?" Meg asked.

"Well, now. First, try not to say any words for just a moment. Think within your own mind. Think of all the things you call people, different kinds of people."

▶ What words does the beast reject for a name and why?

While Meg thought, the beast murmured to her gently. "No, *mother* is a special, a one-name; and a father you have here. Not just friend, nor teacher, nor brother, nor sister. What is *acquaintance?* What a funny, hard word. Aunt. Maybe. Yes, perhaps that will do. And you think of such odd words about me. *Thing,* and *monster! Monster,* what a horrid sort of word. I really do not think I am a monster. *Beast.* That will do. *Aunt Beast.*"

"Aunt Beast," Meg murmured sleepily, and laughed.

"Have I said something funny?" Aunt Beast asked in surprise. "Isn't Aunt Beast all right?"

"Aunt Beast is lovely," Meg said. "Please sing to me, Aunt Beast."

If it was impossible to describe sight to Aunt Beast, it would be even more impossible to describe the singing of Aunt Beast to a human being. It was a music even more glorious than the music of the singing creatures on Uriel. It was a music more tangible than form or sight. It had essence and structure. It supported Meg more firmly than the arms of Aunt Beast. It seemed to travel with her, to sweep her aloft in the power of song, so that she was moving in glory among the stars, and for a moment she, too, felt that the words Darkness and Light had no meaning, and only this melody was real.

◀ What qualities of Aunt Beast's song make it so comforting to Meg?

Meg did not know when she fell asleep within the body of the music. When she wakened Aunt Beast was asleep, too, the softness of her furry, faceless head drooping. Night had gone and a dull gray light filled the room. But she realized now that here on this planet there was no need for color, that the grays and browns merging into each other were not what the beasts knew, and that what she, herself, saw was only the smallest fraction of what the planet was really like. It was she who was limited by her senses, not the blind beasts, for they must have senses of which she could not even dream.

◀ What does Meg realize about her senses as compared to those of the beasts?

She stirred slightly, and Aunt Beast bent over her immediately. "What a lovely sleep, my darling. Do you feel all right?"

"I feel wonderful," Meg said. "Aunt Beast, what is this planet called?"

"Oh, dear," Aunt Beast sighed. "I find it not easy at all to put things the way your mind shapes them. You call where you came from Camazotz?"

"Well, it's where we came from, but it's not our planet."

"You can call us Ixchel, I guess," Aunt Beast told her. "We share the same sun as lost Camazotz, but that, give thanks, is all we share."

"Are you fighting the Black Thing?" Meg asked.

"Oh, yes," Aunt Beast replied. "In doing that we can never relax. We are the called according to His purpose, and whom He calls, them He also justifies. Of course we have help, and without help it would be much more difficult."

"Who helps you?" Meg asked.

"Oh, dear, it is so difficult to explain things to you, small one. And I know now that it is not just because you are a child. The other two are as hard to reach into as you are. What can I tell you that will mean anything to you? Good helps us, the stars help us, perhaps what you would call *light* helps us, love helps us. Oh, my child, I cannot explain! This is something you just have to know or not know."

"But—"

"We look not at the things which are what you would call seen, but at the things which are not seen. For the things which are seen are <u>temporal</u>. But the things which are not seen are <u>eternal</u>."[1]

"Aunt Beast, do you know Mrs Whatsit?" Meg asked with a sudden flooding of hope.

"Mrs Whatsit?" Aunt Beast was puzzled. "Oh, child, your language is so utterly simple and limited that it has the effect of extreme complication." Her four arms, tentacles waving, were outflung in a gesture of helplessness. "Would you like me to take you to your father and your Calvin?"

"Oh, yes, please!"

"Let us go, then. They are waiting for you to make plans. And we thought you would enjoy eating— what is it you call it? oh, yes, breakfast—together. You will be too warm in that heavy fur, now. I will dress you in something lighter, and then we will go."

As though Meg were a baby, Aunt Beast bathed and dressed her, and this new garment, though it was made of a pale fur, was lighter than the lightest summer clothes on earth. Aunt Beast put one tentacled arm about Meg's waist and led her through long, dim corridors in which she could see only shadows, and shadows of shadows, until they reached a large, columned chamber. Shafts of light came in from an open skylight and <u>converged</u> about a huge, round, stone table. Here were seated several of the great beasts, and Calvin and Mr. Murry, on a stone bench that circled the table. Because the beasts were so tall, even Mr. Murry's feet

▶ What does Aunt Beast say about human language?

---

1. **For the things . . . eternal.** Quotation from the Bible, II Corinthians 4:18

words for everyday use

tem • po • ral (tem´pə rəl) *adj.*, temporary; lasting only for a short time. *When Mr. Schmidt died, Helena began to consider the <u>temporal</u> nature of life.*

e • ter • nal (ē tər´nəl) *adj.*, going on forever; timeless. *Romeo pledged <u>eternal</u> love to Juliet.*

con • verge (kən vərj´) *v.*, come together. *Five roads <u>converge</u> at the center of Mills Crossing.*

did not touch the ground, and lanky Calvin's long legs dangled as though he were Charles Wallace. The hall was partially enclosed by <u>vaulted</u> arches leading to long, paved walks. There were no empty walls, no covering roofs, so that although the light was dull in comparison to earth's sunlight, Meg had no feeling of dark or of chill. As Aunt Beast led Meg in, Mr. Murry slid down from the bench and hurried to her, putting his arms about her tenderly.

"They promised us you were all right," he said.

While she had been in Aunt Beast's arms Meg had felt safe and secure. Now her worries about Charles Wallace and her disappointment in her father's human fallibility rose like gorge in her throat.

◄ Why is Meg disappointed in her father?

"I'm fine," she muttered, looking not at Calvin or her father, but at the beasts, for it was to them she turned now for help. It seemed to her that neither her father nor Calvin were properly concerned about Charles Wallace.

"Meg!" Calvin said gaily. "You've never tasted such food in your life! Come and eat!"

Aunt Beast lifted Meg up onto the bench and sat down beside her, then heaped a plate with food, strange fruits and breads that tasted unlike anything Meg had ever eaten. Everything was dull and colorless and unappetizing to look at, and at first, even remembering the meal Aunt Beast had fed her the night before, Meg hesitated to taste, but once she had managed the first bite she ate eagerly; it seemed that she would never have her fill again.

The others waited until she slowed down. Then Mr. Murry said gravely, "We were trying to work out a plan to rescue Charles Wallace. Since I made such a mistake in tessering away from IT, we feel that it would not be wise for me to try to get back to Camazotz, even alone. If I missed the mark again I could easily get lost and wander forever from galaxy to galaxy, and that would be small help to anyone, least of all to Charles Wallace."

words
for
everyday
use

vault • ed (vól´tid) *adj.,* arched. *The music rose high into the <u>vaulted</u> ceiling.*

Such a wave of <u>despondency</u> came over Meg that she was no longer able to eat.

"Our friends here," he continued, "feel that it was only the fact that I still wore the glasses your Mrs Who gave you that kept me within this solar system. Here are the glasses, Meg. But I am afraid that the virtue has gone from them and now they are only glass. Perhaps they were meant to help only once and only on Camazotz. Perhaps it was going through the Black Thing that did it." He pushed the glasses across the table at her.

"These people know about tessering," Calvin gestured at the circle of great beasts, "but they can't do it onto a dark planet."

"Have you tried to call Mrs Whatsit?" Meg asked.

"Not yet," her father answered.

▶ Why does Aunt Beast speak to Meg in a scolding way?

"But if you haven't thought of anything else, it's the *only* thing to do! Father, don't you care about Charles at all!"

At that Aunt Beast stood up, saying, "Child," in a reproving way. Mr. Murry said nothing, and Meg could see that she had wounded him deeply. She reacted as she would have reacted to Mr. Jenkins. She scowled down at the table, saying, "We've *got* to ask them for help now. You're just stupid if you think we don't."

▶ In what way does Aunt Beast explain Meg's rude behavior?

Aunt Beast spoke to the others. "The child is <u>distraught</u>. Don't judge her harshly. She was almost taken by the Black Thing. Sometimes we can't know what spiritual damage it leaves even when physical recovery is complete."

Meg looked angrily around the table. The beasts sat there, silent, motionless. She felt that she was being measured and found wanting.

Calvin swung away from her and hunched himself up. "Hasn't it occurred to you that we've been trying to tell them about our ladies? What do you think we've been up to all this time? Just stuffing our faces? Okay, you have a shot at it."

---

words for everyday use

de • spond • en • cy (di spän′ dən sē) *n.*, loss of hope. *Martina's last hope died out and <u>despondency</u> set in.*

dis • traught (di strót′) *adj.*, extremely troubled. *Rachel was <u>distraught</u> when she heard that Marcel was missing.*

"Yes. Try, child." Aunt Beast seated herself again, and pulled Meg up beside her. "But I do not understand this feeling of anger I sense in you. What is it about? There is blame going on, and guilt. Why?"

"Aunt Beast, don't you know?"

"No," Aunt Beast said. "But this is not telling me about—whoever they are you want us to know. Try."

Meg tried. Blunderingly. Fumblingly. At first she described Mrs Whatsit and her man's coat and multicolored shawls and scarves. Mrs Who and her white robes and shimmering spectacles, Mrs Which in her peaked cap and black gown quivering in and out of body. Then she realized that this was absurd. She was describing them only to herself. This wasn't Mrs Whatsit or Mrs Who or Mrs Which. She might as well have described Mrs Whatsit as she was when she took on the form of a flying creature of Uriel.

"Don't try to use words," Aunt Beast said soothingly. "You're just fighting yourself and me. Think about what they *are*. This *look* doesn't help us at all."

Meg tried again, but she could not get a visual concept out of her mind. She tried to think of Mrs Whatsit explaining tessering. She tried to think of them in terms of mathematics. Every once in a while she thought she felt a flicker of understanding from Aunt Beast or one of the others, but most of the time all that emanated from them was gentle puzzlement.

"Angels!" Calvin shouted suddenly from across the table. "Guardian angels!" There was a moment's silence, and he shouted again, his face tense with concentration, "Messengers! Messengers of God!"

"I thought for a moment—" Aunt Beast started, then subsided, sighing. "No. It's not clear enough."

"How strange it is that they can't tell us what they themselves seem to know," a tall, thin beast murmured.

One of Aunt Beast's tentacled arms went around Meg's waist again. "They are very young. And on their earth, as they call it, they never communicate with other planets. They revolve about all alone in space."

"Oh," the thin beast said. "Aren't they *lonely?*"

Suddenly a thundering voice reverberated throughout the great hall:

"WWEEE ARRE HHERRE!"

◀ What kinds of blame and guilt might Meg be experiencing?

◀ Is it more important to know what things look *like*, or what they are *like?*

◀ Why do the beasts think that Earth must be lonely?

Chapter 12

The Foolish and the Weak

Meg could see nothing, but she felt her heart pounding with hope. With one accord all the beasts rose to their feet, turned toward one of the arched openings, and bowed their heads and tentacles in greeting. Mrs Whatsit appeared, standing between two columns. Beside her came Mrs Who, behind them a quivering of light. The three of them were somehow not quite the same as they had been when Meg had first seen them. Their outlines seemed blurred; colors ran together as in a wet water color painting. But they were there; they were recognizable; they were themselves.

Meg pulled herself away from Aunt Beast, jumped to the floor, and rushed at Mrs Whatsit. But Mrs Whatsit held up a warning hand and Meg realized that she was not completely materialized, that she was light and not substance, and embracing her now would have been like trying to hug a sunbeam.

"We had to hurry so there wasn't quite time. . . . You wanted us?" Mrs Whatsit asked.

The tallest of the beasts bowed again and took a step away from the table and towards Mrs Whatsit. "It is a question of the little boy."

"Father left him!" Meg cried. "He left him on Camazotz!"

<u>Appallingly</u>, Mrs Whatsit's voice was cold. "And what do you expect us to do?"

Meg pressed her knuckles against her teeth so that her braces cut her skin. Then she flung out her arms pleadingly. "But it's Charles Wallace! IT has him, Mrs Whatsit! Save him, please save him!"

"You know that we can do nothing on Camazotz," Mrs Whatsit said, her voice still cold.

---

words for everyday use   ap • pal • ling • ly (ə pôl´iŋ lē) *adv.*, shockingly. *We thought that we had enough food to weather the storm, but the cupboards were <u>appallingly</u> empty.*

"You mean you'll let Charles be caught by IT forever?" Meg's voice rose shrilly.

"Did I say that?"

"But we can't do anything! You know we can't! We tried! Mrs Whatsit, you have to save him!"

"Meg, this is not our way," Mrs Whatsit said sadly. "I thought you would know that this is not our way."

Mr. Murry took a step forward and bowed, and to Meg's amazement the three ladies bowed back to him. "I don't believe we've been introduced," Mrs Whatsit said.

"It's Father, you know it's Father," Meg's angry impatience grew. "Father—Mrs Whatsit, Mrs Who, and Mrs Which."

"I'm very glad to—" Mr. Murry mumbled, then went on, "I'm sorry, my glasses are broken, and I can't see you very well."

"It's not necessary to see us," Mrs Whatsit said.

"If you could teach me enough more about the tesseract so that I could get back to Camazotz—"

"Wwhatt tthenn?" came Mrs Which's surprising voice.

"I will try to take my child away from IT."

"Annd yyou kknoww tthatt yyou wwill nnott ssucceeedd?"

"There's nothing left except to try."

Mrs Whatsit spoke gently. "I'm sorry. We cannot allow you to go."

"Then let me," Calvin suggested. "I almost got him away before."

Mrs Whatsit shook her head. "No, Calvin. Charles has gone even deeper into IT. You will not be permitted to throw yourself in with him, for that, you must realize, is what would happen."

There was a long silence. All the soft rays filtering into the great hall seemed to concentrate on Mrs Whatsit, Mrs Who, and the faint light that must be Mrs Which. No one spoke. One of the beasts moved a tendril slowly back and forth across the stone table top. At last Meg could stand it no longer and she cried out despairingly, "Then what are you going to do? Are you just going to throw Charles away?"

◀ What won't the Mrs Ws do? Why?

◀ Why are Mr. Murry and Calvin not allowed to return to Camazotz?

Mrs Which's voice rolled formidably across the hall. "Ssilencce, cchilldd!"

But Meg could not be silent. She pressed closely against Aunt Beast, but Aunt Beast did not put the protecting tentacles around her. "*I* can't go!" Meg cried. "I can't! You know I can't!"

"Ddidd annybbodyy asskk yyou ttoo?" The grim voice made Meg's skin prickle into gooseflesh.

She burst into tears. She started beating at Aunt Beast like a small child having a tantrum. Her tears rained down her face and spattered Aunt Beast's fur. Aunt Beast stood quietly against the assault.

"All right, I'll go!" Meg sobbed. "I know you want me to go!"

"We want nothing from you that you do without grace," Mrs Whatsit said, "or that you do without understanding."

Meg's tears stopped as abruptly as they had started. "But I do understand." She felt tired and unexpectedly peaceful. Now the coldness that, under Aunt Beast's <u>ministrations</u>, had left her body had also left her mind. She looked toward her father and her confused anger was gone and she felt only love and pride. She smiled at him, asking forgiveness, and then pressed up against Aunt Beast. This time Aunt Beast's arm went around her.

Mrs Which's voice was grave. "Wwhatt ddoo yyou unndderrsstanndd?"

"That it has to be me. It can't be anyone else. I don't understand Charles, but he understands me. I'm the one who's closest to him. Father's been away for so long, since Charles Wallace was a baby. They don't know each other. And Calvin's only known Charles for such a little time. If it had been longer then he would have been the one, but—oh, I see, I see, I understand, it has to be me. There isn't anyone else."

▶ How does Meg feel about going back to Camazotz?

▶ Why must Meg return to Camazotz to save Charles?

---

words for everyday use

min • is • tra • tion (min′is trā′shən) *n.,* act of giving help or care. *The doctor's <u>ministrations</u> eased the pain of the patient.*

Mr. Murry, who had been sitting, his elbows on his knees, his chin on his fists, rose. "I will not allow it!"

"Wwhyy?" Mrs Which demanded.

"Look, I don't know what or who you are, and at this point I don't care. I will not allow my daughter to go alone into this danger."

"Wwhyy?"

"You know what the outcome will probably be! And she's weak, now, weaker than she was before. She was almost killed by the Black Thing. I fail to understand how you can even consider such a thing."

Calvin jumped down. "Maybe IT's right about you! Or maybe you're in league with IT. *I'm* the one to go if anybody goes! Why did you bring me along at all? To take care of Meg! You said so yourself!"

"But you have done that," Mrs Whatsit assured him.

"I haven't done anything!" Calvin shouted. "You can't send Meg! I won't allow it! I'll put my foot down! I won't permit it!"

"Don't you see that you're making something that is already hard for Meg even harder?" Mrs Whatsit asked him.

Aunt Beast turned tentacles toward Mrs Whatsit. "Is she strong enough to tesser again? You know what she has been through."

"If Which takes her she can manage," Mrs Whatsit said.

"If it will help I could go too, and hold her." Aunt Beast's arm around Meg tightened.

"Oh, Aunt Beast—" Meg started.

But Mrs Whatsit cut her off. "No."

"I was afraid not," Aunt Beast said humbly. "I just wanted you to know that I *would.*"

"Mrs—uh—Whatsit." Mr. Murry frowned and pushed his hair back from his face. Then he shoved with his middle finger at his nose as though he were trying to get spectacles closer to his eyes. "Are you remembering that she is only a child?"

"And she's backward," Calvin bellowed.

"I resent that," Meg said hotly, hoping that indignation would control her trembling. "I'm better than you at math and you know it."

◀ Why does Calvin accuse the Mrs Ws of being in league with IT? Do you think he really believes this?

"Do you have the courage to go alone?" Mrs Whatsit asked her.

Meg's voice was flat. "No. But it doesn't matter." She turned to her father and Calvin. "You know it's the only thing to do. You know they'd never send me alone if—"

"How do we know they're not in league with IT?" Mr. Murry demanded.

"Father!"

"No, Meg," Mrs Whatsit said. "I do not blame your father for being angry and suspicious and frightened. And I cannot pretend that we are doing anything but sending you into the gravest kind of danger. I have to acknowledge quite openly that it may be a fatal danger. I know this. But I do not believe it. And the Happy Medium doesn't believe it, either."

"Can't she see what's going to happen?" Calvin asked.

"Oh, not in this kind of thing." Mrs Whatsit sounded surprised at his question. "If we knew ahead of time what was going to happen we'd be— we'd be like the people on Camazotz, with no lives of our own, with everything all planned and done for us. How can I explain it to you? Oh, I know. In your language you have a form of poetry called the sonnet."[1]

"Yes, yes," Calvin said impatiently. "What's that got to do with the Happy Medium?"

"Kindly pay me the courtesy of listening to me." Mrs Whatsit's voice was stern, and for a moment Calvin stopped pawing the ground like a nervous colt. "It is a very strict form of poetry, is it not?"

"Yes."

"There are fourteen lines, I believe, all in iambic pentameter.[2] That's a very strict rhythm or meter, yes?"

▶ What is a sonnet?

---

1. **sonnet.** Fourteen-line poem, usually with a fixed rhyme scheme
2. **iambic pentameter.** Rhythmical pattern common in poetry; in an iambic pentameter poem, each line contains five iambs; each iamb consists of one strongly stressed and one weakly stressed syllable, as in the famous line by poet Christopher Marlowe: "Was this the face that launched a thousand ships . . . ?"

"Yes." Calvin nodded.

"And each line has to end with a rigid rhyme pattern. And if the poet does not do it exactly this way, it is not a sonnet, is it?"

"No."

"But within this strict form the poet has complete freedom to say whatever he wants, doesn't he?"

"Yes." Calvin nodded again.

"So," Mrs Whatsit said.

"So what?"

"Oh, do not be stupid, boy!" Mrs Whatsit scolded. "You know perfectly well what I am driving at!"

"You mean you're comparing our lives to a sonnet? A strict form, but freedom within it?"

◀ To what does Mrs Whatsit compare our lives? Why?

"Yes," Mrs Whatsit said. "You're given the form, but you have to write the sonnet yourself. What you say is completely up to you."

"Please," Meg said. "Please. If I've got to go I want to go and get it over with. Each minute you put it off makes it harder."

"Sshee iss rrightt," boomed Mrs Which's voice. "Itt iss ttime."

"You may say good-by." Mrs Whatsit was giving her not permission, but a command.

Meg curtsied clumsily to the beasts. "Thank you all. Very much. I know you saved my life." She did not add what she could not help thinking: Saved it for what? So that IT could get me?

She put her arms about Aunt Beast, pressed up against the soft, fragrant fur. "Thank you," she whispered. "I love you."

"And I, you, little one." Aunt Beast pressed gentle tendrils against Meg's face.

"Cal—" Meg said, holding out her hand.

Calvin came to her and took her hand, then drew her roughly to him and kissed her. He didn't say anything, and he turned away before he had a chance to see the surprised happiness that brightened Meg's eyes.

At last she turned to her father "I'm—I'm sorry, Father."

He took both her hands in his, bent down to her with his short-sighted eyes. "Sorry for what, Megatron?"

▶ For what does Meg apologize?

Tears almost came to her eyes at the gentle use of the old nickname. "I wanted you to do it all for me. I wanted everything to be all easy and simple. . . . So I tried to pretend that it was all your fault . . . because I was scared, and I didn't want to have to do anything myself—"

▶ What do parents want to do for their children? Why can't they do this?

"But I wanted to do it for you," Mr. Murry said. "That's what every parent wants." He looked into her dark, frightened eyes. "I won't let you go, Meg. I am going."

"No." Mrs Whatsit's voice was sterner than Meg had ever heard it. "You are going to allow Meg the privilege of accepting this danger. You are a wise man, Mr. Murry. You are going to let her go."

Mr. Murry sighed. He drew Meg close to him. "Little Megaparsec. Don't be afraid to be afraid. We will try to have courage for you. That is all we can do. Your mother—"

"Mother was always shoving me out in the world," Meg said. "She'd want me to do this. You know she would. Tell her—" she started, choked, then held up her head and said, "No. Never mind. I'll tell her myself."

"Good girl. Of course you will."

Now Meg walked slowly around the great table to where Mrs Whatsit was still poised between the columns. "Are you going with me?"

"No. Only Mrs Which."

"The Black Thing—" Fear made her voice tremble. "When Father tessered me through it, it almost got me."

"Your father is singularly inexperienced," Mrs Whatsit said, "though a fine man, and worth teaching. At the moment he still treats tessering as though he were working with a machine. We will not let the Black Thing get you. I don't think."

This was not exactly comforting.

The momentary vision and faith that had come to Meg dwindled. "But suppose I can't get Charles Wallace away from IT—"

"Stop." Mrs Whatsit held up her hand. "We gave you gifts the last time we took you to Camazotz. We will not let you go empty handed this time. But what we can give you now is nothing you can touch with your hands. I give you my love, Meg. Never forget that. My love always."

◀ What does Mrs Whatsit give to Meg?

Mrs Who, eyes shining behind spectacles, beamed at Meg. Meg felt in her blazer pocket and handed back the spectacles she had used on Camazotz.

"Your father is right," Mrs Who took the spectacles and hid them somewhere in the folds of her robes. "The virtue is gone from them. And what I have to give you this time you must try to understand not word by word, but in a flash, as you understand the tesseract. Listen, Meg. Listen well. *The foolishness of God is wiser than men; and the weakness of God is stronger than men. For ye see your calling, brethren, how that not many wise men after the flesh, not many mighty, not many noble, are called, but God hath chosen the fool-ish things of the world to <u>confound</u> the wise; and God hath chosen the weak things of the world to confound the things which are mighty. And base things of the world, and things which are despised, hath God chosen, yea, and things which are not, to bring to nought things that are."*[3]

◀ What does Mrs Who say about the foolish and the weak?

She paused, and then she said, "May the right pre-vail." Her spectacles seemed to flicker. Behind her, through her, one of the columns became visible. There was a final gleam from the glasses, and she was gone. Meg looked nervously to where Mrs Whatsit had been standing before Mrs Who spoke. But Mrs Whatsit was no longer there.

"No!" Mr. Murry cried, and stepped toward Meg.

Mrs Which's voice came through her shimmer. "I ccannnott hholldd yyourr hannddd, chilldd."

Immediately Meg was swept into darkness, into nothingness, and then into the icy devouring cold of the Black Thing. Mrs Which won't let it get me, she

---

3. *The foolishness of God. . . to nought things that are.* Quotation from the Bible, I Corinthians 1:25–28

---

words for everyday use
con • found (kən found´) v., confuse or bewilder. *The problem <u>confounded</u> the wisest and most innovative problem solvers.*

thought over and over while the cold of the Black Thing seemed to crunch at her bones.

Then they were through it, and she was standing breathlessly on her feet on the same hill on which they had first landed on Camazotz. She was cold and a little numb, but no worse than she had often been in the winter in the country when she had spent an afternoon skating on the pond. She looked around. She was completely alone. Her heart began to pound.

▶ What does Mrs Which give to Meg?

Then, seeming to echo from all around her, came Mrs Which's unforgettable voice. "I hhave nnott ggivenn yyou mmyy ggifftt. *Yyou hhave ssomethinngg thatt ITT hhass nnott. Thiss ssomethinngg iss yyourr onlly wweapponn. Bbutt yyou mmusstt ffinndd itt fforr yyourrssellff.*" Then the voice ceased, and Meg knew that she was alone.

She walked slowly down the hill, her heart thumping painfully against her ribs. There below her was the same row of identical houses they had seen before, and beyond these the linear buildings of the city. She walked along the quiet street. It was dark and the street was deserted. No children playing ball or skipping rope. No mother figures at the doors. No father figures returning from work. In the same window of each house was a light, and as Meg walked down the street all the lights were <u>extinguished</u> simultaneously. Was it because of her presence, or was it simply that it was time for lights out?

She felt numb, beyond rage or disappointment or even fear. She put one foot ahead of the other with precise regularity, not allowing her pace to lag. She was not thinking; she was not planning; she was simply walking slowly but steadily toward the city and the domed building where IT lay.

Now she approached the outlying buildings of the city. In each of them was a vertical line of light, but it was a dim, eerie light, not the warm light of stairways in cities at home. And there were no isolated

words for everyday use   ex • tin • guish (ek stiŋ´gwish) v., put out. *A gust of wind <u>extinguished</u> the candles.*

brightly lit windows where someone was working late, or an office was being cleaned. Out of each building came one man, perhaps a watchman, and each man started walking the width of the building. They appeared not to see her. At any rate they paid no attention to her whatsoever, and she went on past them.

What have I got that IT hasn't got? she thought suddenly. What have I possibly got?

Now she was walking by the tallest of the business buildings. More dim vertical lines of light. The walls glowed slightly to give a faint illumination to the streets. CENTRAL Central Intelligence was ahead of her. Was the man with red eyes still sitting there? Or was he allowed to go to bed? But this was not where she must go, though the man with red eyes seemed the kind old gentleman he claimed to be when compared with IT. But he was no longer of any consequence in the search for Charles Wallace. She must go directly to IT.

IT isn't used to being resisted. Father said that's how he managed, and how Calvin and I managed as long as we did. Father saved me then. There's nobody here to save me now. I have to do it myself. I have to resist IT by myself. Is that what I have that IT hasn't got? No, I'm sure IT can resist. IT just isn't used to having *other* people resist.

CENTRAL Central Intelligence blocked with its huge rectangle the end of the square. She turned to walk around it, and almost <u>imperceptibly</u> her steps slowed.

It was not far to the great dome which housed IT.

I'm going to Charles Wallace. That's what's important. That's what I have to think of. I wish I could feel numb again the way I did at first. Suppose IT has him somewhere else? Suppose he isn't there?

I have to go there first, anyhow. That's the only way I can find out.

---

words for everyday use   im • per • cep • ti • bly (im´pər sep´tə blē) *adv.,* slightly or gradually. *The snail moved imperceptibly across the floor.*

▶ What does Meg think of Mrs Who's and Mrs Whatsit's gifts?

Her steps got slower and slower as she passed the great bronzed doors, the huge slabs of the CENTRAL Central Intelligence building, as she finally saw ahead of her the strange, light, pulsing dome of IT.

Father said it was all right for me to be afraid. He said to go ahead and be afraid. And Mrs Who said—I don't understand what she said but I think it was meant to make me not hate being only me, and me being the way I am. And Mrs Whatsit said to remember that she loves me. That's what I have to think about. Not about being afraid. Or not as smart as IT. Mrs Whatsit loves me. That's quite something, to be loved by someone like Mrs Whatsit.

She was there.

No matter how slowly her feet had taken her at the end, they had taken her there.

Directly ahead of her was the circular building, its walls glowing with violet flame, its silvery roof pulsing with a light that seemed to Meg to be insane. Again she could feel the light, neither warm nor cold, but reaching out to touch her, pulling her toward IT.

There was a sudden sucking, and she was within.

It was as though the wind had been knocked out of her. She gasped for breath, for breath in her own rhythm, not the <u>permeating</u> pulsing of IT. She could feel the inexorable beat within her body, controlling her heart, her lungs.

But not herself. Not Meg. It did not quite have her.

She blinked her eyes rapidly and against the rhythm until the redness before them cleared and she could see. There was the brain, there was IT, lying pulsing and quivering on the dais, soft and exposed and nauseating. Charles Wallace was crouched beside IT, his eyes still slowly twirling, his jaw still slack, as she had seen him before, with a tic in his forehead <u>reiterating</u> the revolting rhythm of IT.

As she saw him it was again as though she had been punched in the stomach, for she had to realize

---

words for everyday use

per • me • at • ing (pər ́mē āt ́iŋ) *adj.*, penetrating. *The odor of the cooking fish was <u>permeating</u> the entire house, so we opened the windows.*

re • it • er • ate (rē it ́ə rāt ́) *v.*, repeat. *In case Vera had not heard, Glen <u>reiterated</u> that he did not want to go to the movies.*

afresh that she was seeing Charles, and yet it was not Charles at all. Where was Charles Wallace, her own beloved Charles Wallace?

What is it I have got that IT hasn't got?

"You have nothing that IT hasn't got," Charles Wallace said coldly. "How nice to have you back, dear sister. We have been waiting for you. We knew that Mrs Whatsit would send you. She is our friend, you know."

For an appalling moment Meg believed, and in that moment she felt her brain being gathered up into IT.

"No!" she screamed at the top of her lungs. "No! You lie!"

For a moment she was free from ITs clutches again.

As long as I can stay angry enough IT can't get me. Is that what I have that IT doesn't have?

"Nonsense," Charles Wallace said. "You have nothing that it doesn't have."

"You're lying," she replied, and she felt only anger toward this boy who was not Charles Wallace at all. No, it was not anger, it was loathing; it was hatred, sheer and <u>unadulterated</u>, and as she became lost in hatred she also began to be lost in IT. The red miasma swam before her eyes; her stomach churned in ITs rhythm. Her body trembled with the strength of her hatred and the strength of IT.

With the last <u>vestige</u> of consciousness she jerked her mind and body. Hate was nothing that IT didn't have. IT knew all about hate.

"You are lying about that, and you were lying about Mrs Whatsit!" she screamed.

"Mrs Whatsit hates you," Charles Wallace said.

And that was where IT made ITs fatal mistake, for as Meg said, automatically, "Mrs Whatsit loves me; that's what she told me, that she loves me," suddenly she knew.

She knew!

◀ What does Charles say about Mrs Whatsit?

◀ What happens when Meg thinks about her hatred for "this boy"?

◀ What was ITs fatal mistake? What does Meg realize?

---

words for everyday use

un • a • dul • ter • at • ed (un ə dul´tər āt id´) *adj.*, pure. *Clarence's <u>unadulterated</u> happiness was polluted by Martin's negative comments.*

ves • tige (ves´tij) *n.*, trace of something that once existed. *With her last <u>vestige</u> of strength, Paloma pulled herself onto the wide ledge.*

Love.

That was what she had that IT did not have.

She had Mrs Whatsit's love, and her father's, and her mother's, and the real Charles Wallace's love, and the twins', and Aunt Beast's.

And she had her love for them.

But how could she use it? What was she meant to do?

If she could give love to IT perhaps it would shrivel up and die, for she was sure that IT could not withstand love. But she, in all her weakness and foolishness and baseness and nothingness, was incapable of loving IT. Perhaps it was not too much to ask of her, but she could not do it.

But she could love Charles Wallace.

She could stand there and she could love Charles Wallace.

Her own Charles Wallace, the real Charles Wallace, the child for whom she had come back to Camazotz, to IT, the baby who was so much more than she was, and who was yet so utterly vulnerable.

She could love Charles Wallace.

Charles. Charles, I love you. My baby brother who always takes care of me. Come back to me, Charles Wallace, come away from IT, come back, come home. I love you, Charles. Oh, Charles Wallace, I love you.

Tears were streaming down her cheeks, but she was unaware of them.

Now she was even able to look at him, at this animated thing that was not her own Charles Wallace at all. She was able to look and love.

I love you. Charles Wallace, you are my darling and my dear and the light of my life and the treasure of my heart. I love you. I love you. I love you.

Slowly his mouth closed. Slowly his eyes stopped their twirling. The tic in the forehead ceased its revolting twitch. Slowly he advanced toward her.

"I love you!" she cried. "I love you, Charles! I love you!"

Then suddenly he was running, pelting, he was in her arms, he was shrieking with sobs. "Meg! Meg! Meg!"

"I love you, Charles!" she cried again, her sobs almost as loud as his, her tears mingling with his. "I love you! I love you! I love you!"

A whirl of darkness. An icy cold blast. An angry, resentful howl that seemed to tear through her. Darkness again. Through the darkness to save her came a sense of Mrs Whatsit's presence, so that she knew it could not be IT who now had her in its clutches.

And then the feel of earth beneath her, of something in her arms, and she was rolling over on the sweet smelling autumnal earth, and Charles Wallace was crying out, "Meg! Oh, Meg!"

Now she was hugging him close to her, and his little arms were clasped tightly about her neck. "Meg, you saved me! You saved me!" he said over and over.

"Meg!" came a call, and there were her father and Calvin hurrying through the darkness toward them.

Still holding Charles she struggled to stand up and look around. "Father! Cal! Where are we?"

◀ Where do Charles and Meg find themselves?

Charles Wallace, holding her hand tightly, was looking around, too, and suddenly he laughed, his own, sweet, contagious laugh. "In the twins' vegetable garden! And we landed in the broccoli!"

Meg began to laugh, too, at the same time that she was trying to hug her father, to hug Calvin, and not to let go of Charles Wallace for one second.

"Meg, you did it!" Calvin shouted. "You saved Charles!"

"I'm very proud of you, my daughter." Mr. Murry kissed her gravely, then turned toward the house. "Now I must go in to Mother." Meg could tell that he was trying to control his anxiety and eagerness.

"Look!" she pointed to the house, and there were the twins and Mrs. Murry walking toward them through the long, wet grass.

"First thing tomorrow I must get some new glasses," Mr. Murry said, squinting in the moonlight, and then starting to run toward his wife.

Dennys's voice came crossly over the lawn. "Hey, Meg, it's bedtime."

Sandy suddenly yelled, "Father!"

Mr. Murry was running across the lawn, Mrs. Murry running toward him, and they were in each other's arms, and then there was a tremendous happy jumble of arms and legs and hugging, the older Murrys and Meg and Charles Wallace and the twins, and Calvin grinning by them until Meg reached out and pulled him in and Mrs. Murry gave him a special hug all of his own. They were talking and laughing all at once, when they were startled by a crash, and Fortinbras, who could bear being left out of the happiness not one second longer, catapulted his sleek black body right through the screened door to the kitchen. He dashed across the lawn to join in the joy, and almost knocked them all over with the exuberance of his greeting.

▶ How can Meg tell Mrs Whatsit, Mrs Who, and Mrs Which are near?

Meg knew all at once that Mrs Whatsit, Mrs Who, and Mrs Which must be near, because all through her she felt a flooding of joy and of love that was even greater and deeper than the joy and love which were already there.

She stopped laughing and listened, and Charles listened, too. "Hush."

Then there was a whirring, and Mrs Whatsit, Mrs Who, and Mrs Which were standing in front of them, and the joy and love were so tangible that Meg felt that if she only knew where to reach she could touch it with her bare hands.

Mrs Whatsit said breathlessly, "Oh, my darlings, I'm sorry we don't have time to say good-by to you properly. You see, we have too—"

But they never learned what it was that Mrs Whatsit, Mrs Who, and Mrs Which had to do, for there was a gust of wind, and they were gone.

words for everyday use

cat • a • pult (kat´ə pult´) v., launch; hurl. *With the surprising success of her first movie, the young actor catapulted to stardom.*

ex • u • ber • ance (eg zü´bər əns) n., great liveliness and joy. *The older horse could not match the exuberance of the young colt, who galloped and frolicked all afternoon in the pasture.*

Respond to the Selection

Mrs Whatsit, Mrs Who, and Mrs Which come back briefly, but they do not have time to say goodbye properly. They only have time for Mrs Whatsit to say, "You see, we have too—." What do you think they are off to do? What planets and beings might they visit next?

Investigate, Inquire, and Imagine

Recall: GATHERING FACTS

1a. What does Calvin say humans would probably do if beings from another planet landed on Earth?

2a. What does Meg think at first is the only course of action to save Charles Wallace?

3a. What three gifts is Meg given for her return to Camazotz?

Interpret: FINDING MEANING

1b. Why do you think the beasts have a different reaction than humans would have?

2b. Why do Meg and Calvin have difficulty describing Mrs Whatsit, Mrs Who, and Mrs Which to beings on Ixchel? What does Mrs Whatsit mean when she says, "[T]his is not our way"?

3b. In what way do the gifts of Mrs Whatsit and Mrs Which work together to help Meg save Charles Wallace from IT?

Analyze: TAKING THINGS APART

4a. Compare Meg's expectations of Mrs Whatsit to her expectations of her father. Why is Meg the one who must save Charles Wallace? Why won't the three Mrs Ws help her do this?

Synthesize: BRINGING THINGS TOGETHER

4b. What has Meg learned from her fantastic journey? How has she changed?

Evaluate: MAKING JUDGMENTS

5a. The creatures on Ixchel do not have the ability to see; instead, they use their tentacles to sense things around them. Evaluate the creatures' attitudes and decide whether their lack of sight is a handicap or an advantage. Use evidence from chapter 11 to support your answer.

Extend: CONNECTING IDEAS

➤ 5b. One of the themes of *A Wrinkle in Time* is that appearance is often different from reality. Give examples of appearance being different from reality on Ixchel. What might human beings learn from the beings on Ixchel?

Understanding Literature

ANALOGY. An **analogy** is a comparison of things that are alike in some ways but different in others. Mrs Whatsit uses an analogy to help Calvin understand why the Happy Medium is unable to foresee the future. What two things does she compare? In what ways are the two things similar?

CENTRAL CONFLICT AND RESOLUTION. A **central conflict** is the main problem or struggle in the plot of a poem, story, or play. The **resolution** is the point in a poem, story, or lay in which the central conflict, or struggle, is ended. What is the central conflict of *A Wrinkle in Time?* What event resolves, or ends, the central conflict?

Plot Analysis of
A Wrinkle in Time

A **plot** is a series of events related to a central conflict, or struggle. The following diagram illustrates the main plot of *A Wrinkle in Time*.

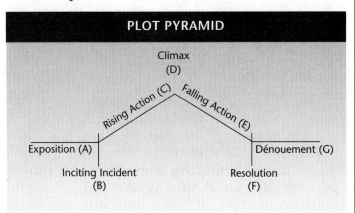

PLOT PYRAMID

Climax (D)

Rising Action (C)

Falling Action (E)

Exposition (A)

Inciting Incident (B)

Resolution (F)

Dénouement (G)

The parts of a plot are as follows. (Note, however, that plots rarely contain all these elements in precisely this order.)

The **exposition** is the part of a plot that provides background information about the characters, setting, or conflict.

The **inciting incident** is the event that introduces the central conflict.

The **rising action,** or complication, develops the conflict to a high point of intensity.

The **climax** is the high point of interest or suspense in the plot.

The **crisis,** or turning point, often the same event as the climax, is the point in the plot where something decisive happens to determine the future course of events and the eventual working out of the conflict.

The **falling action** is all the events that follow the climax.

The **resolution** is the point at which the central conflict is ended, or resolved.

The **dénouement** is any material that follows the resolution and that ties up loose ends.

Exposition (A)

The first two chapters of *A Wrinkle in Time* can be considered the exposition. They introduce the Murry family and the town in which they live, and give some background information. The reader learns that Meg's father, Mr. Murry, has disappeared; that Meg has trouble fitting in at school and thinks she is ugly; and that Charles Wallace is an exceptional boy with some special abilities.

Inciting Incident (B)

The inciting incident is the appearance of Mrs Whatsit, who enters the Murry home in the middle of a stormy night. She casually mentions that "there is such a thing as a tesseract," a remark that reveals she may know something about Mr. Murry's disappearance. Her arrival hints at what will become the central conflict of the story: the battle against the evil forces that hold Mr. Murry captive.

Rising Action (C)

The rising action includes everything that happens after the inciting incident up until chapter nine. The characters of Mrs Who, Calvin, and Mrs Which are introduced and the group travels to Uriel, where Mrs Whatsit transforms into a centaur-like creature and shows them the Dark Thing. Then they travel briefly to a two-dimensional planet and from there, visit the Happy Medium, who shows them through her crystal ball that Earth is being menaced by the Dark Thing. Finally, they go to Camazotz, a planet that has already been taken over by the Dark Thing. There, they meet the Man with the Red Eyes, who hypnotizes Charles Wallace. They free Meg's father, who has been imprisoned by IT; then they go to confront IT. When IT threatens to brainwash Meg, Meg's father is forced to tesser himself, Calvin, and Meg away from Camazotz. They land on the planet Ixchel. Meg is frozen; Aunt Beast nurses her back to health. When Meg is finally recovered she calls upon the three Mrs Ws, who help Meg understand that she must go back to Camazotz to save Charles Wallace.

Climax (D)

The climax occurs in the final chapter, when Meg returns to Camazotz alone to rescue Charles Wallace from IT. As Meg confronts the brainwashed Charles Wallace, she feels hate for him—and in doing so, she too begins to be lost in IT's power. Then suddenly, she realizes that the weapon she needs to use is love. She channels all her love into Charles Wallace.

Falling Action (E)

Slowly, Charles Wallace comes out of his robotic state as IT loses power over him. He runs into Meg's arms, and they both shout "I love you!" The two of them are whisked away in a whirl of darkness.

Resolution (F)

The group lands in the twins' vegetable garden, safely at home and free from IT at last. Charles Wallace hugs Meg, crying out "You saved me! You saved me!" Calvin and Mr. Murry congratulate Meg.

Dénouement (G)

The twins and Mrs. Murry come outside looking for Meg—and discover to their amazement that Mr. Murry has returned. The entire family is joyfully reunited. The three Mrs Ws appear briefly to say goodbye, then go off on their way to new adventures.

The Booklist Interview: Madeleine L'Engle

ABOUT THE RELATED READING

The following is an interview with Madeleine L'Engle that was published in *Booklist* magazine in 1998. That year, L'Engle won the Margaret Edwards Award, a prize given by the American Library Association for lifetime achievement in the field of young adult literature. She talked to interviewer Sally Estes about science fiction and fantasy writing and answered questions about some of the books in her Time Quartet, which includes *A Wrinkle in Time* (1962), *A Wind in the Door* (1973), *A Swiftly Tilting Planet* (1978), and *Many Waters* (1986).

BOOKLIST: *First, I'd like to congratulate you on winning the Margaret Edwards Award.*
L'ENGLE: Obviously, I am very thrilled.

BKL: *. . . I'd like to focus on [the science fiction and fantasy works you've written,] in particular your time-travel trilogy, which isn't actually a trilogy anymore since you've connected it up with other series and added* Many Waters. *Let's start with the classic* A Wrinkle in Time. *I understand that it was turned down by more than 20 publishing houses.*
L'ENGLE: Oh, heavens, many more than 20. It barely got published.

BKL: *Now it has become a children's classic. Would you have thought 35 years ago that all of this would have happened to that little book?*
L'ENGLE: No, I wouldn't. I called it back and said, "Let's just quit."

BKL: *Did you submit the same manuscript each time?*
L'ENGLE: Yes, I submitted the same manuscript. I mean, I thought it was good.

▶ *What is to happen to the grenadier and light infantry companies?*

BKL: *There must be quite a few publishers out there today who wish somebody on their staffs could have recognized that, too.*

L'ENGLE: They thought it was too hard for kids. And the kids will laugh when I say the problem is that it's too hard for the grown-ups. Which really is true, I think.

BKL: *Have you had much interaction with kids who read science fiction and fantasy in general?*
L'ENGLE: Yes, a lot of them say, "I don't like science fiction, but I loved your book." There's a new category now called science fantasy, and I think that's probably a better description than either fantasy or science fiction for my books.

◀ *How does Madeleine L'Engle describe the books in her Time Quartet?*

BKL: *I do see more fantasy than science fiction; however,* A Wrinkle in Time *does have scientific underpinnings.*
L'ENGLE: So does *A Wind in the Door.* I got a wonderful batch of letters from a high-school biology class. The teacher was using the book as her text in a biology class. With what I knew about biology, I was able to get it right about the mitochondria.[1] So there's a lot of science in *Door,* too.

BKL: *What made you depart from the Austin family series, set in "real time,"[2] to write* A Wrinkle in Time? *You had a good thing going with the Austins.*
L'ENGLE: The first Austin book [*Meet the Austins,* 1961] also took almost two years to find a publisher. It's a simple little book, but it starts with a death, and at that time, death was <u>taboo</u>, and children weren't supposed to know it existed. With *Wrinkle in Time,* I just became fascinated with the science of it. I felt that the science was very philosophical. I was reading some Einstein, who said that anyone who was not lost in <u>rapture</u> at the power of mind behind the universe is, and I quote, "as good as a burned-out candle." And I

---

1. **mitochondria.** Mitochondria (singular *mitochondrion*) are microscopic parts of a cell. In *A Wind in the Door,* Meg, Calvin, and a supernatural companion travel inside a mitochondrion.
2. **set in "real time."** The Austin family does not travel through time as the Murrys do.

words for everyday use

ta • boo (ta bü') *adj.,* forbidden; not talked about. *In our family, talking about Uncle Ralph's criminal past is taboo.*

rap • ture (rap' chər) *n.,* experience of being carried away by overwhelming emotion; a feeling of awe while looking upon something divine or godly. *The astronauts looked down at the Earth, an expression of rapture on their faces as they contemplated the miracle of life in a vast universe.*

thought, "Oh, wow, I've found my predilection.[3]" Then I began to read more Einstein and Planck.[4] These scientists are dealing with the nature of being, and I was fascinated by them; of course, I had never read them in school.

BKL: *So you didn't have any science background before you started reading Einstein?*
L'ENGLE: I avoided it as much as possible. We had to take a science in college, so I took psych[ology]. That was as far from science as I could get and still fill the requirement.

BKL: *With your interest in science, did you do your own research on the later books? For example, the biological elements in* A Wind in the Door?
L'ENGLE: Yes, that was the best thing I got out of college, being able to do my own research. I went up to Columbia [University] and got a couple of books on cellular biology. And my eldest daughter helped me go through them. But certainly I had no previous background.

BKL: *Did you plan all along to bring the characters in your different series—the Murrys, the Austins, and the O'Keefes—into contact with each other, or did that just happen somewhere along the way?*
L'ENGLE: It just sort of happened.

BKL: *Are you going to continue with these characters?*
L'ENGLE: Right now, I'm writing a book, and I have no idea what genre[5] it is. It's about Meg, in her fifties, with her kids all leaving the nest, and she's figuring out who she is and where she's supposed to go.

BKL: *Do you use a family tree to keep all your characters straight?*
L'ENGLE: There is one at the beginning of most of the books, which I didn't make. And there are a couple of

---

3. **predilection.** Preferred or loved thing
4. **Einstein . . . Planck.** Einstein and Planck were famous physicists, or scientists who study matter and energy. Albert Einstein (1879–1955) was a German-born American physicist famous for his theories of relativity; Max Ernst Planck (1858–1947) was a German physicist famous for his work on the quantum theory.
5. **genre** (zhän' rə). Type of writing. Some common genres include science fiction, mystery, and romance.

mistakes in it, but it's pretty good. It appears just in the hardcovers.

BKL: *In all of your books, you have the very good versus the very evil, which is the traditional fantasy mode. But how did you* <u>concoct</u> *the ecthroi,[6] and where did you get that name?*

◀ What traditional aspect of fantasy literature appears in L'Engle's Time Quartet books?

L'ENGLE: It's a Greek word, and it means "the enemy." It's an enemy-sounding word, and I didn't want to use any of the words that we had already encrusted with meaning. I wanted something brand new. And I like the sound of the word.

BKL: *How did you develop your concept of evil—that absolute* <u>conformity</u> *is bad?*
L'ENGLE: I went to a boarding school where I was pushed to conform, and I thought it was terrible.

BKL: *Do you read other authors who write for children and young adults?*
L'ENGLE: I do. The nicest thing is that people send me books that I might not get otherwise, and so I read in as wide an area as possible. Yes, I do read [young adult literature]. I think that some of the best literature today is being written in that genre.

BKL: *What do you think of the science-fiction and fantasy genre for children and young adults? How has the genre evolved? What's the state of its health?*
L'ENGLE: I think right now it's in a state of <u>transition</u>—just as the whole planet is, as we head toward another millennium. We're just going to be different; things are changing. Computer chips are changing a lot of things. We're getting more and more used to living in an electronic world, and I

---

6. ***ecthroi.*** Evil forces in the book *A Wind in the Door*

---

words for everyday use

con • coct (kən käkt') *v.,* cook up or prepare; devise. *The villains sat in their hideout* <u>concocting</u> *a plan to take over the world.*

con • for • mi • ty (kən fôr' mə tē) *n.,* the act or state of conforming—that is, molding one's appearance, actions, or personality in order to fit in with an accepted standard of behavior, often in obedience to peer pressure or to an authority. *In the military, a certain degree of* <u>conformity</u> *is necessary.* **conform,** *v.*

tran • si • tion (tran zi' shən) *n.,* passage from one state, stage, subject, or place to another; change. *At thirteen years of age, Lou was in a* <u>transition</u> *from childhood to young adulthood.*

think fantasy is probably the best way to reflect what that means to our lives.

BKL: *Do you get lots of letters from kids?*
L'ENGLE: I do. I get about 100 letters a week, but oddly enough, I would say 75 of them are from grown-ups. They're reading both the grown-up books, the non-fiction books, and the fantasies.

BKL: *What do the children who write you ask—what are they most interested in?*
L'ENGLE: One constant question is, Where do you get your ideas? Almost everybody asks that. And then, there are two kinds of letters: those where the writer explains that he or she must do a study of an author, and "I've chosen you." Then there are the kind from kids who want to write; they just love the books and want to talk about them and ask questions. One I loved was from an 11-year-old saying, "How can I stay a child forever and never grow up?" I wrote back and said, "You can't, and it wouldn't be a good idea if you could. But what you can do, and what I hope you will do, is stay a child forever *and* grow up."

▶ *Where does L'Engle get her ideas?*

BKL: *Very good answer. How do you deal with the* <u>inevitable</u> *question about where you get your ideas?*
L'ENGLE: I tell a story about Johann Sebastian Bach.[7] When he was an old man, a young student said, "Papa Bach, where did you get the ideas for all these melodies?" And the old man said, "Why, when I get up in the morning, it's all I can do not to trip over them."

BKL: *Religion and science are interconnected in your books. Some would see a conflict there. How do you* <u>reconcile</u> *the two?*
L'ENGLE: It's never bothered me. Anything we learn about Earth doesn't change God; it doesn't change

---

7. **Johann Sebastian Bach.** German composer who lived from 1685–1750

words for everyday use
in • ev • i • ta • ble (i ne′ və tə bəl) *adj.*, incapable of being avoided. *The tension between the two countries grew and grew until it seemed war was* <u>inevitable</u>.

rec • on • cile (re′ kən sīl) *v.*, settle; resolve. *The marriage counselor was able to help the couple* <u>reconcile</u> *some of their problems.*

our concept of God. For instance, when we were forced to accept that Earth is not the center of the universe—everything is not revolving around us—that really shook the religious thinking, and so the concept of God was changed. But God didn't change—just what we think.

BKL: *I have read somewhere that one of your most frequently asked questions is about Charles Wallace. Why haven't you written about him as an adult? Is he coming back?*

L'ENGLE: He is definitely coming back, but I have to wait until he does.

BKL: *So your characters drive you more than you drive them?*

L'ENGLE: Oh, heavens yes. They tell me. I'm not in charge; I don't control; I don't <u>dominate</u>; I don't <u>manipulate</u>; I'm not a dictator. I listen to them.

BKL: *Charles Wallace is certainly a strong character, but your books are especially notable for their strong female characters. I would guess you get lots of letters from girls who identify with the young women in your books.*

L'ENGLE: Oh yes, a lot of them do. Lots of people identify with Meg. Certainly I do myself. I made Meg good at arithmetic and bad at English, and I was good at English and bad at arithmetic. And I was an only child, so I gave her some brothers. But other than that, I'm very much Meg. I have all her problems. One absolutely charming letter I got was from someone, probably around my age, saying, "When I die, I really hope to meet some of your characters." I've been lucky in my life in knowing a lot of strong women, and they've been good role models for me, and I come from a family of strong women. My mother was a southerner, and after the Civil War, there were very few men left, and the women had to

◄ How is the character of Meg Murry similar to and different from what Madeleine L'Engle was like as a young adult?

words for everyday use

dom • i • nate (dä′ mə nāt) *v.,* rule; control. *The other students resented the way Kelly <u>dominated</u> their discussion group, never letting anyone else talk.*

ma • nip • u • late (mə nip′ pyə lāt) *v.,* manage skillfully; control or play upon by artful, unfair, or insidious means so as to serve one's purpose. *Shawn <u>manipulated</u> his little brothers to get them to do his chores for him.*

be strong. So that goes back to tradition as well as my beliefs. I've never seen why women should be weaker than men or stronger; we're all human beings, struggling to be human.

BKL: *You're still writing, and you're still writing for youth.*
L'ENGLE: I think I go back and forth. Actually, when I'm writing a book, I'm not really thinking about where we're going to <u>market</u> it; it's sort of a decision we make after the book is finished. For instance, the book I'm working on now, part of it is from Meg's point of view, but part of it is from the point of view of her kids. So we'll make that decision later.

Critical Thinking

1. L'Engle describes the books in her "Time Quartet" as "science fantasy." What kind of science can be found in *A Wrinkle in Time?* What kind of science can be found in *A Wind in the Door?* How did L'Engle become interested in using scientific ideas in her writing?
2. L'Engle says that she was pushed to conform, or to change her behavior to fit in with everyone else, while she was at boarding school. What aspects of *A Wrinkle in Time* might have been inspired by Madeleine L'Engle's experiences at boarding school?
3. Science and religion are interconnected in Madeleine L'Engle's books. Why do you suppose some people would find that an odd combination? Can you think of any ways that religion and science might disagree with one another?
4. What question would you like to ask Madeleine L'Engle?

words for everyday use   mar • ket (mar' kət) *v.,* sell; promote for sale. *Cigarette companies should never be allowed to <u>market</u> their product to young people.*

from *Alice's Adventures in Wonderland*
by Lewis Carroll

RELATED READING

ABOUT THE SELECTION

This selection is taken from the classic story *Alice's Adventures in Wonderland,* written by Charles Lutwidge Dodgson (1832–1898), an English author best known by his pen name, **Lewis Carroll.** Both *Alice's Adventures in Wonderland* and its sequel, *Through the Looking Glass,* tell the story of a young girl named Alice. Like Meg in *A Wrinkle in Time,* Alice is transported to strange lands filled with unusual, fantastic beings.

CHAPTER I: Down the Rabbit-Hole

Alice was beginning to get very tired of sitting by her sister on the bank, and of having nothing to do: once or twice she had peeped into the book her sister was reading, but it had no pictures or conversations in it, "and what is the use of a book," thought Alice, "without pictures or conversation?"

So she was considering in her own mind (as well as she could, for the hot day made her feel very sleepy and stupid), whether the pleasure of making a daisy-chain would be worth the trouble of getting up and picking the daisies, when suddenly a White Rabbit with pink eyes ran close by her.

There was nothing so *very* remarkable in that; nor did Alice think it so very much out of the way to hear the Rabbit say to itself, "Oh dear! Oh dear! I shall be late!" (when she thought it over afterwards, it occurred to her that she ought to have wondered at this, but at the time it all seemed quite natural); but when the Rabbit *actually took a watch out of its waistcoat-pocket,* and looked at it, and then hurried on, Alice started to her feet, for it flashed across her mind that she had never before seen a rabbit with either a waistcoat-pocket, or a watch to take out of it, and burning with curiosity, she ran across the field after

◀ *What is strange about the Rabbit?*

it, and fortunately was just in time to see it pop down a large rabbit-hole under the hedge.

In another moment down went Alice after it, never once considering how in the world she was to get out again.

▶ What happens to Alice?

The rabbit-hole went straight on like a tunnel for some way, and then dipped suddenly down, so suddenly that Alice had not a moment to think about stopping herself before she found herself falling down a very deep well.

Either the well was very deep, or she fell very slowly, for she had plenty of time as she went down to look about her and to wonder what was going to happen next. First, she tried to look down and make out what she was coming to, but it was too dark to see anything; then she looked at the sides of the well, and noticed that they were filled with cupboards and book-shelves; here and there she saw maps and pictures hung upon pegs. She took down a jar from one of the shelves as she passed; it was labelled "ORANGE MARMALADE," but to her great disappointment it was empty: she did not like to drop the jar for fear of killing somebody, so managed to put it into one of the cupboards as she fell past it.

"Well!" thought Alice to herself, "after such a fall as this, I shall think nothing of tumbling down stairs! How brave they'll all think me at home! Why, I wouldn't say anything about it, even if I fell off the top of the house!" (Which was very likely true.)

Down, down, down. Would the fall *never* come to an end! "I wonder how many miles I've fallen by this time?" she said aloud. "I must be getting somewhere near the centre of the earth. Let me see: that would be four thousand miles down, I think—" (for, you see, Alice had learnt several things of this sort in her lessons in the schoolroom, and though this was not a *very* good opportunity for showing off her knowledge, as there was no one to listen to her, still it was good practice to say it over) "—yes, that's about the right distance—but then I wonder what Latitude or Longitude[1] I've got to?" (Alice had no idea what Latitude was, or Longitude either, but thought they were nice grand words to say.)

Presently she began again. "I wonder if I shall fall right *through* the earth! How funny it'll seem to come out among the people that walk with their heads downward! The Antipathies,[2] I think—" (she was rather glad there *was* no one listening, this time, as it didn't sound at all the right word) "—but I shall have to ask them what the name of the country is, you know. Please, Ma'am, is this New Zealand or Australia?" (and she tried to curtsey as she spoke— fancy *curtseying* as you're falling through the air! Do you think you could manage it?) "And what an

◀ *Where does she think she might end up?*

---

1. **Latitude or Longitude.** One way to describe your position on Earth is by giving your latitude and longitude. Look at a globe. Lines of latitude are parallel to the equator, while lines of longitude go from north to south in a direction perpendicular to the equator. London, England is located near 0° longitude and 51° latitude.
2. **Antipathies.** Alice means "antipodes," the lands on the direct opposite side of the earth. In England, the antipodes were usually considered to be Australia and New Zealand.

ignorant little girl she'll think me for asking! No, it'll never do to ask: perhaps I shall see it written up somewhere."

Down, down, down. There was nothing else to do, so Alice soon began talking again. "Dinah'll miss me very much to-night, I should think!" (Dinah was the cat.) "I hope they'll remember her saucer of milk at tea-time. Dinah my dear! I wish you were down here with me! There are no mice in the air, I'm afraid, but you might catch a bat, and that's very like a mouse, you know. But do cats eat bats, I wonder?" And here Alice began to get rather sleepy, and went on saying to herself, in a dreamy sort of way, "Do cats eat bats? Do cats eat bats?" and sometimes, "Do bats eat cats?" for, you see, as she couldn't answer either question, it didn't much matter which way she put it. She felt that she was dozing off, and had just begun to dream that she was walking hand in hand with Dinah, and saying to her very earnestly, "Now, Dinah, tell me the truth: did you ever eat a bat?" when suddenly, thump! thump! down she came upon a heap of sticks and dry leaves, and the fall was over.

Alice was not a bit hurt, and she jumped up on to her feet in a moment: she looked up, but it was all dark overhead; before her was another long passage, and the White Rabbit was still in sight, hurrying down it. There was not a moment to be lost: away went Alice like the wind, and was just in time to hear it say, as it turned a corner, "Oh my ears and whiskers, how late it's getting!" She was close behind it when she turned the corner, but the Rabbit was no longer to be seen: she found herself in a long, low hall, which was lit up by a row of lamps hanging from the roof.

There were doors all round the hall, but they were all locked; and when Alice had been all the way down one side and up the other, trying every door,

words for everyday use

ig • no • rant (ig' nə rənt) adj., lacking knowledge; unaware; uninformed. Centuries ago, people were ignorant of the fact that the earth was sphere-shaped, not flat.

ear • nest • ly (ər' nəst lē) adv., seriously. Alisha listened earnestly to the teacher, while her sister goofed off.

she walked sadly down the middle, wondering how she was ever to get out again.

Suddenly she came upon a little three-legged table, all made of solid glass; there was nothing on it except a tiny golden key, and Alice's first thought was that it might belong to one of the doors of the hall; but, alas! either the locks were too large, or the key was too small, but at any rate it would not open any of them. However, on the second time round, she came upon a low curtain she had not noticed before, and behind it was a little door about fifteen inches high: she tried the little golden key in the lock, and to her great delight it fitted!

◀ Describe the door Alice opens with her little key. What is beyond the door?

Alice opened the door and found that it led into a small passage, not much larger than a rat-hole: she knelt down and looked along the passage into the loveliest garden you ever saw. How she longed to get out of that dark hall, and wander about among those beds of bright flowers and those cool fountains, but she could not even get her head through the doorway; "and even if my head *would* go through," thought poor Alice, "it would be of very little use without my shoulders. Oh, how I wish I could shut up like a telescope! I think I could, if I only knew how to begin." For, you see, so many out-of-the-way things had happened lately, that Alice had begun to think that very few things indeed were really impossible.

There seemed to be no use in waiting by the little door, so she went back to the table, half hoping she might find another key on it, or at any rate a book of rules for shutting people up like telescopes: this time she found a little bottle on it, ("which certainly was not here before," said Alice,) and round the neck of the bottle was a paper label, with the words "DRINK ME" beautifully printed on it in large letters.

◀ Why doesn't Alice drink from the bottle right away?

It was all very well to say "Drink me," but the wise little Alice was not going to do *that* in a hurry. "No, I'll look first," she said, "and see whether it's marked

words for everyday use   alas (ə las') *interj.,* used to express unhappiness, pity, or concern. "*Alas!*" I cried. "I lost *my favorite pen!*"

'*poison*' or not"; for she had read several nice little stories about children who had got burnt, and eaten up by wild beasts and other unpleasant things, all because they *would* not remember the simple rules their friends had taught them: such as, that a red-hot poker will burn you if you hold it too long; and that if you cut your finger *very* deeply with a knife, it usually bleeds; and she had never forgotten that, if you drink much from a bottle marked "poison," it is almost certain to disagree with you, sooner or later.

However, this bottle was *not* marked "poison," so Alice ventured to taste it, and finding it very nice, (it had, in fact, a sort of mixed flavour of cherry-tart, custard, pine-apple, roast turkey, toffee, and hot buttered toast,) she very soon finished it off.

    *   *   *   *   *
      *   *   *   *
    *   *   *   *   *

"What a curious feeling!" said Alice; "I must be shutting up like a telescope!"

And so it was indeed: she was now only ten inches high, and her face brightened up at the thought that she was now the right size for going through the little door into that lovely garden. First, however, she waited for a few minutes to see if she was going to shrink any further: she felt a little nervous about this; "for it might end, you know," said Alice to herself, "in my going out altogether, like a candle. I wonder what I should be like then?" And she tried to fancy what the flame of a candle is like after the candle is blown out, for she could not remember ever having seen such a thing.

After a while, finding that nothing more happened, she decided on going into the garden at once; but, alas for poor Alice! when she got to the door, she found she had forgotten the little golden key, and when she went back to the table for it, she found she could not possibly reach it: she could see it quite plainly through the glass, and she tried her best to climb up one of the legs of the table, but it was too slippery; and when she had tired herself out with trying, the poor little thing sat down and cried.

◀ *Why is Alice crying?*

"Come, there's no use in crying like that!" said Alice to herself, rather sharply; "I advise you to leave off[3] this minute!" She generally gave herself very good advice, (though she very seldom followed it), and sometimes she scolded herself so severely as to bring tears into her eyes; and once she remembered trying to box her own ears for having cheated herself in a game of croquet she was playing against herself, for this curious child was very fond of pretending to be two people. "But it's no use now," thought poor Alice, "to pretend to be two people! Why, there's hardly enough of me left to make *one* respectable person!"

Soon her eye fell on a little glass box that was lying under the table: she opened it, and found in it a very small cake, on which the words "EAT ME" were beautifully marked in currants. "Well, I'll eat it," said Alice, "and if it makes me grow larger, I can reach the key; and if it makes me grow smaller, I can creep under the door; so either way I'll get into the garden, and I don't care which happens!"

◀ *What does she hope will happen when she eats the cake?*

---

3. **leave off.** Stop

She ate a little bit, and said anxiously to herself, "Which way? Which way?," holding her hand on the top of her head to feel which way it was growing, and she was quite surprised to find that she remained the same size: to be sure, this generally happens when one eats cake, but Alice had got so much into the way of expecting nothing but out-of-the-way things to happen, that it seemed quite dull and stupid for life to go on in the common way.

So she set to work, and very soon finished off the cake. . . .

from CHAPTER VI: Pig and Pepper

Alice explores more of Wonderland and meets a number of strange characters, including a baby who turns into a pig. At one point she meets a peculiar cat, sitting in a tree, who grins a great deal and has a habit of appearing and disappearing.

The Cat only grinned when it saw Alice. It looked good-natured, she thought: still it had *very* long claws and a great many teeth, so she felt that it ought to be treated with respect.

"Cheshire Puss," she began, rather <u>timidly</u>, as she did not at all know whether it would like the name: however, it only grinned a little wider. "Come, it's pleased so far," thought Alice, and she went on. "Would you tell me, please, which way I ought to go from here?"

"That depends a good deal on where you want to get to," said the Cat.

"I don't much care where—" said Alice.

"Then it doesn't matter which way you go," said the Cat.

"—so long as I get *somewhere*," Alice added as an explanation.

"Oh, you're sure to do that," said the Cat, "if you only walk long enough."

---

words for everyday use **tim • id • ly** (tim' id lē) *adv.,* shyly; in a way that shows a lack of courage or self-confidence. *Jim stood <u>timidly</u> by the edge of the basketball court, hoping one of the older kids would ask if he wanted to join the game.*

Alice felt that this could not be <u>denied</u>, so she tried another question. "What sort of people live about here?"

"In *that* direction," the Cat said, waving its right paw round, "lives a Hatter: and in *that* direction," waving the other paw, "lives a March Hare. Visit either you like: they're both mad."[4]

◀ *What does the Cheshire Cat say about the people and creatures in the area?*

"But I don't want to go among mad people," Alice remarked.

"Oh, you can't help that," said the Cat: "we're all mad here. I'm mad. You're mad."

"How do you know I'm mad?" said Alice.

"You must be," said the Cat, "or you wouldn't have come here."

Alice didn't think that proved it at all; however, she went on: "And how do you know that you're mad?"

"To begin with," said the Cat, "a dog's not mad. You <u>grant</u> that?"

"I suppose so," said Alice.

"Well, then," the Cat went on, "you see, a dog growls when it's angry, and wags its tail when it's pleased. Now *I* growl when I'm pleased, and wag my tail when I'm angry. Therefore I'm mad."

◀ *What logic does the Cat use to prove that it is mad? Do you agree with its logic?*

"*I* call it purring, not growling," said Alice.

"Call it what you like," said the Cat. "Do you play croquet with the Queen to-day?"

"I should like it very much," said Alice, "but I haven't been invited yet."

"You'll see me there," said the Cat, and vanished.

Alice was not much surprised at this, she was getting so used to <u>queer</u> things happening. While she was looking at the place where it had been, it suddenly appeared again.

"By-the-bye,[5] what became of the baby?" said the Cat. "I'd nearly forgotten to ask."

---

4. **mad.** Insane
5. **by-the-bye.** Old-fashioned term meaning "by the way"

words for everyday use

de • ny (di nī′) v., refuse to accept the truth of. *Nobody can deny the fact that reading is an important skill.*

grant (grant) v., assume to be the truth. "*I grant that the homework was difficult,*" Ms. Rae said calmly, "*but you didn't even try.*"

queer (kwir) adj., differing in some odd way from what is normal or usual. *The sky was a queer greenish color before the storm broke.*

"It turned into a pig," Alice quietly said, just as if it had come back in a natural way.

"I thought it would," said the Cat, and vanished again.

Alice waited a little, half expecting to see it again, but it did not appear, and after a minute or two she walked on in the direction in which the March Hare was said to live. "I've seen hatters before," she said to herself; "the March Hare will be much the most interesting, and perhaps as this is May it won't be <u>raving</u> mad—at least not so mad as it was in March." As she said this, she looked up, and there was the Cat again, sitting on a branch of a tree.

"Did you say pig, or fig?" said the Cat.

"I said pig," replied Alice; "and I wish you wouldn't keep appearing and vanishing so suddenly: you make one quite <u>giddy</u>."

"All right," said the Cat; and this time it vanished quite slowly, beginning with the end of the tail, and

▶ *What part of the Cat is left after the rest of it vanishes?*

ending with the grin, which remained some time after the rest of it had gone.

"Well! I've often seen a cat without a grin," thought Alice; "but a grin without a cat! It's the most curious thing I ever saw in my life!"

Critical Thinking Questions

1. Recall that a **fantasy** is a story that is very imaginative or unrealistic. Fantasy stories may involve imaginary beings such as elves, dragons, or unicorns, as well as magical or supernatural occurrences. Does this selection fit the definition of a fantasy? Explain.
2. Compare and contrast Alice's adventures in this selection with those of Meg, Charles Wallace, and Calvin. Discuss the method of travel described in both works. Are any scientific explanations given for how Alice is able to enter Wonderland?
3. Which parts of this selection from *Alice's Adventures in Wonderland* are alluded to, or referred to, in *A Wrinkle in Time?* Go back to *A Wrinkle in Time* and copy down the passages that refer to Alice's story. Why do you think Madeleine L'Engle chose to make these references to *Alice's Adventures in Wonderland?*

from *Flatland: A Romance of Many Dimensions*
by A. Square (Edwin A. Abbott)

ABOUT THE RELATED READING

The following is an excerpt from the book *Flatland*, published in 1884 by English scholar and clergyman **Edwin A. Abbott** (1836–1926). Like Meg, Charles Wallace, and Calvin, the main character of this fantastical story travels to worlds of different dimensions. He is A. Square—literally, a square, a flat, two-dimensional shape living in Flatland, a world flat as a sheet of paper. Like all the other people in his world, A. Square only knows two dimensions: width and length. The third dimension—thickness, or height—is completely unknown to him. Then, one evening, he is visited by a sphere-shaped creature from "Spaceland," who opens his eyes to the third dimension.

From Part I: This World

Section 1: Of the Nature of Flatland

I call our world Flatland, not because we call it so, but to make its nature clearer to you, my happy readers, who are <u>privileged</u> to live in Space.

▶ *Describe Flatland. What kind of shapes are not possible there?*

Imagine a vast sheet of paper on which straight Lines, Triangles, Squares, Pentagons, Hexagons, and other figures, instead of remaining fixed in their places, move freely about, on or in the surface, but without the power of rising above or sinking below it, very much like shadows—only hard with <u>luminous</u> edges—and you will then have a pretty correct notion of my country and countrymen. Alas,

words for everyday use

priv • il • eged (pri′ və ləjd) *adj.,* having or enjoying benefits or advantages. *The* <u>*privileged*</u> *children of the village had shiny new shoes every year, while the poor, disad-* vantaged peasants went barefoot.

lu • mi • nous (lü′ mə nəs) *adj.,* glowing. *Her eyes were large and* <u>*luminous*</u> *as pools of light.*

a few years ago, I should have said "my universe": but now my mind has been opened to higher views of things.

In such a country, you will perceive at once that it is impossible that there should be anything of what you call a "solid" kind; but I dare say you will suppose that we could at least distinguish by sight the Triangles, Squares, and other figures, moving about as I have described them. On the contrary, we could see nothing of the kind, not at least so as to distinguish one figure from another. Nothing was visible, nor could be visible, to us, except Straight Lines; and the necessity of this I will speedily demonstrate.

Place a penny on the middle of one of your tables in Space; and leaning over it, look down upon it. It will appear a circle.

But now, drawing back to the edge of the table, gradually lower your eye (thus bringing yourself more and more into the condition of the inhabitants of Flatland), and you will find the penny becoming more and more oval to your view, and at last when you have placed your eye exactly on the edge of the table (so that you are, as it were, actually a Flatlander) the penny will then have <u>ceased</u> to appear oval at all, and will have become, so far as you can see, a straight line.

The same thing would happen if you were to treat in the same way a Triangle, or a Square, or any other figure cut out from pasteboard. As soon as you look at it with your eye on the edge of the table, you will find that it ceases to appear to you as a figure, and that it becomes in appearance a straight line. Take for example an equilateral Triangle[1]—who represents with us a Tradesman of the respectable class.

---

1. **equilateral Triangle.** A triangle whose sides are equal in length

---

words for everyday use

cease (sēs) v., stop. *The woodcutter <u>ceased</u> his chopping when he heard his wife call out for him.*

Figure 1 represents the Tradesman as you would see him while you were bending over him from above; figures 2 and 3 represent the Tradesman, as you would see him if your eye were close to the level, or all but on the level of the table; and if your eye were quite on the level of the table (and that is how we see him in Flatland) you would see nothing but a straight line.

When I was in Spaceland I heard that your sailors have very similar experiences while they <u>traverse</u> your seas and <u>discern</u> some distant island or coast lying on the horizon. The far-off land may have bays, forelands, angles in and out to any number and extent; yet at a distance you see none of these (unless indeed your sun shines bright upon them revealing the projections and retirements[2] by means of light and shade), nothing but a grey unbroken line upon the water.

Well, that is just what we see when one of our triangular or other acquaintances comes towards us in Flatland. As there is neither sun with us, nor any light of such a kind as to make shadows, we have none of the helps to the sight that you have in Spaceland. If our friend comes closer to us we see his line becomes larger; if he leaves us it becomes smaller; but still he looks like a straight line; be he a Triangle, Square, Pentagon, Hexagon, Circle, what you will—a straight Line he looks and nothing else. . . .[3]

▶ How do all the shapes look to one another?

---

2. **projections and retirements.** Land that juts out and land that curves inward, as in a bay

3. **a straight Line he looks and nothing else.** In later chapters, A. Square explains that through training, Flatlanders *can* learn to see the difference between lines, triangles, hexagons, and other shapes. Otherwise, they tell each other apart by the sense of touch.

words for everyday use

tra • verse (tra vərs′) v., travel across or over; pass through; extend across. *We tra-versed the river on horseback, getting our boots soaked in the muddy waters.*

dis • cern (di sərn′) v., detect with the eyes or with the other senses; recognize as separate and distinct. *When she tasted the cake, the chef was able to discern the spices of cinnamon, nutmeg, and cloves.*

From Part II: Other Worlds

Section 14. How I vainly tried
to explain the nature of Flatland

Beginning in section 13, A. Square dreams that he visits a place called Lineland, where the people are all lines and dots moving along a line. The men are lines and the women are dots. Because they can never look at each other from the side or from above, they cannot tell by sight who is a line and who a dot—they all see each other as dots. Even more strangely, they cannot pass one another, but must always remain lined up in the same order, so that they forever have the same neighbors. [See the drawing below.] One of the lines declares himself the King of the World—he thinks that the one-dimensional line of Lineland is the entire world. A. Square tries to show him how limited his view is by explaining the concept of a second dimension, but the King is not convinced.

◀ Describe Lineland. How do all the inhabitants of Lineland look to one another?

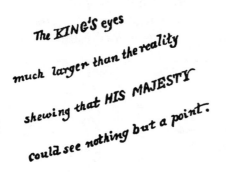

"[P]ermit me to point out that your life in Lineland must be deplorably dull. To see nothing but a Point! Not even to be able to contemplate a Straight Line! Nay, not even to know what a Straight Line is! At least I can discern, by sight, a Line from a Point. And let me prove it. Just before I came into your kingdom, I saw you dancing from left to right, and then from right to left, with Seven Men and a Woman in your immediate <u>proximity</u> on the left, and eight Men and two Women on your right. Is not this correct?"

"It is correct," said the King, "so far as the numbers and sexes are concerned, though I know not what you mean by 'right' and 'left.' But I deny that you saw these things. For how could you see the Line, that is to say the inside, of any Man? But you must have heard these things, and then dreamed that you saw them. And let me ask what you mean by those words 'left' and 'right.' I suppose it is your way of saying Northward and Southward."

"Not so," replied I; "besides your motion of Northward and Southward, there is another motion which I call from right to left."

King. Exhibit to me, if you please, this motion from left to right.

I. Nay, that I cannot do, unless you could step out of your Line altogether.

King. Out of my Line? Do you mean out of the world? Out of Space?

I. Well, yes. Out of *your* world. Out of *your* Space. For your Space is not the true Space. True Space is a Plane[4]; but your Space is only a Line.

King. If you cannot indicate this motion from left to right by yourself moving in it, then I beg you to describe it to me in words.

I. If you cannot tell your right side from your left, I fear that no words of mine can make my meaning

▶ What does
A. Square say "true space" is?

---

4. **Plane.** A flat or level surface

clearer to you. But surely you cannot be <u>ignorant</u> of so simple a <u>distinction</u>.

King. I do not in the least understand you.

I. Alas! How shall I make it clear? When you move straight on, does it not sometimes occur to you that you *could* move in some other way, turning your eye round so as to look in the direction towards which your side is now fronting? In other words, instead of always moving in the direction of one of your extremities,[5] do you never feel a desire to move in the direction, so to speak, of your side?

King. Never. And what do you mean? How can a man's inside "front" in any direction? Or how can a man move in the direction of his inside?

I. Well then, since words cannot explain the matter, I will try deeds, and will move gradually out of Lineland in the direction which I desire to indicate to you.

At the word I began to move my body out of Lineland. As long as any part of me remained in his <u>dominion</u> and in his view, the King kept exclaiming, "I see you, I see you still; you are not moving." But when I had at last moved myself out of his Line, he cried in his shrillest voice, "She is vanished; she is dead." "I am not dead," replied I; "I am simply out of Lineland, that is to say, out of the Straight Line which you call Space, and in the true Space, where I can see things as they are. And at this moment I can see your Line, or side—or inside as you are pleased to call it; and I can see also the Men and Women on the North and South of you, whom I will now enumerate, describing their order, their size, and the interval between each."[6]

◄ Why does the King call his side his "inside"?

---

5. **extremities.** End points

6. **whom I will now enumerate . . . interval between each.** He enumerates, or counts, the men and women and tells how far apart they are from each other.

---

words for everyday use

ig • no • rant (ig' nə rənt) *adj.*, lacking knowledge; unaware; uninformed. *Jesse, who had not yet taken a chemistry class, was <u>ignorant</u> about the elements on the periodic table.*

dis • tinc • tion (di stiŋ(k)' shən) *n.*, the distinguishing of difference. *The four-year-old had trouble making the <u>distinction</u> between his left and right foot.*

do • min • ion (də mi'nyən) *n.*, land under complete control or ownership. *The social studies classroom was the <u>dominion</u> of Ms. Kinney.*

When I had done this at great length, I cried triumphantly, "Does that at last convince you?" And, with that, I once more entered Lineland, taking up the same position as before.

But the Monarch replied, ". . . You ask me to believe that there is another Line besides that which my senses indicate, and another motion besides that of which I am daily conscious. I, in return, ask you to describe in words or indicate by motion that other Line of which you speak. Instead of moving, you merely exercise some magic art of vanishing and returning to sight. . . . Can anything be more <u>irrational</u> or <u>audacious</u>? Acknowledge your <u>folly</u> or <u>depart</u> from my dominions."

Section 16: How the Stranger vainly endeavoured to reveal to me in words the mysteries of Spaceland.

A. Square is "sitting" at home one night thinking about the possibility of higher dimensions, which his young grandson has suggested to him. Suddenly, a stranger enters the house. At first, of course, A. Square perceives the visitor as a line, as all shapes look to each other like lines. Then, looking at the slight shading caused by fog and by using the sense of touch, he concludes that his visitor is a circle.

However, the visitor is not a circle but a sphere, a three-dimensional object which does not exist in Flatland. When A. Square asks where his honored visitor came from, the stranger attempts to explain the concept of three-dimensional space.

words for everyday use

ir • ra • tio • nal (i ra' shə nəl) *adj.,* lacking reason; not making sense according to logic or reason. *My brother has the <u>irrational</u> idea that eating candy is good for him.*

au • da • cious (ò dā' shəs) *adj.,* recklessly bold; going against the law, religion, or manners. *The student's <u>audacious</u> prank got him expelled from school.*

fol • ly (fä' lē) foolishness; foolish act or idea. *Jeanette locked her keys in her car, then shrieked once she realized her <u>folly</u>.*

de • part (di pärt') *v.,* leave. *The hero waved goodbye, then <u>departed</u> into the sunset.*

Stranger. [I come from] Space, from Space, sir: whence else?

I [A. Square]. Pardon me, my Lord, but is not your Lordship already in space, your Lordship and his humble servant, even at this moment?

Stranger. Pooh! What do you know of Space? Define Space.

I. Space, my Lord, is height and breadth[7] <u>indefinitely prolonged</u>.

Stranger. Exactly: you see you do not even know what Space is. You think it is of Two Dimensions only; but I have come to announce to you a Third—height, breadth, and length.

◀ *What are the three dimensions of space?*

I. Your Lordship is pleased to be merry.[8] We also speak of length and height, or breadth and thickness, thus denoting[9] Two Dimensions by four names.

Stranger. But I mean not only three names, but Three Dimensions.

I. Would your Lordship indicate or explain to me in what direction is the Third Dimension, unknown to me?

Stranger. I came from it. It is up above and down below.

I. My Lord means seemingly that it is Northward and Southward.

Stranger. I mean nothing of the kind. I mean a direction in which you cannot look, because you have no eye in your side.

I. Pardon me, my Lord, a moment's inspection will convince your lordship that I have a perfect luminary at the juncture of two of my sides.[10]

---

7. **breadth.** Width
8. **Your Lordship is pleased to be merry.** You are joking.
9. **denoting.** Calling
10. **luminary . . . juncture of two of my sides.** A. Square has an eye in the corner, right where two of his sides meet.

words for everyday use

in • de • fi • nite • ly (in de′ fə nət lē) *adv.,* without a definite end. *The violence in Israel could go on and on <u>indefinitely</u> unless something is done to stop it once and for all.*

pro • long (prə lòŋ′) *v.,* make longer. *My grandparents decided to <u>prolong</u> their visit by another week.*

▶ Why does A.
Square call his side
his "inside"?

Stranger.   Yes: but in order to see into Space you ought to have an eye, not on your Perimeter, but on your side, that is, on what you would probably call your inside; but we in Spaceland should call it your side.

I.   An eye in my inside! An eye in my stomach! Your Lordship jests.

Stranger.   I am in no jesting humour.[11] I tell you that I come from Space, or, since you will not understand what Space means, from the Land of Three Dimensions whence I but lately looked down upon your Plane which you call Space.... From that position of advantage I discerned all that you speak of as *solid* (by which you mean "enclosed on four sides"), your houses, your churches, your very chests and safes, yes even your insides and stomachs, all lying open and exposed to my view.

I.   Such assertions are easily made, my Lord.

▶ How was the
stranger able to see
inside A. Square's
house?

Stranger.   But not easily proved, you mean. But I mean to prove mine. When I descended here, I saw your four Sons, the Pentagons, each in his apartment, and your two Grandsons the Hexagons; I saw your youngest Hexagon remain a while with you and then retire to his room, leaving you and your Wife alone. I saw your Isosceles[12] servants, three in number, in the kitchen at supper, and the little Page in the scullery.[13] Then I came here, and how do you think I came?

I.   Through the roof, I suppose.

Stranger.   Not so. Your roof, as you know very well, has been recently repaired, and has no aperture[14]. . . . I tell you I come from Space. . . .

---

11. **I am in no jesting humour.** I'm not in a joking mood.
12. **Isosceles.** An isosceles triangle; that is, a triangle with two equal sides.
13. **Page in the scullery.** A page is a young boy servant; a scullery is a room off the kitchen where the dishes and other utensils are washed and stored.
14. **aperture.** Opening

**words
for
everyday
use**   jest (jest) *v.*, joke; make fun. *When I saw the grin on his face, I realized he was only jesting.*

ex • posed (ik spōzd') *adj.*, uncovered; displayed, visible. *Before going out into the cold, Marsha pulled her hat down and wrapped a scarf around her face so that only her eyes were exposed.*

The Stranger, a sphere, tries to explain the concept of height, which Flatlanders see only as "brightness." A. Square is unable to understand. Then the stranger explains that Flatland is a Plane, or a flat level surface like the surface of a body of water, and that it is possible to rise above or fall below this Plane. He then demonstrates by rising above and then going below Flatland himself. To A. Square, who can only see him as a circle, it looks as though the stranger is becoming smaller and smaller and then disappearing. [See the drawing below.]

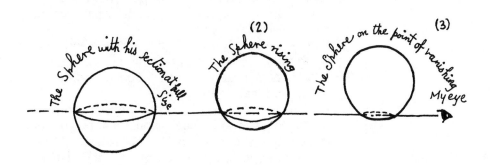

There was no "rising" that I could see; but he <u>diminished</u> and finally vanished. I winked once or twice to make sure that I was not dreaming. But it was no dream. For from the depths of nowhere came forth a hollow voice—close to my heart it seemed— "Am I quite gone? Are you convinced now? Well, now I will gradually return to Flatland and you shall see my section become larger and larger."

. . . All that I could comprehend was, that the Circle had made himself smaller and vanished, and that he had now re-appeared and was rapidly making himself larger.

Watching this occur, A. Square comes to believe that his visitor is a magician or enchanter. As the Sphere goes on to give him more explanation, A. Square attacks him, trying to drive him out of the house.

◀ *What does A. Square see when the Sphere rises and sinks? Why?*

words for everyday use

di • mi • nish (də mi′ nish) *v.,* make or become less (as in size or importance). *My respect for Ben <u>diminished</u> when I learned he had cheated on the test.*

Critical Thinking

1. With a partner, use pencil, paper, and scissors to create models of Lineland and Flatland. Then act out the scene in which A. Square meets the King of Lineland, showing how he is able to "disappear." When A. Square is in the King's line of vision, what does he look like to the King? Explain. Next, find a small spherical object such as a ball or a marble to represent the Sphere who visits A. Square. Act out the scene in which A. Square meets the Sphere, showing how the Sphere is able to disappear. When the Sphere is in A. Square's line of vision, what does he look like? Explain.

2. How is A. Square's reaction to a three-dimensional being similar to the King of Lineland's reaction to A. Square? Why do you think A. Square and the King of Lineland react in this way?

3. Imagine that a four- or five-dimensional being came to visit you. Use your imagination. What do you think this creature might look like to you? How might the being try to prove the existence of a higher dimension? Why might you think the being was supernatural or magical?

4. In chapter 5 of *A Wrinkle in Time,* the Mrs Ws accidentally take Meg, Charles Wallace, and Calvin to a two-dimensional planet. Compare their experience of a two-dimensional planet with the Sphere's experience in two-dimensional Flatland.

5. Mrs Whatsit explains that "tessering" means going beyond the fourth dimension to the fifth, so that they travel in the fifth dimension. Meg has a very hard time understanding what she means by that. What makes it so hard for people to envision a fifth dimension?

Wrinkles in Spacetime:
The Science of *A Wrinkle in Time*
by Jennifer J. Anderson

ABOUT THE RELATED READING

Jennifer J. Anderson is a book editor who lives in Minneapolis. She first read *A Wrinkle in Time* when she was in the sixth grade, and it is still one of her favorite books. She wrote this article to explain some of the scientific ideas that inspired Madeleine L'Engle's classic novel.

Science fiction is imaginative literature based on scientific principles, discoveries, or laws. Madeleine L'Engle based some of the ideas of *A Wrinkle in Time* on the exciting theories of physicists Albert Einstein and Max Ernst Planck. (A **theory** is an idea that has been tested and shown to be true by scientific experiments.) Einstein's theory of relativity and Planck's quantum theory changed forever the way we think of energy, matter, motion, time, and space.

Quantum Theory and *A Wrinkle in Time*

Charles Wallace raises his hand and a solid wall fades away, enabling the children to walk right through it. With the help of Mrs Who's glasses, Meg slips through the walls of her father's prison and delivers him out. It sounds like magic at work, but Madeleine L'Engle offers a scientific explanation. Through the words of Charles Wallace, she explains that solids aren't really solid at all, but mostly empty space. Therefore, the **atoms**, or basic building blocks that make up matter, might be "rearranged" or "pushed aside" to make a solid wall part like a curtain of rice.

◀ *What is an atom, and what is it made up of?*

To understand how this could work, let's take a look at an atom. Not literally of course; an atom is incredibly tiny—one hundred-millionth of an inch—too small to be seen even with the most powerful of microscopes. Look at the diagram below. As scientist

Ernest Rutherford first explained in 1911, an atom consists of a hard central core, called the *nucleus,* and particles that orbit around it, called *electrons.*

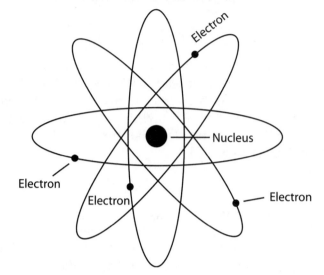

The electrons and nucleus are much, much tinier than the atom as a whole, and the space in between them is enormous. One scientist, Robert Jastrow, writes that if the outer ring of electrons were the size of the Astrodome that covers the Houston baseball stadium, the nucleus would be like a ping-pong ball in the center of the stadium. That is how empty the atom is.

Although atoms are mostly empty space, they are in effect solid because the orbiting electrons form a cloud that acts as a barrier.[1] For example, if you touch a table, the electrons in the surface of the table meet the clouds of electrons in your finger. Where they meet, the negative charges of the electrons push each other away, keeping your finger from going past the surface of the table. The electron clouds prevent us from "pushing aside" atoms with our hands the way Charles Wallace does on Camazotz.

Our modern understanding of the atom has been greatly advanced by the **quantum theory**, a complex theory about energy and matter developed in part by

---

1. In the diagram of the atom, the electrons are shown as individual particles. In reality, however, electrons move more like waves and form what is called an "electron cloud" around the nucleus.

physicists Max Ernst Planck and Albert Einstein.[2] The quantum theory helped lead to the splitting and fusing, or joining together, of the nuclei of atoms to make powerful bombs and to create nuclear energy.

Scientists are still not able to rearrange atoms the way Charles Wallace does. However, quantum theory does provide another idea of how people and objects might be able to pass through solid barriers—through an effect called "tunneling." Electrons and other particles use tunneling to pass through barriers and appear almost as if by magic on the other side. In fact, many electronic devices such as radios and computers depend on this technique. According to quantum theory, larger objects should also be able to tunnel through barriers. For example, there is a very small possibility that a person in jail might suddenly vanish and appear on the other side of a prison wall! Nobody has ever seen such a thing, but the laws of physics do not rule it out. Science can indeed be stranger than science fiction.

◀ *What is one way people might be able to pass through solid walls?*

Einstein and *A Wrinkle in Time*

In *A Wrinkle in Time,* the characters travel to distant planets by "wrinkling" time and space. Could this ever be possible? Incredibly, the answer is yes. Albert Einstein's theories of relativity led to the conclusion that wrinkles, or warps, do exist in time and space. Perhaps someday—not for many, many centuries—humans will be able to use these wrinkles to travel long distances through space, and even into the past and future.

The idea that time or space could have "wrinkles" is extremely hard to imagine. First of all, time and space do not seem to have any physical form at all. We cannot *see* time or space. When we think of time, we normally think of it as a straight line going only in one direction. When we think of space, we think of emptiness with some objects floating around in it. However, according to Einstein, the truth is very different. He changed the

---

2. Max Planck is usually considered the "father" of quantum theory. However, many other scientists, including Albert Einstein, contributed to it.

▶ What are Einstein's two great theories?

world's ideas about time and space with his theory of relativity, which was actually two theories, the **special theory of relativity** and the **general theory of relativity**. These theories came out almost 100 years ago, in 1905 and 1915, but because they are so incredible, people still have a hard time believing that they are true.

Time is Relative

▶ Explain how people might be able to time travel into the future.

Einstein's special theory of relativity, which was published in 1905, showed that time is not the same for everyone. In fact, time slows down for people who are moving at very high speeds. Imagine you are on a spaceship traveling close to the speed of light—that is, close to 186,282 miles per second. You could never actually reach the speed of light, because according to Einstein, it is physically impossible for any person or thing to move as fast as light. But suppose you are going 99.999% as fast. You might leave Earth, visit a distant star, then turn around and be back to Earth in one year. But when you got back, you would find that over two hundred years had gone by! Time slowed down for you, because you were going at such a high speed. But back home, all your friends and everyone you knew would be long dead, and you would be visiting the world of the future. You would have made an incredible journey through time—but there would be no way to go back. This method of travel would not be very practical. It would be better to travel Mrs Whatsit's way, in a higher dimension, or by "wrinkling" space and time.

The Fourth Dimension

Hermann Minkowski, a mathematician who had been one of Einstein's teachers, read Einstein's special theory with amazement. He pointed out that if Einstein's theory was correct, it meant that time was another dimension like those of space. We are familiar with three dimensions of space: length, width, and depth. One space can be represented by a line. Two dimensions can be represented by a square, which has length and width. Three dimensions can be shown as a cube, which has length, width, and depth. Minkowski claimed that according to Einstein's theories, *time* had to be considered as a fourth dimension. Space and time could never again be considered separate—they were combined together in four-dimensional space, or *spacetime*.

◀ What is the fourth dimension, according to Einstein? What is four-dimensional space called?

Although Einstein was the first to show the unity of space and time, the idea of a fourth dimension was not new. In fact, science fiction writer H. G. Wells had explored the idea of time as a fourth dimension in his novel *The Time Machine,* published in 1895. Others had imagined the fourth dimension as just another dimension in space. One such representation of four-dimensions in space is called a hypercube, or tesseract.

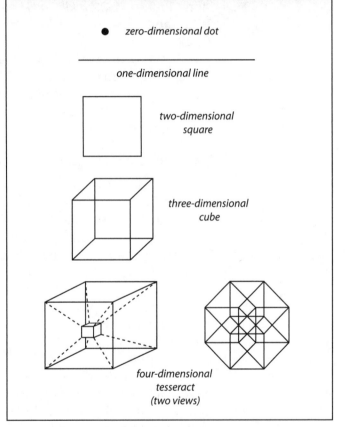

Moving up to Four Dimensions

● zero-dimensional dot

one-dimensional line

two-dimensional square

three-dimensional cube

four-dimensional tesseract (two views)

The Tesseract

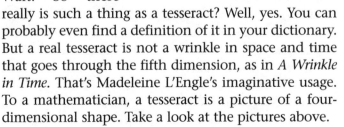

Wait! So there really is such a thing as a tesseract? Well, yes. You can probably even find a definition of it in your dictionary. But a real tesseract is not a wrinkle in space and time that goes through the fifth dimension, as in *A Wrinkle in Time.* That's Madeleine L'Engle's imaginative usage. To a mathematician, a tesseract is a picture of a four-dimensional shape. Take a look at the pictures above.

◀ What is a tesseract?

Looking at a picture of a tesseract might not help a person understand four-dimensional space, however. After all, a picture is only two-dimensional. You might get a better idea by looking at a computer model of a tesseract on one of the Internet sites listed at the end of this article. Or, you can try to imagine what higher-dimensional space is like through examples, such as the story of A. Square in Edwin Abbott's *Flatland* (see page 204).

So far, we have only discussed the fourth dimension. But in *A Wrinkle in Time,* Mrs Whatsit, Mrs Who, and Mrs Which travel in the *fifth* dimension. Could a fifth dimension exist as well? Today, some physicists believe there may actually be a fifth dimension of space, and possibly a sixth, seventh, and many more higher dimensions. As you read this, people are hard at work searching for evidence that these dimensions exist.

Warps and Holes in Space and Time

Can the fabric of space and time—or as we now know it, four-dimensional *spacetime*—really be bent, or wrinkled, like Mrs Who's skirt? The answer is yes, according to Einstein's general theory of relativity. The theory states that spacetime can be warped, or bent, by planets, stars, and other objects in it. Picture a stretched-out sheet of rubber, like a trampoline. Now picture heavy objects, such as bowling balls, placed on this sheet. They will create dents in the otherwise smooth surface, as seen in the graphic on the next page.

▶ Explain what can cause wrinkles, dents, and holes in the fabric of space and time.

The heavier the object, the deeper the dent would be. In fact, scientists now know that extremely heavy objects create holes—"black holes" in space that might lead out into another time and place, or even a whole new universe! Black holes in fact may be our best chance for finding a "shortcut" like the one the three Mrs Ws take through space and time. To learn more about these fascinating—and terrifying—objects, read "Black Holes and Time Tunnels" on page 223.

To find out more about Einstein and time travel, get a closer look at the atom, or see a model of a mind-boggling tesseract, visit the library or log on to

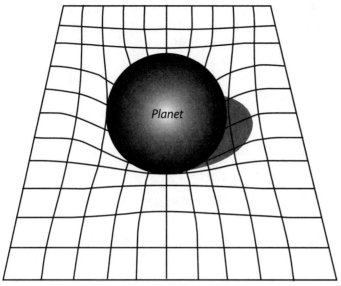

Fabric of spacetime

the Internet. The following books and links can help you get started.

Books

Cooper, Christopher. *Matter.* Eyewitness Science series. London, New York: Dorling Kindersley, 1992, 2000.

Darling, David J. *Could You Ever Build a Time Machine?* Minneapolis: Dillon Press, 1991.

Gribbin, John and Mary. *Time & Space.* Eyewitness Science series. London, New York: Dorling Kindersley, 1994, 2000.

Jastrow, Robert. *Red Giants and White Dwarfs.* New York: W. W. Norton, 1990.

Parker, Barry L. *Cosmic Time Travel: A Scientific Odyssey.* New York: Plenum Press, 1991.

Parker, Steve. *Albert Einstein and Relativity.* New York: Chelsea House Publishers, 1995.

Swertka, Albert. *The World of Atoms and Quarks.* New York: Twenty-First Century Books, 1995.

Internet Sites

"Hypercube's Home Page"
http://www.geocities.com/CapeCanaveral/7997/index.html

MathForum's "Math Spans in All Dimensions"
http://mathforum.com/mam/00/612/index.html
Nova Online's "Atom Builder" and "See Inside a
Diamond"
http://www.pbs.org/wgbh/nova/diamond/
inside.html
Nova Online's "Einstein Revealed" and "Time
Traveler"
http://www.pbs.org/wgbh/nova/einstein/
"The Tesseract, or Hypercube: A Guided
Demonstration"
http://www.geom.umn.edu/docs/ outreach/4-cube/

Critical Thinking

1. If it is true that atoms consist mostly of space, why
   can't we move them aside with our hands as Charles
   Wallace does on Camazotz?
2. What did Einstein's two theories of relativity teach us
   about time and space?
3. In *A Wrinkle in Time,* the characters travel long distances by "wrinkling" space and time. According to
   Einstein, how might wrinkles be formed in space and
   time?
4. Name one element of *A Wrinkle in Time* that is based
   on science. Name one element that is purely
   imaginative.

"Black Holes and Time Tunnels"
by Dr. David Darling

ABOUT THE RELATED READING

Dr. David Darling holds degrees in physics and astronomy and has written many books and articles about science. Born in England in 1953, he currently lives in Brainerd, Minnesota with his wife Jill. They have two children. This selection is taken from his book *Could You Ever Build a Time Machine?* It explains what black holes are and explores whether they could be used as "time machines" to travel to different times and places in the universe.

High in the sky on a clear fall evening is the star group of Cygnus the swan. It is not hard to find. Look for a large pattern of stars in the shape of a cross, or a swan in flight.

A map of the constellation Cygnus is shown below. On this map, the end of the swan's tail is marked by a bright star called Deneb. Slightly ahead of Deneb are three stars in a line. They represent the swan's body and the tips of its wings. Finally, some distance away

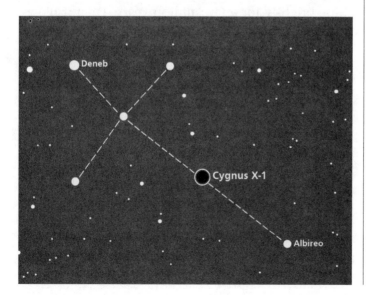

is a fifth, fairly bright star, Albireo. It marks the position of the great bird's head.

Now look halfway along the neck of the swan. There is a point on the map labeled Cygnus X-1. The next time you are outside on a clear, dark fall evening, locate Cygnus and gaze at the spot where Cygnus X-1 lies. Though you will not actually see anything, you will be looking at the exact point in space where scientists believe there may be a black hole.

Crushed Out of Sight

Black holes are popular subjects in films, as well as in many science fiction stories. But there is a good chance that black holes really exist in space. They are places where the pull of gravity is so strong that nothing, not even light, can escape from them. Once inside a black hole, you could never come back out the same way. However, it is possible that you could escape by a different route and arrive at a totally different part of the Universe. What is more, a journey into a black hole might transport you through time, either into the far future or the remote past.

▶ Explain in your own words how black holes are formed.

How can black holes be made? They might be created by the explosion of very heavy stars. A star that weighs 20 or 30 times as much as the Sun can only shine brightly for a few million years. Then it blows itself apart. During this huge explosion, known as a supernova, all the top layers of the old star are blasted away into space at high speed. However, the core, or central part, of the star may remain whole.

In a normal, middle-aged star, such as the Sun, the core is the place where light and heat are made. Here the temperatures are incredibly hot—many millions of degrees. The outward pressure of this light and heat prevents the inward force of gravity from squeezing the core any smaller. For most of a star's life, these two great forces struggle against one another in an evenly matched game of tug-of-war. But in a dead star, there is no longer any light pressure to oppose gravity. As a result, the core is squeezed tighter and tighter and gets smaller and smaller.

When the average-sized stars, such as the Sun, reach the end of their lives, their cores shrink down to hot balls of squashed matter. These are called white dwarfs. Then another force, caused by particles of matter becoming too crowded together, stops gravity from crushing a white dwarf to an even smaller size.

In bigger, heavier stars, the force of gravity acting on the star's dead core is much stronger. Even after the supernova explosion has blown away much of the star's contents, the core that remains may be heavier than the Sun. If the core is more than three times as heavy as the Sun, nothing can prevent gravity from crushing the core smaller and smaller. From an original size of more than 20,000 miles across, the core is squashed in less than a tenth of a second to a ball only 25 miles across. At this stage, a tablespoonful of this matter would weight the same as four billion full-grown elephants. But gravity squeezes it still smaller. In a fraction of a second, more than three Suns' worth of star material becomes crammed into an incredibly tiny space. Now it may be no larger than the period at the end of this sentence.

Within a few miles of the totally crushed star, gravity is so strong that it will pull in anything that comes too close. And it will allow nothing to escape, not even a ray of light traveling at more than 186,000 miles per second. This region around the crushed star is completely black and invisible. That is why scientists call it a black hole.

The Mystery of Cygnus X-1

If black holes are black and invisible, then how can we ever know they are there? In fact, we cannot, unless there is something nearby that can be seen and upon which the black hole has a noticeable effect. This is the case with Cygnus X-1.

From observations made by instruments in space, scientists have discovered that huge amounts of X rays—rays that carry a great deal of energy—are coming from the direction of Cygnus X-1. They have also found that a binary star lies in the same position as

◀ *How can scientists detect black holes?*

the source of the X rays. A *binary star* consists of two stars that are circling around each other. One of these stars is much bigger and brighter than the Sun, but it can only be seen through a large telescope because it is so far away. Astronomers know it is there because of the "wobbles" it causes in the movement of its giant neighbor.

From the extent of the wobbles, astronomers think that the dark star in Cygnus X-1 must weight from five to eight times as much as the sun. This fact alone suggests that it is likely to be a black hole. But the X rays offer still stronger evidence. Careful studies of the X rays have revealed that they are almost certainly coming from a whirlpool of extremely hot gas. This gas, scientists believe, has been stripped away from the bright, giant star by the gravitational pull of a nearby black hole. Just before it disappears down the black hole, the gas is heated to more than 18 million degrees Fahrenheit. At that superhot temperature, it gives off an intense X-ray glow.

Into the Black Hole

Even before scientists found signs of real black holes in the Universe, they had studied the mathematics of what black holes might be like inside. According to their theories, black holes may be like the entrances of tunnels that join different regions of space and time. These strange tunnels are called *wormholes*. At the end of a wormhole is an exit known as a *white hole*. By going into a black hole, traveling along its wormhole, then coming out the white hole at the other end, a spacecraft might be able to leap across huge distances of space and millions of years in time.

But two British scientists, Stephen Hawking and Roger Penrose, pointed out some problems with this wonderful way to travel. For one thing, there seems to be an energy barrier inside a black hole. No normal object, such as a spacecraft, could pass through this barrier without being torn to bits. The two scientists identified a second major problem. It appears that the wormhole tunnel would instantly squeeze shut if a piece of matter tried to move along it.

▶ What is a wormhole? What might happen to a spaceship that traveled through a wormhole and came out a white hole at the other end?

▶ What are two problems with traveling through a black hole?

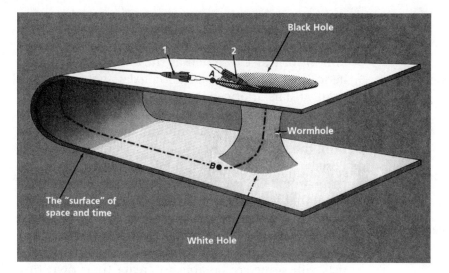

However, in 1988, new results were produced by researchers Michael Morris, Kip Thorne, and Ulvi Yurtsever at the California Institute of Technology. These showed that a wormhole might be kept open with the help of two round plates that carried a charge of electricity. The plates would be located on either side of the "throat" leading into the wormhole. Results from even more recent research have shown that objects entering a spinning black hole might also be able to travel through time.

Yet, just because something is possible in theory does not mean it will quickly, or ever, become fact. We are still not certain that black holes exist. The evidence for them, though, is strong. If they do exist, then the nearest one is likely to be many trillions of miles away. Cygnus X-1 is about 10,000 light-years from Earth. One light-year is the distance that light travels in a year, or about 6 trillion miles. Cygnus X-1, then, lies about 60 thousand trillion miles away!

It is possible that there are closer black holes to Earth that we have not yet found. If they are not members of binary star systems, then they would be extremely hard to detect. Still, it would be surprising if there were a black hole similar to Cygnus X-1 that was closer than a few hundred light-years to the Sun. At such a distance, it would be very difficult to reach such an object. And it would be even harder to use it as a time machine.

Black Holes, Large and Small

▶ Where might we find "supermassive," or extremely enormous, black holes?

Much larger black holes, weighing millions or even billions of times as much as the Sun, are thought to lie in the center of galaxies. *Galaxies* are huge collections of stars arranged in spiral, round, oval, or irregular shapes. We live in a galaxy called the Milky Way. To explain the unusual amount of energy coming from the middle of large galaxies, scientists have proposed the idea of "supermassive" black holes. But these would lie even farther from Earth than black holes that formed from neighboring stars.

▶ How might scientists create black holes?

There may also be mini black holes. These may be smaller than a pea but with the *mass,* or amount of matter, of a mountain. It is also possible that scientists will someday be able to create their own tiny black holes in the laboratory. They might do this by directing extremely intense, pure beams of light into a tiny pellet of matter. If enough energy could be focused onto the pellet at one time, it would collapse to form a black hole so small that it could only be seen under a microscope.

But there is a problem with this plan. Small black holes would tend to rip apart any object that was sent into them. This would happen because the pull of gravity on anything approaching a mini black hole would be much greater at the front of the object than at the back.

▶ Why might supermassive black holes be better choices for travel than small black holes?

In the case of a very large, massive black hole, the difference in gravitational pull across an approaching object would be much less. The supermassive black holes that may occupy the center of some galaxies also appear to be the only kind that human beings might be able to enter and survive.

Scientists today do not know if black holes will ever be used as a means to jump instantly into the remote past or future. The technical problems to be overcome, even if such journeys are possible, are among the most difficult imaginable. Yet the people who lived a century ago might have thought of human missions to the Moon in the same way.

Someday, in some form, the human race is likely to build a machine that can swiftly travel through time. Where that will lead us, no one yet knows.

Critical Thinking

1. What is a black hole, and how is it formed? How do we know black holes really exist?
2. How is a black hole similar to the Black Thing described in *A Wrinkle in Time?*
3. Explain how people might be able to travel through a black hole to reach another time and place. What are some problems with using black holes as time machines?
4. Look at the picture of a rocket going through a black hole. How would traveling through a black hole be similar to and different from the way Mrs Whatsit, Mrs Who, and Mrs Which "wrinkle" through space and time?

Creative Writing Activities

Writing a Sequel

At the end of *A Wrinkle in Time,* Meg and Charles Wallace escape from IT. However, the evil leader is still in power. What do you think happens next on the dark planet? Will the people ever become free? Use your imagination to write a short story that tells what happens to the people on Camazotz.

A Letter from Meg

Imagine you are Meg. Write a letter to the three Mrs Ws thanking them for helping you save your father and telling them how much you have learned on your incredible journey. Be specific: what wisdom have you gained? How are you different now than you were before you met them?

Sci-Fi Fairy Tale

Rewrite a familiar fairy tale as a science fiction story by setting it in the future, on another planet, or with some characters changed into robots or aliens. For instance, you might rewrite "Jack and the Beanstalk" so that instead of climbing a beanstalk, Jack falls through a black hole. You may wish to illustrate your story; or, write it in comic book form.

A Personal Bill of Rights

On Camazotz, people have had their rights taken away by IT. They do not even have the right to think for themselves. What rights do you have? Think about the rights you take for granted. Then write your own bill of rights. You can use the following format: "I _____, being of sound mind and body, do hereby declare the following rights as a law-abiding citizen of _____, bearing in mind that these rights carry with them certain responsibilities. I have the right to _____, knowing it is my responsibility to _____." List ten rights, describing the responsibility that comes with each.

For example, you may write: "I have the right to stay up late, knowing it is my responsibility to get up early for school." Then add the line "This Bill of Rights is hereby signed, sealed, and ratified this day of _____, in the year _____. Signed: _____. Witnessed by: _____."

Critical Writing Activities

The following topics are suitable for short critical essays on *A Wrinkle in Time*. An essay written on one of these topics should begin with an introductory paragraph that states the thesis, or main idea, of the essay. The introductory paragraph should be followed by several paragraphs that support the thesis with examples from the novel. The essay should conclude with a paragraph that summarizes the points made in the body of the essay and that reinforces the thesis.

Science Fiction and Fantasy

Write an essay explaining why *A Wrinkle in Time* can be considered a "science fantasy," that is, a mixture of science fiction and fantasy. In your essay, include definitions of science fiction and fantasy and tell how the book fits each definition. Before you begin, you may want to fill out a chart like the one below to list examples of science fiction and fantasy in the book.

Science Fiction	Fantasy

The Fight between Good and Evil

A Wrinkle in Time is about the fight between good and evil. Write a paper about good and evil in the book. Which characters are good? Which are evil? What "weapons" does each side use? What historical figures are mentioned as being fighters of evil? Explain what the book is trying to say about each person's responsibility to fight evil.

Civil Rights and Liberties

The Declaration of Independence states that all people have the right to "life, liberty, and the pursuit of happiness." In the Bill of Rights in the U.S. Constitution, we are guaranteed freedom of speech and freedom of the press. This means that people can speak or write freely, even criticize the government if they so choose. The government cannot prevent people from expressing their own ideas. Write a paper comparing and contrasting these ideas with the ideas of IT. What rights and freedoms have been taken away from the people on Camazotz?

The Importance of Differences

Charles Wallace says "differences cause problems." In *A Wrinkle in Time*, Meg learns that she must be herself—not try to be like everyone else. What makes her different, and how do her differences help her when she is on Camazotz? When do you feel pressured to dress, think, or act just like everyone else? Write a paper explaining why you think being your real self is important. Use examples from *A Wrinkle in Time* and from your own life.

Reflecting on the "Time Quartet"

Read at least one of the other three books in Madeleine L'Engle's Time Quartet: *A Wind in the Door, A Swiftly Tilting Planet,* and *Many Waters.* Then, write an essay comparing and contrasting the book or books to *A Wrinkle in Time.* In what ways are the books similar? How are they different? Consider the themes, or main ideas, in each book, as well as the settings and the characters.

Projects

Illustrating *A Wrinkle in Time*

Some of the planets Meg, Calvin, and Charles Wallace visit are wildly different from the planet Earth. Because they are so different, every reader may have a slightly different image of these places. Choose one of the planets or scenes from the novel and create a drawing, painting, or diorama to illustrate it.

Good Versus Evil Collage

With a small group, collect images from magazines and newspapers in order to create a collage illustrating the theme of good versus evil from *A Wrinkle in Time.*

Creating a Book of Quotations

With a partner, collect all the quotations from *A Wrinkle in Time,* including those recited by Mrs Who as well as passages from the Bible. Put these together into your own book of quotations. You may decorate the book with designs and illustrations and create a cover with art paper or cloth.

Internet Research

A great deal of information about Madeleine L'Engle and her work is available on the Internet. Visit a search engine such as Google at http://www. google.com and enter the words "Madeleine L'Engle." You should find a number of sites. Visit four of them, and take notes about what you find there. Then, turn in a report to your teacher that explains what sites you visited and what information you found at each one. Tell which site you liked best, and why.

Science Project: Building a Model Atom

In the CENTRAL Central Intelligence Building on Camazotz, Charles Wallace opens up a hole in the wall so that he, Calvin, and Meg can pass through it. When Calvin asks him how he did it, Charles says, "I merely rearranged the atoms." Read the article "Wrinkles in Spacetime" on page 215 and ask the librarian or science teacher for a book that explains in more detail what an atom is. Then, create your own model of an atom. Does it consist mostly of empty space? If so, why do solid things feel solid? Why can't we "rearrange the atoms" as Charles does? Alternatively, you might choose another idea from the article, such as the tesseract or Einstein's special relativity theory, research it, and prepare an oral report for the class.

Debating IT

Divide the class into two groups: the followers of IT and the freedom fighters. The followers of IT should skim over the book and gather all of ITs arguments for why IT should rule. For example: "Differences create problems." The freedom fighters should write counterarguments explaining why IT is wrong. They may use words from the Declaration of Independence and the Gettysburg Address, as Meg does, as well as their own words. When the groups have finished preparing, hold a debate. Each student should present an argument or counterargument in turn. The teacher will judge whether the freedom fighters win or whether they fail and are hypnotized by the power of IT.

Glossary of Words for Everyday Use

PRONUNCIATION KEY

VOWEL SOUNDS

a	hat	ō	go	ə	extra
ā	play	ȯ	paw, born		under
ä	star	u̇	book, put		civil
e	then	ü	blue, stew		honor
ē	me	oi	boy		bogus
i	sit	ou	wow		
ī	my	u	up		

CONSONANT SOUNDS

b	but	l	lip	t	sit
ch	watch	m	money	th	with
d	do	n	on	v	valley
f	fudge	ŋ	song, sink	w	work
g	go	p	pop	y	yell
h	hot	r	rod	z	pleasure
j	jump	s	see		
k	brick	sh	she		

a • ber • ra • tion (ab´ər ā´shən) *n.*, departure from the normal.

ab • horred (ab hȯrd´) *adj.*, hated.

a • cute (ə kyüt´) *adj.*, sharp; severe.

a • gil • i • ty (ə jil´ə tē) *n.*, quick and easy movement.

ag • o • ny (ag´ə nē) *n.*, intense pain; torture.

alas (ə las´) *interj.*, used to express unhappiness, pity, or concern.

a • li • en (ā´lē ən) *adj.*, strange; foreign.

an • guished (aŋ´gwisht) *adj.*, feeling great suffering, as from worry, grief, or pain.

an • gu • lar (aŋ´gyü lər) *adj.*, having sharp corners.

an • ni • hi • late (ə nī´ə lāt´) *v.*, destroy completely.

an • ti • cli • max (an tī klī´maks) *n.*, sudden drop from the important to the commonplace.

ap • pal • ling • ly (ə pȯl´iŋ lē) *adv.*, shockingly.

ap • pre • hen • sion (ap´rē hen´shən) *n.*, dread; uneasy or fearful anticipation of the future.

apt (apt) *adj.,* likely.

as • si • mi • late (ə sim´ə lāt´) *v.,* absorb.

as • suage (ə swāj´) *v.,* lessen; relieve.

at • ro • phied (a´trə fēd) *adj.,* wasted away.

au • da • cious (ȯ dā´ shəs) *adj.,* recklessly bold; going against the law, religion, or manners.

au • thor • i • ta • tive (ə thȯr´ə tāt´iv) *adj.,* having or showing power.

a • vid (av´id) *adj.,* eager and enthusiastic.

bel • lig • er • ent (bə lij´ər ənt) *adj.,* warlike; seeking a fight.

bil • ious (bil´yəs) *adj.,* having a greenish color to the skin, as if suffering from liver disease.

bland • ly (bland´lē) *adv.,* smoothly.

bra • va • do (brə vä´dō) *n.,* pretended courage.

brusque • ly (brusk´lē) *adv.,* abruptly.

cat • a • pult (kat´ə pult´) *v.,* launch; hurl.

cease (sēs) *v.,* stop.

char • ac • ter • is • tic (kar´ək tər is´tik) *adj.,* typical.

chide (chīd) *v.,* scold.

chor • tle (chȯrt´´l) *n.,* gleeful chuckling or snorting sound.

cla • ri • fy (klar´ə fī´) *v.,* make clear.

com • pel (kəm pel´) *v.,* force.

con • ceive (kən sēv´) *v.,* think; imagine; understand.

con • cept (kän´sept) *n.,* idea.

con • coct (kən käkt´) *v.,* cook up or prepare; devise.

con • for • mi • ty (kən fȯr´ mə tē) *n.,* the act or state of conforming—that is, molding one's appearance, actions, or personality in order to fit in with an accepted standard of behavior, often in obedience to peer pressure or to an authority.

con • found (kən found´) *v.,* confuse or bewilder.

con • no • ta • tion (kän´ə tā´shən) *n.,* idea suggested by or associated with a word.

con • sis • tent (kən sis´ tənt) *adj.,* holding always to the same principle or practice; steady.

con • straint (kən strānt´) *n.*, something that forces or compels.

con • sult (kən sult´) *v.*, ask for information.

con • verge (kən vərj´) *v.*, come together.

cor • po • re • al (kȯr pȯr´ē əl) *adj.*, physical, bodily.

cor • ro • sive (kə rōs´iv) *adj.*, eating away.

coun • ter • act (kount´ər akt´) *v.*, act directly against.

crev • ice (krev´is) *n.*, narrow opening.

de • ci • pher (dē sī´ fər) *v.*, translate; make understandable.

de • fen • sive • ly (dē fen´siv lē) *adv.*, protectively.

deft (deft) *adj.*, skillful in a quick and easy way.

de • lin • quent (di liŋ´kwənt) *n.*, person who fails to do what duty or law requires.

delve (delv) *v.*, search deeply.

de • ny (di nī´) *v.*, refuse to accept the truth of.

de • part (di pärt´) *v.*, leave.

de • spond • en • cy (di spän´dən sē) *n.*, loss of hope.

de • vi • ate (dē´vē āt´) *v.*, turn aside from a particular course or direction.

dic • tion (dik´shən) *n.*, manner of expression in words.

dig • ni • ty (dig´ nə tē) *n.*, pride.

di • la • pi • da • ted (də lap´ə dāt´id) *adj.*, falling to pieces.

di • mi • nish (də mi´ nish) *v.*, make or become less (as in size or importance).

dis • cern (di sərn´) *v.*, detect with the eyes or with the other senses; recognize as separate and distinct.

dis • il • lu • sion (dis´i lü´zhən) *v.*, take away one's illusions or false ideas.

dis • so • lu • tion (dis´ə lü´shən) *n.*, breaking up or into parts; dissolving.

dis • tinc • tion (di stiŋ(k)´ shən) *n.*, the distinguishing of difference.

dis • tort (di stȯrt´) *v.*, change from its usual shape.

dis • traught (di strȯt´) *adj.*, extremely troubled.

di • vert • ing (də vərt´ iŋ) *adj.*, amusing or entertaining.

dom • i • nate (dä′ mə nāt) *v.*, rule; control.

do • min • ion (də mi′ nyən) *n.*, land under complete control or ownership.

du • bi • ous • ly (dü′ bē əs lē) *adj.*, doubtfully.

ear • nest • ly (ər′ nəst lē) *adv.*, seriously.

em • a • nate (em´ə nāt′) *v.*, come forth.

en • ve • lop (en vel´əp) *v.*, wrap up or cover completely.

e • phem • er • al (e fem´ ər əl) *adj.*, lasting for only a brief time; short-lived.

e • ter • nal (ē tər´nəl) *adj.*, going on forever; timeless.

ex • clu • sive (ik sklü´siv) *adj.*, keeping out certain people or groups.

ex • posed (ik spōzd′) *adj.*, uncovered; displayed, visible.

ex • tin • guish (ek stiŋ´gwish) *v.*, put out.

ex • u • ber • ance (eg zü´bər əns) *n.*, great liveliness and joy.

fa • cet (fas′it) *n.*, one of a number of sides or aspects.

fal • li • ble (fal´ə bəl) *adj.*, likely to be mistaken or fooled.

fal • ter (fȯl′tər) *v.*, stumble.

flank (flaŋk) *v.*, position to the side(s) of.

fol • ly (fä′ lē) foolishness; foolish act or idea.

fren • zied (fren′zēd) *adj.*, wild or frantic.

fri • gid (frij´id) *adj.*, extremely cold.

fur • tive (fər´tiv) *adj.*, sneaky.

gait (gāt) *n.*, manner of walking.

gam • bol (gam´bəl) *v.*, jump or skip about in play.

gid • dy (gid′ ē) *adj.*, dizzy, confused.

grant (grant) *v.*, assume to be the truth.

ig • no • rant (ig′ nə rənt) *adj.*, lacking knowledge; unaware; uninformed.

im • pe • ne • tra • ble (im pen´i trə bəl) *adj.*, not able to be passed through or understood.

im • per • cep • ti • ble (im′pər sep´tə bəl) *adj.*, not plain or distinct; difficult to see or understand.

im • per • cep • ti • bly (im´pər sep´tə blē) *adv.*, slightly or gradually.

im • per • so • nal (im pər´sə nəl) *adj.*, not related to an individual.

im • plore (im plòr´) *v.*, beseech or beg.

im • pres • sion • a • ble (im presh´ən ə bəl) *adj.*, easily influenced.

in • ad • ver • tent • ly (in´ad vərt´'nt lē) *adv.*, unintentionally; without meaning to.

in • de • fi • nite • ly (in de' fə nət lē) *adv.*, without a definite end.

in • den • ta • tion (in´den tā´shən) *n.*, dent or small hollow.

in • dig • na • tion (in´ dig nā´shən) *n.*, anger about injustice.

in • ef • fa • ble (in ef´ə bəl) *adj.*, too overwhelming to be expressed or described in words.

in • ev • i • ta • ble (i ne' və tə bəl) *adj.*, incapable of being avoided.

in • ex • o • ra • ble (in eks´ə rə bəl) *adj.*, unstoppable; irresistible.

in • so • lent (in´sə lənt) *adj.*, boldly disrespectful.

in • tol • er • able (in täl´ər ə bəl) *adj.*, not able to be endured.

in • tone (in tōn´) *v.*, recite in a songlike way.

in • ver • ted (in vər´təd) *adj.*, turned upside down.

in • vol • un • tar • y (in väl´ən ter´ē) *adj.*, not done of one's own free will.

ir • ra • tio • nal (i ra' shə nəl) *adj.*, lacking reason; not making sense according to logic or reason.

jeo • par • dize (jep´ ər dīz´) *v.*, put at risk; endanger.

jest (jest) *v.*, joke; make fun.

ju • di • cious • ly (jü dish´əs lē) *adv.*, showing sound judgment; wisely and carefully.

lu • mi • nous (lü' mə nəs) *adj.*, glowing.

ma • lig • nant (mə lig´nənt) *adj.*, having a harmful influence; threatening.

ma • nip • u • late (mə ni' pyə lāt) *v.*, manage skillfully; control or play upon by artful, unfair, or insidious means so as to serve one's purpose.

mar • ket (mar' kət) *v.*, sell; promote for sale.

ma • te • ri • a • lize (mə tir´ ē ə līz) *v.*, develop into something real or tangible.

men • ace (men´əs) *n.*, threat.

met • a • mor • phose (met´ə mȯr´ fōz) *v.*, change in form or nature; transform.

mi • as • ma (mī az´mə) *n.*, unwholesome vapor.

min • is • tra • tion (min´ is trā´shən) *n.*, act of giving help or care.

mis • con • cep • tion (mis´ kən səp´shən) *n.*, mistaken thought or idea.

mod • er • a • tion (mäd´ər ā´shən) *n.*, avoidance of extremes.

my • o • pic (mī äp´ik) *adj.*, nearsighted.

non • de • script (nän´di skript´) *adj.*, hard to describe; colorless; drab.

ob • lique • ly (ō blēk´lē) *adv.*, indirectly.

om • i • nous (äm´ə nəs) *adj.*, threatening.

om • ni • po • tent (äm nip´ə tənt) *adj.*, all-powerful.

o • paque (ō pāk´) *adj.*, not transparent: blocking out light.

or • gan • ism (ȯr´gə niz´əm) *n.*, living being.

pe • dan • tic (pe dan´ tik) *adj.*, laying unnecessary stress on minor or trivial points of learning.

per • emp • to • ry (pər emp´tə rē) *adj.*, final; decisive.

per • me • at • ing (pər´mē āt´ iŋ) *adj.*, penetrating.

per • plex • i • ty (pər pleks´ə tē) *n.*, bewilderment; confusion.

phy • si • cist (fiz´i sist) *n.*, expert in the study of matter and energy.

pin • ioned (pin´yənd) *adj.*, bound.

pla • cid • ly (plas´id lē) *adv.*, calmly.

plain • tive • ly (plān´tiv lē) *adv.*, in a sorrowful or sad way.

plunge (plunj) *v.*, move rapidly downward or forward.

po • tent (pōt´´nt) *adj.*, having power.

po • ten • tial • ly (pō ten´shəl lē) *adv.*, possibly.

prac • ti • ca • ble (prak´ti kə bəl) *adj.*, usable; that can be put into practice.

pre • ci • pi • tous • ly (prē sip´ə təs lē) *adv.*, suddenly or unexpectedly.

pre • lim • i • na • ries (prē lim´ə ner´ēz) *n.*, preparatory steps.

prim • i • tive (pri´mə tiv) *adj.*, belonging to or characteristic of an early age or stage of development; little evolved.

priv • il • eged (pri´ və ləjd) *adj.*, having or enjoying benefits or advantages.

pro • bing • ly (prōb´iŋ lē) *adv.*, searching with great thoroughness.

pro • di • gious (prō dij´əs) *adj.*, wonderful; amazing; of great size.

pro • long (prə lȯŋ´) *v.*, make longer.

pro • pi • tious (prō pish´əs) *adj.*, favorable.

prox • i • mi • ty (präk si´ mə tē) *n.*, closeness.

queer (kwir) *adj.*, differing in some odd way from what is normal or usual.

rap • ture (rap´ chər) *n.*, experience of being carried away by overwhelming emotion; a feeling of awe while looking upon something divine or godly.

rave (rāv) *v.*, talk without making sense.

re • cess (rē´ses) *n.*, hollow place.

rec • on • cile (re´ kən sīl) *v.*, settle; resolve.

re • course (rē´ kȯrś) *n.*, that to which one turns for aid or safety.

re • it • er • ate (rē it´ə rāt´) *v.*, repeat.

re • lin • quish (ri liŋ´kwish) *v.*, give up.

re • proc • ess • ing (rē präs´es iŋ) *n.*, the act of processing again.

re • pul • sive (ri pul´siv) *adj.*, disgusting.

re • si • lience (ri zil´yəns) *n.*, ability to bounce or spring back into shape.

re • so • nant (rez´ə nənt) *adj.*, resounding or reechoing; strong or deep in tone.

re • ver • be • ra • te (ri vər´ bə rāt) *v.*, echo.

re • vul • sion (ri vul´shən) *n.*, extreme disgust.

shrill (shril) *adj.*, having a high-pitched, piercing sound.

sin • is • ter (sin´is tər) *adj.,* threatening harm, evil, or misfortune.

smug • ly (smug´lē) *adv.,* in a self-satisfied manner.

snide (snīd) *adj.,* slyly malicious.

som • ber (säm´bər) *adj.,* dark and gloomy; very serious.

sparse (spärs) *adj.,* thinly spread.

sub • due (sub´dü) *v.,* conquer; overcome.

sub • side (səb sīd´) *v.,* become less active.

sul • len (sul´ən) *adj.,* showing ill humor by moody and unsociable withdrawal.

su • pine (sü´pīn) *adj.,* lying on the back, face upward.

ta • boo (ta bü´) *adj.,* forbidden; not talked about.

tan • gi • ble (tan´jə bəl) *adj.,* capable of being touched or felt by touch.

tem • po • ral (tem´pə rəl) *adj.,* temporary; lasting only for a short time.

te • nac • i • ty (te nas´ə tē) *n.,* quality of holding firmly; stubbornness.

ten • ta • tive • ly (ten´tə tiv lē) *adv.,* experimentally; uncertainly.

tim • id • ly (tim´ id lē) *adv.,* shyly; in a way that shows a lack of courage or self-confidence.

trac • ta • ble (trak´tə b'l) *adj.,* easily managed.

tran • si • tion (tran zish'ən) *n.,* passage, or change, from one condition to another.

trans • lu • cent (trans lü´sənt) *adj.,* letting light pass through.

tra • verse (tra vərs') *v.,* travel across or over; pass through; extend across.

trem • or (trem´ər) *n.,* trembling, shaking, or shivering.

trep • i • da • tion (trep´ə dā´shən) *n.,* anxiety; fear.

un • a • dul • ter • at • ed (un ə dul´tər āt id´) *adj.,* pure.

un • kempt (un kempt´) *adj.,* untidy.

un • mi • ti • ga • ble (un mit´ə gə bəl) *adj.,* absolute; not lessened or eased.

un • ob • scured (un əb skyürd´) *adj.,* clear or distinct; easily seen.

un • sub • stan • tial (un´səb stan´shəl) *adj.,* not solid or heavy.

vault • ed (vȯl´tid) *adj.,* arched.

ve • loc • i • ty (və läs´ə tē) *n.,* swiftness, speed.

ver • ba • lize (vər´bə līz) *v.,* express something in words.

ves • tige (ves´tij) *n.,* trace of something that once existed.

void (void) *n.,* empty space.

vul • ne • ra • ble (vul´nər ə bəl) *adj.,* open to attack.

waft (wäft) *v.,* float, as on wind.

war • i • ly (wer´ə lē) *adv.,* cautiously.

whirl • wind (hwərl´wind´) *n.,* current of air spinning violently upward in a spiral that has a forward motion.

wraith • like (rāth´ līk) *adj.,* ghostly.

writhe (rīth) *v.,* twist or squirm as if in pain.

wry • ly (rī´lē) *adv.,* in a drily funny way.

zom • bie (zäm´bē) *n.,* person showing mechanical, listless behavior; literally, a dead person who has come to life.

Handbook of Literary Terms

ALLUSION. An **allusion** is a reference in a literary work to something famous. There are several allusions in *A Wrinkle in Time* to the play *The Tempest* by William Shakespeare and to the book *Alice in Wonderland* by Lewis Carroll.

ANALOGY. An **analogy** is a comparison of things that are alike in some ways but different in others. In chapter 12 of *A Wrinkle in Time,* Mrs Whatsit makes an analogy that compares life to a sonnet, a form of poetry.

ATMOSPHERE. See *mood.*

CENTRAL CONFLICT. A **central conflict** is the main problem or struggle in the plot of a poem, story, or play. The central conflict of *A Wrinkle in Time* is the struggle of Meg, Charles Wallace, and their friends against the forces of evil that have imprisoned their father and threaten the universe. See *plot.*

CHARACTER. A **character** is a person or animal who takes part in the action of a literary work. The main character is called the *protagonist.* A character who struggles against the main character is called an *antagonist.*

Characters can also be classified as major characters or minor characters. *Major characters* are ones who play important roles in a work. *Minor characters* are ones who play less important roles.

A *one-dimensional character, flat character,* or *caricature* is one who exhibits a single quality, or character trait. A *three-dimensional, full,* or *rounded character* is one who seems to be an actual human being.

In *A Wrinkle in Time,* the main character, or protagonist, is Meg. The antagonist is the creature known as IT. Major characters in the story include Charles Wallace, Calvin, Mr. Murry, Mrs Which, Mrs Who, and Mrs Whatsit. Minor characters include Sandy and Dennys, Mr. Jenkins, and Aunt Beast. Mr. Jenkins is an example of a one-dimensional or flat character. Meg is an example of a three-dimensional or full character.

CHARACTERIZATION. **Characterization** is the act of creating or describing a character. Writers create characters using three major techniques: by showing what characters say, do, or think; by showing what other characters say or think about them; and by describing what physical features, dress, and personality the characters display. Madeleine L'Engle uses all three techniques to create the character of Meg.

CONFLICT. A **conflict** is a struggle between two forces in a literary work. A conflict can be internal or external. A struggle that takes place inside a character is called an *internal conflict*. A struggle that takes place between a character and some outside force such as another character, society, or nature is called an *external conflict*. An internal conflict in *A Wrinkle in Time* is Meg's struggle to accept herself just the way she is, with faults and all. An external conflict is the struggle between Meg and IT. See *plot*.

DESCRIPTION. A **description** gives a picture in words of a character, object, or scene. The following is an example of description, which gives a picture in words of Mrs Whatsit: "It seemed small for Meg's idea of a tramp. The age or sex was impossible to tell, for it was completely bundled up in clothes. Several scarves of assorted colors were tied about the head, and a man's felt hat perched atop. A shocking pink stole was knotted about a rough overcoat, and black rubber boots covered the feet."

DIALOGUE. **Dialogue** is conversation involving two or more people or characters. In a piece of writing, dialogue is shown by putting in quotation marks the exact words the characters say. The following is an example of dialogue:

"Hi," he said cheerfully. "I've been waiting for you."

"Why didn't you come up to the attic?" Meg asked her brother, speaking as if he were at least her own age. "I've been scared stiff."

"Too windy up in that attic of yours," the little boy said. "I knew you'd be down. I put some milk on the stove for you. It ought to be hot by now."

FANTASY. **Fantasy** is a type of writing that is very imaginative or unrealistic. Fantasy stories may involve imaginary beings such as elves, dragons, or unicorns, as well as magical or supernatural occurrences. The plot, or storyline, of a fantasy story often has to do with a battle between the forces of good and evil. *A Wrinkle in Time* contains elements of fantasy and science fiction. For this reason, it is sometimes called a "science fantasy."

FORESHADOWING. **Foreshadowing** is the act of presenting materials that hint at events to occur later in a story. Madeleine L'Engle uses foreshadowing when she has Mrs Whatsit remark "there is such a thing as a tesseract." This comment hints that Mrs Whatsit may know something about the disappearance of Meg's father.

INCITING INCIDENT. The **inciting incident** is the event that introduces the central conflict, or struggle, in a poem, story, or play. Mrs Whatsit's visit to the Murry home may be seen as the inciting incident of *A Wrinkle in Time*.

IRONY. **Irony** is a difference between appearance and reality. Irony happens in a piece of writing when reality is the exact opposite of what the reader or the characters would expect. It is ironic that people think Charles Wallace is a moron, when in reality he is a genius. It is also ironic that Meg's faults, the qualities that get her into trouble at home, do the exact opposite and actually help her when she is on Camazotz.

MOOD. **Mood**, or **atmosphere**, is the emotion, or general feeling, created by a piece of writing. A mood can be any kind of feeling—tense or peaceful, suspenseful or silly, gloomy or joyful, happy or sad, festive or lonely. A writer creates mood by using description and details. The details Madeleine L'Engle gives while describing the CENTRAL Central Intelligence building on Camazotz help create a spooky, suspenseful mood.

PLOT. A **plot** is a series of events related to a central conflict, or struggle. A plot usually involves the introduction of a conflict, its development, and its eventual resolution. See page 183 for a description of the elements of plot and an analysis of the plot of *A Wrinkle in Time.*

PUN. A **pun** is a play on words, one that cleverly makes use of a double meaning. The Happy Medium's name is an example of a pun.

RESOLUTION. The **resolution** is the point in a poem, story, or play in which the central conflict, or struggle, is ended. See *plot.*

SCIENCE FICTION. **Science fiction** is imaginative literature based on scientific principles, discoveries, or laws. It is similar to fantasy in that it deals with imaginary worlds but differs from fantasy in having a scientific basis. Often, science fiction deals with the future or with worlds other than our own. *A Wrinkle in Time* contains elements of both science fiction and fantasy. For this reason, it is sometimes called a "science fantasy."

SETTING. The **setting** of a literary work is the time and place in which it occurs, together with all the details used to create a sense of a particular time and place. The setting of chapter one is the Murry home on a dark and stormy night.

SIMILE. A **simile** is a comparison using *like* or *as.* Writers often use similes when they want to describe something in an original way. Madeleine L'Engle uses a simile when she describes the mothers on Camazotz as being "like a row of paper dolls." The women are like paper dolls in that both seem to be perfectly identical. Like a row of paper dolls that are attached to each other, the women also seem to move and act at the same time.

SONNET. A **sonnet** is a fourteen-line poem, usually with a strict rhythm and rhyme scheme. Mrs Whatsit compares life to a sonnet: "a strict form, but with freedom within it." Following is some more information about sonnets.

There are several different kinds of sonnets. The Elizabethan, or Shakespearean, sonnet is divided into three groups of four lines and a final couplet (two rhyming lines). It has the rhyme scheme *abab cdcd efef gg.* The Italian sonnet is divided into two parts, the octave, a group of eight lines, and the sestet, a group of six lines. The rhyme scheme of the octave is *abbaabba,* and the rhyme scheme of the sestet is *cdecde, cdcdcd,* or *cdedce.* The rhythm of most sonnets is called iambic pentameter. That means the poems usually have ten syllables per line. Every other syllable has a strong stress on it, as in the famous line "Was THIS the FACE that LAUNCH'D a THOUsand SHIPS?" from Christopher Marlowe's play *Dr. Faustus.*

SUSPENSE. **Suspense** is a feeling of expectation, anxiousness, or curiosity created by questions raised in the mind of a reader. For example, in chapter 10, Madeleine L'Engle creates suspense about what will happen to Meg as she is carried away by a strange creature.

SYMBOL. A **symbol** is a thing that stands for or represents both itself and something else. In *A Wrinkle in Time,* the Dark Thing can be seen as a symbol of evil forces in the universe.

THEME. A **theme** is a central idea in a literary work. A book can have many themes. One theme of *A Wrinkle in Time* is that a person must accept himself or herself "faults and all," recognizing that no one is perfect. Another theme is that people must keep their individuality, not try to conform to be like everyone else.

Acknowledgments

Booklist. The Booklist Interview: an interview with Madeleine L'Engle by Sally Estes, from *Booklist*, May 15, 1998. Reprinted with permission. Copyright American Library Association. All rights reserved.

David Darling. "Black Holes and Time Tunnels" from *Could You Ever Build a Time Machine?* by David Darling. Copyright © 1991 by David Darling. Reprinted by permission of the author.